ALSO BY TERRI BRUCE

Hereafter (Afterlife #1)

Thereafter

Terri Bruce

◆ Mictlan Press ◆

Thereafter (Afterlife #2)
Copyright © 2014 Terri Bruce

Cover artwork by Shelby Robinson
Cover model Chelsea Howard
Cover design by Jennifer Stolzer

Digital ISBN: 978-0-9913036-3-2
Print ISBN: 978-0-9913036-2-5

Printed in the United States of America
First Edition

To friends, old and new:
How far we travel in life matters far less than those we
meet along the way.

I'm so grateful our journeys brought us together.

ACKNOWLEDGEMENTS

To everyone who supported me during "the dispute" — I can never thank you enough. This book is possible only because of you. Special thanks go to Victoria Strauss at Writer Beware and to David Vandagriff at the Passive Voice.

To Sue Burke whose input and feedback on twelfth-century Spain were invaluable to the creation of Andras and to Jill, Brenda, and Kelsey, critique partners extraordinaire — without all of you, Irene would still be wandering around lost in the forest.

To Yovani Baez, Heather Barrett, and Jennifer Allis Provost, intrepid beta readers — being a first reader is not an easy job, and I both admire and appreciate your courage and your kindness. Thank you! Additional thanks go to Yovani for agreeing to beta read Book #1 in the first place and then returning for Book #2. That I ever had the courage to show *Hereafter* to anyone in the first place was due entirely to you.

To book bloggers and the book blogging community, especially Danielle at Book Whore, Rachel at Parajunkee's View, and Jennifer at the Bawdy Book Babe — I still think you're all consummate professionals, no matter what you might say. ☺

And finally, as always, to my family — I know they say family are the people who *have* to put up with you, but I still appreciate you doing it anyway.

Special thanks go to my production team: artist Shelby Robinson whose amazing artwork graces this book's cover, editor Janet Hitchcock at *The Proof is in the Reading*, cover layout artist Jennifer Stolzer, and e-book formatter, E. M. Havens — I couldn't do this without you guys!

One

Irene Dunphy opened her eyes.

"Oh, crap."

Everything looked strangely familiar — the carpeting, the old-fashioned lamps, the twin beds with their faded and worn coverlets. She turned in place, taking everything in, her heart sinking. She was dead and this was the afterlife. Only...this didn't look like any version of the afterlife she'd ever heard of. In fact, it looked a lot like the hotel room she'd supposedly just left back on Earth when she'd stepped into the warm and welcoming white light that formed the tunnel to the Great Beyond.

She looked down, taking stock of her person. Well, at least she seemed to be all here — two arms, two legs. She was still wearing what she'd died in — the candy-apple red, spaghetti-strapped, thigh-length cocktail dress and three-inch strappy sling back shoes she'd worn clubbing. To this ensemble had been added an olive-green, man's suit coat — courtesy of Jonah, who'd "borrowed" one from his dad to give to Irene.

Same clothes.

Same room.

Her heart sank. She hadn't actually made it to the other side. She was still stuck on Earth.

"Great," she said, turning to Jonah, the fourteen-year-old boy who had improbably become her traveling companion, sidekick, friend, and conscience all rolled into one as she'd tried to navigate life as a ghost and find a way to cross over.

Only…Jonah wasn't there. Neither was Samyel, the mysterious man who had agreed to be her guide in the afterlife.

The image of Jonah's pale blue-green eyes and straw-colored hair came readily to mind, even though he was nowhere to be seen. If she had crossed over, it made sense that Jonah wouldn't be here. Jonah was, after all, still alive and belonged in the land of the living. However, Samyel should be here. Where was he?

As she studied the room, fine details began to come into focus. The floor lamp was missing. The curtains were a different color. The desk wasn't in the same place. In fact, the more she looked around, the more she realized this was not the same room she had inhabited in the land of the living. So where the hell was she?

"Hello?" she called, still turning in a circle, growing more uneasy by the minute. Where was everyone? She couldn't be alone, could she? Surely, there had to be other people — *dead* people — about?

She listened hard, looking for any signs of life beyond the empty room's four walls. Somehow, though, she knew it was fruitless. She was alone. She could sense it. The utter completeness of the silence washed over her, thick and heavy, like a shroud. A chill scuttled down her spine.

She crossed to the door in three strides and pulled it open. The aimless, loitering ghosts that she expected to see populating the hallway of the hotel's thirteenth floor were gone. There was only a deep, vast silence — no muffled footsteps, no voices, no doors opening and closing. Nothing.

"Hello?" she called again, though the hallway was obviously empty.

She suppressed a tremor of uncertainty as she stepped out of the room. She turned left and headed down the windowless corridor, the faded, rose-colored carpet absorbing all sound. On the walls, old-fashioned gas lanterns burned steadily with a muted yellow glow.

In the land of the living, the last room on the left had been occupied by another ghost — one who had become her…well, lover seemed too intimate, too fond, a word for her relationship with Ernest. What did you call someone you slept with to keep the self-loathing, fear, and despair at bay?

She knocked on the door, waited, knocked again, and finally tried the door handle. The brass knob turned easily, and she walked into the empty room. It had the same air of abandon and neglect as everything else.

Her heart thumped unevenly as she fought the rising panic. The stories told of two, possibly three, planes of existence: the land of the living, the land of the dead, and an in-between place that connected the two. Even if she was only in the in-between place, there should be thousands if not millions of other dead people here. After all, how many people died every day? Every week? Every year? They all had to make the same journey, right? So where were they?

She backed out of the room, spun around, and headed for the stairs, breaking into a run as her heart thundered in her ears. She slammed open the door to the stairwell and bolted down the stairs, the sound of her heels on the metal and concrete reverberating in the enclosed space.

She hardly paused as she reached the last stair and yanked open the door. She exploded into the lobby, only to come immediately to a dead stop. The lobby had a ghostly, neglected air of faded opulence and splendor — crystal chandeliers, marble floor, brass and gold fixtures — and the reassuring presence of a lone bellboy manning the front desk.

Irene tried to catch her breath and shake off the panic.

You idiot, she chided herself. *What the hell is wrong with you? Of course you're not alone. It's not like you're the only person who ever died.*

She smoothed down her dress as her eyes roved over her surroundings.

So…this is the afterlife.

The lone bellboy gave it away — if this had been the land of the living there would be more people about. She frowned in disapproval. While she suspected the hotel was supposed to look familiar to be comforting, somehow it just creeped her out. In a strange way, the vast, empty space was more terrifying than a three-headed hellhound would have been. At least that would have been expected.

An almost overwhelming urge to both laugh and cry bubbled up within her. Maybe she hadn't been as ready for this as she thought or as brave as she'd pretended to Jonah. Truth be told, given the option, she'd turn around right now and go home, back to the land of the living. Being a ghost might have been dreadful, but it wasn't as dreadful as being alone.

The bellboy was staring at her. Instantly, the steel came into her spine. She straightened up, shook back her mane of dark, reddish-brown hair, and with a determined set to her jaw, stepped forward.

"Howdy, Miss," the boy said with a wide, friendly grin. By boy, she really did mean a child—he looked like he was twelve. Like everything else, the red wool of his uniform was faded and the gold braid clustered on one shoulder shone with the burnished warmth of old brass.

He stood behind what Irene assumed was the registration desk. However, incongruously, behind him there was a narrow hall leading to a kind of atrium in which she could see trees and a river. Only it wasn't an atrium exactly, because she could also see glistening white sand and clear blue sky. It was more like the hallway simply faded away, leaving the outside exposed. She blinked in surprise and turned to look over her shoulder. Behind her was the hotel lobby. In front of her was a river.

A crowd of people milled about on the sand; they appeared to be waiting for something. None of them seemed in the least bit concerned about anything—about being dead, about standing both in a hotel and outside on a beach at the same time, or about the strangeness of the place they found themselves in. They were chatting amicably, as if they were waiting to catch a bus. One man smoked a cigar.

The boy folded back a hinged section of the counter that separated him and Irene. A fashionable, middle-aged couple—the woman in a luxurious fur coat and the man in a gray suit and hat—pushed past Irene. "Stand aside," the woman said imperiously. "I won't be left behind on account of anyone." Without looking at either Irene or the boy, the man put a finger to the brim of his hat, as if tipping it to them.

"You have your coin?" the boy asked the couple.

"Of course we do," the woman snapped. "What do you take us for?"

The boy let them pass. Irene hesitated for a second and then started to follow the couple through the gap in the counter. The boy put up a hand to stop her.

"I'm sorry, Miss, but this is the express—it's for them that know where they're going." He dropped the counter back into place. "Besides, you don't even have a coin."

"A coin?"

"Of course, Miss. Can't cross without a coin."

"Oh, shit, a coin!"

A sinking feeling settled over Irene as the boy's meaning hit her. All the stories of the afterlife were true—something she'd learned after she'd died. The Norse stories of Valhalla and Valkyries, the Greek myths of Hades and the Elysian Fields, the Sumerian belief in a bleak and faded world of mud and dust—all these and more were true.

Including, apparently, the story of a ferryman.

Coins—especially pennies and dimes—had been immensely valuable to the ghosts in the land of the living, even though Irene hadn't been able to figure out why. For no apparent reason, they were highly sought after and were the currency of choice among the dead.

Irene fingered the pendant at her throat. It was a simple, heart-shaped green stone, suspended on a cheap rawhide cord, like something you'd find at a carnival or fair. She'd gotten it at a dead trader's booth. She recalled the outrage that Amy, her ghostly companion, had expressed at what she claimed was an exorbitant price.

"It's sixty cents," Irene had protested.

"It's six *dimes*," Amy retorted.

Now the strange emphasis Amy had put on the word "dimes" made sense. Irene's stomach turned to lead and dropped like a bowling ball. Jonah, who was a veritable encyclopedia of the afterlife, had warned her—just after she'd given her last coin to a panhandler – that coins were probably valuable for a reason. Now she knew why.

God, I really am an idiot.

Everyone knew the story: when you died, you had to pay the ferryman a coin to row you across the river and sure enough, here was a river.

"Oh, come on," she said. "You're kidding, right?"

The bellboy shook his head. "'Fraid not."

"But –"

"Sorry, Miss, rules is rules," he said without the slightest trace of sympathy.

Irene felt a momentary flutter of panic. Then she laughed. "This is a dream, right? The one where you have to take a test, only you haven't studied, and then suddenly you're giving a presentation naked…this is my subconscious worrying that I'm not prepared."

"It's all right," the boy said. "Everyone says that." He pointed across the lobby to a set of double doors. "I'm afraid I'm going to have to ask you to leave."

"Leave? What do you mean, 'leave'? Where am I supposed to go?"

"You'll have to go to the other crossing." He grinned at her. "Catch the local, if you get my meaning."

"The local?" Irene realized she was parroting everything the boy said and snapped her mouth shut. She stared alternately at the doors and at the bellboy. The kid didn't seem to be joking, and this seemed a little too real to be a dream. She could feel beads of cold sweat pooling between her shoulder blades and struggled to keep her composure. "Are you kidding me?"

"Oh, don't worry, Miss. It takes longer, but you'll still get there in the end." He slipped under the hinged section of the counter, coming to stand beside her. "Now please…if you wouldn't mind –"

"Look, I just got here and I'm *really* confused as to what is happening. Isn't there, like, an orientation program or something? I mean, can you please just explain to me –"

The boy took hold of her arm, right above the elbow. "Come along now, Miss; don't be any trouble, if you please."

"Trouble? What trouble?" she cried. "I'm just trying to ask a question!"

However, he was already pushing her toward the doors. She dug in, trying to stop their forward movement, but her three-inch heels could find no traction on the smooth marble floor. "Wait...will you just wait a minute?" She flailed, trying unsuccessfully to wrench her arm from his surprisingly strong grip. "Hang on a sec—"

He swung open one of the doors and thrust her through it. She wheeled around just in time for the door to slam in her face. The glass of the doors was soaped, preventing her from seeing inside. She grabbed the long, brass handle with both hands and shook the door frantically, but it didn't budge. She threw herself against it, getting nothing more than a bruised shoulder for her effort. With mounting frustration and panic, she banged on the glass with her fist. "Hey!" she hollered. "HEY! Let me in!"

The door remained resolutely closed.

She gave it one last, furious kick and then turned away, swearing under her breath. She ran a hand through her hair and inhaled slowly, trying to retain some vestige of her dignity. The kid was probably inside watching her, laughing his ass off right now. She wasn't doing anything but making an idiot of herself, and she refused to give him the satisfaction.

She tossed back her hair and took a deep breath. *Okay, time to regroup.*

She absently looked around, trying to think what to do next. For the first time she took in her surroundings, and she froze in horror.

She had been in Boston when she'd gone through the tunnel, and while her current surroundings vaguely resembled that city in the sense that the nearby streets were hardly more than alleys and the buildings were a lumpy, unorganized mix of old stone and new glass, she was quite sure she was no longer in the actual Boston.

This city was...dead. There was no other word for it. There was no sound—no cars, no phones, no honking horns, no barking dogs, no shouting voices. There was no movement, nothing—no cars, no people, no trees, not even pigeons.

The sky was gray—not cloudy, just gray. There was a sense of nothingness about the place. Not just empty or still or quiet but a complete lack of life or vitality. It was as if everything—even the stones of the buildings and the asphalt of the street—was lifeless and dead.

No, no, no, no – this can't be happening.

But it was. She really was alone—completely and utterly alone.

Panic flooded through her and she wheeled around to attack the door with renewed vigor. "Let me in!" she yelled over and over as she pounded on the door. "Let me in!"

There was no response. The realization that there was no help coming crashed into her, and her knees buckled. She grabbed the door handle for support as the world began to sway before her eyes.

Oh my God – I'm in Hell.

She doubled over, still holding onto the door handle, and put her head between her knees, trying to stop the scenery from swaying. Spots danced before her eyes. She clung to the coolness of the door handle pressing into her hand and the hammering of her heart in her ears to keep from passing out.

For a wild moment she thought of the bottle of vodka she had carried around with her on Earth. Dear God, if she ever needed a drink, now would be the time. Just as quickly, she remembered she no longer had it. Jonah had smashed it and then made her promise to give up drinking.

That thought was as sobering as a bucket of cold water to the face. The panic melted as quickly as it had come, replaced by a deeper, more complex feeling of grim determination mingled with cold fury. She straightened up, not sure if she was angry with herself for making such a stupid promise, angry at Jonah for asking it of her, or full of resolve not to let Jonah down.

Jonah.

He would know what to do if he was here.

WWJD—what would Jonah do?

Hysterical laughter bubbled up within her and she desperately tried to tamp it down. *Keep it together, Irene.*

A movement in her peripheral vision caught her attention, cutting into her mounting hysteria, and she turned to look. Yes, there was movement at the end of the street. Her heart fluttered with hope.

She squinted, trying to pick out fine details. Whatever it was, it was about a hundred feet away. Then her eyes widened as she recognized the figure. She started forward and then broke into a run, relief flooding through her. Samyel! As weird and creepy as he was—sneaking around alleys, always seeming to be laughing at a joke that only he got, and spending his days on some mysterious search for something—at least he was company.

Just as quickly, Irene's relief changed to confusion. Samyel was kneeling in the street, his back to her, his outspread arms raised to the sky, his head thrown back in silent adoration and exaltation. She slowed to a halt, now less than fifty feet away, her skin prickling with unease.

"Samyel?" she called, her voice quavering with uncertainty. Why was he kneeling? And what was he looking at?

She glanced up at the sky, but it was empty.

She took two cautious steps forward. "Samyel?" Surely he heard her calling his name or, at the very least, had heard the sound of her heels clattering on the pavement? Why didn't he look at or acknowledge her? "What the hell are you doing?" she asked, fear sharpening her tone.

Samyel didn't respond. Instead, he stood up, his back still to her. He threw off the baseball cap she had never seen him without, dropping it to the ground with a careless flick of the wrist. The back of his coat moved, as if live snakes writhed and swirled under the fabric. The material wrinkled upward, horizontal stripes of bunched material marring the smooth surface. With a jagged sound, the coat split down the back, the fabric pushed aside by the unfolding of...wings— giant, black, feathered wings.

Irene stumbled backwards, her brain refusing to believe what she was seeing. Giant wings covered in glossy black feathers as dark as his waist-length hair stretched out from Samyel's bare back, spanning twenty feet or more.

He tossed something away and then turned his head to look at her over his shoulder. She realized the item he had tossed must have been his sunglasses — the other accessory she had never seen him without — because they were nowhere to be seen.

He looked right at her; she was too far away to see his eyes, but she had no doubt he saw her. He turned away and then, his back still to her, bent his knees and, with a mighty heave, launched himself into the air. The impossible wings beat twice and then he soared overhead, higher and higher, circling out of sight.

"Wait!" Irene cried, one hand reaching for him. It was a reflex only, an automatic impulse; she wasn't really sure she wanted him to stay.

It was too late anyway; he was gone.

Two

Wings

She'd known all along that Samyel was something "other" — not alive, not dead. He referred to "humans" and "men" as if he wasn't one of them. Since the moment she had come across him roasting a rat on a spit in an alley, she had sensed something malevolent and dangerous about him lurking just below the surface. Something in his manner, his voice, his scornful derision and mocking words had put her on edge. However, since she'd had no other choice, she'd struck a bargain with him anyway — she would bring him across to the afterlife with her in exchange for his help in getting safely to...well, wherever it was she was supposed to go.

She'd assumed that between traveling with Samyel — even if he turned out to be a psychopath — and being lost in an afterlife that contained demons, hellhounds, and God only knew what else, Samyel was the lesser of the two evils. Never in her wildest dreams, though, could she have imagined wings.

She had a sudden memory of her and Samyel stopped in Boston Common to look at a graceful statue of a serene and beautiful angel pouring out a bowl of water.

"This is an angel?" Samyel had asked, something mocking and dangerous in his voice.

"More or less," she replied. "Sometimes they have halos."

11

"You believe in such a thing?"

"Me? No."

"Very wise," he replied. Then he'd laughed.

Now she understood why.

Relief and panic clashed. She was terrified of being alone in this strange deserted place, but she was just as terrified of this strange winged version of Samyel, as well. A shudder ran through her — *wings*. She covered her mouth with a hand as her stomach suddenly heaved. She mentally kicked herself again.

Jonah was right. Jonah was always right.

Jonah had thought that Samyel was some kind of underworld demon, and he'd worried about Irene's safety if she crossed over with him. While Irene might have had a vague, subconscious notion that Samyel wasn't quite human, she hadn't really believed it possible that he could be a demon. She still didn't believe — not really — that all the afterlife stories were literally true. How could they be? Most of them were incompatible. How could you both "eat of every good thing" and have no need for food? Live in a dismal gray realm where the food was "as mud" *and* carouse in the hall of Odin? It made no sense. However, Samyel's wings changed everything; if they were real, then what else must be real, too?

She rubbed her arms, trying to get the blood flowing. Then she kicked herself again. She was dead — there was no blood to flow. She dropped her hands with a sigh and looked around. So where was she? What was she supposed to do now? Where the hell was she supposed to go?

Good grief, she must really be falling apart — she was starting to sound like Scarlett O'Hara.

Get a grip!

Did it rain here? Did it snow? Did it get dark? Were there wild animals? Her knees buckled once more, but now she didn't even have a building to grab onto.

At that moment a noise startled her out of her panic. She whipped around, a fight or flight response kicking in. She tensed, the roar of adrenaline in her ears.

The hotel door was standing partially open.

"Hey!" Irene cried, wild hope surging through her. She started forward, but in that same moment a bag—her bag—was unceremoniously thrown out onto the street by an unseen hand, and then the door slammed shut again.

When Irene had stepped into the tunnel she had been carrying a large, rattan beach bag stuffed full of carefully collected "dead" items—things that had crossed into the spirit realm—and Jonah's hand-drawn map of the land of the dead. Knowing he would not be able to go with her, Jonah had spent their last two weeks together meticulously combing through books about the afterlife to create a map to guide her. In the panic and confusion since arriving here she hadn't even noticed she didn't have the bag with her.

She ran to the door and shook it, but wasn't surprised to find that it wouldn't open. She scowled and gave the door a short, vicious jab with her foot before turning away and dropping to her knees beside her bag and its scattered contents. She ignored the discomfort of the rough surface of the sidewalk against her bare skin as she collected everything together, cataloging all of the items.

That bag and map were all she owned—all she had been allowed to take to the afterlife. Without that bag, she had nothing—no weapons, no blanket, no flashlight, nothing. Granted, she might be dead, with no body and therefore technically no need of food or drink or shelter from the cold, but she *remembered*. She remembered being alive, being hungry and tired and all the other sensations one experienced when one had a body, and even now, when it rained, she felt wet; when it was hot, she became thirsty; when the wind blew, she grew chilly.

She sat back on her heels and exhaled a long, controlled breath. As best she could tell, everything was still here—blanket, wind chimes, candles, lighter, tire iron, pepper spray, perfume, suntan lotion. It was a muddled, motley assortment of items—a mixture of things she'd had with her when she died and items she had picked up later. Not sure what she would need in the afterlife—Jonah had repeatedly emphasized that in the "olden days" people were buried with mountains of things they were supposed to need, including food, clothing, tools, weapons, and even pets — she had just taken everything she'd come across.

However, now that she looked at the stuff and compared it to her situation, it all seemed so useless, like so much junk. What good were candles and matches if it never got dark? What use was a blanket if it was never cold? What use were weapons if she was the only person here? Sure, items could be used to remind her what it was like to be alive, but would such memories be enough to keep her from going crazy if she was doomed to spend eternity here alone?

She shuddered and felt another pang of regret that she'd promised Jonah she'd give up drinking. Even a wine cooler would come in handy at this point.

Instantly Jonah's face came to mind, and she felt a twinge of guilt. She'd been here all of thirty seconds, and she was already on the verge of both breaking her promise and throwing in the towel.

Put on your big girl pants, she chided herself. *Now, think!*

Okay, so her goal was to get to the afterlife — the *real* afterlife — which was apparently reached by boat. The bellboy had said that she would have to take another boat — "the local" — and had indicated it was to be found at another crossing. Only he hadn't said where, exactly, that other crossing was.

She found Jonah's map, crumpled and crushed within the bag. She smoothed it out and smiled at the crude drawing — green triangles for mountains, blue squiggles for water, and — she squinted, trying to decipher Jonah's handwriting — ah, yes, black crosses to indicate ground as sharp as glass. Awesome.

When Jonah had first mentioned the stories of the dead being ferried across a river, she'd resisted the idea that the dead *had* to do anything. "Why?" she'd asked him. "Why do I *have* to cross the river?" Now it seemed so obvious: you had to cross the river to get to the other side. It was like a bad metaphysical pun; apparently the universe, for all its lack of orderliness, had a sense of humor.

She looked at the map again. Uncertainty fluttered in her stomach. The map wasn't really all that helpful — the river she needed to cross was supposedly to the east. Not east of anything in particular, just east. However, that information was only helpful if she knew which way east was — and did she have a compass? Of course not.

She looked up scanning the sky for the sun, hoping it would give her some clue. *Oh for God's sake — do I look like Magellan? Like I know how to navigate by the sun.*

Well, it was a moot point anyway; there was no sun — just the dull, heavy, gun-metal gray.

Great.

She sighed and tried to focus on the positive. *Okay, don't give up. Other people manage to find their way and they don't have maps.*

No, they usually have a guide. Only her guide had up and...flown away.

Something furry brushed against her leg. Irene jumped to her feet and let out a shriek, backing blindly away from whatever it was. She looked down and was arrested by the sight of a cat — a perfectly ordinary black and white cat. It sat on its haunches, looking up at her with vibrant green eyes.

Irene blinked in surprise and then frowned. How odd to see something as ordinary as a cat in such a desolate and barren place. She looked around, but the cat seemed to be alone, the only other living thing in sight.

She looked down again and realized the cat was staring at her. Irene shifted uneasily from foot to foot. She wasn't particularly fond of cats to begin with and now this one — strange and out of place — was staring at her.

"What do you want?" she asked it.

The cat blinked at her.

"I don't have any food."

It continued to stare, obviously wanting something.

Irene turned away, putting her back to the cat and its unnerving gaze. However, she could feel its eyes boring into her. "Shoo!" she said over her shoulder. When the cat didn't move, she turned back around and nudged it with her foot. With a disgruntled look, the cat got up and walked off.

Irene frowned as it retreated across the street. When she was sure it was gone, she looked at the map again. With no way of knowing which direction east was, the map wasn't really any use. She stuffed it back into her bag.

She halfheartedly tried the hotel door again, but, as expected, it didn't open. She turned around and stood for a moment, looking right and then left. "Eeney, meeney, miney, moe."

She turned right and started walking. She wandered down the street, poking into buildings at random. They were all empty, stripped of even furniture and decorations. The desolation was unnerving. The unbroken stillness, so beautiful and serene in a forest, was alarming in a city. Cities weren't meant to be noiseless and empty.

The streets seemed to lead in circles, or maybe it was just that the landscape looked the same no matter how far she traveled. Real cities had districts and neighborhoods, zones that each had a distinct feel and character — the financial district, the upscale residential area, the enclaves of ethnic neighborhoods like Chinatown and Little Italy. In such a place, you could tell you were getting somewhere by the change in the scenery.

There was none of that here. Instead, there were ancient looking wooden and stone structures — barely more than primitive huts, stately-looking colonial- and federal-style mansions, ornate stone edifices that might be courthouses or museums, and modern-looking high-rises of glass and steel all jumbled together. The streets were just as eclectic a mix — cobblestone, brick, asphalt, concrete, even bare dirt at times — ranging in size from barely more than a cow path to wide, sweeping avenues. This wasn't so much a city as a storage area or dump for abandoned buildings.

Irene knew that people crossed over to the land of the dead seven days after death and that anything with the body crossed over as well — including buildings. She remembered being told that this was a common occurrence in the "olden days" when the custom was to wake the dead, standing watch at their coffin for a week. Apparently, wherever she was now was where all the buildings ended up afterward. She supposed this accounted for the feeling you got sometimes when you were in a building and it just felt

16

"off" — sort of soulless and dead. Turns out, it was dead. The physical shell of the building might remain in the land of the living, but its spirit or essence had been transported to the Great Beyond.

She pushed open the door to yet another building — this one an ancient, many-gabled house, and peered inside. The single room was adorned only by a large fireplace on the far wall. Like all the other buildings she'd investigated, it was stripped of everything — furniture, decorations, lamps, even rugs. She paused long enough for her eyes to sweep the room again. Then she turned around...and shrieked.

There was an...animal, of sorts. It was just shy of knee height, upright and vaguely humanoid, ugly, and covered in hair. She didn't know where it had come from, but now it squatted in the middle of the room, looking at her with a disconcertingly human face set amidst dense, dark brown fur. It sort of reminded her of a very large, tailless Tamarin — a kind of small monkey she'd seen in a zoo once.

The creature hissed, let out a screech, and then skittered away on two legs to a corner, where it chittered balefully at her. She blinked, too surprised to do much more than stare. It wasn't exactly repulsive, but it wasn't cute either. She didn't know what it was — she'd never seen anything like it — and she had no idea if she should be terrified or not. The thing hissed again and bared its sharp, little teeth, and Irene decided retreat would be the best course of action.

"It's okay," she said soothingly as she slowly backed away. "No one's gonna hurt you, little fella."

She turned for the door and the thing flew at her, scrabbling around to drive her from the exit with hisses and shrieks, its long nails clicking against the bare wood of the floor. It scrambled up her leg, its claws pricking like needles, sending a cascade of fire down her legs. She shrieked with a mixture of surprise and pain and swatted at it, trying to get it off. When that didn't work, she jigged across the floor, shaking her leg in a desperate attempt to dislodge it. In response, it climbed higher, using the fabric of her dress like a ladder to clamber up to her shoulder, where it proceeded to rip at her hair, pulling clumps of it out by the roots.

Surprise gave way to genuine panic as Irene realized she was in serious trouble. Frantically, while trying to protect her face from its claws, she took another swipe, and this time, she connected. The ferocious little ball of fur hit the floor with a heavy thump, and Irene dashed blindly for the door, having enough presence of mind to slam it shut behind her.

For a moment, she just stood there, dazed, trying to collect herself. She took deep, wrenching breaths, trying to slow her racing heart. Her legs and waist were a mass of welts from a thousand tiny needle pricks. Her scalp burned and throbbed. She clasped her arms around herself to control their shaking.

The thing hit the window with a thump. Irene jumped. She took several hasty steps back, but the thing just sat there motionless, watching her with its beady eyes, its face pressed to the glass.

Irene backed away and then realized something was missing. She looked down. Her bag was gone.

"Son of a bitch!" She must have dropped it inside when the creature scrambled up her leg. She weighed the idea of just abandoning the bag, but she couldn't bring herself to do it. It was too valuable.

Her eyes met the two tiny black ones. The thing pawed at the window with its tiny hands as if in anger or frustration. Then it stopped. Everything seemed to move in slow motion as it turned its head, looked over its shoulder, and then looked back at Irene. She almost thought she saw a flash of triumph on its face. She knew it had seen the bag.

The horrid little thing disappeared from view, and in her mind's eye, Irene could see it scamper across the room to her stuff, intent on destroying it. She let out an inarticulate cry of outrage and stamped her foot.

She stood in front of the door, one hand on the doorknob, and took several deep, fortifying breaths. She had no weapons. She would have to simply run in, grab the bag, and race out again. She mentally fixed the position of the bag in her mind—she didn't know where exactly she had dropped it, but the room hadn't been that large and she had pretty much stayed in a straight line from the front door to the middle of the room.

She took another breath, held it for a second, and then let it out in a long, controlled exhale. With an explosive movement, she threw open the door and sprinted for all she was worth. A second later, she skidded to a halt beside the bag, its contents strewn like splattered guts across the floor. Frantically, she grabbed items and stuffed them in the bag while trying to simultaneously keep an eye out for the critter and move in a circle so the thing couldn't sneak up behind her.

Her gaze was arrested by several items on a nearby windowsill, and she paused as her mind tried to comprehend what she was seeing. It was several seconds before she realized that the cluster of items was her bottle of perfume, bottle of suntan lotion, and her tube of lipstick. The items seemed to have been arranged neatly, almost like a display. She blinked at the oddity of the sight. She straightened and cautiously crossed the room. She looked to the left and to the right, searching for danger or signs of a trap, before snatching the items off the windowsill. On her second pan of the area, she noticed the wind chimes hanging from a nail on the wall. Other items were arranged around the room—the tire iron resting in a corner like a forgotten umbrella, candles on the mantle, and the blanket folded in half and spread neatly on the floor along one wall as if it were a bed.

She strode across the room and snatched up the blanket, noticing as she did so that a large piece had been ripped from one corner.

"Son of a bitch!" Jonah had given her that blanket. In fact, he had very chivalrously traded a sweatshirt away in the dead market to get that for her, and now some filthy over-sized rodent had torn a hole in it.

A noise to the right made her turn; the *thing* was up on a window sill. It was rubbing something against the glass in wide circles. Irene blinked in surprise; the critter appeared to be polishing the window, and it was doing so with the missing corner of *her* blanket.

As she stared at it, completely disconcerted by its actions, it turned its head, the button eyes regarding her for a moment. It thumped the blanket against the window and cried, "'Erk! 'Erk!" as if it was making some kind of factual statement. Then it thumped the window again and went back to polishing.

Without thinking, Irene jumped forward and seized it with both hands, holding it tightly. She expected it to put up a fight—to kick and bite and scratch. Instead, it went still and placid, silently gazing at her with dark, button-like eyes that reflected her face back at her. It had long, spindly arms capped with fat, three-fingered hands, which it waved absently in the air like an underwater plant swaying in the current.

"Just what the hell are you supposed to be?" She gave it a good shake, like a Magic 8 Ball. It blinked at her and made a croaking sound.

She wasn't sure what to do with it now that she had it; it was like having a wasp trapped under a glass. She walked to the door with the intent to carry it outside into the light so she could get a better look at it, but as she crossed the threshold, the thing began to writhe and scream as if in pain. Startled, she dropped it, and it scurried back inside where it turned and screeched what were undoubtedly invectives at her while it waved a tiny fist.

She stared at it, baffled by its behavior. It didn't seem to like the door, for whatever reason. Jonah would have been fascinated and would have insisted on staying to study it, but Irene's only thought was to get the hell away from it as quickly as possible. She looked down at her legs. The crosshatching of tiny, wet, red lines reminded her of the viciousness it had displayed only moments ago.

"Little fucker," she muttered, glaring at it. Then, very deliberately, she backed out of the house and yanked the door shut.

Three

Her legs still felt like jelly, but she managed to continue down the street, poking her head into various structures, desperately hoping she'd find some people or maybe something that was familiar.

After a few minutes, the jelly legs wore off and the terror faded—which was good, because she had several more run-ins with the creatures. In the first instance, the creature stood in a corner, glaring balefully at her and muttering to itself, while Irene slowly backed out of the house; in the second instance, there were several creatures inhabiting the house and they surrounded her, croaking, "'Erk! 'Erk!" She'd had to kick her way free and dash for the door to escape.

Finally, she stopped to rest, checking that the building was empty—she didn't want any of the creatures sneaking up behind her from inside—before leaning against it. She rested one tired foot against the clapboard siding and surveyed the buildings across the street. The risk of running into more of the creatures now far outweighed the lure of finding anything of value in any of the houses. She wasn't sure what to do next, however. She had no idea how big the city was—she could wander aimlessly for days, weeks, even months, and never find the river. She was getting the sense that when the bellboy had said the alternate route was "the long way," he meant in terms of time, not distance.

Slowly, a smell began to filter into her consciousness. She sniffed—wood smoke. She craned her neck, searching all around for the source of the odor, and then paused when she realized there was smoke curling from the chimney of a tiny stone cottage across the street.

Irene hesitated for a moment — it could just be more of the creatures. However, she quickly dismissed the thought. Though they seemed to have some rudimentary intelligence on par with, say, a dog, she didn't think the things were smart enough to build a fire. So that must mean people.

Deciding it was better to be safe than sorry, Irene pulled the tire iron from her bag. She pushed away from the building, shouldered her bag more securely, and crossed the street, her excitement mounting. She knocked on the door and held her breath. There was a flurry of activity from inside — excited chittering and the sound of a chair scraping against the floor.

After a moment, the door opened a crack and a suspicious eye appeared, peering at Irene with crackling hostility.

"What?" a voice barked, though it was nearly drowned out by a chorus of high pitched sounds that Irene recognized as the cries of the hairy, brown creatures that had attacked her.

Irene took a step back, her fingers tightening on the tire iron. "Uh...hi?" She paused, realizing that everything she wanted to say made her sound like an idiot. "I'm lost"; "What the hell are those horrid brown things?"; and "Is this the land of the dead?" all seemed equally moronic.

The door flew open, and Irene was confronted with a tiny, wizened old woman, her skin as furrowed as that of a Shar Pei, quivering in indignation. Around her feet was clustered a small group of the creatures, all tugging on the hem of the woman's dress like a flock of overeager grandchildren begging for attention. "What?" she barked at Irene again. "What do you want?"

"'Erk! 'Erk!" the things cried.

"Yes, damn you, work, work!" The old woman aimed a half-hearted kick at the nearest creature. "Hell and damnation, do I have to do everything myself? Go wash the floor if you're bored." The things scampered off, chirping joyfully. "And clean the chimney while you're at it!" She turned away, seeming to have forgotten about Irene, and made to close the door.

Irene put out a hand. "Wait! Please, can I just have a second?"

The woman stopped, turned, and looked Irene up and down. "What are you supposed to be?" Before Irene could respond, the old woman bristled, her face turning an indignant shade of splotchy red. "You get!" she shouted to something behind Irene.

Irene looked over her shoulder and saw the little black and white cat, sitting calmly on the sidewalk across the street. The old woman shook her finger at it. "I told you before, you're not wanted here so take your tricks elsewhere."

The crone made to shut the door for the second time, and in desperation, Irene held the door open. "Wait! Please…just tell me where I'm supposed to go. How do I get to the river?"

The woman leered at Irene. "Why don't you ask your friend there?" Then she slammed the door in Irene's face.

Irene stared at the door for a moment, dumbfounded. *What friend?* She looked around, but there was only the cat, which was still sitting across the street, watching her. Its tail swished back and forth. Irene eyed it for a moment, her eyes narrowing in thought. The cat reminded her of one she'd seen before. Back on Earth, she and Jonah had sat in a park, eating sandwiches, and a cat had come up to stare at Irene. She'd felt as if the cat was judging her and had been disconcerted by it. She'd fed it a bit of sandwich and then it had disappeared.

The cat across the street matched Irene's stare for a moment and then got up and walked away. Irene watched it go. To her surprise, the cat stopped, looked over its shoulder at her, and then sat down, as if waiting for her. Irene regarded the cat warily, one eyebrow cocked. She waited to see what it would do next, but it just sat there. After a minute, Irene started toward it. It got up and set off once more.

Was she really supposed to follow a cat? Well, honestly, what other options did she have? It wasn't like she had anything better to do.

She supposed, in an odd way, it made sense; she'd often compared her life since dying to *Alice in Wonderland*.

I guess this is my white rabbit.

The cat disappeared around a corner, and Irene followed. Strangely, there was a small pile of rocks in the middle of the street constructed of flat, smooth stones, such as those found at the beach. She had often seen such stones laid on graves to mark that someone had been to visit. She stopped to study it, but close scrutiny didn't yield any clues as to its purpose, so she walked on.

The scenery continued to be populated with a motley collection of abandoned buildings, and Irene had the vague, queasy feeling of being trapped in some kind of post-apocalyptic movie; she half expected zombies to come lurching out of the nearest doorway, moaning for brains.

The cat was waiting for her at the next intersection. It sat across the street, watching her, its tail swishing thoughtfully back and forth. As she crossed the street, it got up and trotted away.

Irene's thoughts clattered around in her head, clamoring for attention almost as loudly as the rising sense of dread in the pit of her stomach. Jonah had said that the journey through the different levels of the afterlife were a way to test a soul's worthiness to enter Heaven. What did it say about her that she couldn't even find her way out of this city by herself?

Irene had always thought of herself as tough and capable. However, ever since she'd died, she had started to realize she was neither of those things. She'd also thought she'd had a really great life and that she was a pretty decent person. Neither of those things had turned out to be true, either.

She swallowed the lump in her throat and sped up, trying to outrun the feeling that she was in big trouble.

Eventually, she caught up to the cat again. It was waiting at an intersection, and this time it turned right before trotting away. Irene followed.

There was no way to tell how much time was passing, but soon she felt as if she'd been walking for miles. The throbbing pain of her run-in with the shaggy, brown creatures faded away to a dull ache, replaced by a blistering sting in her feet. Time slowed as the unrelenting emptiness of the city dragged on. Her weary, trudging footsteps were the only sound in the gray, silent city. The only break in the monotony was when the cat appeared to show her when to turn. The panic of being alone ebbed away and was replaced by a resigned numbness. She began to feel as empty as her surroundings.

She might have been walking for five minutes or it might have been five hours, she wasn't sure which, when the dense silence was broken by a soft noise. At first, she wasn't sure it was real. However, the sound grew louder and closer with every step she took. Her heart picked up speed, fueled by half hope and half alarm.

She rounded a corner and her heart leapt to her throat — people! There were only three of them — a man, a woman, and a little girl of about ten — but at least they were real, live, actual people. She hurried to catch up to them.

Not one of the three — Irene assumed they were a family — acknowledged her when she drew abreast of them. The adults each had a broken, hopeless look about them, and silent tears tracked down their cheeks as they walked, their eyes determinedly staring straight ahead. The little girl looked solemn and grave, her eyes on the ground in front of her. All three were dressed very formally — the man in a dark suit and the woman and child in pretty, modest dresses. A tremor ran through Irene. These people were dead — those were their funeral clothes. They had died together. An entire family — mother, father, child — laid to rest at the same time.

A chill swept over her. She hadn't encountered anything like this before. In the land of the living, the only dead she had come across were individuals who clung tenaciously to life — those who loved the sensual joys of living, had grudges to settle, feared judgment or retribution in the afterlife, had loved ones they wanted to watch over, or those, like herself, who just plain refused to admit that they were dead and move on.

She realized now, looking at this family, that there were many other kinds of dead — the resigned, the relieved, the heartbroken. These parents were walking their child through the land of the dead, knowing she would never grow up, never fall in love, never become a doctor, an astronaut, a policewoman or whatever other dreams they held for her. To have to then march her through the land of the dead — like the long walk to the gallows — to whatever fate awaited, seemed uncommonly cruel.

Irene didn't speak to the family; their grief seemed too close, too personal, too real. She dropped back, following a few paces behind them.

The cat appeared at the next intersection, indicating Irene should turn right. When the family continued straight, Irene called to them, saying, "I think it's this way." Her voice seemed harsh and overly loud in the stillness, and she cringed.

They didn't seem to hear. Irene hesitated, wanting to insist, but uncertainty stopped her; she was, after all, following a cat and only because it was better than being alone. She didn't actually know where she was going. In a moment the family had disappeared, swallowed up by the gray landscape.

The long, slow, death march feeling returned. She walked for a long time now without seeing the cat, continuing in a straight, uninterrupted line. The landscape eventually emptied out. The pavement faded away to a hard, gray ground that crunched underfoot, as if covered by frost, and the buildings became sparser until they were replaced with stark, black, leafless trees with twisted trunks, dark and pitted like they had been burned.

Soon even this scenery became vague and ill-defined. Irene wasn't sure if it was simply that the dull gray sky melted into the dull, gray ground giving no sense of a horizon, or if the world really was fading away, but she could only see about a hundred yards ahead. Beyond that, the landscape simply melted away. Not fog or mist, exactly; it was more like there simply wasn't anything there, as if the scenery was being created as she went.

Occasionally, she would see a pile of the beach stones on the ground or another person flashing between the black trees at a distance. Some instinct kept her following the cat, even though she desperately longed for some company. This eerie, somber wood was starting to wear on her; she felt weighed down, as lifeless and gray as her surroundings, filled with an unnamed melancholy.

After a while, she stopped for a rest. She had no idea how long she'd been walking. According to the Mickey Mouse watch strapped to her wrist—another present from Jonah—it had been a few hours. However, she had no way of knowing if the watch was still working, and the unchanging light around her gave no indication of whether time was actually passing.

She dropped her bag to the ground and then slid down to join it, using one of the dead trees as a back rest. She riffled through the bag, looking for something to eat or drink. She found a few Chinese red bean paste buns and a pack of chewing gum. She remembered with a pang the items she had traded or given away while still on Earth— two chocolate bars and a bottle of gin. God, what she wouldn't give to have one or the other with her right now. There was no help for the chocolate bars, but stupidly, as a grand gesture that she was ready to face the challenges ahead on her own two feet, she had given the bottle of gin to Jonah before she had crossed over. *Idiot*, she castigated herself.

She stuffed the buns back in the bag; they had to last all eternity, no sense in wasting them. Suddenly, she was exhausted. She wrapped the suit coat more tightly around herself, burrowing into its protection, and closed her eyes.

Sometime later, she awoke to an odd scrabbling noise. She was still for a moment, trying to identify the source. She turned her head and spied her bag, which seemed to be undulating gently. Then she noticed a tail sticking out of it.

"Hey!" she cried. The tail grew longer as the cat backed out of the bag. It froze and looked at her, its eyes wide with surprise. Irene blinked twice. The cat had a pen in its mouth—one of her pens from her bag. The cat seemed to grin at her, and then it turned and fled with its prize.

"Hey!" Irene yelled, scrambling to her feet, but the little thief was gone. She shook her head. *What the hell was a cat going to do with a pen?*

She sat back down, feeling vaguely uneasy. The picture of the cat holding the pen kept returning. She turned the incident over in her mind, but it just didn't make any sense. Like everything else here, it was completely insane. She scowled and wished there was something she could kick, then she wished Jonah was here. He'd know why the cat wanted the pen.

Instantly, she hated herself for that thought. How had she become so utterly dependent on a fourteen-year-old? She was a grown woman for God's sake!

Still, she couldn't help but miss him—to miss his wisdom; his calm, rational approach to everything; his dry sense of humor. Hell, she even missed the endless recitations of facts and stories about the afterlife, which were his consuming passion.

She smiled despite herself. It was strange how you could get so attached to someone so quickly. She had only known him a few weeks—or had it been a few months? Days had all flowed together at the end. Either way, whenever she'd been frustrated or ready to throw in the towel, he'd always stepped in, logical and unflappable, and pointed out an obvious next step. She'd been impatient with him at the time, annoyed that he always had an answer for everything, that he'd been more competent than her. Now she'd give anything to see him again.

Tears prickled her eyes, and she impatiently wiped them away.

She drew her knees up to her chest, curling herself into as tight a ball as she could. The weird, drab light made her both sleepy and unable to sleep—it was too dark for day and too light for night. Her body didn't know what to do. She rested her head on her knees and sat there for a long time, resenting the light and the missing horizon and the black trees and the stupid cat and the brown, hairy things, and the old woman, and the bellboy, and a hundred other things before she finally drifted back into a restless slumber.

When she awoke, the cat was sitting a short distance away, flicking its tail impatiently. When it saw that she was awake, it rose to its feet, turned, and starting walking. It went a few feet, looked at her over its shoulder, took two more steps, and then sat down with an expectant air.

"Yeah, alright." Obviously it was time to go. She sighed and got up, wincing with pain at the stiffness in her joints. Then she set off again.

Four

Irene stopped to survey the landscape, trying desperately to note some landmark, something that looked familiar or different, or at least indicated she had moved from her original spot. They had been walking for what felt like days, and the unchanging landscape was both draining and grating. Crazy thoughts started darting through her mind: maybe she was only imagining that she was moving. Maybe she was standing still, and it was the trees that were moving.

Maybe, there aren't any trees. Maybe I'm imagining it all.

Perception could change how you looked to other people; she'd had proof of that in the land of the living. There, she had run into the Uglies — people who hated themselves so much, whose self-perception was so warped, that after death they became actual monsters, dark shadows that stalked the dead.

So, maybe, just maybe, perception could change what you saw around you, too. Maybe she had never left the dead city. Maybe she was just imagining this entire forest.

Cold beads of perspiration tickled the small of her back.

She listened hard, searching for any proof that this was real, that the forest existed, that something other than her existed. Once more, the idea that this was Hell and that she was being punished arose, stronger than before.

Something brushed against her ankle and she jumped.

The cat.

Irene tried to nudge it out of the way with her foot. "Look, I don't even know where you're leading me. How do I know you're not a *bad* cat? You could be leading me off a cliff for all I know. Or maybe you just need a can opened."

The cat threaded itself through her legs, purring so vigorously it vibrated.

Irene had been joking when she'd said that the cat might be leading her off a cliff, but now she hesitated. It could be true. If she was indeed in Hell, then it could be a bad cat...demon...creature...thing, right? She racked her brain, trying to remember if Jonah had told her any stories about cats and the afterlife.

Warily watching the cat, she reached into her bag for the wind chimes. The most important thing she'd learned in her time on Earth as a ghost was that bells of any kind — and that included wind chimes — drove away evil spirits. Tentatively, she shook the wind chime at the cat. It gave her a quizzical look, as if wondering what the hell she was doing, but didn't otherwise seem affected. Irene relaxed, feeling stupid. Well, you couldn't be too careful.

"Look, how about a rest break?" she asked. Her head, so recently recovered from the vicious hair pulling, throbbed anew, her legs felt like cooked spaghetti, and her feet ached. She was a city girl — long hikes in the woods were not a large part of her regular routine, and even if they were, her three-inch heels were not really the right footwear for this kind of excursion.

She headed for the nearest tree, dropped her bag, and plopped down on the ground. Almost as soon as the bag was on the ground, the cat ran to it and stuck its head inside.

"Hey!" Irene pulled the bag away. "Stop that!"

The cat gave her a disgruntled look, staring at her through narrowed eyes.

"What?" She eyed it for a moment. "Look, there's nothing in here that a cat would want. See?" She started pulling items out. "Blanket. Candle. Matches. Pepper Spray. Perfume. Bracelet."

As she pulled out the bracelet, the cat perked up. It looked first at the bracelet, then at Irene, and then back at the bracelet again.

Irene surveyed the bracelet doubtfully. It was just a thin, silver bangle. As far as she knew, there was nothing special about it. She wasn't even sure where she'd gotten it; she'd probably picked it up during Ghost Festival.

"You want this?" she asked.

The cat scooted closer. Irene shrugged and held the bracelet out. The cat grabbed the bracelet in its mouth and took off, streaking away into the grayness. Irene shook her head. *Stupid cat.*

She lay down on the ground, covering herself with the blanket, and within minutes she was asleep. When she awoke, the cat was there, sitting nose-to-nose with her, staring unblinkingly at her. She reared back in alarm, scrambling to a sitting position. "Jesus!" she cried. "You scared the crap out of me."

The cat didn't seem the least disturbed by this. It sat up, licked a paw, and then looked at her expectantly.

"Yeah, okay, okay." She got up, stretching and twisting to work out the stiffness that had invaded her body while she slept. She ached all over. She gathered up the blanket and was stuffing it into the bag when she heard a noise. It was so small and soft she almost missed it, but the cat tensed, alerting her that something was different. She heard the sound again and recognized it as a footstep on the hard, crisp ground. She squinted, looking hard for the source. In the distance, where the landscape dissolved into a seamless curtain of gray, something seemed to be moving. She stared, her eyes burning with the strain, trying to make out shape, color, or movement.

It was a woman—Irene could see her now, coming closer. Relief surged through Irene at the sight of another person, only to be replaced by alarm a second later. Something was wrong.

The woman walked with a slow, shuffling, almost uncertain gait, and the fixed look with which she regarded Irene was unnatural in its intensity. A dark, unkempt curtain of hair fell in limp hanks to the woman's waist. The idea of zombies rose again in Irene's mind, and Irene took a step back, unconsciously pulling the suit coat tight around her. "Uh, hello?" she said, trying not to panic.

The woman had stopped and was tilting her head at odd angles, as if she was having trouble seeing Irene clearly. Irene froze. The woman wasn't a zombie; she was feral.

Irene took another step back and then another. The bag bumped against her hip and she jumped. She pulled it close, clutching it to her chest.

The woman zeroed in on the bag in Irene's arms, her gaze changing instantly to one of ferocious, fixed intent, and she rushed forward, arms outstretched. Irene took two faltering steps back, groping in the bag for the wind chimes. Her hand connected, and she yanked them out. Holding them high, she shook the chimes vigorously and kept shaking. The chimes tinkled melodiously, the sound harsh and loud in the thick silence of the dead woods.

The other woman paused for a moment, and Irene's heart leapt. It was working!

She shook the chimes harder as she gathered herself, preparing to turn and run. Then, a nanosecond before everything changed, Irene realized the other woman wasn't being held at bay by the chimes—she was just momentarily confused by them. Irene's heart plummeted as the woman's face twisted with rage, and she rushed at Irene, sweeping toward her like one of the Furies of Greek legend.

Irene was already in motion, turning and launching herself into a sprint. She slammed into something hard. As she recoiled, she looked up into a man's face as blank and fixed as that of the woman behind her.

Icy cold terror poured through Irene's veins. She tried to step back, to turn, to run, but the man grabbed her arm. His fingers were like a vice, crushing the tender flesh of her upper arm through the fabric of the coat.

There was a momentary struggle as she tried to pull out of his grip. She lost her hold on the wind chimes and they clattered to the ground. Her bag swung wildly, spilling items left and right. Reflexively, she raised a knee, driving it hard into the man's groin. Her eyes widened in shock as the man let out a slight grunt but was otherwise impervious to the blow.

With all her might, Irene frantically pulled against the man and, with a painful wrench, managed to yank herself free. She backed away, her head swinging from side to side, as she tried to keep both the man and the woman in sight. Blind horror swept over her as she realized more of the blank-faced people had appeared from behind trees, lurching out of the gray nothing.

Many, many more.

Irene spun in a circle, but she was surrounded by a ring of people, all silent and unkempt, their expressions fixed, radiating malevolence.

She thrust a hand into her bag, searching for something, anything with which to protect herself. Her hand tightened around something smooth and hard. The tire iron. She yanked it out and raised it, tensing for battle. As if by some unseen signal, the crowd rushed forward with a sudden roar.

With a guttural cry, Irene swung the tire iron, connecting with whatever she could — heads, shoulders, arms. Everything was a blur; it all seemed to shift and move before her eyes, mixing into a bleary slur of color and noise. She heard enraged grunts of pain, and for a millisecond the weight pressing around her lightened as the crowd pulled back.

She was winning!

In the next instant, however, the crowd gave a united roar of rage and attacked in earnest — grasping, clawing hands reaching out to tear her apart.

The woman with the dark hair launched herself at Irene, catching hold of the bag and pulling it from Irene's arms. Irene tried to jerk away, but there was nowhere to go. The crowd pressed closer against her back, pinning her in place.

Hands were on her now, fingering the material of her dress, groping at her exposed skin, stroking her hair. She twisted this way and that, flailing her arms, trying to brush them off and break free of their invading hands. The blood thrummed in her ears, blotting out all other sounds. Dimly, she felt the tire iron wrenched painfully from her grip. She threw her hands over her head and tried to curl into a ball to protect herself but there was no room—the crowd pressed too close.

Were they going to maul her? Kill her? Tear her apart like wild animals?

She squeezed her eyes shut, blotting out the horror surrounding her. The hands became rougher—tearing at her dress, pulling her hair, clawing at her skin. The monsters surged against her relentlessly, crushing and suffocating her. Irene squeezed her eyes shut even tighter, waiting for the death blow she knew was about to come.

Someone grabbed her shoulder, gathering jacket, dress, and skin in a painful grip, and yanked her sideways, up and out of the crowd. Then she slammed into something hard. The shock of the impact caused her eyes to fly open. They widened as she stared into the face of a man. Not one of the crowd attacking her and not the man who had first grabbed her; this was an ordinary man. His dark eyes flashed with anger, and that single show of emotion was enough to distinguish him from her blank-faced assailants.

The impact had been from slamming into his chest. Now he roughly thrust her aside with one hand as he scooped something—a magazine—from the ground and tossed it to the crowd of angry spirits.

"Pax verbotem. Pax tecum," he said, his voice low and deep. "Solace and peace. Be calm. Pax vobis." His voice was flat and steady, without intonation, and he wove a soothing, almost hypnotic, rhythm with his words.

The suddenly calm and docile ghosts clustered around the one holding the magazine, their attention no longer on Irene. Irene's rescuer grabbed her wrist and drew her away without a backwards look at the angry mob. She tried to break into a run, but the stranger held onto her tightly.

"There is no need to run," he said. "They will not follow now." His voice was rough and deep, almost guttural.

"What the hell were those things?" she cried, trying to free her wrist from his crushing grip. Her heart still pounded and her mind swirled with a furious mixture of adrenaline and terror making it impossible to think straight. She wanted to run. She wanted to vomit. She wanted to sit down and cry. "Who are you? Where are we? What is going on?" She knew she sounded hysterical, but she couldn't seem to stop herself.

"They are the Fantasmas Hambrientos. The hungry dead. *They* are lost, not in their right minds, and cannot be held accountable for their actions."

She felt as if she'd been slapped. The unsaid—but implied—"unlike you" rankled as it hung in the air. The harsh words snapped her out of her mounting hysteria, evaporating the terror and shock.

She came to a dead stop, forcing the man to stop as well. She stared at him in mute outrage. Finally, she managed to grind out, "How nice for them." She yanked her wrist from his hold and rubbed it, giving him a pointed look, but he didn't seem the least fazed by the insinuation that he'd hurt her. "Those things tried to kill me!"

He eyed her up and down for a moment before replying. "It is not the Fantasmas' fault. They only want to remember."

Irene's face flamed at his icy disdain. "Could have fooled me." She pulled the suit coat tight, feeling fortified by the flimsy fabric, and crossed her arms. She was on the verge of a meltdown, she could feel it. Since she'd arrived here, she'd been denied access to the boat to the other side, thrown out of the hotel, abandoned by her guide, scratched and clawed by overgrown rodents, and nearly torn limb from limb by "Hungry Ghosts." She wasn't sure how much more she could take. She'd left Earth, in part, to get away from scary monsters and, instead, had jumped straight from the frying pan into the fire—this place was, by far, much, much worse than what she'd left behind.

This was such a mistake, she thought wildly. *Coming here was the absolutely wrong decision.*

No surprise there. She was the queen of wrong decisions, starting with the one that had landed her in this mess to begin with. If only she hadn't gotten behind the wheel that night…

She turned away and took several deep breaths, trying to pull herself together. She knew what Jonah would say if he were here — she needed to be calm and rational right now, needed to understand what was going on. Her first instinct was to simply turn around and head back the way she came, but she knew, despite how angry and frustrated she was, that the likelihood she could find her way back to the city was pretty low.

She turned back to the man, who was watching her carefully. She realized she probably looked a fright — she was dog-tired, battered and bruised, and her dress was torn, her hair a mess. She fought the reflexive urge to smooth her hair and instead, with as much dignity as she could muster, asked, "Are there many of those things around here?"

The man's dark eyes narrowed and his stance changed to one of impatience. "The Fantasmas do not attack unless provoked. They only wanted something to help them remember. Are those trinkets you carry so important that you could not spare one for an unfortunate soul, lost in this unholy place?"

Irene's mouth dropped open. "How dare you! How the hell was I supposed to know what they wanted?"

He was still regarding her as if she was something disgusting that he'd stepped in. She snapped her mouth shut and looked him up and down, eyeballing him as he had her. He was about her age and height, with a sort of Mediterranean look, what her mother would have called "swarthy" — dark complexioned with wavy brown hair so dark it was almost black, a full but neat mustache, and a closely cropped beard.

Her eyes stopped in surprise at his feet, which were clad only in rough woolen socks. She looked hard at his clothes and noted that he was wearing what looked almost like tights with a knee-length linen shirt of off-white. She blinked at the strange pajama-like outfit but didn't comment. She was wearing a skimpy cocktail dress with a too-large man's suit coat in a vomit-inducing shade of olive green. Who was she to judge?

"Okay, fine," she said frigidly. "Would you mind telling me where we are?"

"I am a Guardian of the Way. I will see you safely to the crossing."

Irene blinked at him as she tried to decipher this cryptic message. "Uh...thanks? I'm fine. I can find my own way from here. I've got a—" she looked around, "cat...somewhere..." However, the cat had vanished.

"Come," he said, still watching her closely, as if she was going to morph into a two-headed space alien at any second. "I will lead you to the river."

"Ah. So by crossing, I take it you mean the place where we can catch the boat to the other side, right?"

"It is the place where we wait."

"Wait? For what?"

"For God to accept our penance and open the gates of Heaven."

Irene stared at him, her eyes almost popping out of her head. Was he joking? He had to be. Only, he didn't look like he was joking. She eyed him from head to foot again, studying his strange clothes. Maybe he was talking about the place of final judgment—the place where the Egyptian goddess Ma'at, the Hindu god Yama, and all the rest determined if a soul was worthy to enter paradise.

A sudden suspicion, accompanied by a creeping sensation of dread, slithered over Irene. "Are you a priest?" she demanded.

"I am a brother of the Holy Order of Santiago."

"Is that a yes?"

A wave of crimson washed over his face and he stiffened angrily. "It would be vanity to assume they speak of us still," he said, "though we were defenders of the faith, protectors of the shrine of Sant Iago, of the Holy Sepulcher, and of the Holy See..."

She floundered along in the wake of this litany, trying to find something familiar in his words. She shook her head to show she didn't understand.

The man sighed heavily and waved a dismissive hand. "It is vanity, that is all. It matters not that I was a knight. Whether I be knight, farmer, merchant, or a whoreson drunkard, death has leveled us all."

"Wait, what? You were a knight? Like...a knight? Like, with armor and a sword and all that?" She had, of course, seen them in movies, and she had a vague idea who King Arthur was. Other than that, guys with tin cans on their heads smacking each other with swords was a hazy concept from ancient history that generally held little interest. Irene had never wanted to be a princess in a castle, rescued by a knight on a white horse. No, when she'd played make-believe, she'd been a gymnast, a cowgirl, a race car driver — something fierce and solitary — and when she'd envisioned her dream guy, he'd been in a three-piece suit and decidedly horse-free.

"Yes, a knight — in the service of God. Members of my order were holy warriors — skilled fighters and men of purity who served the Lord."

How did they keep finding her? First there was Jonah, with his puritanical views on drinking, sex, and swearing, and now some kind of religious fanatic from the Middle Ages.

"Jesus," she muttered, "I am in Hell."

This must be just another example of the universe's sense of humor.

Irene cast him an assessing look and mulled over her options. Given the choice between continuing on or going back, she supposed she'd rather continue on. She had no idea if she could even get back to the dead city, and she already knew there was no help for her there. The city was a dead end.

However, continuing on meant accepting this guy's help. The cat had disappeared, and without it she wasn't sure she'd be able to find the river on her own. That is, if the cat was even leading her to the river. She still wasn't entirely convinced the cat was on her side. Plus, there were the "Hungry Ghosts" to deal with, despite what Hercules here might say about them being harmless.

So, on the one hand, the knight's company might not be a bad thing. On the other hand, being saddled with this guy—and all the associated proselytizing and sneering judgment she would most likely have to put up with—didn't seem terribly appealing.

There was also the small matter of what, exactly, this guy meant about "waiting" at the river. The bellboy had said there was another boat, another way to cross. So why was everyone just waiting around?

The creeping feeling of dread returned. She flashed back to the image of Samyel flying away. He had told her, back on Earth, that they were going to different places. At the time, she'd accepted Jonah's theory that Samyel was some kind of demon. She had assumed, therefore, that if they weren't going to the same place, he was going to Hell and she'd be going to Heaven. However, if Samyel was an angel...*fuck*.

Okay, calm down, she told herself. *You don't know this is anything other than the in-between place Jonah told you about.* Or maybe it was purgatory. Yes, she'd done something incredibly stupid by driving drunk, but she hadn't hurt anyone. Well, anyone other than herself. It wasn't like she'd committed suicide...exactly; she hadn't meant to die after all. So, in the grand scheme of things, was her mistake really Hell-worthy?

Don't answer that.

She looked the knight up and down again and sighed. "Okay, fine. I'll just go back and get my stuff, and then we can be off."

"You do not need those items. Leave them."

She folded her arms across her chest again and raised an eyebrow. "I thought you said the Hungry Ghosts weren't dangerous?"

"Woman," he said, impatience vibrating in his voice, "I have been in these lands for eight hundred years. I can assure you that it will hurt you not if you divest yourself of a few worthless items."

She clenched her jaw to keep from saying something she'd regret and, instead, said, with as much calm as she could muster, "Well, I'd like them nonetheless."

He obviously didn't know the value of dead objects or he would have shown a little more concern. Dead objects not only helped you remember, they formed the only acceptable currency, other than coins, among the dead — and if he didn't know, she wasn't about to tell him.

She turned on heel and went back to collect her stuff. The crowd of Hungry Ghosts had disappeared, melting away as quietly and quickly as it had formed. To her surprise, it looked like they had left all of her belongings behind: the bag, the tire iron, the wind chimes — she could see all of it, scattered across the ground. Even the magazine.

Irene grabbed her bag and began stuffing items into it as she went. In a few moments, the knight appeared. He didn't speak; however, he did help her to pick up everything. They worked together for several minutes in unbroken silence.

Once all of the items had been collected and safely stowed in the bag, Irene gestured broadly. "Fine. Lead the way."

The knight set off and Irene followed. She was so turned around now that she had no idea if they were continuing on her original trajectory or a new path. They walked in silence for some time. The quiet began to grate on Irene's nerves so she attempted to strike up a conversation. "So, do you have a name?"

He neither slowed nor turned. "My name would mean nothing to you."

"What the hell is that supposed to mean?" She remembered Samyel's reaction the first time she had introduced herself. He'd been surprised that she had freely shared her name, as if names were secret things, holding some kind of special, mystical significance. She was getting that same sort of vibe from this guy, and once again she felt as if everyone but her knew some great cosmic secret.

"My name means something; it is that of a proud and noble house. It tells of my rank, my estate, my lineage, my allies, my enemies — if you know of such things, which you do not. How could you? You are not from Spain; I can tell. Besides, I know my line died out hundreds of years ago.

Therefore, my name would mean nothing to you. For what, then, should I speak it?"

She imagined hitting him over the head with a rock, and she glared at his back even though she knew he couldn't see her. "Well, for starters, I have to call you something. How about Fred? Fred's a nice name, don't you think? Fred suits you. Yeah, Fred it is. So, Fred, tell me…"

She was gratified to see his spine stiffen, but he sounded remarkably unperturbed as he spoke. "Generally, if people address me, they call me '*Sir*.'"

She nearly walked into a tree at that.

"Sir?" she choked out. Several responses went through her mind in rapid succession, but she tamped them all down, saying instead, "So…*Sir Knight*…can I ask you a question? You said you've been here for eight hundred years. How do you know that?" She glanced up at the bleak gray sky that blended into the trackless gray ground. "It's not like time here is…definite." *Or even discernible.* She glanced at the Mickey Mouse watch. Well, the hands had moved since the last time she looked, but she had no way of knowing if a few hours or a few days had passed. It was already starting to feel like she'd been here forever.

She thought she detected a trace of smugness in his voice as he said, "I ask each soul that I encounter what year it was when they left Earth."

That was actually pretty…clever. She narrowed her eyes. "So what year was it when you left Earth?"

"Year of our Lord, eleven hundred and ninety-five," he responded, sounding weary — as if he had said it many times before.

She turned his answer over. *Eleven ninety-five.* She thought hard, struggling to remember something — anything — about that time period.

In fourteen ninety-two, Columbus sailed the ocean blue.

Right country, wrong year. This guy had lived three hundred years before America had even been discovered. Three hundred years before Isabelle and Ferdinand and Christopher Columbus and the *Nina*, the *Pinta*, and the *Santa Maria*, Spain had been doing…what?

Her mind was blank.

She rolled her eyes skyward. *You never told me this stuff was going to be important.*

"So...," she said, searching desperately for a topic of conversation, "if you're a knight, aren't you supposed to have a sword...armor...stuff like that?" She didn't know the least thing about burial customs of the Middle Ages, but from the little she knew about knights—and what she had learned from Jonah about the burial customs of warriors in general—their armor and weapons were their most prized possessions, something they wouldn't want to be parted from even in death. It was the one thing, above all others, a knight would want to take to the other side.

The knight grunted and kept walking. Irene sped up so she could draw abreast of him. "Okay, what is with the ignoring me? Were questions taboo in the twelfth century or something?"

He stopped short and she almost ran into him. "I am not used to being questioned in such a manner."

She understood the unstated, but implied, qualifier immediately. "By a *woman?*"

"By anyone."

Irene shook her head in disbelief. "Christ! I was just trying to make some conversation."

"Conversation is not necessary."

"Maybe not, but it's usually nice, anyways."

"Seek your comfort from God. I have no words of solace or wisdom." He turned and continued on.

Irene stared at his retreating back. "That's just great," she muttered. If the universe was trying to tempt her into committing murder then it was doing a great job. She swore under her breath and then reluctantly, wondering if she had made the right choice in going with him, set off again.

Five

The silence returned. Irene tried to keep her mind busy so she wouldn't have to feel the quiet pressing down on her. At first she tried to amuse herself by envisioning what the afterlife—the *real* afterlife, the one she'd get to when she crossed the river—would look like. She tried to conjure up images of sun-drenched beaches with half-naked cabana boys serving her fruity umbrella-decorated drinks, but the bleakness of her surroundings kept intruding, so she gave up.

They walked for some time. Finally, when Irene couldn't take the silence anymore, she called out to the knight, "How about we stop for a bit?"

The knight slowed, but didn't stop, as he said to her over his shoulder, "For what reason?"

"For being tired. I'd like a rest break."

The knight stopped, turned around, and frowned at her as if confounded by her words. "We are free of the chains of the flesh. There is no fatigue, no pain, no cold, no discomfort. It is self-indulgent to nurture such feelings."

"Yeah, well, try telling that to my feet." Without waiting for his permission, Irene headed for the nearest tree and plopped down beside it, resting her aching back against the hard, rough surface.

The knight heaved a theatrical sigh and moved closer, standing a few feet away, hands on hips. Irene cocked an eyebrow. "Pull up some ground. We're going to be here for a few minutes."

The knight glared, his frown deepening. Irene ignored him and rested her head against the tree, but it was impossible to relax completely with him looming over her. She opened one eye and peered up at him.

"So, how does one get to be a knight in the holy order of…whatever? Is that punishment for a crime, like community service or something?"

Outrage swept over the knight's face and he seemed to swell with rage. Irene thought he might actually explode, and she reared back in alarm, smacking her head painfully against the tree.

"It is an honor to serve. The ranks of the holy orders are filled with the flowers of the nobility. I am a nobleman, descended from a long line of noblemen and from a pure and unblemished lineage. I chose to enter the Order, as was customary for those of my station and rank."

Irene didn't dare say anything else, since it seemed everything she said just pissed him off. The knight began to pace. After a moment, he tensed and looked into the distance.

"Did you hear a noise?" he asked.

Irene's heart jumped. She sprang to her feet, clutching the bag to her chest as if for protection. "No. Why, did you?"

The knight frowned. "I am not sure. However, it is folly to linger in one place too long. We should go."

As much as her feet still hurt, Irene had to agree. She didn't really want to run into the Hungry Ghosts again— she'd barely survived the last fight, and she was so tired now she doubted she would stand any kind of chance.

As before, they didn't talk as they made their way through the forest. Irene let her thoughts wander as she tried to sort out everything she'd seen and learned since arriving here. Soon, however, a sound intruded, worming its way into her consciousness. She cocked her head, listening hard. It sounded like singing, in the far distance.

"Do you hear something?" she asked, veering to the right and angling toward the sound.

It was a choir; she could hear it more clearly now, and it was beautiful. They were singing an exquisite, wordless melody that spoke to her of love and longing and peace and hope and a thousand other things she had no names for but could sense and feel vibrating deep inside.

The music captured her and tugged her forward. Unconsciously, she sped up.

"That is not the way," she heard the knight say, the sound seeming to come from far away. She tried to pause, to turn and answer him, but found she couldn't stop. Her feet were moving of their own volition, as if she was being pulled by an invisible force. She wind-milled her arms in an attempt to slow herself down and tried to cry out, to call for help, but things were moving too fast, and the words were snatched from her before she could utter them.

She caught another snatch of the beautiful music.

Do not mourn me because I am not gone...

They were singing about death.

No, not about death. Not exactly. They were singing about life and death, sorrow and delight, hope and despair.

I am a thousand winds that blow. I am the diamond glints on snow...

She stopped fighting the force pulling her down the path as emotions surged through her. *Home. Comfort. Longing. Contentment. Joy.* She picked up speed and hurtled headlong as if flying, the trees rushing past in a blur. Panic and fear warred with reassuring calm.

I am the sun on ripened grain...

The trees and the weird gray light disappeared as the world around her faded away, and then there was a sensation of sliding down a long, dark tunnel, though her feet never left the ground. The only thing visible was the path, and she was rushing along it in a darkness so thick and stifling she could feel it pressing against her.

I am the gentle autumn rain...

The beautiful music rose up in an overwhelming swell, breaking over her and washing away all thoughts, all feelings, lulling and consoling, easing her panic. It filled her, replacing fear with a deep sense of calm and well-being.

I am the soft starlight at night…

It *was* a choir. She could make out individual voices now—some sweet and high, some deep and low. Her heart gave a kick of joy. Had she made it? Was this Heaven?

She wanted to sob with relief.

Do not stand at my grave and weep…

Suddenly, she could see stars. For the first time since arriving in the land of the dead, the sky was speckled with shimmering, dancing pinpricks of light. Tears bubbled up and threatened to spill over. Was she home? Was she back on Earth?

I am not there; I do not sleep…

There was a glow up ahead and she raced toward it, the bag banging against her hip. Over a small rise, a village came into sight, as if materializing out of thin air. The falling, rushing, headlong sensation slowed and then dissipated, leaving her walking sedately along as if nothing had happened.

Do not stand at my grave and cry…

She stopped, trying to catch her breath. The music's beauty and a sense of infinite love overwhelmed her. She couldn't breathe, feeling as if she was being suffocated by beauty and kindness. She panted, trying to draw air into her lungs.

I am not there, I did not die…

"I'm not dead!" her heart cried out desperately, as if begging the universe to acknowledge her. "I'm here. I'm still here."

Through the pain and joy, the presence of other people began to filter through.

She wasn't alone.

Irene looked hard, trying to take in everything around her. She was in some kind of rustic Indian village. Everything was suffused in the orange light of a large central bonfire around which tents and teepees—she squinted…yes, teepees—were arranged at uneven intervals. Other, smaller, fires—or perhaps torches—were interspersed throughout the area, providing enough light for her to see a general picture but not to pick out fine details.

She could also see that some of the fires were for cooking. Women bent over kettles hung from wooden tripods, poking or stirring. Other people carried stacks of wood or pushed wheelbarrows or strode past with purpose. No one took any notice of her.

The beautiful music filled the air, coming from everywhere at once, breaking over her and filling her with both joy and sorrow.

She turned in a circle; the knight was nowhere to be seen. That fact gave rise to a momentary panic, but before it could fully form there was a touch on her arm. She spun around, expecting danger, but, instead, found only gentle, smiling faces surrounding her. Unlike with the Hungry Ghosts, Irene sensed no hostility — only kindness. A woman smiled and wrapped a blanket around Irene's shoulders. Someone else put a mug in her hand and Irene took a sip. It was strong, it was bitter, and — thanks be to God! — it was alcohol. She took a long, sloppy drink, gulping it down for as long as she could tolerate the searing in her throat and then finally lowered the mug with a choking cough.

"Thanks," she managed to gasp out. She wiped her mouth with her sleeve and took a deep open-mouthed breath to cool the burning of her throat. "Where am I?"

The woman with the kind face simply smiled. The music swelled.

Irene's brow furrowed. "Who are you? What is this place?"

Again, the music swelled but no one spoke. Gentle hands were guiding her now, pushing and steering her across the clearing, past the bonfire, toward a large tent. She felt something warm and soft in her hands and looked down. It was a piece of freshly baked bread. Her stomach rumbled, and she tore into it, suddenly ravenous. Memories slammed into her, flickering so fast across her mind's eye that she could hardly make them out — being lifted in the air by her father — sitting at Grandma Larson's kitchen table with a cookie and glass of milk — high school graduation — college graduation — on the beach with Jonah — a rainbow — a bird in flight cutting across the sun — and a thousand other images, too beautiful, too comforting, too affecting to hold onto.

She tried to shove the memories and feelings away, but they crowded into her mind, blotting out everything else. She was dizzy now, lightheaded and confused. The gentle hands were now leading her. Everything seemed to be getting dim, and she couldn't see where they were going. She wasn't sure if she had been drugged or was just exhausted, but she was slipping into unconsciousness and couldn't bring herself to care. She felt too safe and comforted, cocooned in warmth and joy. She felt something brush her face and thought it was a flap of canvas.

Her head was spinning, her eyes heavy. Her foot caught on something, and she tripped, falling forward. Hands guided her and slowed her descent. She landed on all fours on something soft. A blanket? She was too weak, too dizzy, too tired to hold herself up, and she flopped down onto her stomach. The fibers under her were soft and inviting against her face. She struggled for a moment, resisting the urge to sleep. A blanket was drawn over her, and the tension in her shoulders turned to liquid and flowed away.

Against her will, her eyes drifted closed and she slept.

Six

Irene floated to consciousness and was soothed back to sleep by gentle hands several times over the course of the next few...hours? Days? Weeks? She had no way of knowing. Always, the music surrounded her, comforting her, filling her up. In her dreams, the music took form, pulled her into its arms, and together they danced. It cradled her while she wept. It stroked her body until she was made liquid with need, and then it made raw and primal love to her.

As she rose to consciousness once more, she fought to surface, resisting the urge to sink back into comfort of oblivion. She rolled away from the soft hands and pushed off the blanket with a groan. She forced her eyes open as she sat up, blinking at the soft light cast by a low-burning torch.

A shirtless man, fresh off the cover of a romance novel, sat by her feet. He smiled at her. She blinked, stupefied, her brain not quite sure how she should react — hunky, yes, but completely out of context. The music surged for a moment, soporific and soothing. The man reached for her, grazing her exposed collarbone lightly with his fingertips. She shivered as the light touch raised goose bumps and sent a thread of molten warmth through her. His fingers pushed at the jacket, sliding it down one shoulder.

For a moment, she was mesmerized, and the warmth running through her pooled deep and low. His hand returned to her collarbone, stroking it lightly, then slid to the thin strap of her dress, pushing it off her shoulder.

A sudden flame of alarm shot through her, breaking the spell, and she jerked away. She grabbed the front of her jacket, pulling it protectively closed. "Get away from me!" She spied her bag nearby, and, in an instant, flipped over, grabbed the bag, and dove for the tent flap. The cooler air outside the tent blasted away the last of the cobwebs, clearing her thoughts. Feeling vaguely unsettled, she clutched the jacket to her chest and race-walked away from the tent, looking over her shoulder. The man didn't follow.

Irene looked around, taking in the village again. "Where the hell am I?" The weird—and erotic—dreams, the haunting music, and the wordless people were making her feel odd—dizzy and slightly off-balance. Her head felt thick and fuzzy, like she had a bad head cold. Her thoughts moved like molasses, and she didn't seem able to work up the energy to care where she was, let alone be alarmed by any of it.

She moved through the village, studying the people at work. No one seemed the least bit interested in her. Her vision seemed to go in and out of focus as she walked—at times she could see the village spread out before her, uncrowded and serene. At other times, everything around her seemed dim and foggy, as if the fires were smoking. The people were the haziest of all. She had noticed before, when she first arrived, that everyone looked blurry and indistinct, but she'd thought it was due to the lighting. Now she realized everyone *was* out of focus, as if she was looking at them through a Vaseline-smeared lens. The man in her tent, the woman who had given her a drink—she had been able to see them clearly when they were interacting with her.

Most unsettling of all was that, even when no one was in sight, it seemed like there was a crowd around her, pressing against her as it undulated with frantic purpose, the to and fro bustle of rush hour commuters trying to catch a train. It was as if everything existed out of the corner of her eye. She sensed things around her, but when she turned to look, there was nothing there.

She felt more frustrated than frightened, like there was something obvious she was missing—a thought just out of reach or a word on the tip of her tongue – and she grew more annoyed by the second.

As she wandered through the village, she tried talking to the few people she could see – women tending cooking fires, men carrying wood, a young woman carrying a bundle of fish on a pole. Some smiled at her but didn't pause what they were doing. Most didn't acknowledge her at all.

"Hello," she said to one kindly-looking woman stirring a pot. The woman smiled and the ever present background music seemed to swell slightly. "Yeah, okay, I get it," Irene said. "You're the ones singing and you can't talk. Great. But where the hell am I and why am I here?"

The woman's eyes slid away from Irene as her attention returned to her pot. Irene waved a hand in front of the woman's face, but the woman didn't so much as blink. Irene blew out her breath as her hands clenched. She stalked away from the woman, shifting the bag to her other shoulder. She headed for the nearest tent. She twitched back the flap and poked her head in. It was nearly pitch black inside. She could just make out a prone figure on the ground, asleep. Pale blue light flickered against the canvas walls, winking in and out. After a minute of squinting, she realized the light was actually images – washed out, like a slide show in a brightly-lit room – and they weren't on the walls; they were hovering in the air, filling the space from edge to edge.

A smiling woman hugging a curly-haired child.

A light spring rain.

A girl galloping across a meadow on horseback.

The images flashed before her like the pages of a flip book. Irene shook her head and backed out of the tent. Her recent – and muddled – dreams rose up in her mind and she shook her head again to dislodge them. A creeping anxiety crawled over her skin and she trembled. She was getting the distinct feeling she was not meant to be here.

Irene dug into her bag and pulled out the flashlight. She switched it on and re-entered the tent. She shone the light around the interior to make sure there was nothing hiding in the corners before crouching down next to the prone figure on the ground. It turned out to be a man.

"Hey," she said, shaking him slightly. He didn't stir. She shook him harder. "Hey!" Still no response. The images around her continued unabated. She reached for the man's wrist and tried checking for a pulse.

Stupid, she chided herself when she felt nothing. First of all, like you know what a good pulse rate is. Second of all, he's dead, just like you. Third of all, this is clearly not real.

She stood up, dusted herself off, and stepped out of the tent.

The next tent was the same—a prone figure on the ground, pale images dancing in the air. This time, though, there was a young woman kneeling on the ground next to the sleeper. The kneeling woman looked up when Irene entered, but then promptly went back to watching the sleeping person. The images above this sleeper's head were different, but just as random and abstract as the man's had been.

"What are you doing?" Irene asked the watcher, but the woman ignored her. Irene shifted uneasily from one foot to the other. Was this the place of judgment Jonah had talked about? Were these images scenes from the person's life? She thought of the man who had been in the tent when she'd awoken. What images had flashed over her head? The same as she'd seen in her dreams? Had the man watched her dancing and weeping and having sex? If so, what had he thought of her?

She turned and burst out of the tent, needing air. She forced herself to keep going, to keep checking tents, hoping desperately that she would find something that made sense. However, tent after tent, it was all the same. The only variation was in the images over each sleeper's head and whether or not there was a watcher.

Fine, she thought, struggling to control her mounting frustration and fear. As much as she hated to admit it, the knight had been right—there was nothing for her here. This was not where she was supposed to be.

She surveyed the village once more, trying to remember from which direction she had come. She hefted her bag more securely on her shoulder and then set out, pretty sure she was retracing her steps back toward the dead forest.

She passed the perimeter of the camp, the line of tents and teepees fading into the distance. In the next instance, the village reappeared in front of her.

Irene stopped. She looked over her shoulder; there was nothing but a vast expanse of bare ground and the star-lit sky behind her.

"What the...?" Hadn't she just walked *out* of the village? So how could she be walking *into* it again? She turned around, putting the village behind her and set off once more. In an instant, the village materialized in front of her again. Her heart sank. She knew this game. She'd had bad dreams before, had seen horror films — the kind where the door was locked and you couldn't get out, where you ran and ran but safety only got farther away while the thing chasing you got closer and closer.

She squared her shoulders and continued walking, not ready to give up just yet. She walked straight through the center of the village and kept going. If she walked in a straight line, then, logically, she would have to leave the village behind. However, again, the village reappeared before her as if she had simply walked through a revolving door. Her heart fluttered, harder this time, and she took a deep breath to fight the rising panic. *Okay, keep calm. Exhaust all logical possibilities before you panic.*

Maybe it was a different village, and it just looked really similar to the first one.

And was only two steps away from the first one?

Well, maybe it was another strange tunnel thing, like the path that had brought her here. Maybe she was crossing from village to village and it just seemed like it was a couple of steps.

Irene's gaze wandered over the bonfires, the torches, the tents. How the hell would she know if it was the same village or not? There were no landmarks, no distinguishing people or objects to either confirm or refute the identity of this particular village.

She stalked over to the tent she thought had been the one she'd occupied and threw back the flap. A woman lay on the floor, sleeping. Images danced in the air above her. For a moment, Irene's heart stopped. Was that her lying there?

She shone the flashlight on the woman's face, her heart in her throat, terrified she would see her own face there. The light caught the woman's hair—blond, not red.

Irene sagged with relief. She lowered the flap and caught her lip between her teeth. *Well, what the hell am I supposed to do now?*

She wandered across the center of the village. Again, she had the strangest feeling she was in the middle of a hurrying crowd, people brushing against her from all directions, but there was no one in sight. She could feel them, though, sense them, almost hear them in fact, but it was as if her eyes just didn't register them. She felt a cup being pressed into her hand and she snatched at it, pulling it from thin air. It materialized in her hand, and she tipped the contents down her throat, washing away her qualms and confusion in the searing burn of straight vodka.

She continued moving aimlessly through the village, taking long, breath-snatching gulps from the cup in her hand.

So…this was Hell.

Despite the indescribable beauty of the music and the fact that there was unlimited alcohol—and possibly even sex, if Mr. Overly-Touchy-Feely in her tent was any indication—this clearly was not Heaven, after all.

There was a brief flare of disappointment and then…nothing. She felt a weird sense of disconnect—she should be more frightened, possibly even despondent. At the very least, she should be mad as hell—if she had wanted to spend eternity drinking and having mindless sex, she could have stayed on Earth. There she would at least have also had friends, a comfortable bed, and sunshine.

Maybe I'm in shock.

She thumped down on a large boulder. She went to take a swig from her cup and realized it was empty. She banged it against the rock. "Hey, a little service here!" She shook the cup again and was gratified to hear the slosh of liquid, though surprised by it as well. She hadn't really expected the whole shouting at thin air thing to work. She supposed this proved she wasn't completely losing her mind — there were invisible people around her. At least they provided decent service.

She took another long, satisfying drink. She felt a twinge of guilt, knowing she was breaking her promise to Jonah, but didn't stop.

"Well, you're certainly not the usual," a large, deep voice said.

Irene nearly choked on her drink. She lowered the cup and looked up, blinking in surprise at the man standing there. No one would call him handsome, that was for sure. He was short, round, and bald, and had a garish, multi-hued sheet twined around him like a toga — the wavy stripes of yellow, orange, blue, and purple making Irene's eyes water. He reminded her of a circus tent: big and colorful.

The dead looked how they thought they looked, and most people seemed to have a bit of a blind spot in this area — they either thought they looked average or slightly above average. The end result was that the dead tended to be rather uniform looking — not too tall, not too short, not too thin, not too fat. This guy was either a hell of a realist or he was something altogether different.

Irene lifted her gaze to his face. Her eyes locked with his, and she suddenly knew he was in the "something different" category. A warm, comforting benevolence flowed from his large, liquid eyes; it was as if she was drowning in warm chocolate. It was love, pure and absolute, and she had never felt anything like it before. The sensation was too earnest, too generous, too kind, and she had to look away.

He ambled up and leaned against the rock, his back to her. "So, what did you dream about?"

Irene took a long, slow drink, trying to decide how she wanted to respond. She wasn't an idiot. She could see him clearly and he talked. He was real — probably the only real thing in the entire place. Something about him invited — no, compelled—absolute confidence and trust, but Irene resisted, part of her fearing a trap.

"What are you supposed to be?" she asked.

He didn't seem in the least perturbed by the question. "Just a sign post, someone to keep your feet on the path."

Something clicked in her brain. Jonah had talked about Buddhas—wise sages that guided people in the afterlife. Apparently, here, at long last, was her guide—her *real* guide, the one she'd thought Samyel was supposed to be. She gave him a sideways look, assessing him.

"So how do I get out of here?" she asked.

"What did you dream about?"

She took another drink, stalling for time. The question was too intimate, too personal. It was none of his business.

She kept drinking. He stayed silent.

Besides, the dreams were probably some kind of Rorschach test, and she had no interest in being psychoanalyzed.

She gave him another sideways look. Something about his demeanor suggested he was willing to wait all eternity for an answer.

She tried to hold out, to force him to give in first, but she ran out of patience. She might be stubborn, but she wasn't good at games and she was sick of this place. She wanted to leave.

"Dancing and sex," she muttered into her cup.

"And how did that make you feel?"

She couldn't suppress an eye roll. "I don't know…" She shrugged impatiently, feeling suddenly embarrassed. "…confused. It felt…good, but it was like, at the same time, I didn't want to be doing…" She felt herself blush and was horrified at her sudden discomfort. She was certainly not squeamish when it came to talking about or having sex. "…those things."

Or doing them with some nameless, faceless person.

That realization shocked her.

"Hmm, interesting," he said.

When the man in the tent had reached for her she had felt…disgusted. Not by him, per se, and not by the thought

57

of having sex with him, but by the thought of him touching her, even if it was only the slightest contact. She'd had a deep, shuddering sense of being violated in some way. It had seemed obscene that someone she didn't know, someone who didn't know her, should touch her—which was the terrifying part, because she didn't know why she should feel that way. She'd never had a problem with casual sex—had, in fact, enjoyed plenty of it during her lifetime. So why should she suddenly be overly fastidious about a simple touch?

She felt a deep, stabbing ache of longing that took her by surprise, followed immediately by a wild flare of panic. She shouldn't feel this way—something was very, very wrong. Death had changed her somehow.

No, not death; Jonah. Jonah had changed her. She remembered the exact moment when things had changed — that moment when she'd hurt him and had felt…guilt. For the first time in her life, she had engaged in self-censure, had wanted to change herself not in response to someone else's expectations or demands but because *she'd* wanted it— because his approval, his friendship, had meant more than her freedom to do just as she pleased.

"That's what self-respect feels like, in case you're wondering," the man said.

Irene stared at him, her eyes wide. Her friendship with Jonah had been something entirely different and new, unlike anything she'd ever had with anyone else—with her "friends," her family, her boyfriends. It had been a true friendship, complete with absolute honesty, unwavering loyalty, and acceptance of the other person's faults as well as his or her good qualities. For the sake of that friendship, she had made promises—that she'd be brave and strong and honest—and had even set off on this stupid journey. Now it appeared that friendship had opened some kind of door, a terrible, awful Pandora's box that was changing her in unexpected ways, to the point where she couldn't even stand the thought of a casual touch from a stranger.

Her fingers convulsed around the cup in her hand, reminding her it was still there. She felt another wild flare of panic, and she set her jaw, pushing down the jumble of feelings that had risen so suddenly. "So what am I supposed to do now?"

The man nodded toward the tents. "Probably go back to sleep, finish the dream, figure out what it is you want."

She didn't need mystical, fortune-telling dreams for that. "What I want is to leave."

What I want is another chance.

That thought surprised her. Even more surprising was the realization that it was true. For some time a feeling she couldn't name had been creeping up on her, stalking her, hovering just out of sight, growing even before she'd left Earth. She had managed to keep it at bay by keeping busy, keeping distracted—and drinking a lot, when that didn't work. However, here it was at last, staring her baldly in the face: regret.

She wanted to do better, be better, and it was too late; she was dead. *Better late than never, my ass.* She had an urge to laugh hysterically or, perhaps, to cry. She took a drink to stop herself from doing either.

The man was watching her intently, as if he could read her thoughts. "So leave. No one asked you to come here. You did this to yourself."

Irene shook her head. "That's not true. I didn't choose to come here, it just happened."

His voice was gentle but firm. "Everything that happens to us is a result of our choices, Irene."

His words were like a slap, and she reared back in shock. "I know that," she said. "Do you think I don't?"

His eyes moved to the cup in her hand. "Do you?"

She looked down, and then a bolt of white-hot anger jolted through her. She raised her eyes, meeting his level look with a steely one of her own. "So if I put this down, everything will be okay? I won't be dead anymore?"

His gaze didn't waiver.

"Then I don't see what difference it makes. What's done is done."

The corners of his mouth lifted in a gentle smile. "That might be part of your problem."

"My only problem," she ground out, "is that I'm stuck here, in the village of the damned, and I want out. Are you going to help me or not?"

"No one is keeping you here. If you want to leave, then leave."

"As far as I can tell, no one is doing anything!" she cried, finally losing her temper. "This is the most unorderly version of the afterlife I've ever heard of. There's clearly no one in charge, nothing makes sense. People and cats and freaky little monsters appear and disappear at will..." The panic was threatening to engulf her again so she raised the cup to her lips and took a long, steadying drink until she felt calmer.

The man was studying her with a critical, assessing look now. "You really should go back to sleep and finish figuring out what you want."

With a cry of frustration, she threw up her hands, accidentally tossing the contents of the cup as she did so. "You already said that. I know what I want. I want to get the hell out of here, that's what I want!" She tossed the now empty cup to the ground and kicked it for good measure.

He tilted his head, as if contemplating something. "It's interesting that you managed to get here at all."

"What's that supposed to mean?"

"It means..." — he seemed to be considering his words carefully — "it's unusual for someone to be able to get in without being able to get out."

"That doesn't really help."

His eyes, though still full of love and gentleness, now held a touch of reproach. "You know, the world is a beautiful place if you have the eyes to see it."

She glowered at him. "Technically, I don't have eyes at all. I'm dead."

"Exactly. Yet, you're still trying to *see*."

That made her pause.

Samyel had mocked her once, saying, "You see with no eyes, you hear with no ears." Later, he had ridiculed her belief that he understood 'the tongues of men' — "My English must be very good, indeed," he'd said. "You speak with no mouth."

She'd understood what he meant in a literal sense but hadn't really absorbed the ramifications. If she had no eyes, how did she see? If she had no mouth, how did she speak? At the time, she'd wondered how it was she was communicating but had pushed it out of her mind. The thought was too big, too overwhelming. She'd had no room to grapple with the possibility she might have developed some form of ghostly telepathy. She had wanted to be alive and hadn't wanted to acknowledge that death had changed anything. Having no physical body and developing psychic powers would have definitely meant things were different.

However, here it was once more: the unwelcome idea that death had resulted in a great many changes and that she was going to have to change too, in order to come to grips with this new "life."

Something the knight said tickled her memory—he was from Spain. Since she didn't speak Spanish, he must have been speaking English, right? After all, he'd had like eight hundred years to learn it. However, she knew the answer to that: not very likely.

Other thoughts began to intrude—if she had no body, she had no legs. So how did she walk? If she had no arms, how did she pick up stuff and carry her bag? If she had no body, why did she feel pain when the creatures in the city had bit and scratched her and feel aroused when the guy in the tent had touched her? While the dead couldn't actually feel physical sensations, they could remember what they felt like. Were those feelings just memories? Did she just imagine the pain?

The knight had told her it was impossible that her feet could hurt or that she could be tired or hungry. However, if she wasn't supposed to have any sensations related to her physical self, then what, exactly, was she supposed to be feeling? What was left after you took away sight and sound and taste and touch?

"So what does that mean, exactly?" she asked. "Am I just imagining that I'm—" She blinked in surprise and quickly looked around, but the man had disappeared.

"Why does that keep happening?" she asked out loud, trying to stay calm.

All the unanswered questions rose up together, pushing all other thoughts aside. An answer, too dreadful to contemplate, presented itself. If you took away all the physical sensations, then there was nothing left—and maybe that was what death really was. Maybe by holding onto the memory of her physical self, she was holding herself together. If she let go of that, then maybe she'd just...fall apart, dissolving into nothing.

No, she told herself fiercely. *That's not the answer. I refuse to let it be the answer.* The Guide must have meant something different; there had to be a way—a real way—out of here.

Irene dredged her memory, cobbling together everything she had learned about being a ghost since she'd died. She knew self-perception could change the way you looked to other people. The Guide had said that the world was a beautiful place, "If you have the eyes to see it." Perhaps that implied that perception could change what you saw as well. So did that mean she was imagining the village?

She looked around. No, the village was real—in a sense. This wasn't a dream, of that she was certain. Her brow furrowed. So what of the vast crowd of people she sensed, just beyond her range of vision? Could it be that there was actually a teeming crowd of people out there, just out of sight? Could the reason she couldn't see them be because she kept trying to look at them with physical eyes—which she no longer had?

Maybe she hadn't been alone this whole time. Maybe there were millions of other people here, and she was just looking at everything the wrong way. She'd had the same problem finding the tunnel to the afterlife—it had been right in front of her, only she hadn't been able to see it.

She concentrated harder, digging deeper into her memory, trying to understand.

The living people back on Earth who had been able to see or hear her — Jonah and Madame Majicka the psychic — obviously knew how to "see" and "hear" in a different sense of the words, the same way she now saw and heard in a very different way. She had no idea what that way was, and how she was supposed to tap into it...way beyond no idea.

"I'm so screwed."

Instantly, Jonah's disapproving face came to mind. He had accused her, on several occasions, of giving up before she had even tried. He would, no doubt, say this was one of those times.

Okay, fine, big girl pants.

Somehow that didn't seem to be enough. *You can do this if you just put your mind to it*, she told herself. She ignored the little voice that said, "Yeah, right."

Okay, so according to the Guide, she just had to "see" differently. *No problem.*

She made sure to pick up the cup and put it in her bag, which she settled securely on her shoulder, before setting off. She took a deep breath, fixed her gaze on a far distant point, and thought of the forest. She marched across the village square and kept going past the teepees, holding a picture of the forest in her mind.

The village faded away to black and in the next instant reappeared before her as she reentered the encampment.

She gritted her teeth and tried again.

And again.

It's okay, she told herself. *You're still learning. Don't give up. You can do this.*

She walked forward, chanting to herself, "Dead forest. Dead forest. Dead forest." On the next pass, she tried saying, "Take me to the dead forest. Take me to the dead forest." She attempted to clamp a lid on her rising panic as she tried every variation she could think of: she walked forward and backwards, she clicked her heels together, she tried "following the light" as she had to cross to the land of the dead by staring into one of the camp fires. Each time, the village would simply reappear before her as if it had run up behind her and thrown itself into her path.

Finally, so exhausted she could hardly put one foot in front of the other, she had no choice but to give up. Blindly, her eyes bleary and heavy with fatigue, she stumbled back to the center of camp and sought out an empty tent. She threw herself down on the soft blanket that covered the tent's floor. Sleep came hard and fast, washing over her like a tidal wave, and with it came another round of unsettling dreams.

Seven

Irene awoke and crawled out of the tent, feeling sick and uneasy. Her stomach churned with uncertainty and something else, a kind of empty, aching need — unfulfilled longing? Unsatisfied desire? She couldn't quite put her finger on it.

She looked up at the sky. It was still dark — she hated to call it night since it seemed to be perpetual — and the stars shone cold and bright high overhead. *Just one more example of how the English language isn't equipped to handle life after death*, she thought. There was the entire funkiness of referring to her current existence as "life" when she was technically "dead," and now there was no way to keep track of time in a place that had no sun.

For simplicity's sake, she decided to call the time when she was awake "day" and the time she was asleep "night." Assuming her "body" was still on a twenty-four hour clock and tended to want to sleep at roughly the same time it had when she was alive, she had been here for at least two days.

"Well," she said, smoothing her dress. "What shall we do today?"

The question was, of course, rhetorical. There was nothing to do. Sleep had not brought any additional clarity about how to leave the village. She was still stumped.

She dug in her bag and pulled out the cup. She held it out. "Coffee, please." The cup filled to the brim with steaming, hot liquid. She took a sip. *Huh.* It was good, and it was just the way she liked it.

Sipping the coffee thoughtfully, she circled the village, looking for anything different from the day before. Everything was still the same. She spied a large, flat stone, probably the one where she'd met the Buddha on the previous day. She scooted up onto it and dropped the bag down beside her. The bag hovered upright for a second and then tipped over, spilling the contents all over the ground. Irene stared at the scattered items stupidly for a minute, feeling a burst of hysteria bubbling up. She fought the urge to laugh.

Was it even worth picking the stuff up? What the hell did she need any of it for now? She kicked at the pile. Maybe the knight had been right. Useless crap. How could she have been so stupid as to not keep a coin? One of the first things she and Jonah had talked about was the Greek myth of Charon, the ferryman who rowed people across the river Acheron. She had referred to it as the river Styx and Jonah had corrected her.

Jonah.

God, how she missed him. She felt tears prickle in her eyes, and she studied the objects on the ground, trying to distract herself. She poked the nearest one — her purse — with a toe. She slid to her knees and dumped the rest of the bag's contents on the ground. She spread the pile with her hand.

She picked up the suntan lotion, flipped open the cap, and held the bottle under her nose. Instantly, she was flooded with memories of sun-drenched beaches, the tang of hundreds of different bodies of water — fresh, salt, and chlorinated — and the feel of sand between her toes, in her bathing suit, and dried in her hair.

The memories came so fast and hard they were like physical blows. She doubled over, nearly sick to her stomach. She dropped the suntan lotion and wrapped her arms around her waist.

Oh, God, I want to go home.

She rocked back and forth for a moment until she was certain the contents of her stomach were going to stay where she had put them.

She surveyed the other items and knew it was useless to think of getting rid of any of it. These were her memories. These were her life. Compartmentalized and secreted in finite, tangible objects, but her life nonetheless, and unless there was a way out of this place, they were all that would keep her sane, keep her from fading away into nothingness as the time stretched on endlessly.

Her hand touched a rock, one of the flat beach stones she'd seen on graves. She picked it up, laying it flat in her palm. She didn't remember picking this up. In fact, she had been careful not to take any. It had seemed disrespectful and too much like stealing to remove them, and while she'd seen a few here—both loose and piled in cairns—she hadn't picked any of them up. There had been no point. What would she do with a rock?

No wonder her bag was so heavy.

She tossed the rock over her shoulder and heard it hit the ground with a satisfying thud some distance away. It felt good to be rid of something, to make a decision and be sure it was the right one.

She surveyed the pile again and then grabbed a small handful of paper animals. She picked one up between a finger and thumb. It was a horse. Irene had been in Chinatown during Chinese Ghost Festival, a holiday in which the living left offerings for the dead. These offerings included paper replicas of things people thought the dead would need in the afterlife—money, clothes, television sets, and even animals. Irene had admired the precise and delicate folds of the Origami figures and had picked some up to admire them more closely. Without thinking, she had dropped them into her bag and apparently been carrying them ever since.

Well, even Jonah couldn't argue with her on this—there was no way she was going to need a paper horse on her journey through the afterlife. Plus, these didn't hold any sentimental value. She cast the horse onto a nearby fire and watched as the paper curled and blackened in the low-burning flames.

The fire leapt and seemed to glow blue for a moment. Irene tensed — what was happening?

Thick black smoke began to rise slowly from the flames, spiraling upward in a thickening column. The smoke grew denser and then elongated sideways. Irene leapt to her feet and backed away, her heart pounding. Something was forming in the fire.

The smoke was taking shape now; there was purpose and design in its movements. She could see a long, horizontal back, four legs, a neck, and finally a head and a tail. The smoke swirled with a final flourish and then shuddered into the solidity of a smoke-colored horse. The animal blinked passively. Then it violently shook its head, blew out a breath, and delicately picked its way forward out of the fire. It immediately put its head down and began to lip the ground, looking for food.

Irene stared stupidly at it. "Are you shitting me?" She started to laugh and knew she sounded hysterical. *This is it. I've finally cracked. I've gone completely off my rocker.*

Well, who could blame her? She'd gone from one crisis to another since arriving here. The strain would be enough to drive anyone over the edge.

She pinched her arm through her jacket and then yelped at the resulting pain. *Okay — so not a dream.* She heard the crinkle of paper and looked down. She had crushed the remaining paper figures in her fist. She opened her hand and stared at the crumpled items. A crane. A swan. Two more horses. Three items that might be temples or possibly houses. A filigreed rectangle that might be a decorative screen.

She looked at the horse again and then at the items in her hand. She couldn't seem to get a handle on her thoughts. The living could send items to the dead — that she was already aware of. However, the fact that little paper items could be turned into the real thing was entirely new.

Another memory surfaced — she had worried that her mother might cremate her body, rather than bury it. Jonah had reassured her that she'd still be fine; burning items also sent them to the land of the dead.

Irene stared at the horse. After a moment, she crept forward, ready to run if the horse decided to attack her. It lifted its head, watching her with a wary eye, and then returned to nibbling the ground.

Irene poked its shoulder. The horse snorted, shook its head, and moved a few steps away.

Okay, so not a hallucination, either.

She frowned and bit her lip, at a loss as to what to do. The horse didn't seem terribly interested in her, so she retreated back to the rock. Her eyes absently roamed over the pile of items from her bag, as if the answers she sought lay there.

Her gaze fell on the words "SO YOU'RE DEAD" emblazoned on the cover of a thin black book. She snatched it up, dropping the paper items, all thoughts of the horse instantly shoved aside; she'd forgotten she had this. She'd gotten the snarky self-help book from Madame Majicka before leaving the land of the living—gone through a lot of trouble, in fact, to get it, including attempted breaking and entering.

She cracked the book open but was prevented from reading it by the sudden appearance of a large velvety nose in the middle of the page. The horse, apparently bored, had wandered closer and now stuck his nose in the middle of the book, sniffing wetly at it as though hoping it might be food.

Irene sprang up. "Shoo!" she cried, flapping the book at the horse. "Go on. Get away from me." The horse snorted, put its head down and began nuzzling the pile of items from Irene's bag. "Get!" she cried. "No! Bad! Bad horse! Sit! Stay! Uh…" She flailed wildly, at a loss what to do. She was a city girl—what the hell did she know about horses?

The horse responded by sticking its nose into her hand and snuffling, leaving a trail of thin, clear snot behind.

"Ugh!" she cried, wiping her hand on its neck. "God, you're a disgusting creature. Get! Yuck! Go on!" The horse was unperturbed by the chastisement and wandered off with a flick of its tail to graze a few feet away.

With one last suspicious glance at the horse, Irene stuffed everything else back in her bag for safe keeping. Then she settled herself and the bag on the rock, hopefully putting both out of the horse's way.

She opened the book and ran her eyes over the page. It contained only three lines, printed in a large, stark font:

1. You're dead.
2. No, really, you're dead.
3. But life goes on.

The first time she had read these words she'd been incredulous, wondering if it was a joke. Now the words took on a different meaning – life did go on. Death was not an ending; it was a change in state of being. Somewhere along the line, mankind had lost this knowledge. Humans used to prepare their dead for the next stage of life. They had stories that told you what to expect, and when they buried you they included a care package of necessities. Somewhere along the line, views had changed. Death had become more about the living – helping them cope and carry on – and the dead were left to fend for themselves.

Irene turned the page and skimmed the FAQ, hoping desperately that it held some answers.

Q: Is this Hell?
A: It depends on your point of view.

Irene grunted. *Yes*, she thought sourly, *it really did*.

Q: Why haven't I crossed over?
A: Death isn't about a right and a wrong way to do things; it's about having options.

Since she'd died, she had been faced with a multitude of choices: stay on Earth as a ghost – which was incredibly boring while also simultaneously surrounding her with reminders of everything she'd lost – or cross over – where she'd face the possibility of things like Hell, eternal torment, and final judgment, not to mention the various exciting climatic and geographic features, such as freezing winds, lakes of fire, and razor sharp mountains; stay in the dead city — all alone except for the vicious little monsters that kept attacking her — or traverse a forest full of insane ghosts in the vague hope of finding a place to cross the river; stay here in the village — where it was safe, yet she'd have no hope of ever moving on — or find her way back to the forest — which was unsafe and held only a vague promise of helping her reach her goal of continuing on to the land of the dead. Oh, yes, the afterlife was definitely full of options. Unfortunately, they all sucked.

"Nice horse."

Irene started and turned her head. The Guide looked just the same as before, including the brightly-colored toga.

"*Don't* start," she said.

"I thought you were leaving."

"I tried, but I couldn't do it." She shrugged. "I guess I'm just not smart enough."

"Oh, baloney! Don't give me that. You don't get to just give up and then sit around sulking until someone hands you the answer."

"Oh, come on," she said. "Can't you at least give me a hint? I'm clearly floundering here."

"Why should I give you a hint?"

She glared at him. "Because you're my guide, right? You're supposed to help lead me into the light or Nirvana or whatever."

He raised an eyebrow. "Whatever gave you that idea?"

Her mouth dropped open, and she slid off the rock so she could stand, hand on hips, facing him. "If you're not my guide, then who are you?"

He gave her a gentle smile. "Oh, just a guy." At her look of mute outrage, he laughed, the sound a warm, deep, comforting rumble. "Okay, fine, here's the thing: you're on the right track, but you have to walk with purpose. You have to know where you're going and you have to *want* to get there."

Irene stared at him with a mixture of dismay and shock. It was true she didn't really want to go back to the woods or to the river. What she really wanted was to go home. To Earth. To her life. To wake up in her bed, safe and alive, and find that this was all the aftereffects of a night of heavy drinking. To have a second chance to do things right — to be a better person, a better daughter, a better friend, to love and be loved. But how had he known that?

She stared at him for a moment, and then realized it didn't matter. Somehow, in this strange, incomprehensible place, rational explanations didn't matter. He was here, and he was trying to help. If she wanted that help, she was going to have to start being honest.

She looked down and toyed with a button on her coat, twisting the hard, olive-green plastic under her fingers until she had nearly broken the threads holding it in place. "I want to go home," she confessed, feeling like a four-year-old admitting she was scared of the dark.

"So go home."

She shrugged her shoulders impatiently, as if trying to shake off a fly. "Home means Earth."

"Yeah...so?"

She hesitated. "Can I do that? Can I go back to Earth?"

"You're already on Earth."

Her head snapped up and she raised an eyebrow in surprise. "Really?"

"Of course. Where did you think you were?"

Irene shrugged helplessly. "How the hell should I know where I am? It's not like I ever died before."

The liquid brown eyes crinkled with laughter. "You haven't moved through time and space, Irene; this isn't the TARDIS. You're still in the same place. You're just seeing it differently."

She gave him a suspicious look. "Different how?"

"Think of how a leg looks on an X-ray or how blood looks under a microscope — different ways of looking at the same thing."

She stared at him, trying to reconcile the incongruity of a man in a toga talking about X-rays and microscopes.

"Okay," he said, "you don't like that? Well, then, how about...you know how you go to the financial district and the city is full of beautiful skyscrapers and the sidewalks are made of brick or granite and everyone's wearing business suits? Then you go to, say, the garment district, and the buildings and the sidewalks aren't so nice? Same city, different facet."

She gave him an exasperated look. "So, what? You're saying dying is like wandering into a bad part of town?"

He returned her look with an impatient one of his own. "We're talking facets, Irene. Layers. Work with me, here."

Irene pursed her lips. "Okay, fine. Well, what I want is to go back to *my* facet, back to the land of the living."

"Irene, you can go anywhere you *want*."

Her eyes narrowed in suspicion. "As a ghost, though, right?"

"As *anything* you want."

Her heart leapt but she held it in check, still sensing a catch of some sort. "Anything except me, right? I can't be me again. Alive, I mean."

The horse wandered closer to the Guide, sniffing him over wetly in a search of treats. "Irene, you *are* alive," the Guide said gently, stroking the horse's neck. The horse closed its eyes and heaved a satisfied sigh.

"You know what I mean."

"You know, ancient man understood that everything — including life and death — is connected."

"Yeah, yeah, the circle of life — "

The Guide's look changed to one of almost pity. "We are all part of the same whole. The peel, the seeds, the flesh — they are all the apple, and there is no distinction between the whole and its parts. They are one and the same."

She gave him a dry look. "Listen, Obi-Wan, I get what you're saying...sort of — Kumbaya, the circle of life, and all that — but from a practical standpoint, you can't put an apple back together once you've dissected it, and you can't make a new apple from the peel. So they're not the same thing. I'm missing a very big part of my apple — it's in a grave somewhere, decomposing as we speak."

"Just because *you* can't make a new apple from the peel, doesn't mean it's impossible. The blueprints for that apple live inside every single cell of its being. As long as one atom of it exists, the entirety of its being exists."

She blinked at him. Surprise and hope washed over her. "Yeah, okay, I guess. You're talking about cloning and such, right? But...I don't really see a science lab around here." His look made her stop. "Oh. You're not really talking about science, are you? Is this about God?"

He gave her a gentle smile. "I'm talking about everything, Irene. There are no distinctions. The whole is the part and the part is the whole. The universe is a closed system of infinite simplicity and beauty. Everything works together, the gears of the great machine fitted with precision and care. Nothing is without purpose. There are no extraneous parts, no waste, no excess. Trees make oxygen. People breathe oxygen. Hot air rises. Cold air sinks. Animals eat plants and make manure that grows more plants. A perfect circle; a closed system in which neither matter nor energy is created or destroyed, only endlessly recycled and renewed."

A wave of frustration and despair washed over Irene. "Look, I was a marketing executive, not a science major. I have no idea what you're talking about from a practical standpoint. From a philosophical one, it's really hard to get on board with the whole sense of wonder and joy thing when I've lost...everything."

"Irene, you haven't lost *anything*."

She shifted impatiently, dismissing his words with a careless wave of her hand. "That ashes-to-ashes stuff is not the same as me being alive, on Earth, in my own body, with my own life, again. You keep asking what I want. Well, *that* is what I want."

The Guide smiled. He made a motion with his hand and a perfect little acorn appeared in his palm. "An acorn has many different purposes. Obviously, its main purpose is to become an oak tree. However, it can also be food for squirrels or pigs, it can be ground up and made into flour, and it can rot and provide nutrients for other plants. There is change, yes—rebirth, renewal, transformation—but at all times the essential core—the acorny-ness, if you will—

remains the same. Eventually, with the fullness of time, it becomes an acorn again."

Irene crossed her arms over her chest. "Yeah, that's my point. It's not the *same* acorn."

He raised an eyebrow. "How do you know?"

She opened her mouth to argue and then snapped it shut. She supposed she couldn't say with one hundred percent certainty that it wasn't the same acorn, but, still…that wasn't really the point. "Okay, so you're talking about reincarnation, right? Well, then how do I ensure that I become the tree-making kind of acorn and not the pig-food kind?"

He shook his head. "You're thinking about this all wrong. There's no value judgment. The universe values acorns that make trees the same as those that feed pigs."

She glared at him. "The acorns might feel differently about that."

He smiled. "Not if they understand that they're simply taking different paths to the same destination."

"And what destination is that?"

"To be an acorn again."

Irene's brain cramped. "So, it's just a big circle? The entire point is to go from an acorn back to an acorn again? Then why bother? Can't we just skip all the parts in the middle and stay an acorn?"

He chuckled. "Then how would the pigs get fed?"

Irene compressed her lips into a thin line. Say what he might, this wasn't sounding very good for her future. Even if she got to the river and managed to find a way across, apparently the best she could expect was to then be taken to some kind of karmic recycling plant. She tried scouring her memory for everything Jonah had told her about the afterlife, but none of this sounded like any of the myths or legends she'd heard.

"So where does this place fit in?" she asked, a knot of dread forming in the pit of her stomach. "Am I being punished? Have I been sent to the pig food factory?"

The warmth in his eyes almost undid her. "You haven't been sent anywhere," he said gently. "You did this to yourself, remember?"

A sudden overwhelming feeling of shame and embarrassment washed over her, as if she had let down someone incredibly important. She stared at the Guide, the despair so thick she thought she might drown in it. So she really was in Hell. Tears sprang to her eyes, and she had to turn away to hide them. "So that's it, then? This is my punishment? I made one stupid mistake and I have to pay for it for the rest of eternity?"

"Was it just one mistake?" he asked.

"Too mean," she said softly. "Didn't anyone ever tell you not to kick a girl when she's down?" She felt naked and exposed, and the urge to retreat, to hide, to lash out in order to deflect the scrutiny filled her.

"Irene," he said softly. When she looked, he showed her the acorn again. "Not the exact same acorn, true, but an acorn nonetheless, and that is what is essential to know. All acorns are the same acorn, in their hearts. They all share the same core of acorny-ness."

So the answer was no. She would never again be Irene Dunphy—as she was—on Earth.

He saw her look of disappointment and shook his head. "Have faith," he said gently. "You'll have to go forward to go back, and it will be a long, hard journey, but if that is what you want, *truly* want, then it is possible."

"Faith in what?" Her voice rose to a near-wail.

"In me. In you. In that boy you believe in so much. In strangers. In the universe. In the miracles all around you. In the purpose and design of the great machinery of life. It's all the same thing, really."

She felt very small and insignificant and more than a little confused. She wasn't quite sure if they were talking religion or science or philosophy or maybe just utter nonsense.

She met his warm, gentle eyes, and a tremor ran through her. No, not nonsense. Whatever or whoever he was, he was absolutely sincere, and she knew—though she didn't know how she knew — that he spoke only truth, had only her best interests at heart, and would never hurt or trick her.

She swallowed back the tears. "Are you..." she hesitated, feeling both foolish and frightened. "Are you...God?"

He chuckled softly. "No. And yes. But mostly no. I am all things. Nothing more and nothing less. I am everything that lives and everything that dies. I am everything that was and everything that will be."

Irene's heart skipped a beat. The words were familiar. They were the first words that Samyel had spoken to her. She had thought at the time they sounded like a password of some sort, and now, she had that feeling again.

The Guide seemed to be expanding, a shimmering white glow haloing his body and radiating from him in expanding waves. Irene raised a hand to shield her eyes as the light became blinding. "I am diamond glints on snow and a thousand winds that blow. I am sunlight on ripened grain and the gentle autumn rain. I am the sound of birds in flight and the soft star-shine at night." The last thing she saw was his gentle smile as it deepened. "As are you. As are we all." He faded from sight, the light winking out as suddenly as it had come, leaving his words to hang in the air.

A feeling washed over Irene — so big, so suffocating, there were no words to describe it. She didn't understand exactly what had just happened, but she knew she had been in the presence of something bigger, vaster, more eternal than anything she could have ever imagined. She felt so small in comparison. Even worse, he had said that he believed in her, her of all people, and had put her fate directly into her own hands. Nothing could have terrified her more.

The damn burst; tears she'd unknowingly held inside since long before she'd died were freed at last, and she sank to the ground and wept.

Eight

She cried for a long time. At some point, the horse came to stand beside her. It rested its chin on her shoulder and gently blew in her ear, offering wordless comfort. When the tears finally slowed, she leaned back against its thick, soft warmth.

So what did she want?

She wanted to go back to Earth, that was true, but how badly? Badly enough to be ground up several times over and then finally spit out in some new shape? The Guide seemed to be implying she'd retain some essence of "Irene-ness" at the end of the process. How much Irene, though, and in what form? The idea of being a tree with the consciousness and memory of her human self did not seem in the least appealing. It seemed more likely he had meant some form of reincarnation, where her consciousness or "soul" was recycled, used to make a new person, and some facet of her personality would be passed on, but that was it.

Yet, he'd said, "Have faith," as if she would emerge at the end of the process whole and intact. However, that could have just been a way of pacifying her, fobbing her off like a child.

Have faith — in what, exactly? God? The universe? Herself? Two of those she didn't believe in, and she had no proof that the third had control over anything.

Well, the good news was that she didn't have to know right this instant what she wanted, because, for the moment, all options lay down the same road. He'd said she would have to go forward to go back—which meant, no matter whether she wanted to continue on to her final destination or try to get back to Earth, the choice was the same: she had to get to the river, find a way across, and then deal with whatever happened after that.

She wiped her eyes with the sleeve of her coat and climbed to her feet. She double-checked that she had everything, stowed the magic cup in the bag, and settled the bag more firmly on her shoulder.

She stopped and turned, however, when she heard footfalls behind her. The horse was following. It stopped when she stopped and stood staring expectantly at her.

"Shoo!" she said to it. "I mean it. Shoo." As far as animal sidekicks went, she already had her hands full with the klepto cat. She didn't need a horse, too.

When the horse didn't move, she shouted and waved her arms wildly. When that only resulted in it tossing its head with a nervous, wide-eyed stare, she ran up to it, flapping her arms like a chicken. It shied away from her, jogged a few feet off, and then stopped, staring as if waiting to see what she was going to do next.

She gave up. With a resigned shrug she set off once more for the center of the village. The horse followed.

Will trade horse for guide cat, she thought.

She concentrated on her longing for home, the vast, empty, ever-present aching need. She waited until it was the only thing in her mind, until she could feel it with every fiber of her being. She closed her eyes, letting the feeling fill her. Then she started walking.

Again, there was the sensation of rushing through a long tunnel. She kept her eyes squeezed shut, clinging to thoughts of home like a life raft. The feeling of movement stopped. Everything went still and quiet. Cautiously, Irene peeked at her surroundings through one eye. The cat was sitting before her in the middle of the gray nothing, as if it had been waiting for her all along. It seemed to grin at her for a moment. Then it stood up, tail held high, and walked away, leading her out of the nothingness.

"Good to see you, too," Irene muttered, following it.

The world opened up again, the gray lightened and receded, and she was back in the forest. She heard the soft crunch of footfalls behind her and looked over her shoulder. The horse had managed to follow her out of the village. She looked around, but the knight was nowhere to be seen. She couldn't say she was really sorry that he was gone.

The cat had kept walking. Irene looked at the horse, which was hanging back, gazing at her with a hopeful look. Irene sighed. "Come on, Trigger," she said, sarcastically calling it the only horse name she knew, and even that one she wasn't sure about — was Trigger the Lone Ranger's horse or John Wayne's?

She and the cat quickly fell back into the old routine of ceaseless walking through a landscape that continued to be unvaried and unchanging: thick, black, leafless trees, their brittle branches reaching out like skeletal fingers; gray, rough ground; and always, the gun-metal gray sky, heavy and thick around her.

With the return to the forest came the return of the fear of the Hungry Ghosts. She was tense and nervous, sure that the insane dead hid behind every tree, looming just ahead in the gray nothing, ready to materialize, fully formed, as she drew closer. However, she neither saw nor heard any sign of them, though occasionally she thought she heard footsteps or voices somewhere out of sight.

Finally, she grew tired, the emotional and physical strain too much, and had to stop for a rest. She only meant to sit for a few minutes, but somehow managed to slip into an uneasy sleep. She jerked awake, bolting upright, looking around wildly, expecting to see a ring of Hungry Ghosts surrounding her.

Instead, the horse grazed placidly nearby. The cat sat a few feet away, its tail swishing across the ground as it stared at her. She relaxed, exhaling in a rush, and then climbed stiffly to her feet. She didn't feel at all rested. Her feet ached, her back ached, her head ached; she felt like she'd been awakened mid-nap. No amount of impatiently reminding herself that all of these aches and pains were imaginary helped in the least. God, what she wouldn't give for a hot shower and some coffee. *Coffee!*

She pulled out the cup, held it out, and asked for some. The cup instantly filled. Irene realized she'd been holding her breath, not sure the cup would work outside the village, and now she let it out as she held the steaming liquid under her nose and inhaled the comforting aroma.

She looked at the cat, which had an air of impatience about it. "Lead on," she said resignedly. The cat moved off, and she and the horse followed.

Even after hours of walking, there was still nothing to see.

"Are we actually getting anywhere?" she called to the cat and then felt stupid for talking to it. It didn't seem to notice that she'd spoken.

Finally, after another interminably long afternoon of trudging through the forest without interruption, she called out, "Rest break!" She didn't really expect the cat to respond, but it looked at her over its shoulder and then stopped walking.

Irene headed for the nearest tree. She dropped her bag and sank to the ground, resting her aching back against the tree's rough surface for support.

Even the horse was tired; it snorted, and then with awkward, ungraceful movements, it flopped down on the ground with a long-suffering sigh. It lay on its side for a moment, chest heaving, as if too weak to move. Then, with a snort, it hurled itself over on its back and proceeded to roll. It thrashed on the ground, legs up in the air, in horsey ecstasy. Irene watched it, amused.

There was a rustling sound near her elbow; she looked down. The cat was there, its face and one paw in her bag, fishing for something.

"Hey!" Irene swatted at it. It jumped and then streaked off, disappearing into the gray beyond.

Irene frowned. What had the damn cat stolen now? Who ever heard of kleptomaniac cat, anyway?

She pulled the bag closer and looked inside. On top was an envelope.

"What the....?" She pulled it out. It was sealed, and on the front, in scrawling, untidy letters, was her name.

She hesitated as she turned the envelope over, a flutter of uncertainty making her hands shake. This was new — she was sure of it. Where had it come from? While it was true the cat had stolen one of her pens, she was pretty sure it couldn't write. Yet, it had been pawing the bag, and then this envelope had appeared.

Irene braced herself as she slid a thumb under the flap.

Inside the envelope was a letter — addressed to her. She scanned the bottom of the page, and her heart stopped. It was from Jonah. The writing blurred as her eyes filled with tears, and it was several long minutes before she could see clearly enough to read.

Dear Irene,

I don't know if you'll get this. I'm putting it on your grave. Even if you don't, it makes me feel better to write it, so I'll leave it anyway.

I hope you found the river okay. I wonder what it looks like there. Is Charon really a skeleton or just an old man? I hope everything is okay with Samyel.

~Jonah

Irene started to cry again and then laughed, too, through her tears. The letter was so typically Jonah — he said nothing about himself. Reading between the lines, he sounded sad — and, of course, worried about her. She wasn't fooled by the casual mention of Samyel; she knew that was the whole reason he was contacting her — half burning curiosity as to who or what Samyel was and half dread that Samyel had hurt her once the two of them had reached the land of the dead.

She wished she could write back, that she could reassure him she was fine. Well, okay, maybe not reassure; more like lie. There was already too much worry packed into that fourteen-year-old brain of his, and she didn't want to add to it. Besides, there was the very real concern that Jonah would try to follow her to the land of the dead if he thought she was in trouble, and she didn't want to give him the least encouragement. Jonah seemed to think he'd be able to pop back and forth between the two realms, but Irene was pretty sure it was a one way trip, despite what the Guide might say.

Irene hunched down into the jacket, the letter clutched to her chest like a talisman. Eventually, her eyes drifted closed and she dreamed of the beach. She awoke the next morning thinking she felt the spray of the ocean on her face, only to realize it was the salt of tears. She had been crying in her sleep.

As before, when she awoke, the cat was impatiently waiting for her, and as soon as she was up, they set off.

Every once in a while, she spotted a lone flat stone on the barren ground, which she assumed had been dropped by some dead person who, like her, had suddenly and inexplicably found themselves in possession of a rock.

Why rocks? What the hell use was a rock to anyone, anyway? Why couldn't it be coins? Actually, it was common to leave pennies on a grave, too, wasn't it?

She stopped and pawed through her bag, finally dumping the contents on the ground just to be sure Jonah hadn't sent a penny along with the letter, but she was out of luck.

Maybe it was just Benjamin Franklin's grave that people left pennies on, she mused as she repacked her bag. She had been to Philadelphia once, had seen the mountain of pennies left on the grave of the man who coined the phrase, "A penny saved is a penny earned." Irene groaned. Franklin had to be the richest person in the land of the dead. She shook her head and tried not to think about the endless supply of pennies he had access to, the bastard.

She shouldered the bag and set off after the cat, which was now out of sight.

When she stopped to rest, the cat came close and poked at her bag. Irene peered into it, hoping the cat's actions signaled another letter from Jonah. It didn't. The cat gave her guilt-inducing glares until Irene resignedly reached into the bag and pulled out something — another pen — to give it. The cat took it and streaked off.

Irene sighed and leaned her chin on the bag. She thought about Jonah's letter again. He said he'd left it on her grave. Yet, somehow, it had found its way to her. She wished she could send back a reply. If only there was a way.

If she could, what would she say?

Dear Jonah,

Having a blast, wish you were here.

Yeah, right. Even she couldn't lie so outrageously.

So what would she say? She turned various responses over in her mind until, at last, she had composed something she would actually send, if she could.

Dear Jonah,

Turns out Samyel is a jerk (big surprise). He flew away and left me as soon as we reached the other side (he has wings). This might sound weird, but I think he's an angel. Once again, I'm reminded that all the afterlife myths are true, just not in the way we think they are. Sure, there's such a thing as angels, only they aren't very nice.

I hope you didn't get in too much trouble for skipping school to help me.

~Irene

She sighed again and pulled the coat closer around her, huddling inside its sheltering safety. She suddenly felt the quiet. Knowing that the insane spirits were out there, the sudden stillness had a sinister quality to it. Was that a rustle behind her or had she imagined it?

You imagined it, she told herself fiercely.

She shivered, trying to resist the urge to look behind her. Even now, the insane ghosts could be there, creeping up on her. The hairs on the back of her neck prickled and goose bumps erupted along her arms.

She tried to force herself to think of something else. However, the feeling of unease grew. The need to look behind her became irresistible. She looked.

There was nothing there.

She kicked herself. *Stupid!*

Dear Jonah,

I have become a paranoid schizophrenic. Send anti-psychotics A.S.A.P.

The knight's warning not to linger anywhere too long rang in her ears, and she soon set off again. The next time she stopped to rest, Irene tossed a book of matches to the cat, which took them and trotted off, and then flopped down on the ground and eased off a shoe to rub an aching foot. The horse came closer, stretching out its neck to stick its nose in her ear. "Ugh, get off," she said, more resigned than adamant as she pushed it away.

It shook its head, nearly beaning her in the process, and then, with a heavy sigh, it flopped down on the ground beside her. It heaved another, long-suffering sigh, and then leaned against her, using her as a support for its back.

"Uh, yo, Trigger, I think you have this backwards." She leaned away and the horse finished sagging to the ground. Irene slipped her shoe back on and then leaned against the horse, back-to-back, enjoying its soft, strong support.

She rested her chin on her knees and let her mind wander. After a moment, though, a movement off to her left caught her eye. She turned her head...and froze.

The long-haired woman was there—the insane one—about fifty feet away.

Irene clutched at her bag, dragging it to her chest like a shield. The two women stared at each other, fear and uncertainty telegraphing back and forth between them. Irene started to get to her feet and then, thinking better of it, halted in place in a half-rising, half-sitting position. The other woman had started to move toward Irene, but froze in an arms-and-legs-akimbo stance of wariness the moment Irene did. Irene's heart thumped once, twice, three times. When the other woman didn't move, Irene risked a glance around, looking for other Hungry Ghosts; the dark-haired woman seemed to be alone.

Irene shifted uncomfortably, sliding back down to the ground as she weighed her options. She could try running, but in three-inch heels how far was she really going to get? Plus, she was tired, her feet and legs already spent. Okay, sure, she technically didn't have feet or legs, so they couldn't be tired, but try telling them that. Irene's eyes darted around, searching for escape routes as she surreptitiously slipped her hand into the bag, searching for the tire iron or pepper spray.

The long-haired woman suddenly dropped into a squat, watching Irene carefully as she moved her fingers lightly across the ground, as if stroking it. Irene tensed, bewildered by the other woman's actions. The horse didn't seem the least alarmed by the woman's presence. It was snoring gently beside Irene. The minutes ticked by, ever so slowly. The woman showed no signs of either attacking or leaving; she seemed perfectly content to remain where she was.

Irene's grip on her bag tightened, the flimsy protection giving her a small measure of comfort, as she watched the other woman with unease. The knight had said the Hungry Ghosts just wanted stuff to help them remember. Slowly, watching the woman carefully for any signs of aggression, Irene reached into her bag and pulled out a magazine.

"Here..." she said, tossing it to the woman. It landed halfway between them.

The woman stared at Irene for a moment and then darted forward. She grabbed the magazine and retreated back to a tree. Irene watched as the woman ran her hands over the magazine's smooth surface and then turned it over and over in her hands, as if trying to absorb the contents through her fingers.

The muscles in Irene's legs burned from holding the crouch, so she eased back down into a sitting position. The long-haired woman no longer seemed interested in her, but Irene couldn't be sure the woman wouldn't chase her if she tried to run. So she waited, hoping the other woman would take the magazine and leave.

Despite the adrenaline pumping through her, fatigue returned, and Irene felt herself growing sleepy. She fought to stay awake, but at some point sleep overtook her. She started, jerking awake in a panic. The horse had its nose in the bag in her arms, using jerky, uncoordinated movements to widen the opening. Irene wrenched the bag away, shouting, "Get!" as she surged to her feet.

The long-haired woman was nowhere to be seen. The magazine lay by Irene's side. The cat sat nearby, impatiently swishing its tail.

Irene couldn't believe the woman was really gone. She circled the area, checking behind every tree. She felt unsettled and anxious for the rest of the day, not entirely sure the whole incident hadn't been a dream. She kept the jacket pulled tightly around her and walked with the bag hugged to her chest for comfort.

She resisted stopping for rest until she absolutely couldn't go any farther. She tossed the cat a tube of lip balm and then settled down against a tree. She snuggled into her jacket, tense and wary, absently watching the horse as it grazed nearby. Just as her eyes were drifting shut, she sensed she wasn't alone. Her eyes flew open. The long-haired woman was about twenty feet away, lurking near a tree. Irene watched her warily for a few moments. When the woman didn't seem inclined to come any closer, Irene tossed her a candle to examine. As before, the woman was gone in the morning, the candle left behind.

The next night, as soon as the little band stopped to rest, the woman—who Irene was starting to think of as Elvira—appeared. This time, she brought friends—two men with the same ragged, unkempt appearance and vacant, fixed stares. All three kept their distance.

Irene, made nervous by the presence of the two men, tossed her lipstick to the group and then sat, tense and wary, to see what they would do. Elvira darted forward, grabbed it, and retreated back to the two men. The three formed a small circle, heads together, as they fell to examining the object. They seemed to have no interest in Irene, so she went to sleep.

In the morning, the lipstick was beside her. Even more surprising, the three Hungry Ghosts were still there, sitting against trees only a few yards away. When they saw that Irene was awake, they all became focused and intent, watching her every movement as if waiting for some signal or sign.

Irene tried to ignore them as she got up and prepared to leave. However, their presence became impossible to ignore when she started walking and the Hungry Ghosts followed her. As she walked, Irene kept glancing uneasily over her shoulder, expecting that they were sneaking up on her. However, the ghosts kept their distance, trailing some way behind the entire time.

When she stopped for the night, the Hungry Ghosts stopped as well. Irene tossed the cat another bracelet and the Hungry Ghosts the bottle of suntan lotion and then huddled deep into her coat.

Dear Jonah,

I am being followed by a group of ~~crazy~~ mentally-ill spirits. I don't know if they were like this when they died or if it's this place, but either way, it's really creepy. I've nicknamed one of them Elvira. You're probably too young to know who that is. Look it up on the Internet.

Irene's feet ached. No, it was beyond ache; they felt like pounded meat.

She slid off her shoes and wiggled her toes in relief. She set the shoes aside and stretched out her legs, enjoying the feeling of cool air between her toes.

A movement out of the corner of her eye drew her attention. Elvira had crept closer. Now she watched Irene warily as she snaked out a hand and grabbed Irene's shoes.

"Hey!" Irene cried, starting up.

Elvira set something on the ground with her other hand and darted off. She stopped a safe distance away and watched Irene.

Irene looked down and saw a pair of shoes. She looked back at Elvira, who was still watching her carefully, and then down at the shoes again. They were sensible, flat-soled lace-ups—walking shoes. Apparently Elvira was proposing a trade. Irene wasn't sure if the other woman just wanted the pretty shoes or if she was seeking to ease Irene's discomfort. Since Elvira was out of her mind, it was very likely the former; still, Irene was oddly touched. Elvira could have tried to steal the shoes but instead was offering a fair trade.

Irene gave Elvira a reassuring smile. "Thanks." She dug in her bag, found a pair of socks, pulled them on, and then slipped her feet into the new shoes. They were a good fit.

Elvira seemed satisfied, and she slipped away into the gray mist, followed by the two men, leaving Irene and the horse alone.

Over the next few days, the ragtag band steadily increased until it consisted of a cat, a horse, and twelve Hungry Ghosts—Elvira, Larry, Curly, Moe, Jasper, Cindy, Mindy, Trindy, Original Bob, Bob 1, Bob 2, and Jane.

Dear Jonah,

I have become the Pied Piper of the afterlife.

The Hungry Ghosts were still skittish—more like feral cats than people—and kept their distance, both while walking and when stopped for the night. Every night Irene would give them something from her bag to examine, and in the morning it would always be lying nearby. None of the ghosts ever spoke, and Irene didn't try to engage them in conversation. She still wasn't entirely comfortable with their presence and secretly hoped she'd wake one morning to find they had gone.

Gradually, the landscape began to change. The world started to resolve itself into an actual landscape—a horizon appeared, the gray receded. Finally, they reached a place where the trees ended and the hard, featureless ground was replaced by sand — soft, brown sand.

Irene sensed a disturbance behind her and looked over her shoulder. The Hungry Ghosts had all stopped at the tree line, where the gray ended and the sand began.

Irene gave them a questioning look. "What?" She scanned the way ahead again, looking for some sign of danger. The uninterrupted sand rose gently before them, building up to a small, gentle hill. She looked back at the ghosts.

"Come on." She motioned them forward, but still they hung back.

She chewed her lip for a minute, torn between exasperation and bewilderment. She wasn't sure what to do. It didn't feel right to just abandon them, but if they didn't want to continue on, there was no way to make them.

The cat sat on the rise of the hill, flicking its tail impatiently. The horse was looking at something in the distance, over the rise, and gave a long, low, deep-throated whinny. It tossed its head and whinnied again, sending a shiver down Irene's spine. She didn't know what the horse saw, but obviously it was excited. It was probably just a meadow full of grass; still, that at least was something.

"Come on," she said coaxingly to her companions, growing impatient to see what was over the hill. "It's only a little farther."

Still, they didn't move.

Irene tried changing tactics. "Listen. There's no point in stopping now. We're almost there." She glared at the group, trying to show she meant business. "Okay, fine. Stay here if you want, but I'm going to keep going."

There was some shuffling movement among the group, and Irene realized they were retreating, slipping back into the forest. "Wait," she cried. "I was kidding. I didn't mean it." However, the Hungry Ghosts were already disappearing back into the grayness. Elvira was the last to go. She looked at Irene, fixing her with a steady stare for a long moment, and then with three backwards steps, she, too, was gone.

Irene stared at the spot where the Hungry Ghosts had been, stunned and bewildered that they'd left. Their alliance might have been an uneasy one, but at least it was companionship — of a sort. At least it was better than being alone. Irene realized she had grown a little attached to the ragtag band, and she frowned, wondering if she should go after them.

Something bumped her shoulder and Irene started. It was the horse, grown impatient with standing around. Irene gave its forehead a vigorous rub, which the horse accepted with a contented sigh.

She realized there was no way to find the Hungry Ghosts in the forest. Even if she went after them, she could wander there for a lifetime and never be able to track them down. She turned away with a pang of regret and continued on her way, nagged by a sense of vague guilt. It only took her and the horse a minute to crest the hill. As she reached the top, she stopped cold in her tracks, all thoughts of the Hungry Ghosts washed away.

She had found the dead.

Nine

Below her, endlessly spreading to the horizon, was a sea of people—hundreds, thousands, possibly millions. Her skin prickled, as if touched by a cold breeze. Once again, the stories were wrong. Oh, everyone who had gone before you was here alright, she could see that at a glance. However, there was no city, no palace, no pearly gates. If there was a river, it was beyond the distance she could see. There was only one way to describe the scene spread before her—a refugee camp.

Her heart beat in time to her faltering steps as she slipped and slid her way down the sandy embankment. Behind her, the horse snorted as it floundered through the sand. The cat lightly ran on ahead.

As she drew closer, Irene was able to make out fine details: people huddled in sparse clumps, one person here, two there, three or four together over there; a few makeshift tents made out of clothes or blankets; a few actual tents; and stationed every hundred feet or so along the perimeter, a sentry standing guard.

The sentries were a mixed-up playing-card deck of people from throughout history. Here, closest to her, was a man in a loin cloth, holding a spear planted firmly against the ground. Farther down there was a cowboy, complete with boots, hat, and gun belt. In the other direction, she could see a knight in full armor, a shield held firmly in one hand and a sword with the point resting on the ground in the other.

Inside the protective circle of warriors, there was confusion everywhere. She could hear the high-pitched chord of near-hysteria in a thousand upraised voices, all shouting to be heard.

Irene slowed, approaching warily. "Uh, hello?" she said to the guards, expecting that they would stop her, but they didn't seem in the least interested in her. The loin-clothed warrior's eyes flicked to her and then returned to watching the forest. "Is it okay if I...I mean..." She wasn't sure what she wanted to ask. Not that it mattered—these guys didn't seem like the type to answer questions. She decided to settle for, "Is it okay if I come in?" When none of the guards answered, she edged past them into the outer edge of the camp. None of the guards reacted.

To Irene's right, a twenty-something woman was clinging to an irate older woman's arm. "What are we supposed to do now? Where am I supposed to go? Do you know? What about you? Do you know?"

To Irene's left, a middle-aged man, hunched with anxiety, was wringing his hands. "This isn't right," he said, repeating the words over and over. "I don't understand." He didn't appear to be speaking to anyone in particular.

In front of Irene stretched a row of what appeared to be pan-handlers: men in suits, men in rags, children with large sad eyes, old women with hard angry faces. A young woman in a long, white, Empire-waisted gown clutched Irene's arm. Tears streamed from her large, cornflower-blue eyes. "Please, Miss, take me," the girl cried. "Please! Choose me!"

Irene was bewildered and tried to pull away, but the girl clung to her with unnerving tenacity. Two boys—Dickensian characters with unruly hair, ragged clothes, and a dusting of freckles across their pug noses—burst upon Irene, skidding to a halt in front of her, interrupting the question Irene had been about to ask.

"Penny, Miss?" the taller one said in a thick Cockney accent.

Irene looked from one to the other as she tried to disengage herself from the woman clinging to her arm. "Are you buying or selling?"

"Oh, ballocks, she ain't got nothin'," the shorter, more angelic-looking one said. The taller one made a rude gesture, and then the two scampered off, disappearing into the crowd.

Irene felt her temper rising. This was all too much. It was too loud, too frenzied, too chaotic.

"I'm sorry," she said, prying the girl's hands from her arm. She pushed the girl away and walked off as quickly as she could through the interminable sea of people.

The farther in she went, the denser the crowd became. Occasionally, she would hear the horse snort behind her as it protested the narrow space it had to maneuver. The cat had long since disappeared.

Irene had no idea where she was going at this point. There didn't seem to be any rhyme or reason to the crowd. If there was a river, it was miles away in an unknown direction. She hoped she was continuing in more or less a straight line which should lead her to the "front" of the crowd, but she was so turned about now she had no way of knowing which direction she was actually headed.

As she slowly pushed her way forward, she occasionally asked those she passed about the river—how far away was it, in what direction did it lie? Most looked confused and shook their heads; those who did speak all asked the same thing: what river?

After a while, Irene changed the question; she asked them what they waited for. No one seemed to know. Fear and dread mingled, making an awful soup in her stomach. It seemed that everyone had simply plopped down to wait, without even knowing what they were waiting for. What if the reason was because there was no next? Maybe there was no way across, or worse, maybe there wasn't even a river. Maybe this was the end of the line.

It is the place where we wait.

The knight's words echoed in her head. Irene's heart thumped unevenly in her chest, and unconsciously, she pulled her jacket tighter around herself as she pressed on. Soon she realized that walking through the camp was like moving through a time capsule. The farther she walked, the farther back in time she went. After passing through those who had arrived within the last few years, things settled down. The chaos and hysteria of the new arrivals was replaced with a quiet resignation, tinged with despair. A few eyes would turn Irene's way as she approached, but no one spoke to her. A few people prayed, a few sang — mostly those crooning lullabies to children.

Eventually, the familiar fashions and hair styles of the twentieth century gave way to old-fashioned dresses with tight waists and long skirts and Gibson Girl hair styles. After a while the waistlines got higher — the Empire style — and then she passed through a period where all the women wore wide, hooped skirts, their hair parted in the middle with ringlets in the front and a tight bun in the back.

The strata of time thinned after this, and it was almost as if she could see the exact moment when the living had stopped preparing the dead for passage across the river. It was a like a dam had been built somewhere around the mid-eighteen hundreds, stopping the flow of the dead to the next stage of the afterlife like a log jam.

The more ornate fabrics of the eighteen hundreds gave way to stiffer, drabber more homespun fabrics. Then knee breeches, ponytails, and wigs began to appear on the men. Irene recognized these fashions as being from the time of the American Revolution. It was here that people started to move aside, muttering and crossing themselves as she approached

A prickle of fear went through her and she tried to move faster, wondering how much farther it was to the river. As the clothing began to get heavier again, the skirts wider and fuller, the necks higher — often ending with a ruff or high collar — Irene realized she wasn't even out of the middle ages yet. There were thousands of years of history to go.

She stopped for a brief rest, and found a letter from Jonah in her bag.

Dear Irene,

Things are pretty much the same here. I hope you found the river okay.

She took this to mean Jonah was having a rough time at home or school, and a wave of sadness washed over her as she read it. She wished she could help in some way.

She didn't linger long; not only was she anxious to find the river, but the people here didn't seem particularly friendly. She set off again, her heart heavy. The burble of background noise died away completely. As she and the horse trudged through the stillness, the scenery all seemed to blend together. The clothes became simpler and plainer until both the men and the women were wearing little more than long robes. Then the men's robes grew shorter and hose or leggings were added. It reminded her a little of the clothing the knight in the forest had worn and she guessed she must be in the late eleven hundreds.

Irene felt as if she had been walking for days. At some point she passed into the remnants of ancient civilizations, the men wearing short skirts or robes, the women wearing long robes fastened on one shoulder. The people here all silently watched her, looking at her with empty, expectant eyes as she passed. She could have heard a pin drop.

Then she crossed into early civilization and the people began to look more and more primitive. Clothes all but disappeared, save for basic coverings made of animal hides or fur. Everyone looked at her with suspicion and at her horse with hunger. She held the tire iron tightly, walking as quickly as she could. The horse seemed to agree, because it snorted and pranced with nervous energy until they were well past.

Still, there was farther to go. The dead began to look like shadows—gray, pale, and faded, their clothes nothing more than tattered rags. Some lay prone, while others sat with their knees drawn up to their chests, staring at nothing. They looked more like statues than people, as still and lifeless as stone. She and the horse were the only things that moved.

Finally, she couldn't walk anymore and had to stop to rest. The eerie stillness of the petrified people unnerved her. She fished in her bag for the cup and found, instead, another letter from Jonah. She had no idea how long it had been since the last one, how long she had been traveling through the camp—she'd lost all track of time and none of his letters were dated.

She read his letter and laughed.

Dear Irene,

It's the feast of Parentalia. The stories say we should send the dead salt, cereal, beans, wine, milk, and violets. I'm sending the first three items; I wasn't sure if the milk would go bad and I didn't have the other things.

With the note was a family-size box of Captain Crunch and a can of green beans. Irene didn't see any salt so she assumed Jonah had simply sprinkled a handful of it over her grave. Jonah had neglected to send a can opener, so the beans were pretty useless, but she kept them anyway.

She popped open the cereal, the rustling of the crunchy, sugar-coated bits against the plastic liner bringing a flood of childhood memories. She smiled as she pulled out a piece, studying it in wry amusement. She popped it in her mouth and chewed slowly. She wasn't a fan of this particular cereal, but it felt good to do something so mundane, so normal.

She looked around, studying the landscape as she chewed. The dead were more spread out now, few and far between. She felt something wet on her hand and looked down. The horse was sniffing the box of cereal, trying to stick its nose in. Irene pulled the box away before the horse could get its head stuck.

"I don't think that's horse food," she said.

The horse snorted and thrust its nose into her other hand, the one she had pulled the cereal out with. It must have detected some trace of the sugary treat there because in a long, slow, smooth stroke it licked her palm.

"Eww!" she cried, even as she laughed. She stared at her now sticky hand for a minute, and then, shaking her head, wiped it on her jacket. The horse ignored her and reached for the box, straining its neck as it reached across her, lips quivering, to grab the carton from her hand.

Irene raised an eyebrow. "I don't think you're supposed to have this." She paused to consider. Actually, she had no idea if the horse should have it or not, and since the horse was already dead, what harm could it do? With a resigned sigh, she pulled out a few bits of cereal and held it out to the horse.

The entire handful disappeared in one scoop of the tongue. Eyes closed in ecstasy, the horse chewed slowly, clearly relishing this rare treat. Irene laughed. "You're ridiculous, you know that?"

She popped another piece of cereal into her own mouth and surveyed the landscape once more. They were running out of history; if there was a river, then surely they must be close.

She looked at the nearby people, studying them thoughtfully. How had these people gotten this way? Were they dead or just sleeping?

Cautiously, she climbed to her feet, securing the cereal in her bag and then headed for the closest person, a man, sitting upright, his legs drawn to his chest with his face resting on his knees. She shuddered as images of an exhibit on Pompeii came to mind—bodies frozen forever in the victim's last moments under layers of ash.

"Hello?" she said, touching his shoulder. A shudder ran through him, and then with a soft "whoosh," he expanded slightly and then imploded, turning into a cloud of sand that rained down on the ground. Irene screamed and jumped back, colliding with the horse which danced away with a snort of alarm.

Irene stared at the settling pile of sand, frozen with horror. What had just happened? She'd barely touched him. How could he just disintegrate like that?

She whirled around, expecting someone to grab her with a shout of "Murderer!"

However, all was quiet. Nothing stirred.

She looked down at the sand under her feet and then back at what remained of the man. Comprehension slithered over her and her stomached clenched. She raised her eyes and looked at the sand stretching endlessly for miles in all directions — sand that had once been people.

Irene became numb with shock as the last of her hope sputtered and died. There was no way out of here. This was the end, the ultimate destination of the dead, the literal truth of "dust to dust." This was the transformation the Guide had spoken of — this place was a giant grist mill, grinding everyone down to nothing.

Irene stared at the pile of sand that had so recently been a man. A shudder of revulsion ran through her and she moved away, unable to stand being so close to it. Then, because it was easier to keep going than to stop, she just kept walking, empty inside, mindlessly putting one foot in front of the other. There were no thoughts now, just blind, dumb shock, her brain barely registering the world around her.

Eventually, there were no more huddled, petrified people, just a vast, desert-like expanse of sand, and then, at last, she was at the river. Rather than elation, however, she felt…nothing.

The river filled the horizon in every direction, more like an ocean. The embankment stood a foot or two higher than the water's surface, and Irene went right up to the edge to get a closer look. The water was almost black and as smooth as glass. Nothing marred its surface — not waves, not boats, not birds. The sound of the water lapping at the land was the only noise. It was the most desolate and empty place Irene had ever seen.

She stared at the water, feeling as flat and empty as its surface. There was no ferryman, no landing, no indication of how to get across. The river stretched endlessly into the distance, far too wide to swim. It was vast and insurmountable.

Dear Jonah,

Whatever you do, don't die — not ever. This place is terrible, more awful than any of the stories.

She was still numb, unable to process the great, overwhelming truth that there was no way out of here. She stared at the water for a long time, unable to make any sense of it.

It's all a trick, she thought, *this idea that there's another way across or around, a lie to keep people going.*

Her hands closed reflexively into fists as a small flame of rebellion rose up within her. *Bullshit!* There had to be a way out of here. There just had to be.

What was it the Guide had said — you have to go forward to go back? Or was it you have to go back to go forward? Maybe it worked both ways: she had to go forward by continuing her journey, in order to get back to the land of the living, but maybe she also had to go back to the dead city in order to go forward. The bellboy had said she'd have to "take the long way around," but he hadn't actually said the river was far away. She'd just followed the cat and it had led her here, but maybe this was a completely different — and wrong — river.

She squeezed her eyes shut for a moment as the circular thoughts caused her brain to spasm.

"Hello, Acorn."

Her eyes flew open as she turned toward the sound. The Guide stood beside her, looking the same as he had in the village — garish toga and all.

"Please don't call me that." She frowned at him as a jumble of emotions battled within her — despair, anger, elation, hope, dismay, exasperation. She had too many questions, too many accusations, too many bargains she wanted to strike. She didn't even know where to start.

He acted like he hadn't heard her. His hands were clasped behind his back and he was staring at the water as if he were on holiday. She waited for him to say something, to set the tone for the conversation. If he was here, there was a reason.

However, he said nothing; he just continued to gaze at the water. Irene couldn't hold her questions in any longer.

"So, is it all a trick? Just a lie? There is no way across?" *This really is Hell, and you're some kind of Hell-spawn demon who delights in torturing us, in offering us hope and then ripping it out from under us.*

"Oh, there's a ferry all right."

Her heart leapt with joy, but she tried to calm it and temper her sudden hope. He could be lying, or there could be a catch. "So where is it?" she asked, gesturing with both hands to the broad expanse of trackless sand stretching in both directions. "How do I find it?"

"Oh, he finds you. The ferry only appears if there's someone waiting to cross."

"What am I, chopped liver?"

The Guide finally looked at her. He turned and gave her a soft smile, and that unwavering love in his eyes reminded her why she had trusted him to begin with, why she believed him when he said this wasn't a trick or a game. Gently, he said, "You have to know where you're going, Irene, and you have to want to get there."

Her mouth dropped open. "Didn't we have this conversation already? I told you, I want to go home."

"Yes, but you don't actually have any concept of what that means." His smile broadened. "Plus, you don't have a coin."

Irene's dismay deepened. "I was sorta hoping the guy would take trade."

The Guide shook his head.

"Really?" Irene cried. "It literally has to be a coin?"

The Guide nodded.

"So what am I and all these other people supposed do to? What happens if you don't have a coin—you're just stuck here forever?"

The Guide raised an eyebrow. "If you thought about it for a moment, I'm sure you could figure out who to ask about that."

"Yeah, well, I'm asking you."

The Guide held up his hands. "Hey, I'm just a signpost. I just point out the various paths before you. I don't actually have any answers."

Something bumped against Irene's other side; she turned. It was the horse head-butting her for attention. She pushed its face away impatiently and turned back to the Guide. However, he was gone, melted into thin air as before. She stared at the spot where he'd been, dumbfounded.

"Thanks," she said drily to the air. "Well-oiled machine, my ass." Then she sighed and ran a hand through her hair. Whatever reason the Guide had had for showing up, he'd obviously felt he'd done what he came to do. Which was what, exactly? What had he been trying to tell or show her?

Think, Irene, think. The Guide said there was someone she could ask to find out what happened to those who didn't have a coin, to find out how they got across the river. Her brow furrowed with thought. Who on earth could she possibly ask—

The answer hit her before she even finished her thought. Of course! She could go straight to the source.

Irene turned away from the river, studying the endless stretch of sand the led back to the millions upon millions upon millions of people waiting for whatever came next.

The story of the ferryman and the coin was Greek, and the Greeks were out there, somewhere, in that morass of human history. The key word was "somewhere." She had no idea how to find the Ancient Greeks.

Since everyone seemed to be more or less arranged by geography and time period, she just had to figure out when they'd lived, then she could probably find them. Of course, other than "a long time ago," she was coming up blank. Um...before Christ, right? So B.C.E. sometime. Well that narrowed it down.

A gentle nudge at her elbow brought her back to the present. The horse stood waiting patiently, its head held at just the right height for a scratch. Irene laughed despite herself.

"Yeah, alright." She scratched the spot right under its forelock. The horse heaved a contented sigh and its eyes drifted closed. Irene laughed again. "You better hope the ferry isn't a rowboat. I don't know how we'd get you on it." She gave the horse another rub. "Come on," she said, "let's go find some Greeks."

Ten

A man stood at the river's edge, gazing down into the water.

Irene had been walking for two days and in that time had encountered nothing but sky, sand, and water. If she had a fruity umbrella drink—and could forget that the sand underfoot was the remains of thousands of people—she could almost imagine she was on vacation on some tropical island.

She had followed the river, not ready to give up the idea that the ferryman might show up or that she might find something of interest. Occasionally, she would catch sight of sails in the far distance. The first time, her heart had leapt as she thought the ferry was coming for her. However, the sails had soon disappeared, never coming within hailing distance of the shore.

It occurred to Irene that these ships couldn't possibly be the ferry. The dead were supposed to be rowed across the river, so one could safely assume the ferry was a small boat. The ships in the distance were huge, full-sailed galleons.

They must be dead ships—crossed over with a dead person. It had never occurred to her that ships would cross to the afterlife, too, but of course they could—if cars and buildings could cross over, why not ships?

Now that Irene thought about it, she realized there were probably a lot of boats here in the land of the dead. The bodies of people who went down with vessels lost in deep water were rarely recovered. Irene imagined the Titanic, World War II submarines, and pirate galleons all sailing together in an armada and shook her head. This place really was insane.

The only other interesting thing she'd encountered had been a strange altar of some sort. At first she thought it was a desiccated and decapitated tree, the stump sticking up from the water. However, as she drew closer she had seen that it was a crude plinth or pedestal of sorts as big around as a dinner plate. Constructed out of sand and hardened by time, it was now as solid as stone and covered in candle wax and dark streaks that Irene hoped were wine. A stick had been stuck in the top of it and to this was affixed a large bronze medallion engraved with the figure of a winged woman with an ugly, pig-like face. Irene had studied it for a long time, trying to determine what it was for. However, there was nothing to indicate the altar's purpose, so she'd finally given up and moved on.

Now she was confronted with a solitary figure, the first person—other than the Guide—who she'd seen in days. He stood poised on the edge of the river, so still he might have been a statue. If he noticed her, he gave no indication of it.

"Hello?" Irene said.

Moving closer, she could see that the man was Chinese, dressed in the black silk suit and long hair-braid that epitomized pictures of California railroad workers in the eighteen hundreds. She looked down to see what he was staring at. The water was black and all she could see was light reflected on its surface.

"Hello?" she said again.

The man turned to look at her. His eyes spoke of suffering.

"Perhaps T'ien requires a leap of faith," he said, as if coming to some sort of conclusion.

Irene squinted at the water. With a thoughtful frown, she reached down with a toe, balancing carefully on her other leg, and touched the water's surface. It rippled, just as normal water would.

"I don't see anything," she said. She looked at the man again, but he had turned his gaze back to the river. The horse was hanging back, seemingly afraid to approach the water, though it was craning its neck and impatiently pawing the ground like it wanted to.

"Is there something down there? Do you see something?" Irene asked the man.

She leaned over, trying to get a better look. Suddenly a vice-like grip clamped onto her arm, jerking her away from the water.

"Hey!" she cried, striking out blindly with a fist, only to have her wrist seized. She struggled against the rough hands as she was pulled around to face her assailant. She went rigid with shock as she looked into the frowning face of the knight from the forest. "You!" she said, her jaw dropping. "Where the hell did you come from?" She wrenched free of his grip and took a step back, putting space between them.

"Touch not the water," the knight said.

"What? Why? What's in there?"

"Hippopotamuses."

"Hippopotamuses?" she said, incredulous. "Are you nuts?" She stared at him for a moment, trying to decide if he was joking. "You're from Europe in the Middle Ages—you don't even know what a hippo is." She jerked her jacket back into place with an impatient huff. Before she could say anything else, there was a soft, wet sound behind her. She turned. The Chinese man was gone. She looked at the water and saw the top of the man's head bob and then disappear beneath the surface.

She cried out and started forward, but the knight grabbed her. "Let be," he said quietly.

"But—"

The man in the water resurfaced for a moment. Then two long, dark shapes appeared, like a pair of surfacing submarines. Irene knew what was going to happen a split second before it did. She started forward again, but the knight tightened his grip, holding her fast.

"No!" Irene screamed, struggling futilely to break free. It was all over in a second. There was a flurry of violent movement as two sets of powerful jaws closed on the man in the water, tossed and tore him as if he were a rag doll, and then disappeared beneath the water with their catch. The water's surface grew smooth and still again, erasing all evidence of the violence that had just taken place.

Irene went limp with shock, unable to believe what she had seen. The knight released her and she stumbled away from him, turning to mutely stare at him, too stunned to ask why. He looked like he wanted to speak; however, he said nothing.

Without thinking, she lashed out with her hand, the slap ringing in the air. "How could you?" she cried, finding her voice again. "How could you just stand there and let him die?" Angry tears spilled over, tracking down her cheeks, and she swiped them away with her hand.

The knight remained impassive, her slap not even appearing to register. "What would you have had me do?"

"I don't know. Something. Anything!"

He shook his head. "I had not the power to save him."

"How do you know? You didn't even try!"

The knight gave her an unreadable look. "He despaired."

"So?"

The knight shifted his weight and his face said that he thought she was being willfully ignorant. "Faith is the only proof against despair. I could not give him that. Only trust in God can."

"Yeah, well, God didn't seem to be helping him—the guy looked like he'd been here for a couple hundred years."

"God delays but He does not forget."

Irene stared at the knight, so angry she couldn't even speak. Finally, she managed to choke out, "You're insane. You know that, right?" She backed away from him, shaking her head in disbelief.

The knight eyed her for a moment, and Irene had the sense that, for the first time, he was really seeing her. His eyes lingered on her dress and then the coat and a small furrow appeared between his eyes.

Irene tugged the jacket closed, feeling a swell of righteous indignation overtake her. "Don't comment on my outfit unless you want me to comment on yours," she said with a pointed look at his stockinged feet and the pajama-like pants and top. Instantly, the knight's face hardened and his lips compressed into a thin line.

Irene and the knight glared at each other for a moment. Finally, Irene turned away and studied the water again. There was no sign of the Chinese man. He really was gone.

Irene's jaw tightened. What a stupid way to die. She might have been careless with her life, but at least she hadn't purposely thrown it away. Of course, she hadn't been stuck here for several hundred years. How long would she be able to hang on to her will to live after she'd been trapped here for a year? Or ten? Or a hundred?

It's not going to come to that, she told herself fiercely.

Irene turned back to the knight, grim determination surging through her. "Any idea where I can find the Ancient Greeks?"

His brow creased with confusion. Somewhat warily, he lifted an arm and pointed. Irene settled the bag more securely on her shoulder. "Thanks." She turned and started off.

"Where are you going?" he asked.

She didn't even pause. "I'm getting the hell out of here."

A moment later, she sighed in exasperation as the knight fell in beside her and the horse. "Are you following me?" she asked.

"The legends foretold of this place — the lesser Hell where we await judgment for our sins."

"How nice for you."

He either didn't notice the sarcasm or didn't care, because he showed no sign of being dissuaded from following her. "It means that we are where God intends us to be."

"Yeah, well what if I don't believe in God?"

"Belief does not change what is."

Irene cast him a sidelong glance as she bit back a response. Arguing with him seemed about as useful as beating her head against a wall, so she held her tongue. Maybe if she ignored him he'd give up and go away.

The knight didn't take the hint. After a protracted pause, as if he was waiting for her to say something, he said, "The children are the worst. They do not know any better than to hope."

This time she couldn't help herself. "Didn't you say just a moment ago that despair is wrong? So which is it?"

"In between hope and despair is acceptance."

Irene rolled her eyes. However, the sight of a figure up ahead, balanced on the edge of the riverbank, prevented her from answering.

"Not another one!" she cried. She dropped her bag and took off at a run. "Hey," she cried, frantically motioning for the man to move away from the water, "get away from there. Stop! Hey! Hey, you!"

The man turned. His face was a mixture of surprise and confusion, which shifted to full-out astonishment as Irene barreled into him. Her momentum carried them sideways, and they landed in a spray of sand, safely away from the water's edge, him on his back and her on top of him.

"What in tarnation are you doin'?" the man sputtered.

Irene pulled back and found herself staring into the cherubic face of a tall, lanky cowboy — complete with hat and spurs. She blinked in surprise, her mouth gaping open. He flashed a dazzling smile and a dimple appeared.

"Where on God's green earth did you come from?" he asked.

"I'm sorry," Irene stuttered, feeling like an idiot. She rolled off of him and scrambled to her feet. "I thought you were going to jump."

The man hooted with laughter as he climbed to his feet and used his hat to dust himself off. "Aw, heck, no. I was just admirin' the view."

"Oh. Sorry." Irene cringed and her face heated with embarrassment.

The dimple appeared again. "Well, shoot, I don't mind much. It makes for a nice change." He considered her for a moment, and then his eyes warmed as a slow, lazy smile spread across his face. Warmth of a very different kind spread through Irene, and she bit her lip as she met his appraising look with one of her own. She smiled and held out her hand. "I'm Irene, by the way. Irene Dunphy."

The cowboy wrapped her hand in one of his. "Ian McFarland. Pleased to make your acquaintance." He smiled at her for a moment and then suddenly frowned. "What's a pretty girl like you doin' round here, anyhow? It's dangerous, you know."

Irene's lips twitched, but she managed to suppress the laugh. "Yeah, hippos; so I heard."

The knight chose that moment to make his presence known. Irene wasn't sure how long he'd been standing there—she had forgotten about him—but now he thrust the bag at her. "Come, let us continue on our way."

"*Our* way?" Irene said, gaping at him. "What 'our'? *I* was going to see the Greeks. I don't remember inviting you."

"Twice now I have come to your aid. Clearly, you are meant to be my responsibility."

"Your *what*?"

"You goin' somewhere?" Ian cut in, apparently oblivious to how close Irene was to choking the knight. "Well, why don't I come along? I know this territory pretty well."

"Your assistance is not required," the knight said, barely acknowledging Ian with a flick of his eyes. Instead, his gaze was fixed on Irene in silent challenge.

Irene set her jaw and crossed her arms. "Yeah, well, I rescued Ian, so that makes him *my* responsibility. So I guess he has to come along, too."

The knight's eyes narrowed. "He was not in any danger."

"Oh, since when did that become a criteria? According to you, I wasn't in any danger from the Hungry Ghosts."

"You...are exceedingly ungrateful."

Irene sucked in air hard as she goggled at the knight in mute outrage. She threw up her hands, gave a suppressed shriek of rage, and stomped off without a word.

"Are you leavin'?" Ian called after her. "Hey, wait...uh...you're not waitin'. Come back...please?" He jogged up next to her. "Okay, look...can you slow down...please? Please? I just want to talk to you...just for a minute, I promise. Just talk to me for a second, and then you can go wherever it is you're going."

Irene sighed and stopped. She turned and nearly slammed into the knight who was right at her elbow. She took a step back and hissed impatiently at him.

"Do you like music?" Ian asked.

The non-sequitur threw her. "What?"

"Do you like music? Cause there's a lady guitarist not too far from here who's real easy on the ears. Also, there's these black fellas about five hundred years thatta-way," he pointed back the way she had come, "with these long...tube....things," he gestured with his hands, indicating a span from his mouth to the ground, "that ain't half bad."

Irene flashed an apologetic smile. "It sounds great, really, it does. Maybe another time, though. We're — *I'm* — kind of on a mission at the moment."

Ian lit up. "Mission? What kind of mission?"

Irene started to shake her head, but Ian cut her off. "I'll go with you," he said. "Wherever it is you're going, I'll go, too. We can go together. You and me. But first...can I just show you one thing?" He held up a finger. "One thing. I promise."

Irene was torn between amusement and exasperation. Ian was like an overeager puppy, exuberant and with the attention span of a gnat. The combination of his effervescent good humor and the knight's scowling disdain was overwhelming, and she felt a little suffocated. She glanced at the knight, and the storm clouds descending over his face increased her desire to get away from him as quickly as possible.

"Look, Ian..." She hesitated — Ian seemed sweet, and he was incredibly good looking. In the face of his thousand-watt smile, she felt her resolve weaken. It would be nice to have some company. She glanced at the knight — *pleasant* company, she amended.

She smiled in spite of herself. "I have to do this one thing first, okay? But after that, I'm all yours. You can show me whatever you want."

Ian let out a whoop. "Yes, ma'am! You won't regret this. I promise."

Eleven

Irene quickly explained to Ian the need to speak to the Ancient Greeks, and then they set off. The knight, glowering but silent, followed. Irene ignored him, though she occasionally cast glances over her shoulder to see if he was still behind them. He and the horse seemed to have become friends, because it walked placidly beside him.

Maybe it was because she was excited or maybe it was because she was no longer alone, but it seemed to take no time at all to travel to the Ancient Greeks' layer of history.

Despite the fact that their burial customs included burying their dead with a coin, a large number of the Ancient Greeks appeared to be stuck at the river. The area they had carved out for themselves in the strata of time was like Woodstock and a drunken college frat party all rolled into one. There were mostly, and even completely, naked bodies everywhere—passed out, drinking and eating, wrestling, playing soccer, and, of course, having sex.

Disapproval rolled off the knight in thick, silent waves, and even Irene—who wasn't easily shocked or discomfited—didn't know where to put her eyes. Of course she'd heard of the Bacchanalias, the hedonism, and the love of nudity—she just hadn't expected it all to be true. Ian, on the other hand, proved to be completely unflappable, and though he kept exclaiming, "Well, I'll be damned," he did so in a way that indicated enthusiasm, rather than horror.

Irene looked around, trying to find someone she might be able to talk to. Ian came in close to her, concern etched on his face. "I ain't so sure this is a fittin' place for a lady."

"Okay, look, maybe you should take Galahad here," she jerked her thumb at the knight, "and wait for me back before we got to the Greeks. The Egyptians looked pretty..." —she corrected herself—"mostly...harmless."

"Andras," the knight said.

Irene's brow knit in confusion. "What?"

"My name is Andras de Cordova," he repeated.

"Uh, okay. Fine. Ian, take Andras—"

"I will remain," the knight said in a tone that brooked no argument.

"Well, hell's bells, then I'm stayin', too!"

"Won't you go to Hell just for being within a thousand miles of all this?" Irene asked Andras.

"I will do penance later."

Irene eyed him suspiciously; she wasn't sure, but she thought he might have been making a joke. His face gave away nothing. She turned away, lips pursed, and surveyed the crowd. Just passing by were three middle-aged men— two wore togas and the third was naked.

Irene figured this was as good an opportunity as any. "Hey, can I ask you a question?" she called out to them.

The three men stopped and looked her up and down. The naked one waggled his eyebrows at her, wiggling his hips suggestively.

"Eww, yuck!" Irene said. "Don't do that. No, really, don't." She wasn't sure if she was disgusted or amused. She had to fight to keep her eyes from straying downward, drawn more from a sense of the bizarre than from curiosity or, God forbid, interest. It wasn't like she'd never seen a naked man before; this, however, was just plain weird.

The three Greeks all looked downcast by her rejection, and Irene instantly felt bad, like she'd kicked a puppy. She was just going to apologize when the three men spoke.

"We know why you've come—" one of the toga-wearing ones said.

"To ask about the legend—" the other one added.

"About Charon and the coin," the naked one finished.

They spoke quickly, in sing-song voices, one after the other, so that the words were layered upon each other, the previous speaker's still hanging in the air when the next spoke.

Irene exchanged a confused look with Ian and then with Andras, but neither seemed to have any better clue than her as to the strange way of speaking.

"Many cultures have such a legend — " the second man who'd spoken said.

"Like the Egyptians with their ferryman Face-Behind — " said the third.

"So don't blame us," the first said.

"Blame? No, I'm not here to blame anyone," Irene said, bewildered by the strange trio. "I just want to know about the coins."

"Seems obvious — " the third said.

"Pay a coin — "

"Get passage."

"Okay, fine, but does it have to be a coin?" Irene asked.

"The coin is a metaphor — " said the first.

"Signaling the shades' acceptance of death — "

"And readiness to move on."

Irene frowned. "So, then, no? Charon won't take some other form of payment?"

She received three scowls in response.

"Only a coin," Andras said emphatically.

Irene shot him a dark look. "Okay, fine. Well, what do the stories say about those that don't have a coin — what happens to them?"

"Isn't it obvious — "

"You're here, aren't you — "

"With all of us."

"Yeah, okay," Irene said, "but is that it? No coin and you're screwed; you're just stuck here forever?"

"The stories say — "

"Those without a coin — "

"Must wander the banks of the river Acheron — "

"Cocytus," the second cut in.

"The legends don't say that!" the first retorted.

"That's speculation," said the third.

"Doomed to wander the banks of *a* river for one hundred years," the first said, raising his voice slightly to speak over his fellows.

Okay, well, that explained about the two rivers — the one at the hotel and the one here. There really were two rivers and two ferries; people had just gotten the stories confused and, over time, the two rivers had become one.

Irene thought back — the Guide had said you had to know where you were going, and the bellboy had said that the river at the hotel was for those who knew where they were going. She hadn't really paid attention at the time — she'd been distracted by the whole getting thrown out of the hotel thing. Later, she had simply thought maybe he meant it was for those who had already been judged, who knew what their final destination was. However, the Guide's words at the river — that she had no concept of what returning to Earth would look like — made her think it might mean something else. Maybe it meant that if you had a really good sense of what awaited in the afterlife, you could hop directly on the boat at the hotel. If, like her, you were struggling to figure out what this whole being dead thing was about, you had to take "the long way" as the bellboy had called it. She thought she was starting to understand — this journey was as much metaphor as it was physical.

She thought again of the self-help guide. *"Death isn't about a right and a wrong way; it's about options."* At the village, the Guide had told her everything that happens is the result of a person's choices.

"Okay, so then what?' Irene asked the Greeks. "What happens after you wander the banks of the river for a hundred years?"

This was met with silence.

"Okay, but some of these people have been here for thousands of years. Clearly there's got to be more to the story."

The Greeks gave a collective shrug. "It's just a story —"

"You take things too seriously —"

"Don't be so literal."

Irene huffed impatiently. "But it's a true story — the river, the ferryman, the coin, it's all real, so why not the rest of it?"

"What do you want us to say —"

"If we knew any better —"

"Do you think we'd still be here?"

Irene scowled. "Fine. So what happens now?"

"What do you mean?"

"I mean, where do we go from here?" she asked.

"There is nowhere else —"

"This is all there is —"

"This is the afterlife."

Irene turned to Andras and Ian in mute appeal.

Andras shook his head. "There is nothing else."

Ian shrugged.

"There's got to be something other than the forest and the river. It doesn't make any sense that this is all there is. Have you walked the entire length of the river? Have you checked that there's no way across?"

The knight gave her one of his unreadable looks.

"Okay, well, what about the ships I saw on the river? Is there a way to signal one of them to come pick us up?"

The knight shook his head. "Nothing here is real, just visions to tempt and torture us."

"The ships are real!"

Andras gave her a pitying look. "Sometimes, in their desperation, people try to swim out to them. They never make it."

Irene took a deep breath to control her rising frustration. "Is there wood? Can we build a raft or a boat?"

Andras gave her a dry look. "With what tools? What to navigate by? Where would we go?"

"Well, to the other side for starters," she said and then realized how stupid she sounded. The river was so vast that there was no way of knowing exactly where the other side lay.

"God wills that we wait," Andras said.

"Oh, and you know that for certain, do you?"

"If it was His will that we cross, then we would be on the other side."

Irene threw up her hands. "You know, you're about as helpful as a wet blanket."

She took a deep breath and ran a hand across her face. Jonah would know what to do. Whenever she'd gotten stuck, he'd always had an idea about what to do next. The thought of Jonah was instantly followed by the memory of Samyel.

Samyel!

"Wait, hang on a sec!" she said. "I know this guy...well, not exactly a guy...he's...got wings...but I bet he could fly us across the river."

Samyel's exact words had been, "I will come when you call." He'd been reluctant, as if agreeing to such a thing against his will. She'd thought he was simply promising to help her if she asked, but now, as she thought about it, she wondered if he meant something different, something much more literal.

Samyel had intimated that names had power, and he had been reluctant to give her his. Perhaps, what he had really given her was the power to call him whenever she needed him. Given the literal nature of everything else in the afterlife, the idea didn't seem that far-fetched.

Andras grabbed her arm, squeezing hard. "Nephilim," he said, nearly spitting the word. "Do not speak its name. They bring only death."

"What's Nephilim?" she asked.

"Winged deity of the afterlife —" one of the Greeks said.

"You'll find alters to them —"

"Along the river."

"Oh, hey, I think I saw one of those!" Irene recalled the bronze medallion affixed to the stone plinth by river. "Pig-faced woman with wings?"

"Manea," the three Greeks said together.

Irene looked from one man to the other in confusion. "So wait...deity? You mean like a god?"

"Ereshkigal, Nephthys, Ishtar —"

"Alpan, Culsu, Tukhulkha —"

"Manea, Karun, Vanth — "

"Hermes, Iris — "

"Yeah, okay, I get it." The recitation was like fingernails on a chalkboard. Irene shook her head to clear it and then tried to get the conversation back on track. "I'm confused. I was talking about a guy who looks like an angel — big, feathery wings coming out of his back."

"Yes, angels — " the naked guy said.

"Nephilim — "

"Winged deities of the afterlife."

"There ain't no such thing as angels," Ian said. "That's superstitious clap trap."

The Greeks shook their heads. "Monsters — "

"With wings — "

"That rule over the dead."

Irene's brow knit with confusion. "Wait, I thought you said they were gods. Now you're saying they're monsters."

"Were *worshipped* as gods — "

"They weren't actual gods — "

"That's a translation error."

"The images were meant — "

"As a warning."

Irene's brow furrowed even further. The only name she'd recognized on the list they'd recited was Hermes. She racked her brain, trying to dredge up what little she knew of Greek mythology. "Hermes was the messenger one, right? But he didn't have wings, and he wasn't a monster. He was gorgeous. All the Greek gods were."

"He had wings — "

"All Nephilim do — "

"We had to move them — "

"To his shoes — "

"In the pictures."

"Wings on the back — "

"Ruined the aesthetic."

Irene goggled at them. "Wait…so let me get this straight. You guys decided to change the pictures warning us that there were scary, winged monsters in the afterlife to make them...prettier? Then, because of that, we all forgot they were monsters and instead thought they were angels?"

"We value beauty_"

"And intelligence—"

"Above all else—"

"Besides—"

"It's not like this was cartography—"

"It was art, not science—"

"Aesthetics over accuracy—"

"It's not meant to be literal."

Irene gave them a dour look while her brain furiously turned over this information. Apparently, she should just forget about any help from Samyel, and—joy of joys—the number of scary monsters populating the afterlife was starting to multiply exponentially. So now we had hairy overgrown rodents, Hungry Ghosts, hippopotamuses, and Nephilim. *Awesome.*

So, where did this leave her in terms of getting out of here? Apparently, nowhere. "Great. So you're telling me that I'm stuck here and there's no way out?"

"That's correct."

"'Bout sums it up."

"Sorry."

"There has to be a way out of here!" She looked at Ian and then Andras again.

Ian shrugged. "Beats me."

Andras shook his head slowly, his gaze full of pity. "There is not."

Irene's frustration boiled over. "So what do you propose I do—just hang around and wait to end up like these people?" She grabbed a handful of sand, held it up, and let it run through her fingers. She was not going to end up like that. The universe might have decided that what it really needed was more beach material, but she had no intention of playing along. The Guide had said there was a way for her to go back—to go home—and that's where she intended to go.

"Woman," Andras said, "eternity is a long time to spend with a restive spirit. It is the will of God that we should enter the Kingdom of Heaven when *He* allows. The wait is bearable only with the peace that comes from accepting this. You would do better to spend your time balming your soul than railing about that which you cannot change."

"You know what—you can save your sermons," Irene snapped, irritated as much by the rebuke as she was by his passivity and unwillingness to try.

"It was not a sermon. It was advice."

She waved a finger in his face, punctuating her words with short jabs to the air. "I know there's a way out of here. There has to be—the world doesn't make sense if there isn't—and if I have to find a way to walk on water to get across that river, then you can be God-damned sure I will."

The knight snorted. "God's teeth, woman, your arrogance knows no limit! Are you so exalted that you alone of all God's creations can subvert His will? That you can countermand all His laws to arrange the world to your accord? Will you obtain Heaven by destroying its gates? Your conceit overbounds all if you think you alone can succeed where all others have failed."

"Now, now, now," Ian said, trying to insert himself between them. "No need to fight. I'm sure it will all work out."

Irene crossed her arms over her chest and glared at Andras, determination surging through her. "Oh, you have no idea, trust me. If there's one thing I have in spades, it's determination." She shouldered the bag more securely and shoved past him. "See you on the other side."

"If it is God's will," he said in that insufferably placid way of his.

She stormed off, her mind working overtime to plot her next move. It didn't matter what Andras said about the river; what did he know? Just because he'd been here for eight hundred years didn't mean he knew everything, or even anything. His judgment was clearly clouded by religious faith, and he was just blindly hanging around—like everyone else—passively waiting for something to happen. Had he even tried to find a way across the river in all that time?

Ian fell in step beside her. "So, where are we going next?"

Irene risked a peek over her shoulder. The horse had followed. Andras had not.

She chewed her lip as the realization that she had no idea where to go from here washed over her. She tried to recall all the other afterlife myths she'd learned before leaving Earth — who else had a story about a ferryman and coins?

"Irene?" Ian said, a worried frown puckering his forehead.

Jonah would know. God, how she wished he was here or that she could send him a letter. Of course, if she could send him a letter, then she'd just have him send her a coin and the problem would be solved.

She felt like kicking something.

"Can you at least slow down a mite?" Ian asked.

Irene came to a dead stop, realizing she'd been ignoring Ian. "I'm sorry," she said.

"So, where we going?"

"I don't know," she admitted.

"Oh, well, in that case, can I show you what I wanted to show you now?"

Before Irene could answer, they were interrupted by two young women dressed as if they had just left the set of *Little House on the Prairie*, horribly out of place among the naked Greeks. Each was carrying a basket.

"Book, Miss?" one asked her.

"Huh?" Irene said, looking from one to the other.

The girl reached into her basket and pulled out a book. It was a cheap paperback romance novel from the twentieth century. Irene frowned in confusion.

"Would you like a book to read? Or perhaps you have a book to share?"

Apparently this was the afterlife's version of a library. Irene had to admire their ingenuity. There was something else there, too; she couldn't quite put her finger on it — a kind of hope, maybe, or a refusal to give up. These girls were doing something with their time, rather than just hunkering down on the bank of the river and waiting for someone or something to save them. At the very least, it was a concerted effort to stave off boredom. Hope, indeed.

Irene felt a tingle of smugness, as if she had somehow been vindicated. She reached into her bag and pulled out a magazine. "Here," she said to the girl, "in case anyone wants the latest news from the land of the living."

"Thank you, Miss!"

Irene couldn't help grinning as she watched the two young women walk away.

"So, how about it?" Ian asked.

"How about what?"

"Can I show you something?"

Irene's grin widened. "You know what? Why the hell not?"

"Well, let's go!" Ian said, breaking into a grin of his own. He grabbed her hand and set off at a run. Irene clutched at the bag, holding the strap on her shoulder as she was pulled along after him, laughter bubbling up inside.

Twelve

"Do you hear music?" Irene asked. Ian just smiled and sped up.

Unlike the ethereal, transcendent music of the village, this was a boisterous, hundred-voice-strong Southern Gospel choir, singing what her friend LaRayne referred to as "get up" music. Suddenly, they were in the middle of it, and Irene realized it wasn't a choir so much as a million-person party. Everyone was clapping and singing and dancing. She stopped and stared, watching the exuberant crowd as the music washed over her.

Ian grinned, and she figured this must be what he'd wanted to show her. She had barely caught her breath when he grabbed her hands and began moving with the music, leaving her no choice but to follow. He led her in a complicated set of steps that seemed to be the kind of dance done at an old-fashioned hoedown. He'd pull her in close for some fast-paced, rollicking steps and then spin her away to lead her at arm's length in weaving in and out of the other dancers.

As she tripped over her feet for the hundredth time, Irene laughed. "I'm actually a pretty good dancer, believe it or not, but this is a little out of my league."

"Hey, now," Ian replied, a delighted grin spreading across his face. "I knew I could make you laugh."

Irene realized that for the first time since she'd died, the suffocating pressure inside her chest had dissipated. She felt more relaxed than she had for as long as she could remember. She smiled at Ian. "Thank you. I needed this. It's been a long time since I really laughed."

Her feet were tired, though, and there was still the little problem of getting across the river, so she led a reluctant Ian away from the spirited crowd.

"So, where to now?" Ian asked.

Irene didn't have an answer; she just walked, hoping that maybe something would come to her. The horse bumped her arm as they walked, nudging her hand until she gave it a scratch on the forehead. They walked for some time in silence, Irene resting her hand on the horse's neck, drawing comfort from the velvety softness. *What would Jonah do?* Or, more correctly, what would he tell her to do?

Thoughts of Jonah raised an image of the cairns she had seen in the forest. In the land of the living, any shrine to the dead acted as a sort of "post office," a conduit that let the living send things to the dead. She had seen many impromptu shrines while on Earth—a brick wall where people left letters for their loved ones, formal ancestor temples in Chinatown, crosses on the side of the road, clusters of candles and pictures on mantels, and, of course, the most obvious one—a tombstone.

She had forgotten about the cairns—she hadn't seen any of them since she'd left the dead forest. Now she realized something about them had been unconsciously bugging her. She supposed they could really just be piles of rocks, stacked up by bored ghosts who had found themselves with a lot of time—and rocks, sent by their loved ones—on their hands. However, it seemed much more likely they were meant to be shrines—afterlife mailboxes; but why would the dead build shrines to themselves? And why out of the rocks left on their own graves? That didn't make any sense—wouldn't such an altar just send stuff to the dead person who had built it?

"Do you know why people here make cairns—piles of rocks? Are they altars of some kind?"

Ian shrugged, and Irene had the impression he had no idea what she was talking about. She sighed.

They came to a bonfire surrounded by a small crowd that, while not exactly friendly looking, wasn't hostile either, so they stopped to rest.

Irene surveyed the area, trying to figure out what time period they were in. She did have to admit that the camp was interesting in that it was a study in human nature. Over the centuries some type of sifting and sorting seemed to have happened. People somehow found their way into enclaves of like-minded folks—there was a group, kneeling, heads bowed, in prayer. To one side she could see a group, surly and distrustful, bunkered down as if expecting an attack at any moment. On the other, a group of families with children, the adults somber and watchful as the children darted in and out of their legs.

For the most part, people were grouped within bands of time, arranged with their contemporaries, but every once in a while she had seen an anachronism—some sort of aboriginal warrior in a loin cloth and holding a spear, in conference with what looked like a bunch of twentieth-century, college frat boys. A tweed-coated college professor-type socializing with a contingent of Romans. A Ghangis Khan look-alike relaxing with what could have been a group of extras from the set of *Gone With the Wind*.

There was one thing that bothered her, though. Everyone was so placid, so calm. For many—hell, most—coming face to face with different cultures, different races, different beliefs from all of history should be shocking, even horrifying. At the very least, the shattering of all their expectations about the afterlife should have caused anger, grief, or mayhem of some sort. However, everyone seemed to take it in stride. There should be riots, wars—at the very least fortified encampments.

What had happened to the superstitions, the zealotry, the xenophobia? Where were the religious fanatics, screaming for the sinners to repent and convert? Where were the primitive beliefs about foreigners being demons or emissaries of the gods? Didn't anyone worry that this place was actually Hell? She knew she still did.

But no; there was none of that. There was a man in a crimson toga-like robe sitting in the lotus position, twisting a Rubik's Cube. There was a group—four Native Americans, two Samurai, five guys with blue face paint, and one guy in a business suit—playing golf. Here was an Arab sheik, a maharajah, and a Canadian Mountie, laughing together as if exchanging knock-knock jokes. It was strange and tragic and funny and horrifying all at once.

Well, if life gives you lemons…she supposed that for a certain type of personality the ability to mingle with people from any place and any time would seem like the best thing since sliced bread.

In fact, she knew one such person who would love this.

Dear Jonah,

> *The river bank is interesting. There are people from every time period and every place on Earth. In the time I've been here, I've seen Vikings, Mongols, Romans, Egyptians, and God only knows what else. We all seem to understand each other somehow. It's kinda crazy, but cool.*

She'd never tell him any of that in an actual letter, of course. She didn't want to encourage his interest in the afterlife—he already spent way too much time with the dead, and she hadn't forgotten that she'd seen him purchase a book about communicating with those who had crossed over. Jonah needed to learn how to get on with the living. She hadn't received any more letters lately, so maybe that was a good sign; maybe he'd moved on, found a new hobby.

"Penny for your thoughts?"

Irene smiled as Ian's words pulled her out of her reverie. He was watching her carefully across the campfire. Irene shifted position; she and the horse were using each other as a mutual backrest, and she wiggled against it, trying to find a more comfortable position.

Irene shook her head. "Just thinking about the cairns; I was wondering why someone would build an altar in the afterlife. If they are shrines, wouldn't each one just send stuff to the person who built it?"

"People pray to their gods. One assumes they are closer here," a high, thin voice at her elbow said.

Irene started. She looked up and then did a double take. The speaker was a middle-aged Chinese man. His long, black robe, Fu-Manchu mustache, and waist-length beard were straight out of a Hollywood movie.

He gave her a reassuring smile and a low bow. "Your pardon. I did not mean to startle." As he straightened up, he suddenly brightened, a smile blooming across his face.

"Ah!" he said, gesturing to the horse. "Gives new meaning to the saying, 'trying to save the dead horse as if it is still alive.' Ha!"

Irene looked at the horse, but since she had no idea what the man was talking about, she didn't know how to respond. She looked at Ian for help.

"Howdy!" he said to the newcomer. "Pull up some ground." He sat up, moving his legs to make room, and patted the space next to him. "I'm Ian and this is Irene."

The man gracefully dropped to a kneeling position. He gave Ian a slight bow and then turned to Irene. He smiled as he bowed to her. "Ah! Irene. A very good name."

Irene raised an eyebrow. "Is it?"

"Oh, yes. Irene of Thessalonica, Irene of Rome, Irene of Macedonia, Irene of Athens, Irene of Hungary…yes, a very good name. Very auspicious."

"Wow, I had no idea." She hesitated and then added, as if revealing an embarrassing secret. "I was named for an actress."

"Ah, yes, " the man cried with delight. "Irene Dunne. Very nice lady."

Irene eyed him up and down once more, certain the guy was not from the twentieth century. "You…know her?"

The man gave her a gentle smile. "I have been here a very long time." Then he bowed again. "I am Gao. A seeker of truth."

"What kind of truth?"

Gao's smile widened. "There is only one truth. I am…" He spread his hands as if the word he searched for might appear in the air between them. "…a scholar. I seek to know man's true nature and to understand our relationship with the cosmos."

Irene's eyebrows rose again. "How's that going for you?"

Gao made a "so-so" gesture. "Eh."

Irene laughed.

"Irene here was just goin' to tell me all about the future," Ian said.

"I was?"

Ian grinned. "Sure, why not?" He stretched out his long legs and propped himself on one elbow with an expectant air.

Gao looked interested. "Ah. Yes?" He looked Irene over, forehead wrinkling with thought. He turned his head as he scanned the nearby crowd, and then looked her over again. "Ah. Forgive me, but may I ask — when are you from?"

Irene understood his confusion. At the moment, she was one of those anachronisms she had noted throughout the camp. She judged that they were probably in Europe — she thought the people around them might be Italians — around maybe the eleven or twelve hundreds. She looked at Ian and Gao and almost laughed — all three of them were clearly out of place. "Early twenty-first century," she said.

Gao's brow wrinkled even more, and he looked her up and down again. Then he brightened "Ah!" He nodded sagely. "The new calendar." He produced a leather-bound journal from somewhere within his robes. He flipped it open and squinted at a page for a moment. Then he smiled. "Ah! You are from the Golden Dragon Time, perhaps? Four thousand, six hundred, ninety-eight?" He ran a finger across the page. "The year two thousand in your calendar."

"Yeah, around there."

"Ah! Very auspicious."

"If you say so. It wasn't auspicious enough to keep me from dying." She tried to hazard a guess as to when Gao was from but quickly gave up — her knowledge of history wasn't anywhere good enough. "What about you, how long have you been here?"

Gao shrugged. "The life of a man is as a second, and the life of a dead man is as of a minute, to the life of a star."

Irene gave him a dry look. "So, a while then?"

Gao chuckled. "All things are relative. Does not your philosophy say this?" Gao consulted the journal again while Irene exchanged a confused look with Ian. "I have been here for two and a half thousand years...give or take."

Irene stared at him, not sure she'd heard right. "Two *thousand* years?" When Gao merely shrugged, horror washed over her.

She'd been shocked when Andras had said he'd been here for eight hundred years. Now, looking out over the sea of people, she finally understood the full ramification of being stuck here. Stuck was for eternity. Stuck was for forever.

"Bet you seen some things," Ian said to Gao, apparently unfazed by this piece of information. "I bet it ain't nothin' compared to what Irene's seen, though." He grinned at her. "So, come on!" He slapped his thigh. "Tell us about the future."

"I doubt I could do it justice," she said, her mind still stuck on the fact that Gao had been here for two thousand years.

"Oh come on," Ian cried. "Tell us something." Irene felt a flicker of annoyance, but now Gao added a polite request to Ian's pleading for tales of the future.

"I don't know how to describe roads and cars and electricity and airplanes and computers and television and office buildings to someone who's never even seen anything remotely like that stuff," she said.

However, even that little bit seemed to impress Ian, even though Irene was pretty sure he hadn't understood a word of it. He slapped his thigh again and gave a low whistle. "That sure does sound amazin'!"

Irene laughed in exasperation. "You don't even know what I'm talking about!"

Ian grinned. "Sure, but it still sounds good."

"Wait a sec..." Irene pawed in her bag and pulled out her last magazine. She tossed it to Ian. "Here. A picture is worth a thousand words." She had a small qualm about letting him base his entire impression of the future on a copy of *Cosmopolitan*, but since Ian was dead—and therefore not likely to ever visit Twenty-first Century Earth—she reasoned it couldn't really make much difference.

There was an awkward pause in the conversation as Ian burrowed into the magazine, leaving her and Gao nothing to talk about. Irene suddenly felt embarrassed for giving Ian something but not Gao, so she fished in the bag, looking for something appropriate. Her hand brushed paper. She pulled out one of the origami birds and passed it to Gao. Gao appeared even more delighted by this gift than Ian had with the magazine.

"Ahh!" he cried with an ear-to-ear grin. He gave her a low bow of gratitude.

"If you set that on fire," she said, still rummaging through her bag, "it will turn into a real bird."

Gao gave her a quizzical look, as if he thought she was joking. She nodded to the horse. "It's how I got the horse." Her hand encountered a red bean paste bun. She pulled it out and passed it to Gao.

"Ah," he said, suddenly growing serious. He was slow to take the sweet from her, hesitating as if he was about to refuse. "It has been a very long time, indeed, since I have seen one of these." He studied it for a long moment and then, taking it from her, broke the pastry in half and handed half back to her with an incline of the head.

"Please," he said, gesturing for her to take a bite.

Irene smiled, took the proffered half, and bit into it. Gao watched her chew for a moment, and then he solemnly took a bite of his own half. Irene had never had a red bean paste bun in her life, and she chewed slowly, trying to decide if she liked it or not. The taste and texture were completely alien, unlike anything she'd ever eaten before—sweet and a little gritty.

"Is that food?" Ian asked.

Irene broke her share in half and passed a piece to Ian. He took one bite and made a moue of distaste. "Ack! That is terrible! What is it?"

Gao laughed. "Perhaps it is an acquired taste."

Ian shook his head. "Sorry, friend, if that's your national food and all, but that truly is terrible."

Gao leaned forward, looking at the magazine in Ian's lap. "What is that?" he asked. Irene wasn't sure but thought he was pointing to an advertisement for an iPod. She supposed, to someone unfamiliar with the device, the picture of a teen with wires sticking out of her head probably looked more like she was flinching in extreme pain rather than dancing rapturously.

Ian laughed and pointed at something else. Gao leaned closer, and soon the two men were huddled together, pouring over the magazine, Irene clearly forgotten. She watched them for a while, amazed and slightly worried that maybe she shouldn't have let them see it. Wasn't there some rule about not telling people from the past about the future? Did that apply to the dead, too, or was it just for time travelers? She felt a twinge of sadness; Jonah would know. In fact, keeping track of the characteristics of various tropes had been a sort of running joke with them. *In-jokes — another thing I miss about the land of the living.*

Beside her, the horse shifted its weight, flopping down to stretch out fully on the ground. There was a sound of protest as it stretched out its legs, accidentally kicking someone nearby.

She became aware of how unnaturally quiet everything was—the only sound was the occasional low murmur of voices. There weren't any other noises—no bushes rustling, no wind blowing, no crickets chirping, not even the sound of the campfire crackling. She stared at the fire, feeling a prickle of unease at its silence. Andras has said that nothing here was real, and it had never seemed more true than in this moment.

A great weight of melancholy settled over her. Ian had been here for a hundred and fifty years; Andras—eight hundred; Gao—twenty-five hundred. She hated to admit it, but if there was a way out of here, they would have found it already. Her stomach roiled with a sick ache, and she pulled her jacket tighter around her.

Irene became aware that Gao was staring at her, and she flushed with embarrassment. He inclined his head. "Your pardon. I did not mean to stare. It is just that you look...pained."

Irene sighed and rubbed a hand over her face. "Oh, sorry. I was just thinking is all."

"Must be very serious thoughts to cause such a face."

Irene chuckled. "Oh nothing much...apparently I'm just trying to reorder the universe to my liking." She couldn't keep a note of sarcasm from creeping into her voice.

Gao grinned. "Well, then...may the universe hear your prayers."

A pair of scruffy-looking characters shuffled by. "Tobaccy? Anyone got any tobaccy?"

Irene shook her head and they continued past. Ian called Gao's attention to something in the magazine and the two men went back to studying the pages intently. Irene sighed and rubbed her forehead again, feeling the beginnings of a headache. Suddenly, she was bone tired. Behind her, the horse rubbed its face against the ground and gave a contented sigh. Irene felt an unaccountable wave of sadness wash over her.

Despair is a sin.

Andras's words echoed in her thoughts.

She was about to push him out of her mind when something clicked in her brain.

Sin. God. Prayer.

One built an altar with the expectation of sending something, whether it was an item or a prayer, to a particular person — to a loved one or to a specific god — regardless of where that person might be. So, in essence, the afterlife "post office" system had two parts: the "mailbox" or altar where you left items for the dead, and the "mailbox" where you received items.

On Earth, items left for the dead had just turned into ghost items — passing into the hidden world of the dead, but remaining at the altar where they had been left. So why had the ghost version of Jonah's letters come directly to her, instead of simply remaining on her grave?

Because they were left at my grave – a shrine dedicated specifically to me.

All the other ghost items that she'd encountered had been left at a general shrine for the dead, not at one dedicated to a specific person. Apparently, that distinction dictated where the items would go – remain in the land of the living or pass into the land of the dead.

Irene's heart jumped. *I'm still connected to the land of the living – I'm connected to my grave!* Well, more likely, not so much the grave as the body buried in it.

The flesh, the peel, the seeds – they are all one.

Damn it! She slapped herself in the forehead. The Guide had known. He had been trying to tell her back in the village. The answer was obvious, right there in front of her. Death had split her into parts, had separated her body and her spirit, but the parts were still connected. So, if messages could be sent one way, then they must be able to be sent the other as well, right?

"Are you all right?" Gao asked, breaking into her train of thought. He was staring at her with a mixture of concern and amusement. So was Ian.

Irene flushed with embarrassment. "I'm sorry – it's just that I think I've figured a way out of here."

Ian stared at her in astonishment, the magazine sliding from his lap to pool on the ground beside him. "Really?"

"I...I don't know," she said. There was still something missing from this plan. How, exactly, did she send a message back through the conduit? Her gravestone – an "altar" built above her body – was the mailbox to send messages from that side; what was the mailbox on this side? What was something she had that might still be connected to the land of the living that she could use as an altar?

She was too excited, too worked up. Her thoughts were racing, her mind jumbled. She sat up and wrapped her arms around her knees, rocking slightly to dispel the nervous energy building inside of her.

Ian leaned forward. "Don't keep me in suspense!"

Irene shushed him with a wave of her hand. "I'm trying to concentrate."

The cairns.

The essence of the rocks here, in the land of the dead, was connected to the physical rocks, still in the land of the living, the same way her spirit here was connected to her body. The dead had been using the rocks left on their graves to build mailboxes to send letters back home.

Irene groaned. *Stupid, stupid, stupid*, she chided herself. It was all so obvious when you stopped to think about it. *How the hell else had all the stories of the afterlife made it back to the land of the living?* Didn't anyone ever wonder where the stories had come from? Even if everyone thought they were just made up, myths contain a grain of truth – didn't anyone ever wonder how people could know the truth about the afterlife? For the stories to leak out, the dead had to have been communicating with people in the land of the living for millennia. So they must have had a way to ask for coins, too. Like with the funeral rites and the practice of sending goods with the dead, everyone had just forgotten how it was done.

She tried to temper the excitement building inside her, which was threatening to spill out in whoops of joy. The Guide had said the universe was a well-oiled machine in which everything had a purpose, that everything was designed to work together in a simple and elegant manner. So there had to be a way across the river. If there was any order or logic to the universe, then there was no way someone had designed a system with such a fatal flaw as this one seemed to have. Maybe the solution really was as simple as a pile of rocks.

Oh…crap.

A *pile* of rocks. She stopped mid-thought, her body stilling in mid-motion as her excitement ground to a halt. The number of rocks was a moot point. She didn't even have one rock – she had tossed the one she'd found in her bag, probably sent by Jonah, back in the village – and she certainly didn't have enough to build a cairn. Even if one rock was enough, she doubted she could find her way back to the village to retrieve it.

Once again, she was reminded that Jonah was always right – he had warned her not to throw anything away because she didn't know what she would need in the land of the dead.

She dropped her forehead to her knees.

So...she needed rocks to contact Jonah and she needed to contact Jonah to get rocks.

Great.

Who said the universe didn't have a sense of humor?

Her brain cramped and her eyes watered as her thoughts banged against her skull in a frustrating loop.

"Irene?" Ian said.

She lifted her head.

Ian's face fell. "Oh."

She sighed and rubbed her eyes, trying to think harder. Maybe there was a way to get a message to Jonah. It would be kind of roundabout — she could use the existing cairns to send a letter to Jonah with a note asking whoever found it on the other side to deliver it to Jonah. The biggest challenge, of course, would be finding a cairn that was still active. There was no way to know how old any of those cairns were — they could be thousands of years old. If the grave on the other side had been destroyed or the rocks removed then the cairn wouldn't work. Even if the grave and the rocks were still intact, it still might not work. If the grave was really old, it was unlikely that anyone — living or dead — visited it; there would be no one there to receive her letter.

Frankly, there were a whole lot of "ifs" to this plan — *if* her theory was right that the cairns could send things back to the land of the living, and *if* she could find an active cairn, and *if* the cairn connected to an active cemetery the dead still visited, and *if* the person who found her letter was willing to deliver it, and *if* Jonah had ignored her and still continued to enter the meditative trance state that let him see ghosts and ghost objects — but it was the best she could do. And yet she felt like whooping for joy — she had a plan!

Irene jumped to her feet. "I've got to go."

"What, now?" Ian asked.

"Uh, yeah, sorry." Flustered, her thoughts racing, she gathered up her stuff. Gao looked confused. "Uh, it was nice to meet you," she said in a rush, knowing she was babbling and incoherent, but unable to stop herself.

Ian rose to his feet, dusting himself off. "I never met such a girl for tearing off in a hurry all the time."

Gao held out the magazine. "Your book."

"Uh...keep it."

Gao looked surprised but pleased at this and gave her a low bow. "It has been a pleasure and an honor. May you find what you seek. I hope our paths may cross again."

The horse seemed to sense that something was afoot because it, too, climbed to its feet.

Irene hastily scanned the area, Gao already fading from her mind as she tried to get her bearings. Then she shouldered her bag and set off, her mind racing. How many cairns had she seen in the forest? A dozen? Two dozen? How would she ever find them again? They had been sprinkled randomly about.

"Uh, Irene? Can we slow down a mite?"

She'd almost forgotten about Ian. She stopped and let him catch his breath.

"So where we goin'?"

She frowned, suddenly realizing she hadn't asked Ian if he wanted to go with her. Maybe he didn't.

"I'm sorry, Ian. I didn't think." She gave him an apologetic smile. "I'm going back to the forest."

"Well, okay. But why? What are we goin' to do there?"

Her heart leapt at his use of "we," but just to be sure she said, "You don't have to come with me."

"Sure I do! There's monsters and stuff out there."

"Oh, and you're going to protect me, cowboy?" She smiled at the thought of Ian trying to protect her from angels and the Hungry Dead.

"Hell, no!" He flashed her a crooked grin and winked. "I'll come along just the same, though." Then he frowned. "Uh...how is this gonna help us get 'cross the river?"

Irene laughed and looped her arm through his. "Don't worry your pretty little head none about that. You'll see."

"Aww, shoot," Ian said. "That's my line."

Thirteen

Irene eventually found herself back among people she recognized as those she had encountered when she'd first entered the camp. Only now they weren't on the edge of the camp. Thousands more had died in the time she had been to the river and back. Instead of a clear expanse of sand to the tree line at the edge of the forest, Irene saw a sea of people stretched out endlessly, the forest far out of sight.

There was a shriek of "horsie!" from somewhere, and an instant later the horse disappeared under a swarm of small children. Two little girls each wrapped herself around a front leg, a gangly boy hoisted himself onto the horse's back, a younger boy hung off the horse's neck, and a timid girl patted the horse's side at arm's length.

For a second, Irene thought the horse was going to be crushed or suffocated by the bodies, but it merely twitched and let out a great, heaving sigh of contentment. Irene smiled, even as she felt a twinge of sadness. Well really, what was she supposed to do with a horse? It seemed much more content where it was, the focus of so much adoration and attention. It was probably best to leave it here. It would most likely be happier.

Irene turned away, trying to ignore the symbolism of leaving behind such a tangible reminder of the land of the living. She shouldered the bag and nodded to Ian, who was watching the horse and children with a silly, fond grin.

"Ready, cowboy?" she asked.

"Ready," he agreed easily enough.

As they set off, there was a commotion behind them. Irene turned. Children were shrieking with laughter as the horse gently shook them off. It gave one long shuddering stretch and then looked at Irene — with reproach, she thought. It put its head down, snorted, and then picked its way through the crowd to stand beside her.

"It's all right," she said. "You can stay."

It just stood there, head lowered, looking half asleep. She smiled and scratched its forehead, surprised by the sudden tenderness she felt for it. "Alright, come if you want to. I'm just saying you don't have to."

The horse snorted in reply.

Irene turned and made her way through the crowd, which very quickly thinned but also became more animated, full of hysterical shrieking and sobbing. A mercifully short while later she, Ian, and the horse could see the edge of the encampment, the border guards, and the uninterrupted sand stretching out to the dead forest.

She took a deep, steadying breath, steeling herself to leave the safety of the encampment. Doubt fluttered in her chest; what if she couldn't find any cairns? What if they didn't work? Without the cat, would she be able to find her way back here if she left? What if it was like the village; what if you could only find this place using the special non-eye kind of seeing, which she hadn't exactly figured out yet?

She squared her shoulders. *Then you'll figure it out. You have all the time in the world,* she reminded herself. *You have forever.*

She sucked in a deep breath and took one ponderous step forward. A hand clamped down on her shoulder, bringing her to an abrupt halt. Anger flashed through her and she spun around. Her anger dissolved into disbelief. It was the knight, Andras.

"Oh, God, not you."

"Hey, hey, hey!" Ian said. "Hands off the lady, if you please."

Andras ignored him. "Where are you going?" he asked Irene.

She tried to shrug out of his grip. "None of your business."

Andras seemed taken aback by this response. Several emotions passed over his face. Finally, he released her arm and took a step back, putting a little distance between them, as if making a concession. "Why would you return to the forest? There is nothing there."

"You know why," she said, a note of challenge in her voice. "I've found a way to get out of here."

"Irene, you don't got to talk to this fella if you don't want to," Ian said, his eyes dancing anxiously back and forth between her and Andras. Irene, her gaze locked on the knight in a silent battle of wills, motioned with her hand that it was okay.

Andras tilted his head, studying her for a long moment. "It is not safe."

A bark of laughter escaped from Irene before she could stop it. "Listen, Galahad, I appreciate the concern. Really, I do. You almost sound worried rather than just annoyed. However, the way out lays thatta-way. So there's nothing you can say that will dissuade me from going out there. Not that it's any of your business what I do."

The knight looked toward the forest, studied it a moment, and then looked back at her. She couldn't help but notice the uncertain, tentative hope in his eyes.

"Look, if it's the Hungry Ghosts you're worried about," she said, "it's fine. We made friends."

Andras quirked an eyebrow. She gave him a smug smile in return. "Some of us learn a little faster than others."

He grunted and a muscle in his jaw flexed. She almost thought he wanted to laugh. However, when he next spoke, it was with his usual solemnity. "There are other things." His eyes flicked back and forth between her and Ian.

"I'll be fine, really." She made a flourish with her hand, as if brandishing a magic wand. "I release you, Sir Knight, from your debt. Please feel free to no longer consider me your *responsibility*."

Andras grimaced again. "What of the Nephilim?"

"There ain't no such thing as angels," Ian insisted.

Andras shot him a dark look.

"I'm not scared of the angels," Irene said. "I've only seen one since I've been here, and he flew away. Besides, I have this." She wrapped her fingers around the heart-shaped pendant at her throat.

"What is that?" Andras asked.

"I don't know, but the one I encountered back on Earth was awfully interested in it. That must mean something."

Andras narrowed his eyes and regarded her for a long moment. "You seem over sure that you have found a way to cross."

Irene laughed. "What's that I'm hearing? It couldn't possibly be that sinful thing called hope, could it?"

He blew out his breath and looked away. She laughed again.

"I will go with you," Andras said, as if he had just reached a momentous decision.

"Hey, hey, hey!" Ian said, holding up a hand. "Now hold on a minute. The lady is with me."

Andras ignored him. "If the Nephilim know your name, then you will need help."

"*One* Nephilim knows my name," she countered.

"If one, then all."

"I can handle it," Ian said, a note of belligerence in his voice.

"I, too, am returning to the forest," Andras said to Irene, as if Ian had not spoken. "I will walk with you. For a time."

Irene nearly doubled over with laughter at that. "Yeah, okay, as long as it's for *my* benefit." She shook her head, still chuckling. "Look, I don't suppose there's any way I can dissuade you?"

Andras's eyes narrowed.

"Yeah, that's what I thought. Fine, since I can't stop you, then come along, Galahad. We'll see if we can get you to the Emerald City, too."

"Andras," he corrected.

"Whatever," she said, setting off. "Just remember that I'm only letting you tag along because the horse likes you."

She turned and set off. Ian was now at her elbow, stuck like glue. Irene suppressed a smile.

The horse snorted. Ian cast it a look. "Hey, why don't we ride?" he asked.

Irene stopped, looked at the horse, and then looked at Ian. "What, that? No way!"

"Sure!" He put his hands on her waist, as if he was going to pick her up. Her look turned murderous.

"If you put me on that thing, I will stab you through the eye with my shoe." Even as she spoke, she realized the statement made no sense since she had traded shoes with Elvira and no longer had the stilettos.

It didn't matter; Ian laughed and let her go, raising his hands in a placating gesture. "Now, now! Don't get riled. I just thought you might like to ride, is all."

Irene shook her head. "If God had meant us to ride horses, he would have equipped them with brakes and power steering."

Andras was standing nearby, arms folded across his chest with a disapproving frown. Irene felt a hot flash of embarrassment mixed with irritation. She felt her smile slip, and she turned away. "Come on," she said to Ian.

Ian eyed the horse for a moment. "Well...if you don't want to ride, mind if I do?"

Irene paused. "Don't you need, like...stuff?"

Ian dismissed this with a wave of his hand. "Ah, heck, no. Watch this."

"Why do we linger?" Andras asked, shifting impatiently from foot to foot.

Irene and Ian both ignored him. Ian approached the horse, grabbed a handful of mane in one hand, hefted himself up, threw a leg over, and settled himself in the middle of the horse's back. The horse swung its head around to eye Ian as if incredulous to find him there.

Ian thumped his legs against the horse's sides. "Git up!" he said. "Hey, what's this horse's name, anyway?"

Irene shrugged. "Name? I don't know. I've just been calling it Trigger."

"Trigger?" Ian hooted. "That ain't no name for a horse!" He studied it for a moment. "How about Zeb. That's a good horse name."

Andras, who had drifted closer, snorted. "Zeb? What kind of name is that? A horse's name should reflect its character: Diablo, Beneplacito, Despreocupado…"

Ian was tapping the horse's sides with his heels, urging it forward. The horse reached around, grabbed Ian's pant leg in its teeth, and tugged.

"Here, here, stop that!" Ian cried. He thrashed his leg, freeing it from the horse's mouth. The horse snatched at Ian's pant leg again, trying to recapture it. Ian thumped his legs harder against the horse's sides. "Hie! Git, Zeb! Git!"

The horse went still for a moment and then suddenly its head went down and all four feet came off the ground. The horse gave one great, heaving buck. Everything seemed to go in slow motion. Ian went sailing over its head and hit the ground.

"Oh my God!" Irene cried, frozen to the spot as she watched Ian tumble end over end.

Ian came to a stop and lay still, gazing up at the sky.

Irene stood there, hands over her mouth, unable to move. The horse shook itself from nose to tail then surveyed Ian placidly as if admiring its handiwork. Andras seemed unconcerned. His mouth quirked down, as if to say, "I told you so," and then he moved off, heading for the forest. "Come," he said, striding past Ian without a second glance.

With a groan, Ian rose to a sitting position. "Damn me!" he said, brushing himself off.

Relief flooded through Irene. "Are you alright?" she asked, hurrying to his side.

Ian climbed to his feet and slapped at his arms, raising a cloud of dust. Then he gave her a cheeky grin. "Was you worried for me?" When she gave him a disgusted look, he grinned even more broadly. "You were, weren't you? Admit it. Come on…you were worried."

"You're already dead," Irene said dryly, but her lips twitched with amusement.

"Shoot!" Ian exclaimed, looking around. "Did you see how far I went? Man, it was just like flying!"

Ian didn't appear to have suffered any ill effects from his fall, so Irene shook her head and followed after Andras, who had stopped to wait for them. The horse trailed after and the small group headed up the sandy slope to the tree line. They crested the hill and the forest lay before them. They stopped at its edge. Dread flooded through Irene at the sight of the bleak, barren landscape. How could she have forgotten how awful this place was? It had only been a few — days? weeks? — since she'd been here.

She sighed, her shoulders sagging at the thought of the monumental task before her. Then she set her jaw and stiffened her spine. If home lay this way, then this was the way she was going. She stepped into the forest.

"Where are we going?" Andras asked.

"We need to find cairns — you know, piles of rocks."

"Yes, I have seen them..." There was hesitancy in his voice.

"But?"

"There is no way to find them. Things are not...fixed, in the forest."

"Well, if they're not 'fixed,' how do you find your way around?"

Andras blew out his breath. "I...feel my way."

"Okay, well, we'll just have to *feel* our way to some rocks."

He closed the distance between them and grabbed her arm. "*This* is your plan?"

"Hey, hey!" Ian said, trying to insert himself between them. "I'll thank you to unhand the lady."

Irene met Andras's hard look with one of her own. "You're going to need to stop grabbing me," she said, her voice like fine-honed steel.

Andras let her go with a frown. Irene glared at him. "Do you have a better idea?" She raised an eyebrow in challenge. "Besides, no one asked you to come along."

"That's right," Ian said. "Why don't you go on back to camp, where it's safe? We'll take it from here."

Andras cast Ian a withering look but it was to Irene he directed his comments. "You try my patience."

"Do you have something better to do with your time?" she asked. "I can assure you, it's going to take a lot less than eight hundred years for us to find a cairn, even by random chance."

Andras shook his head again, his face etched with aggravation. "God's teeth, woman—"

"'Sides," she said tapping him on the chest with the back of her hand as an idea occurred, "there were a lot of cairns in the dead city. We just need to get back there."

Andras frowned and shifted uncomfortably. "What city?"

"You know…the dead city…"

"There is no city."

"Look, when you woke up here…you know, after you died, where were you?"

"I was in a desert."

"I was in a saloon," Ian said.

Irene frowned. "A desert? Huh. That's weird."

"There is nothing here," Andras said softly but firmly, holding her eyes with his own. "Just dreams and hallucinations, sorrow and longing."

She shook her head. "I don't believe that. I woke up in a city, and that's where I'm going."

She turned away. Andras made to grab her arm but she shrugged him off, anger sizzling through her.

"Hey, hey, hey!" Ian said. "Let's all keep our hands to ourselves."

Furious at both his patronizing demeanor and his questioning of her judgment, Irene said to Andras, "*This* is the plan. You can come or not, I don't care, but it's not up for discussion."

Andras's face went dark with rage, and for a moment, Irene thought he was going to strike her. Without waiting for a response, she turned and set off. There was a muffled oath behind her. She ignored it, turning her attention to the task at hand. She needed to focus now, to put all of her energy into finding a cairn that would let her talk to Jonah. Screw Andras and his alpha male bullshit.

Walk with purpose, the Guide had said. Know where you are going and want to get there. See without eyes. Feel your way through.

Jonah. What I need is Jonah.

Jonah, who believed in her, who had faith in her, and who could send her coins, was out there somewhere, a simple letter away. She concentrated with all her might on one thought: *I want to be able to talk to Jonah.*

She put the entire focus of her being into that one thought, holding Jonah's face in her mind's eye for a moment,. Then, from somewhere deep inside, she felt it — a Ping-Pong-ball-sized warmth, solid and real, like a lump of burning coal. Her heart leapt.

Jonah!

She could feel it, a flame inside her, like a compass, tugging, leading, pointing the way.

Hope surged through her. She was going to get out of here. She was going home.

Fourteen

They walked in silence, Irene focusing on Jonah, Andras warily scanning the trees for danger, and Ian cavorting like a puppy.

"Hey! Look at that tree—it looks like a face, doesn't it? Do you see? You aren't even lookin'…"

She glanced at the tree and then shot Ian a disparaging look and shook her head.

"Well, okay…how about that one…"

Irene let him ramble and focused, instead, on sifting her own thoughts.

"This way," she said, setting off again.

They had long since left the place where the scenery had looked somewhat normal, with a distinct horizon and a definite up and a definite down. Once more, everything was a seamless, formless gray dissolving into nothingness.

The flame in Irene's chest flared, a bolt of heat sizzling through her, and then there was something in the grayness ahead. As they drew closer, it came into focus—the cat. It sat there smugly, as if it had been waiting for her the whole time.

"Is that a cat?" Ian said.

Andras made a sound like a hiss. The cat gave him a slow unblinking look and then returned its gaze to Irene. It began purring, the sound so loud Irene could hear it from where she stood.

"I don't like cats," Ian said.

Andras hissed again. The cat narrowed its eyes and moved as if it was going to get up. Irene shushed both men with a wave of her hand.

She crouched down so she was eye level with the cat. "Hey," she said softly. "I need to find piles of rocks. Can you help? I'll give you anything from my bag that you want."

The cat stood up, stretched, and kneaded the ground with its paws. When it was done, it gave Irene a long slow blink. Then it turned around and looked like it was going to start walking. Hope flared in Irene's chest—maybe it really was a magic cat. Then, just as suddenly, her heart plummeted as the cat took off, streaking out of sight.

"Hey!" she shouted, but it was gone.

"Cats," Ian said. "Can't stand 'em."

Andras grunted.

"Oh, shut up," she said, not directing her comment to anyone in particular. She gritted her teeth and set off once more.

The forest seemed to grow darker and drearier the farther they went.

"For what purpose do we search for these rocks?" Andras asked. "They have magical properties?"

Irene looked at him in wonder. "I thought it was sacrilegious to believe in magic and such?" She realized as soon as she said it that it probably wasn't an accurate statement—after all, they had killed people suspected of practicing witchcraft and stuff during the Middle Ages, so even good Christians must have believed in magic. It was simply that it was a sacrilege to practice it.

"I don't believe in witches but I know they exist," Andras replied.

"What's that supposed to mean?"

"It is a saying...in my time."

"Oh." Irene studied him for a moment and then raised an eyebrow. "So you believe in things for which you have no proof they exist—like God, and don't believe in the things you can plainly see do exist—like witches. That's a rather complex belief system you got there."

He raised an eyebrow, mirroring her look back at her. "Belief does not change what is. Would you cease to exist if I simply chose to stop believing that you did? Is God any less than you, that his existence should depend on our belief? He exists; that is all."

"Huh." Irene turned this over and then cast him a sidelong glance.

"What?" he asked.

She shrugged and looked away. "Nothing."

"Hey," Ian called, "there's a tree over here that looks like a pumpkin!"

"You did not answer my question," Andras said.

"What question?"

"The rocks?" he prodded gently.

"Oh, right, the rocks." She huffed, her breath ruffling her bangs. "It's kind of hard to explain, but we're going to make an inter-dimensional phone call."

Andras's brow wrinkled.

She grinned at him. "We're going to send a message to someone—a friend of mine—back on Earth. He can send us coins."

Andras's brow wrinkled even further. "He is condemned to walk the Earth?"

"He's not dead."

The furrows grew even deeper. "Then how will he get your message?"

"Trust me. He will."

"He is a mystic?"

Irene laughed. "No. Well...sort of, I guess. It's as good a word as any to describe him. He's got a way of seeing dead people." Irene was pretty sure there was no way to explain that Jonah had found a book in his school library that contained mystical meditations, including one that let him separate his spirit from his body—a kind of astral projection—which let him see and interact with the dead stuck on Earth as ghosts. She especially didn't think she could explain it in terms Andras wouldn't find suspect. It wouldn't break her heart if he thought witchcraft was involved and decided to distance himself, but such a belief might also lead him to try and stop her.

"Hey," Ian called, "you got to see this. This tree looks like a cup or two people kissing, depending on which way you look at it."

Before Irene could respond, the air was rent by an ear-splitting shriek and then by another and another. Andras swore and took off at a run.

"Wait!" Irene cried, but he had already disappeared into the gray nothing. "Damn it!"

She sprinted after him, muttering under her breath, "Yeah, sure, why not? Let's run *toward* the danger, rather than *away* from it."

"Hey! Hang on…" Ian called from somewhere behind her.

She rounded a tree and burst upon a scene of chaos. Two women and a child were huddled together behind Andras, who was driving off what appeared to be a pack of Hungry Ghosts. Irene scanned the hard, unfeeling faces of the insane dead. She didn't recognize any of them and, though it hardly seemed possible, these ghosts seemed harder, more unfeeling than the ones that had attacked her. They radiated an aura of menace, and Irene shivered, an icy chill sweeping over her.

Andras was speaking gently to them, as he had when he'd rescued her, but the Hungry Ghosts didn't seem in the least placated. They stared past him, their hollow unseeing eyes dark with rage as they stared at the little boy cradled between the two women. Irene could feel the hostility rolling off the Hungry Ghosts, thick and palpable.

Without thinking, she stuck a hand in her bag and pulled out the first thing she touched — the pepper spray.

"Here," she cried, holding it out to the closest ghost. "Here, take it! Go on."

As one, the Hungry Ghosts all turned toward her, and Irene realized her mistake. There was a roar of sound, and then, as a group, they rushed her, their rage hitting her like a wall an instant before they reached her. She was knocked down, the impact of the fall emptying the air from her lungs.

The ghosts were on her in an instant, a dark, malevolent cloud that surrounded her and blotted out the light. Screams were torn from her as she was buffeted, pummeled, and kicked. She squeezed her eyes shut and tried to cover her head, tried to roll into a ball.

She was freezing and burning, suffocating and drowning. The Hungry Ghosts had turned into a shrouding darkness, burning her with cold as they covered and enveloped her. She could hear screaming all around her, the enraged shrieks of the insane dead mixing with Andras's and Ian's yells. Something hard closed on her arm, and she was yanked sideways, up and out of the suffocating dark. Her fingers convulsed on the pepper spray, and she heard the hiss of its release. Ian yelled.

The hissing of the pepper spray went on for a long time, even after she had released the trigger. Blinded by terror, she flailed without seeing what held her. She was crushed against something hard and unyielding as iron bands encircled her, and though she struggled hard against them, they held her fast.

She was being shaken, and then she realized there were words. It was Andras, repeating her name, over and over. She opened her eyes.

The hissing was coming from the cat. Its back was arched and it danced forward on its tiptoes, hissing and spitting in an unearthly, high-pitched wail. The Hungry Ghosts were retreating in the face of this onslaught. The cat was driving them.

Ian was down on the ground—half crouching, half kneeling—wiping furiously at his face. Irene pulled against the restraints holding her, twisting to see what she was pinned against, and realized it was Andras. He was holding her, clamped tight against his chest. She froze and stared at him, their eyes connecting. Terror was etched on his face.

His eyes went wide, and he bellowed. Before Irene could turn her head to see what he was looking at, Andras took a stumbling step backwards and then something slammed into Irene. Everything went black.

When she came to, she was on the ground, her head cradled in Ian's lap. He was stroking her cheek, his fingers feather light on her skin, calling her name softly. Andras crouched beside her, his face stern and unreadable.

"Hey, there she is," Ian said softly. Relief washed over his face, and he gave her his trademark lopsided grin.

"What the hell happened?" Irene asked, struggling to sit up. She put a hand to her head as a wave of dizziness washed over her.

"Easy, now. Easy," Ian said, gently pushing her back down. "You just rest a moment."

She looked at Andras. His lips compressed into a thin line.

"You said they weren't a danger. That they're placated by...stuff. Stuff to help them remember. But it didn't help!" She was shaking now, somewhere between sobbing and yelling, and the memory of the terror washed over her anew.

Andras's frown deepened. "It was the child."

When he didn't say anything more, she glared at him. He blew out his breath.

"The Fantasmos hunger greatly for children."

She blinked at him, horror and revulsion snaking through her. "They eat children?"

He shook his head. "No. They do not eat children." His face was unreadable, and he suddenly stood up, pacing away from them.

Irene sat up, despite Ian's protests. She patted her head—partly to make sure it was still attached—and then ran a hand over her face. Ian climbed to his feet and held out a hand. She shook her head, which made everything swim.

"Thanks, but I think I'll sit here for a minute." Her voice wobbled, and she cleared her throat, trying to remove the lump of fear lodged there.

The sensations that had flooded her when the Hungry Ghosts attacked were familiar—she'd felt the same thing when she'd been attacked by the Uglies on Earth. It was death. Not the ripping and rending that came with separating your spirit from your body—which was unpleasant enough; no, this was actual death, the end of self, the destruction of thought and feeling, the abyss of nothingness. It wasn't a quick snuffing out—a curtain of darkness—and it wasn't a slow fading away. No, this was utter destruction. The dissolution of the bonds holding each molecule together, one by one—the crushing and grinding of each thought, each feeling, each memory, and feeling them torn asunder and blotted out, until none remained. It was dying and knowing you were dying; no, not dying exactly. That sounded too peaceful. No, it was annihilation. It was being taken apart, bit by bit, until nothing remained.

Irene's stomach heaved and she shuddered, waves of horror spasming through her. She wrapped her arms around herself, cold to the bone.

"God damn!" Ian said, interrupting her thoughts. "What on God's green earth is this stuff anyway?"

She looked up. He was holding the pepper spray. Irene's eyes widened. "Oh God! Did I get you?"

Ian smiled. "Aw, shoot. Don't worry none 'bout it. Damn my eyes, though, that sure is some terrible stuff!"

Irene laughed, but as that made her head throb, she quickly stopped. She looked around and spied the horse a short distance away, seemingly unfazed. "Well, at least they didn't hurt the horse."

"Are you kidding?" Ian said. "That crazy thing is what knocked you down."

Feeling steadier, Irene held out a hand, and Ian grabbed it, hauling her to her feet. He held her for a moment, while she tested her legs. They shook like Jell-O, but she was able to stand on her own. Ian's hands lingered on her waist for a moment. Then one slipped around to rest on the small of her back, holding her against him. He was warm and solid, and it felt good to lean against him. She could feel his breath in her hair. He leaned closer, and she realized he was going to kiss her. Her stomach fluttered.

Andras reappeared at that moment, and Irene sprang back from Ian guiltily, as if caught doing something wrong.

"The women and child are gone," Andras said.

Irene looked around. "Did the Hungry Ghosts get them?"

Ian shook his head. "Naw. They run off."

"We should search for them," Andras said.

"Are you nuts?" Irene cried. "How would we even find them? You were the one that didn't think we'd be able to find any cairns, and they don't move around."

Andras's mouth thinned. Irene sighed. She hadn't meant to sound so strident. He had, after all, just saved her life. Again. She recalled his earlier complaint, that she was ungrateful. She took a deep breath, forcing herself to sound calm and reasonable, and tried a peace offering.

"Look, you know what, we're all exhausted and freaked out from what happened. Why don't we just rest here for a while?"

She expected Andras to argue; however, he only blew out his breath and gave her a curt nod.

"I don't relish staying here much, I don't mind tellin' you that," Ian said.

Andras gave him a deprecatory look. "We are not children. The Fantasmos have no interest in us."

Irene reclaimed her bag, which was lying on the ground a short distance away. She pulled out the blanket, spread it out, and then patted it, indicating the men should join her. Ian plopped down, a grin replacing the sour expression he had been directing at Andras. He propped himself on one elbow and stretched out his long legs with a contented sigh. Andras chose to seat himself on a nearby rock. The horse wandered off to graze.

Irene eyed Andras with exasperation and then shook her head. If he was too good to sit on the blanket and associate with them, so be it.

"So, tell me, where do the Hungry Ghosts come from exactly? Were they crazy when they died or did this place make them crazy?"

Andras grunted. "Some cannot forget—their prejudices, their anger, their sorrow, their lives. It becomes a kind of madness—an obsession. They leave the comfort and safety of the camp and wander until they lose the madness."

"And gain another kind?"

Andras gave her a grim smile. "Now you begin to understand about death."

She shook her head. He was nothing if not consistent. "You must be a great drinking buddy, you know that?" She stopped as the meaning of his words hit her. "Wait, what? You mean...they're all out here—with us—all the really angry and violent people?" The people she'd been wondering about back at the camp—the xenophobes, the religious zealots, the people driven by greed and anger and selfishness. Andras was saying they were all out here, in the forest.

Andras gave her a level look, and though there was no trace of smugness, she suspected it hovered just below the surface. "I did warn you there were dangers in the forest."

She shivered, revolted by his unrelenting grimness. Ian saw it and drew closer.

"Are you cold?" he asked.

"We are dead," Andras said flatly.

Irene shot Andras a dark look and then said to Ian, "No, just creeped out."

"Aw, it ain't so bad," Ian said, putting an arm around her and rubbing vigorously to warm her up. "You don't got to worry. I'm here."

She shot him a grateful look, leaning against him as he rubbed her arm. She turned to Andras again. "Look, something still doesn't add up about the Hungry Ghosts. If they don't eat children, then what was it with the kid, then?"

Andras shifted on the rock, clasping his hands and bending forward with a frown. "The souls of innocents are generally taken straight to Heaven. The Fantasmos stick close to them, in the hopes of traveling with them."

Irene turned this over. Now that she thought about it, she hadn't seen many children in the camp. Certainly not babies. The children she had seen were all older—at least six or seven, with most of them over twelve or thirteen.

"So they're like hitchhikers?" she asked. "The Hungry Ghosts, I mean. They try to latch onto kids so they can get teleported to the next level?"

Andras's brow furrowed. "Yes."

Irene contemplated this for a minute. Then she lifted her eyes and met his. "You're awfully forgiving of them."

"What do you mean?"

"They're not angry when they leave the camp; they're despairing." She wanted to throw something at him. He'd called it madness, and to him, it was. To his mind, it was totally crazy to despair, to lose hope, to think that nobody was listening or looking out for you, even after hundreds or possibly thousands of years. He had so little comprehension of the emotion that he pitied those who felt it, as if they were defective or inferior in some way. She was amazed, truly amazed, at how someone could be so lacking in basic human understanding.

Andras was watching her closely, as if trying to read her mind. "That is why they deserve our pity."

She bit back the urge to scream with frustration. Instead, she glared. "How very condescending of you. It's reassuring to know that you're so much better than the rest of us. That you never lose faith or hope, that you never have any doubts or worries. That you're so much better than everyone that you're allowed to *pity* others and feel sorry for them for being so much beneath you."

Abruptly, Andras stood. "I will stand guard against their return." He turned and stalked away.

Irene would have almost thought he'd been angered by her words except she knew he didn't give a shit what she thought of him. To him, she was less than nothing—a heathen and an unbeliever, and that was before they even got to the fact that she was a woman, and a twenty-first century one at that. Inwardly, she laughed ruefully. How everything about her must offend him. It was a surprise he hadn't thrown her in the river rather than saving her from falling in.

"What's so funny?" Ian asked.

Irene shook her head. "The universe—it's ridiculous at times."

Ian smiled. "Aw, shoot. I could have told you that."

Fifteen

Dear Irene,

Your mom is doing okay. I go by after school and help with the yard and stuff. I told her I had to as part of my punishment and she believed me.

Irene's hands trembled as she read the words. She had found the letter in her bag when she'd gone to put the blanket away.

The words blurred as the tears came hard and fast. Jonah was still trying to take care of her, still watching out for her, even though she had crossed over and, as far as he knew, he would never see her again. In lieu of taking care of her directly, he'd taken on caring for her mother.

Andras stopped beside her. "What ails you?"

"Go away," she said, brushing away the tears. She blinked to clear her vision and kept reading.

She talks about you sometimes.

Oh God, she just hoped her mother wasn't telling him embarrassing stories of Irene's childhood. However, the next sentence confirmed her worst fears.

She showed me your baby pictures. You were kind of ugly. You look better now.

She laughed; from Jonah that was a high compliment indeed. No one could ever accuse Jonah of being a flatterer. The few times he had paid her a grudging compliment he had seemed embarrassed, the tips of his ears turning pink as he ducked behind his curtain of hair.

That seemed to be the entirety of the letter. She turned it over to be sure, but there was nothing else. No mention of school. No mention of home. No mention of what kind of punishment he had received for skipping school — not to mention lying to his parents and forging a note from them — in order to help her.

Andras was studying her carefully. She turned her head away as she wiped her eyes. "It's a letter from Jonah."

"The man we're trying to contact?"

Irene nodded.

"This man…he is your husband?"

Irene shook her head as she laughed. "He's not a man, exactly. He's fourteen."

"A boy?" Andras's surprise was evident. "Your son, then?"

Irene laughed outright at that. "No."

"What's all the jawin'?" Ian asked, crossing to them from where he'd been examining another interesting tree. He paused when he saw Irene's face.

"What's wrong?" he asked quickly, his look of annoyance changing to one of concern.

Irene shook her head. "Nothing. I had a letter from home is all."

Ian relaxed but still looked confused. "Everything's all right, then?"

Irene forced a reassuring smile. "Yes." Alright for them, she thought. The painful, crushing wave of homesickness and longing, however, threatened to overwhelm her.

Conscious of both Ian's and Andras's eyes on her, she turned away, hurriedly stuffed the letter in her bag, and thrust the blanket in after it. Head down so they couldn't see the unshed tears still swimming in her eyes, she set off.

Something soft bumped her arm. It was the horse. It had crept up behind her and was now trying to put its head under her arm. She wasn't sure if it was trying to comfort her or just wanted a scratch. She chuckled and rubbed its neck. Then fished a handful of cereal out of the bag, feeding it to the horse a bit at a time as they walked.

"I do not understand," Andras said after a bit. "Who is this boy?"

Annoyance flashed through her. Suspicion and hostility vibrated in every syllable of his question.

"Just a boy." Jonah had the typical fourteen-year-old's need to prove himself, to be seen as an adult, an equal. Calling him a boy seemed disloyal, even if was true, so she quickly added, "Just a friend, someone I met." She tried to think how to explain Jonah in terms Andras might understand. "He...can communicate with the dead. He's got...mystical powers." Okay, technically the mystical powers came from a book of meditations, but whatever. She didn't really understand how the book worked herself so there was no way she could explain it to Andras. Besides, it was just needless details—Andras was never going to meet Jonah, never going to talk to him. He didn't have to understand the mechanics of the relationship. He just needed to know that Jonah was able to help them—perhaps was the only person who could.

She turned her head and met his eyes with an earnest look. "He can help. I would bet my life on that."

Andras regarded her for a moment and then relented with a curt nod.

She focused on the landscape for a moment, checking in with her internal compass, and adjusted their course.

"So, what about you?" she asked. "You've been here long enough that all your family and friends must have crossed over. Have you ever looked for them? You must have had time to find them by now."

A muscle twitched in his jaw. "We are dead."

"Uh, yeah. So?"

"Life has ended and we must leave all such attachments behind."

She stopped. "Are you nuts?"

Andras slowed. For a moment, Irene thought he was going to keep walking, but then he also stopped. He turned toward her slowly, as if reluctant to answer. "Reminders of our earthly life can bring only sorrow. That life is gone. It is better to look forward, to clear your heart and mind in order to prepare them for God, than to cling to the past."

"Yeah, but…" Irene was so flabbergasted she couldn't even form words. She put her hands on her hips and stared at him, her jaw hanging open. "So you never looked for them? You just…cut yourself off? Done." She dusted her hands together to illustrate the point.

"I do not expect you, of all people, to understand."

"What's that supposed to mean?"

His eyes held hers for a moment. "You are holding onto the past with both hands."

"Damn right! Despite what you might think, that's an attribute, not a flaw." She shook her head. "I guess you and I just have very fundamentally different ways of looking at the world."

Andras dropped his eyes, but not before Irene saw a look of puzzlement and perhaps disappointment in them. "Agreed."

Disconcerted, Irene turned to Ian. "What about you? Did you ever look for your family?"

"Well, there weren't no family and not much in the way of friends. There was really just the wife…"

"Wife?" Irene cried. "You're married?"

Ian made a placating gesture with his hands. "Now, hold on….just hold on a second. I was wedded, that's true, but the vows say 'til death do us part. And we died, so we parted. So it's fine, see? Ain't no problem."

"Wait…what? So she's out here somewhere? And you, what? Just left her? You never tried to find her?"

Ian looked deeply offended. "The vows are very specific—'til death do us part. It says it, says it right there in the holy book. The good Lord couldn't be any clearer."

Irene's look could have burned a hole through steel. She wasn't sure what it was about Ian's attitude that bothered her, but somehow, it seemed wrong. She'd spent time speculating—as did most people—about what awaited in the afterlife for widows and widowers who remarried. Did the first spouse, waiting in the Great Beyond for his or her partner, feel betrayed? Would there be recriminations and accusations? Or, instead, did the second spouse have the right to be at his or her partner's side for all eternity? Or, maybe, all three ended up co-existing peacefully?

However, nowhere in all the speculation had she ever heard it said that all marriages dissolved upon death and everyone went his or her own way.

She looked back and forth between the two men. "This sounds like a whole lot of man-bull to me."

Andras frowned. "Man-bull?"

"Yeah—a convenient excuse for guys to just do whatever it is they want."

Ian bristled. "Listen…now just hold on and listen! What is marriage, anyway? Huh? I mean, when you get right down to it? It's about sharing the work and supporting each other and protecting each other. It's a partnership, right? But look around. What's the need for any of that? Huh? No, really, I'm askin'—there ain't no house needs tendin', no babies needs raisin', no joys or sorrows need sharin'."

Irene opened her mouth to protest and then snapped it shut again. He had a point—sort of. So, instead, she spun away from him and stalked off.

"So, see, it's fine. Ain't no reason to be mad," Ian called after her. "So, everything's okay, right? Uh, Irene? Irene?"

She turned to Andras, who had fallen in beside her, with a glare. "What about you? You got a wife stashed around here somewhere, too?"

Andras stared straight ahead. "Members of my order were allowed to marry, but I had not yet taken a wife."

Ian had caught up to them. "Aww, come on, Irene," he wheedled. "Don't be mad. Come on. Please?"

Irene shook her head.

"Are you mad 'cause I married someone else? Well, shoot, I'd marry you too—in a heartbeat. Just say the word."

"I thought you said there wasn't any point to being married now that we're dead."

"Now, don't go twistin' my words," Ian said. "I never said that... not exactly that."

Irene stared at him and felt her anger dissolving. It was hard to stay mad at someone so ludicrous. "You're ridiculous," she said. "Do you know that?"

Ian grinned. "Aww, that's a girl! Shoot, you sure do have the best smile I ever seen."

Irene laughed and shook her head. She supposed it really was ridiculous to be mad; none of it really mattered anymore, anyway. And it wasn't like she had an interest in marrying Ian or anyone else for that matter.

However, she felt a small bubble of doubt. Jonah had asked her once if she thought people could fall in love after they died. She hadn't known, but she had come to realize, the longer she was dead, that she really hoped they could — eternity was a long time to spend alone. And yet, Ian seemed to be saying that even those who found love before they died still ended up alone — even marriage wasn't forever. It wasn't so much an "earthly pleasure" as Andras would call it, but more a thing — like food and sleep — that simply became irrelevant once you died.

Irene lapsed into a moody silence as she pondered what seemed like an increasingly bleak future. When she had left the camp, she'd had such hopes, had felt triumphant and eager. Now, she just felt tired and beat down again.

The rest of the day passed without interruption. They didn't find any cairns, and Irene began to feel that they were wandering aimlessly. As the day wore on, self-doubt assailed her. What if she was wrong? What if they couldn't find any cairns or their way back to the dead city? Was she leading them on a wild goose chase?

Though they made no outward show, Irene suspected Andras and Ian were growing impatient.

"How about we stop for a bit?" she finally said, thinking maybe a short rest would help her regroup.

In response to Andras's scowl, she said, "Yeah, yeah, yeah — there's no fatigue, no pain, self-indulgent nonsense, yada, yada, yada. However, I'd like a cup of coffee, if it's alright with you." She scouted the area, looking for a good place to spread the blanket.

"There ain't no harm in stoppin' for a little bit, if Irene wants to," Ian said, immediately coming to stand protectively beside her.

Andras glared at him.

"It's two to one," Irene said, shooting Ian a grateful look. "You're out-voted." She dropped the bag to the ground and threw herself down beside it, curling her legs under her in as ladylike a pose as she could manage. Ian flopped down beside her. Andras came more slowly, stiffly and reluctantly lowering himself into a sitting position.

Irene riffled through the bag and found the battered tin cup from the village. She really wanted a drink—a real drink—but didn't think either man would approve; Ian might not be against drinking for himself, but she suspected a "lady" downing shots would horrify him — so, instead, she tapped the cup against a nearby tree and said, "Coffee, please."

She held the steaming hot cup to her lips and inhaled, feeling relief and comfort flow through her, easing the tension from her muscles. She exhaled slowly, enjoying the warmth on her face and in her hands.

She opened her eyes to see Andras watching her with a critical look. She quirked an eyebrow in challenge.

"You know, I didn't die yesterday," she said. "I've been dead for a while, actually, so I do know a little bit about it. Fine, I don't have a body so I'm probably not actually tired, but you know what? I don't mind being tired — it's actually good. It reminds me of what it felt like to be alive, to be human. Some of us, like Ian and me, think that's a good thing, something that shouldn't be forgotten."

Ian gaped at her in surprise then a delighted grin crept across his face. "That's right," he said. "*We* do." He put a hand on Irene's knee. She gave him a quelling look and passed him the coffee, which required him to take his hand off her knee.

"You seek to preserve the worst parts of being human," Andras said, his hands convulsing into fists. "We have been freed of the flesh, so that only our true selves remain, the parts most sacred and holy—our thoughts and our soul, which are part of the Divine and belong unto God."

Irene snorted. "You really are something else, you know that?" She shook her head. "Didn't you like anything about being alive?"

"Many things. However, there is no use dwelling on them now."

Ian passed the cup back, and she took a long, slow sip, enjoying the tangle of bitter from the coffee and sweet from the sugar. "If you really believe that everything is God's doing then you have to believe that God gave us bodies for a reason."

"We are made flesh so that we can understand suffering."

Irene rolled her eyes. "Holy Christ! The God you believe in is a real S.O.B., you know that? I can't even begin to fathom how, after eight hundred years, you could still have faith in such a God. I really can't."

Andras gave her a dry look. "Perhaps, in eight hundred years, you will."

Irene was aghast. "God forbid!"

To her surprise, Andras laughed.

Sixteen

After a short time, Andras became restless, clearly eager to be off, so Irene put away the coffee, and they resumed their journey.

Her strength—and her spirits—renewed, the flame in her chest grew strong once more, and there was no conversation as she honed in on her target. They rounded a large tree and stopped. There was a cairn and beside it, to Irene's surprise, was the cat—looking particularly smug. When it saw Irene, it stood up, stretched on its tiptoes, and began a self-satisfied rumbling like a bulldozer. Irene gave it a disgusted look.

"It doesn't count if I found it without you," she said flatly.

"This is what we seek, is it not?" Andras asked. Irene noticed he seemed to be warily avoiding the cat.

Ian rubbed his hands together. "Okay, now we get to see some magic. So, what next? You say 'abracadabra' or something like that and some coins appear?"

Irene shook her head, her lips twisted in a half smile. "If only, but no. I'm going to write Jonah a note and put it under the rocks, and then we wait to see if he gets it."

Ian made a face, clearly indicating this was neither what he expected nor all that scintillating.

She pulled the bag closer and reached in, looking for paper and pen. She reached deeper, her groping hand touching perfume, the tire iron, her purse, and suntan lotion, but no paper or pen. She had a sudden flash of memory, and the image of handing her last magazine to the girl in the bonnet tangled with an image of the cat running off with a pen. Her heart sank.

Her hand trembled and she dug more frantically. Finally, she yanked the bag from her shoulder and upended its contents onto the ground. She sifted through the pile, her hands shaking so hard she sent items scattering as she knocked them aside.

"You sure are carrying a lot of junk," Ian said, leaning over her shoulder.

Irene spread everything out, and then, to be sure, patted each item as she went over them again and again. She groaned.

Andras instantly appeared at her side. "What is wrong?"

She looked up, meeting his eyes with difficulty. "I don't have pen and paper. I can't write a note."

Andras was silent, his dark eyes burning into hers. A muscle twitched in his jaw. "You did not think of this before?" There was a smolder of anger in his voice.

"I'm not an idiot!" she snapped. "I had pen and paper. I just..." Her eyes drifted to the cat, who was sitting nearby, watching them, still rumbling contentedly.

"What about smoke signals?" Ian asked, picking up a book of matches from her pile. "Would that work?"

When Andras gave him a thunderous look, Ian bristled and said, "What? At least I'm trying, just tossin' out ideas, tryin' to get the brain juices flowin'."

Andras looked at Irene for a long, silent moment. Finally, breathing out hard through his nose, he said, "We must return to the camp. Your plan has failed."

Irene shook her head, refusing to give up so easily. "No, just wait a second. Give me a minute to think." She ran a hand over her face as her mind raced. Her gaze fell on the cat once more. Her eyes narrowed as she studied it. It perked up, its half-closed eyes opening wide, and it met her scrutiny with an almost expectant look.

"I need a pen," Irene said to it. Its eyes scanned her face, as if it was actually trying to understand what she was saying. "Do you understand? I need my pen back. It's important...more than important. It's critical. And urgent."

Andras made an impatient sound, but Irene waved him away. She pointed to the items on the ground as she spoke to the cat.

"I'll trade you. Anything you want. I just need a pen."

The cat seemed to consider the offer for a moment. Then it stood and stretched. Hope surged through her, her heart flying up into her throat.

Then the cat turned in a circle, laid down, and went to sleep.

A lead weight slid through Irene, bringing her back to Earth with a thud. She looked helplessly at Andras. His eyes said he thought she was a fool. She looked away.

"I guess there ain't no help for it but to go back," Ian said reluctantly. "Those ghost things are still out here, and I don't relish another run-in."

"Well, maybe we can get some paper and pen back at the camp and then come back again." Even as she said the words, she knew there was no way she'd convince Andras, or even Ian, to return with her. She'd lost all credibility.

Irene avoided looking at either of them as she shoved items back into her bag. The uncomfortable prickle of humiliation crept across her skin. She wouldn't go back — she couldn't. There was nothing for her at the camp. Besides, home lay this way — through the forest and back to the city.

She stood up and faced the two men, her jaw set. She didn't need either Andras's or Ian's permission or help. This was, after all, her plan. She'd come up with it on her own, and she'd execute it on her own. "Fine," she said to them. "Go back if you want, but I'm not giving up that easily."

"What would you have us do?" Andras asked.

"Well..." She paused for a moment, searching for options. Then she raised her eyes to his. "For starters, you could pray for a miracle."

A nerve ticked in Andras's jaw, and she half expected that he would simply turn around and leave. However, to her surprise, he pursed his lips and gave her a curt nod.

"Fine. We will wait...for a miracle."

Irene laid out the blanket and pulled out the tin cup. Despite the even greater than ever need for a drink, she only filled it with coffee. Ian and Andras joined her on the blanket, arranging themselves in various poses—Ian sprawling, Andras compact and upright. The horse ambled over and flopped down behind Irene, who used it for a backrest. She sipped from the cup until her hands stopped shaking from nerves, then offered it to both men. Ian accepted; Andras refused.

The stillness of the forest settled over them, so heavy and thick it could have been a blanket. Irene became aware that Andras was watching her closely, his eyes dark and unreadable.

"What?" she asked.

"You remind me of a woman I once knew."

Irene quirked an eyebrow. "Oh, really?"

His lips compressed into a grim smile. "She was burned for a heretic. She spat on her captors as they led her to the stake and she sneered as she burned."

Irene was horrified. "And what part of this story reminds you of me?"

His gaze was steady and unwavering. "She did not beg. Not once. Nor did she weep."

Irene studied him for a moment, trying to figure out just what he was thinking. "You admired her," she said at last.

His reply was swift and adamant. "She was a heretic. She denied the sovereignty of Our Lord and the divinity of the Savior."

Irene gave him a pointed look.

He was silent for a long moment, clasping his hands between his knees and staring into space as if he was watching the past. Finally, he said, "Yes. I admired her." He returned her pointed look with one of his own. "I only wish she had repented and accepted God."

Irene's expression turned exasperated. "Don't hold your breath."

Andras grunted, but Irene thought she detected a faint trace of a smile. She reached into her bag and pulled out a handful of cereal. She offered some to Ian who gave it a suspicious look and refused. Irene shifted position, snuggling into the horse's warmth. She ate a couple of kernels of the cereal and then offered the rest to the horse, which savored the treat. Then it stretched out prone on the ground and heaved a contented sigh.

For some time, there was no sound but occasional snorts and sighs from the horse. In the stillness, the surrounding gray shroud of the forest pressed down on Irene, stifling and suffocating. God, what she wouldn't give to see the stars, to hear crickets — something, anything, to break the vast and crushing nothing.

Thoughts closed in — regret, panic, desolation — and she squeezed her eyes shut, trying to beat them back or blot them out. She had rushed off, careless and messy, leaving the world of the living behind like a half-eaten peach, running from, rather than toward, something when she'd crossed over. Jonah had tried to warn her. So had others. There had been a trader who had told her he wasn't leaving the land of the living until he'd seen and done everything — bungee jumping, wind surfing, visiting Paris and the Great Wall. Now, all the things she'd left undone — people she should have visited, words she should have spoken, things she should have seen or done or at least tried to do — crowded in upon her. Too late, she realized she should have stayed and dealt with her problems, rather than running away. What she wouldn't give for a second chance, to go back and finish everything left undone.

You'll get back, she told herself fiercely, because the alternative was unbearable. *You will.*

She felt Ian's arm go around her, comforting and warm. He leaned in close and said in her ear, "You all right?"

She opened her eyes and tried to give him a reassuring smile. She couldn't tell him what she was really thinking, so she changed the subject. "So what do you imagine Heaven looks like?"

"That's easy," he said. "It's a saloon full of dancin' girls."

Irene shifted position so she could gape at him. He wiggled his eyebrows suggestively, and she laughed despite herself.

Ian grinned and sat back, looking self-satisfied. "There...see? I made you laugh."

Irene turned to look at Andras. "What about you?"

"It matters not what I think. Heaven is what it is, and I will discover its measure in the fullness of time."

Irene snorted and shook her head. "Well, I can say one thing for you—you're consistent."

Ian waved a dismissive hand at Andras. "Oh, the *padre* here is going to one of those boring afterlives, full of prayer and psalm singing."

Andras gave Ian a deprecating look. "At least I am headed for salvation."

Sensing a spat brewing, Irene quickly cut into the conversation. "Well, you know what, it's late and I'm tired, so I'm going to shut my eyes and try to get some sleep. 'Night."

She turned on her side and snuggled up to the horse. She heard Andras rise and walk away and knew he had gone to keep vigil. The need to keep a lookout made her tense, but somehow, knowing Andras was keeping watch was strangely comforting.

Ian snuggled up to her, fitting himself against her, spoon style, and that was comforting, too. Soon she was lulled to sleep.

Her dreams were a tangled mess—once more she dreamed of the beach, but now it was populated with slimy, black, desiccated trees, and the noise of the waves rolling onto the shore sounded like singing. As before, when she awoke there were tears on her cheeks. She was alone, curled in a ball on the ground. The horse had gone to graze at some point. Ian snored gently nearby, stretched out straight as a rod. Andras was nowhere to be seen.

The cat was sitting beside her, a pen at its feet.

Irene blinked at it, too stunned for her brain to fully register what she was seeing. Then her brain kicked in, and she bolted upright, the depression of the previous night washed away in a flood of hope. "Good cat! Good, good, good kitty."

She reached for the pen. Behind her, she heard Ian's breathing change, stutter, stop, then start again more quietly. "Morning," he mumbled.

The cat arched its back and hissed, defensively covering the pen with its body. Irene drew back, confused. She hesitated and then realized the cat wanted payment. The message was clear: you'll get yours when I get mine.

She was too relieved to dicker. She pointed to the bag. "Help yourself."

The cat didn't move. Irene sighed and pulled the bag close. "Where's the trust?" She dug through the bag and pulled out several items in quick succession. The cat turned up its nose at each one. Finally, when she offered it a book of matches, it hesitated and then grabbed them out of her hand and backed away, watching her warily. Then it turned and fled. Irene shook her head, still not understanding what the cat wanted with the items it took. What could it possibly do with matches — it didn't have opposable thumbs.

Irene picked up the pen and found her hand was shaking. She was excited, but she was also scared — now she was going to find out if her plan would actually work.

"Hey, you got a pen!" Ian said, his grinning face appearing over her shoulder. Andras must have heard him, because he came into view, striding toward them with his usual grim look.

Irene rummaged through her bag, searching for paper. *Stupid*, she scolded herself. She should have asked the cat for paper as well. Come on, there had to be something in here she could use.

Her hand brushed something soft and crinkly, and she pulled it out. It was one of the paper birds she had picked up at the Ghost Festival.

Her heart sank. She held the crane in her palm and studied it, emotions warring within her. Her hand shook, causing the bird to tremble. Andras crouched down beside her. "What is the problem?" he asked.

She lifted her eyes to him. "This is a bird. I mean...there's an actual bird in this thing. Well, the spirit of one."

Andras frowned. "I do not understand."

"It's how I got the horse. It was one of these paper animals; when I burned it the horse came out. If I unfold this so I can use the paper for a letter, what happens to the bird inside?"

Andras stared at the object for a moment and then looked at her again. "What happens to us if you do not?"

Slowly she breathed out, releasing the mounting tension inside as she realized he was right: she was going to have to sacrifice the bird if she wanted to get out of here.

She uttered a silent apology to the bird as she unfolded the paper. She smoothed out the tiny square and realized how little space she had to communicate everything she wanted to say.

Dear Jonah,

You were right — I've been getting the letters you leave on my grave. I need you to send me a bunch of rocks — like twenty of them; I can use them to build a shrine here, and then I'll be able to send you letters directly. Please hurry. I will explain more in my next letter.

~Irene

P.S. Also send paper.

She wrote slowly and deliberately, trying to both be legible and fit everything in. She'd had to use both sides of the paper. She folded the note in half and then wrote *If Found, Please Deliver To:* on the empty space she had left. Underneath, she wrote Jonah's name and address.

She kneeled in front of the cairn. With a silent and fervent prayer, she lifted the top rock, laid the letter on the pile, and then replaced the rock.

She looked up into Andras's and Ian's expectant faces.

"Now what?" Ian asked.

"Now we wait," she said.

It turned out that none of them were particularly good at waiting. Andras paced and Ian amused himself with imaginary quick draw gun fights with trees. After about ten minutes of that, Irene was ready to scream.

She also realized she'd been so eager to contact Jonah, she'd completely forgotten to send the general request for coins to whoever found the letter. *Stupid!* she chided herself.

Wanting a distraction for herself as much as for Ian, she pulled a deck of cards out of her bag. "How about a game of cards?"

"Well, shoot, why didn't you say you had cards?" Ian returned to the blanket, dropping down beside her. "All right! Now you're talkin'. What'll we play?"

"Poker?" Even as she said the words she realized they had no chips.

"Poker?" Ian cried. "That ain't no fittin' game for a lady."

Irene gave him an exasperated look. "What do you suggest then?" She looked to Andras for a suggestion but he had walked away. No doubt, playing cards was yet another sin.

Ian reached for the pack, gently taking the cards from her hand. "Here, how about this?" He quickly went through the cards and pulled out three — the queen of hearts and two aces — which he laid side by side between them. He then turned the cards face down and swapped them back and forth in a dizzying pattern.

"All you got to do is find the queen," he said.

"Three Card Monty," Irene replied. "I know this game."

Ian beamed. "There ya go." His hands stopped moving. "Okay, pick the queen."

"What do I get if I win?" she asked.

"Anything you want. Just name it."

Irene laughed. "Those are pretty high stakes. I don't think I can match them. What do you get if you win?"

"If I win I get...a kiss."

Irene laughed. Ian was giving her a sweet, hopeful look, and she laughed even harder. "You're serious? Okay, fine. A kiss against anything I want. I accept your wager."

She studied the cards for a moment and then tapped the one on the right with her finger. Ian flipped it over to reveal an ace.

"Aww..." he said, "that's okay. That was just for practice. Now we'll play for real."

Irene laughed again. "Best two out of three."

They ended up playing until they both had lost track of who was winning.

"Well, let's call it a tie," Ian said, picking up the cards and shuffling them back into the deck.

"Oh no," Irene replied with a mischievous grin. "I always keep my word. A promise is a promise." She smiled and leaned toward him. Ian's eyes widened, and then he leaned forward, closing the distance between them. Irene pressed her lips to his in a sweet, almost chaste, kiss. She leaned back, suppressing the urge to giggle. She felt like a teenager again — not in the sense that a simple kiss could set her heart fluttering; it was more the fact that this love affair was pretty much on par with those she'd had when she was eleven.

Wow, look how far I've come, she thought wryly. She'd gone from wild, drunken hook-up sex to an adolescent love affair consisting of pecks on the cheek and sly excuses to cuddle. Awesome.

Ian was looking at her with wonder in his eyes. "You really are the most amazin' girl I ever did meet."

She smiled and shook her head, feeling a blush creep up her neck. "I think it's more culture shock than anything, trust me."

"No, sir, it's you all right. You're one in a million." Ian gave her a slow, lazy grin, and her stomach fluttered in response.

She returned his smile, adding a bit of teasing seductiveness to it. However, if Ian had any desire to rip her clothes off then and there, he didn't show it; he just sat there smiling at her, drinking in her face with his eyes. Feeling vaguely disappointed, she said, "Okay, well now, it's your turn to pay up, cowboy."

Ian brightened. "Sure thing! What do you want? Just name it. Anything at all. You want the stars? I'll lasso the stars for you. Or how about I build you a castle made of diamonds? Anything at all."

Irene suppressed another laugh. "How about...you owe me a favor, one I can call in later?"

Ian rose to his feet and held out a hand to her. "Sure!" he said, pulling her up. "I'll be here. I ain't goin' nowhere."

She and Ian were toe-to-toe, a mere whisper apart. Ian had held onto her hand, and now he tucked it against his chest, pulling her in close. His other hand came up to rest lightly on her hip. She could feel it's warmth through the thin fabric of her dress, and she was suddenly hot and uncomfortable, wanting to feel his hand against her bare skin.

"Shoot," Ian said softly, gazing down into her face. She thought he was going to kiss her, and her stomach tightened with anticipation, but then, unexpectedly, he released her and stepped back, clearing his throat as if suddenly embarrassed.

Irene opened her mouth to ask what was wrong when Andras came into view. She frowned, aggravated that the moment was ruined. *My white knight*, she thought with disgust, watching Andras with a scowl. She shook her head. Just one more story the books had gotten wrong. Knights were definitely *not* romantic — in fact, just the opposite. They were mood killers.

She flopped down on the blanket, exhaling the pent up emotions in a long, hard breath. Ian joined her a second later and, to her surprise, so did Andras. Andras seemed to be watching her and Ian, his eyes flicking back and forth between the two of them.

A burst of rebellious anger welled up inside Irene. It was nobody's business but her own who she did what with. It had been bad enough when Jonah had interfered out of jealousy, but this was too much. Andras, she had no doubt, was trying, in his conceited, superior way, to save her immortal soul—for her own good and against her wishes. She ground her teeth and shifted position, putting her back to him, seething with rage. Clearly, if she and Ian wanted to get anywhere, they were going to have to get rid of Andras.

"What do you miss most about being on Earth?" she asked Ian, hoping Andras would get annoyed enough to leave.

No such luck. "That is a fruitless question," Andras said. "It is needless melancholy, and it is a sin to indulge such feelings."

Irene couldn't help herself—she spun around to face him, her mouth hanging open in disbelief. "That's awfully convenient—a sin being anything you don't want to talk about."

"Oh, don't mind him," Ian said.

Andras gave her a level look and spoke over Ian. "It is a sin because it is selfish. It is better to spend your efforts on worthwhile endeavors than on self-indulgent and fruitless ones."

She gave him a dry look, too exasperated to be angry. "I love how you have an answer for everything."

He flashed her a brief smile. "God provides."

Irene couldn't help it: she laughed, even as she shot him an infuriated look. "Well, I miss the stars," she said, tucking the jacket securely under her arms and shifting to find a more comfortable position, her resolution to drive Andras off forgotten.

Andras grew thoughtful. "There was a shrine in Galicia—the holy tomb of Saint James. Pilgrims came from all over to pay homage to the saint. We called the stars 'The Road to Santiago,' because it was said that they were actually the dust raised by the travelers."

Irene studied him for a moment. Just when she thought she had him pegged, he surprised her.

His eyes met hers, open and searching. Finally, she said, "Tell me about being a knight. What was it like?"

Ian cut in. "Well, what I miss the most is meatloaf."

"Meatloaf?" She gave him a mock disgusted look. "That's a sad commentary on your life, my friend."

"There is not much to tell," Andras said, drawing her attention back. "We lived by the word and the sword. Hard. Austere. Devout."

"So what happened?"

"What do you mean?"

Irene gave a half-shrug. "I mean, how did you die?"

"It is folly to think on it. It was a long time ago."

Irene felt like she was trying to dissect a porcupine. Every time she got past one quill, she got stabbed by another. "Okay, fine," she said with a sigh of exasperation, "if we can't talk about the past, what about the future? What do you think awaits us on the other side of the river? Is it our final stop or do you think there are more challenges to come?"

"That is also fruitless—it is needless speculation. God will reveal all in the fullness of time."

Irene flopped over, turning her back to him, silently castigating herself for letting him draw her into a debate. She should have just ignored him, as she had originally planned. "Okay, fine, whatever."

"Meatloaf's not so bad," Ian said, crossing his legs. "Not the way Mrs. Molly made it."

Irene laughed. "You're ridiculous, you know that?"

He grinned. "Yeah, but I make you laugh."

Irene started to laugh again and then stopped when she realized he was serious. He was asking her something or maybe offering her something. His face was solemn and she could read in it sincere intent.

Irene gave him a reassuring smile. "Yes, you do."

Seventeen

"How long must we wait?" Andras's lips were compressed into a thin line and his eyes flashed.

They had been at the cairn for three days. The time had passed very slowly. Cards and short exploratory walks to see if there were any other cairns in the immediate area only ate up so much time. The rest of the time had been spent getting on each other's nerves. Especially since it seemed as if each time she and Ian were alone long enough for Ian to work up to the point where he seemed about to kiss her, Andras would inevitably interrupt.

Irene looked up from the "SO YOU'RE DEAD" book, which she had been studying. "What's the hurry? We're not getting any older."

Andras eyed her for a moment, and then a wolfish grin spread across his face and he gave a short bark of laughter. He grinned at her for a minute, clearly enjoying the stunned surprise on her face. Then the smile faded, replaced by a puzzled look. "You are very...." He looked her up and down, as if the word he was searching for might be found in the folds of her coat. "I do not remember the last time I laughed."

Irene waved him away. "Yeah, yeah, I know—I have a way of surprising people. I've heard that before...several times in fact." She grinned. "It's nice to know you can laugh, though, when the occasion calls for it. At this rate, we might actually be able to be friends in a millennia or so."

He suddenly looked uncomfortable. "I have taken sacred vows of marital chastity—"

She held up a hand to stop him. "I didn't say fuck-buddies, I said *friends*." She gave him a dry look. "Which, I'm sure is a totally foreign concept to a guy from the Dark Ages, but whatever. Just stop calling me woman, keep your eyes up top, and remember that I'm the one who knows where we're going."

His eyes narrowed and the grin was wiped from his face. Inwardly, Irene groaned. She had meant it as a joke, but it had come out harsh, like a reprimand.

Andras scowled at her. "We should leave. Seek other shrines. It is dangerous to linger in one place for so long. It invites trouble."

Obviously their friendly moment had passed and it was back to business. Irene closed the book with a sigh. Her instinct was to stay—she felt closer to Earth, to her life, here than she had anywhere else since she'd crossed over. This was a link to the land of the living, and she didn't want to lose it.

However, Andras was right. She didn't have to be at the cairn to receive a message from Jonah. If the cairn was active, he'd get her letter and send back a reply via her grave, which she would receive no matter where she was. If the cairn wasn't active, then they were wasting time hanging around it. The best bet was to keep moving, find as many cairns as possible, leave as many notes as possible, to increase the odds that one of them would get through.

Paper—or, more specifically, the lack thereof—however, was still a problem. She could re-use the notes from Jonah—though she hated to lose those—and she had a few more paper animals she could destroy, but she hated to do that, too. Now that she knew those paper items held the spirits of living things, she wanted to keep them—they were another link to the land of the living, and the thought of giving each one up hurt too much to think about. True, she'd been aghast at the sudden presence of the horse at first and, having no special love for horses—or animals in general—she hadn't wanted the thing. However, now...well, now it was a friend, a companion, a source of comfort and amusement. It was something to care and think about, other than herself. It was a way to keep from getting lost, from forgetting. When the day came that she began to forget what bird song sounded like, she wanted to have the ability to bring a bird to life and remember.

Andras didn't understand; he thought them worthless, just pieces of paper. She suspected he thought she was mad or speaking metaphorically when she'd explained that the papers held living beings. He hadn't seen the magic that transformed the horse from a palm-sized piece of paper to a living, breathing animal, so how could he understand?

Still, he'd been right when he pointed out that the paper in those animals was the essential ingredient to her plan. She'd hoped for…what, exactly? A miracle? Well, if she was honest, she'd hoped to get lucky on her first try — had based her entire plan on it, really. Now she realized how naïve she'd been — as usual, she'd run off half-cocked without really thinking things through.

She stuffed the book in the bag, avoiding Andras's eyes.

"Ian," she called as she double-checked that she had packed everything away. Ian ambled into view. "Come on," she said. "We're heading out to look for more cairns."

"That cat's back," he said.

Irene perked up. "Is it? Where?"

However, when she went to look for it, it was nowhere in sight.

"I'm tellin' ya, it was here," Ian insisted.

"I'm sure it was." Who could fathom the inscrutable ways of magic cats? Certainly not her, and she'd given up trying. She hoisted the bag more securely onto her shoulder and set off, certain the cat would be back.

They walked all day without finding anything. The flame in Irene's chest seemed to sputter erratically, growing stronger one minute and then nearly disappearing the next. She started to suspect they were going in circles. As the day progressed with no sign of the cat and the fluctuations in her internal compass growing more extreme, she began to panic. Something was wrong. She'd been so sure she could find cairns. All she had to do was focus and walk with purpose, but it didn't seem to be working.

Finally, frustrated, tired, and cranky, she called a halt for the night. Andras scowled at her, but Ian and the horse were more than happy to flop down on the blanket and rest.

Irene rummaged in her bag.

"What are you looking for?" Ian asked.

Without answering, Irene pulled out the candles, set them down, and lit them. It was time to call in some help.

"You will attract the Hungry Ghosts," Andras said wearily, as if it was becoming an intolerable burden to continually explain the most basic of concepts to her.

"I know," she said, struggling not to bite his head off.

"They may be harmless, pitiable creatures, but it is folly to draw their attention."

Irene bit back a self-satisfied smile. "We'll see." She finished with the candles and settled herself on the ground, wrapping the jacket tightly around her.

They sat in silence for some time. The horse grew bored, got up—jostling Irene in the process—and went off to investigate the candles. It burned its nose, scuttled backwards, snorted, and then went off to graze in the opposite direction.

Irene cocked her head and looked at Ian, thoughtfully. "So tell me about life in the eighteen hundreds."

Ian grinned. "Aw, shoot. I bet you already know all about it. Bet you read it in history books and such."

Irene grinned back. It was true that it was a little unfair—she probably had a pretty good idea of what his life had been like, and he had no understanding whatsoever of hers.

"All I know is what I read in books. I want to hear what it was really like."

Ian seemed suddenly shy. Irene laughed and coaxed some more. "Come on, I told you about the future. Your turn. Now spill."

"Well...I worked on a ranch—horses. It was hot. It was dusty. It was a never-ending battle. Always more work than hours to do it. But the pay was good, the food was good, and

Saturdays there was always Miss Lydia's Dancing Girls Emporium."

Irene threw back her head and laughed. "You must have been a handful. What did your wife think of those visits?"

Ian's grin widened. "That's how I met my wife."

Irene gaped at him. "What? Your wife was a...a..." —she groped for a tasteful, historical word — "saloon girl?"

Ian held up a cautioning hand. "Irmaguard was a lady and a damn fine woman."

Irene back-pedaled quickly. "I'm sure she was."

Ian grinned. "She also would have clawed out my eyes if they had wandered any. After we was married there weren't any more visits to Miss Lydia's, which was a damn shame."

Irene laughed. "You're incorrigible!" She shook her head.

She felt Andras's eyes on her, and she looked at him. "I suppose it's 'fruitless melancholy' to ask about your life?"

He gave her a flat look.

For some reason, she couldn't stop from goading him, even though she knew she should just ignore him. "Okay, well if I'm not allowed to ask about your life on Earth and I'm not allowed to speculate about the future, then that doesn't give us a whole lot to talk about. It's a shame, too—I was actually kinda curious."

"About what?" he asked with a note of deep suspicion.

"About your life...about Spain. That's where you're from, right? I don't really know that much about history, and I've never been to Spain."

"It is folly to focus on such things. It brings only sorrow."

She was exasperated by his determination to be so miserable. "Surely you must have some happy memories?"

"Perhaps I had, once. Now all that remains is longing and regret." His right hand flexed convulsively.

Irene studied him for a moment, her curiosity piqued. She wondered what he was thinking about—clearly something had happened to him. "Well, at least tell me how you died."

Andras's lip curled in a sneer. "I died in a place no one remembers fighting a long-forgotten enemy over a long-forgotten cause. It matters not."

His words stung, and she flushed. "Okay, fine, Mr. Porcupine. Whatever. You've got God to keep you company, so I get that us mere mortals are pretty poor companions in comparison. I was just trying to be nice so you didn't feel excluded, but I'll save my breath from now on."

She jerked her jacket closed and turned on her side, putting her back to him. Ian was there, smiling at her. He studied her for a moment and then reached out and caught her hand, snaking his fingers through hers. His gaze was soft and tender. A gentle smile touched the corners of his mouth. "Irmaguard snored," he mouthed to her.

Irene laughed. Ian grinned in response. He gave her hand a squeeze, and Irene felt the tension drain away. Everything was going to be alright. She'd recharge her batteries with a good night's rest and then tomorrow they'd find another cairn. No matter how snarky and difficult Andras was, Ian was always there to put things right.

"Thank you," she mouthed to him.

He brought her hand to his lips and kissed her knuckles tenderly. "Anytime."

Eighteen

Irene refolded the blanket and stuffed it in her bag, along with the candles. It was "morning" and she was the last to get up. When she'd awakened, the horse was grazing, Ian was checking out interesting looking trees, and Andras had wandered off, presumably to stand guard or maybe scout the area.

An alarmed shout from Ian made her nearly drop the blanket. "Holy mother of cats!"

She whipped around to see Ian backing away from Elvira, who was stepping out from behind a tree. Relief flooded through Irene.

"No, it's okay!" she called to Ian, hurrying forward. "She's a friend."

Elvira hesitated, clinging to the tree uncertainly, as if for protection. Irene held the blanket out to her. Elvira darted a glance at Ian and then warily took the blanket. She hugged it to her chest for a moment, looking at Irene expectantly.

"Hey!" Ian said.

"Don't worry, she'll give it back," Irene replied, holding up a hand to silence him. She smiled encouragingly at Elvira. "Can you help us?"

Elvira's eyes searched Irene's face. Irene wasn't sure the other woman understood but pressed on. "We need to find rocks—small piles of them. About this big." She indicated with her hands.

Elvira watched Irene's movements for a moment. She gave no sign that she understood. Then she backed away, the blanket slipping from her fingers.

"No, wait!" Irene said, but Elvira disappeared into the gray void.

"Is it me?" Irene asked, turning to Ian. "Do I smell or something? Why is it everyone I ask for help runs away?"

"Hey, I'm still here," he said.

Irene gave him an exasperated look. "I didn't ask for your help."

Ian grinned. "Well, what else do you call throwing me to the ground and jumping on me like that?"

"An unfortunate mistake," she said with a laugh, retrieving the blanket.

His face fell. "Aww shoot, you don't mean that."

She laughed again. "No, I don't. I was just teasing."

She turned and nearly walked into Andras, who was staring at her with a strange, intense, puzzled look. Irene impatiently cocked an eyebrow at him. "What?"

Andras shook his head. "Nothing."

"No, really — what?"

"You are...," he seemed to be groping for a word, as he had the last time she had surprised him.

"Unusual, yeah. So you've said." She put a hand on her hip. "Why? Because I was nice to Elvira? I'm not —" She'd been about to say, "a jerk" and to point out that she was actually capable of normal human emotions — unlike him — but she bit back the words. Something rankled in the realization that Andras was astounded by her being the least bit nice to anyone. A kind of fierce hurt made her change her words to what she knew he expected to hear. "It's really not that astounding. I was nice to her in the woods so she wouldn't attack me, and I was nice to her now so she'd help us. See? The world makes sense again."

She turned away, a deep scowl on her face, fighting the urge to punch something. She folded up the blanket and stuffed it roughly in her bag. "Come on," she said to Ian, more angrily than she'd meant to.

The inner flame was stronger today, as she'd hoped, and her anger soon faded as she became intent on the task at hand. She decided to return to the original plan of finding the dead city, foregoing a search of the forest for more cairns. With that as her goal, she was more focused, more hopeful, and the flame seemed to respond accordingly.

Just as they decided to stop for the night, Elvira showed up, lurking behind a tree.

"God damn!" Ian shouted, starting up with fright.

Andras cast him a dark look. "There is no need to fear."

Ian gave him a dark look of his own. "Easy for you to say. They don't find you interestin' in the least."

The horse snorted, as if in agreement, and kept its distance, its eyes rolling with fear so that the whites showed every time it looked at Elvira.

Elvira beckoned with a hand for Irene to follow her. Silently, the trio complied and shortly a cairn appeared out of the grayness. Irene gave a shout of triumph. Impulsively she threw her arms around Elvira in gratitude. The other woman flailed wildly in an attempt to get free. Irene released her and stepped back. "Sorry."

Elvira backed away, looking altogether alarmed, and disappeared into the forest. She was gone before Irene could try to stop her.

Irene riffled through her bag for the pen and one of the few remaining paper items. She dashed off a general request for coins to anyone who found the note and then added another copy of her letter to Jonah below that, folded the paper, and stuck it under the top rock. The small triumph buoyed her enough that she decided to forego a rest break, and they continued on their way.

Irene checked her bag frequently, looking for rocks or a letter from Jonah at least indicating he had gotten her message. She found neither.

When they finally stopped to rest, Irene fell asleep quickly. She dreamed of a dark-haired woman who turned into a tree, her hair lengthening and hardening until it became the protective black bark of the dead trees. In her dream, Irene beat her fist against the trunk, crying, trying to save the woman from her suffocating tomb. Every thump of her hand against the tree loosed a burst of heavenly music, a choir singing the song from the village, until she was hammering uncontrollably on the tree and the music sounded non-stop.

Irene started awake, clawing at the blanket which seemed to be smothering her. Her heart thumped in an uneven rhythm.

Andras was watching her from a nearby rock. Ian was nowhere to be seen.

"If you must rest, you should at least avoid sleep," Andras said without inflection. "There are unsavory things in the dreaming."

Irene rubbed at her eyes, trying to clear the nightmare from her brain. "Yeah, no shit, Sherlock," she muttered. She reached for her bag and pulled out the cup. She cast a sidelong glance at Andras and then requested coffee. Softly, under her breath so he couldn't hear her, she added, "With a shot of Kahlua."

Her head pounded unmercifully and she felt sick and unsettled. She sipped the coffee, trying to argue herself into believing that she couldn't, in fact, have a headache or an upset stomach because she technically didn't have a body. Her body, however, didn't believe her.

Andras was watching her. She could feel his disapproving eyes boring into her. She swallowed the last of the coffee and then reluctantly climbed to her feet, squaring her shoulders and threatening to stab her stomach if it dared up-chuck the coffee—or, at least, if it did it in front of him. Andras already thought she was an idiot and a weakling because she needed to stop and sleep; she could only imagine the lecture he'd give her if she told him she wanted to take the day off because she felt ill. Well, she'd be damned if she gave him the opportunity.

"Where's Ian?" she asked.

"He is attempting to ride the horse." Andras's tone made it abundantly clear what he thought of this activity.

Irene groaned. "Didn't he learn his lesson last time?"

A surprised shout, which sounded suspiciously like the one Ian had given when the horse had bucked him off before, answered that question. Irene shook her head and headed toward the sound.

Ian was climbing to his feet and dusting himself off when they arrived. He grinned at her. "Well, I stayed on for a whole minute this time!"

"You're going to break your neck."

Ian shook his head and frowned thoughtfully at the horse. "You know, I don't know where you got this horse. I don't think it's broke."

Andras glowered at Ian from under lowered brows. "It is broke; it just does not like you."

"Oh, yeah? Well, if you're so smart, let's see you ride it."

Irene clenched her teeth and stepped between the two men. "Come on," she said. "Let's go." She set off, hoping they followed her without continuing the argument—her head wouldn't be able to take it. To her relief the two men, and the horse, followed without another word.

Andras was stalking along, apparently still angry because he looked grim and annoyed. Irene was reluctant to talk to him when he was in such a mood, but she couldn't shake either the memory of her bad dreams or the nagging questions she still had about the incident with the crazed Hungry Ghosts.

"Can I ask you something?" she asked hesitantly, drawing closer to Andras. She fully expected him to rebuff her with some kind of exhortation to talk to God about whatever was troubling her, but he only nodded. "About the Hungry Ghosts—or, more specifically, about dead children? You said that little kids go straight to Heaven or whatever, but then you also said that the Hungry Ghosts are drawn to them, which implies that they don't go straight to Heaven from Earth. They spend some time here, right?"

"Sometimes, not often, I have seen children in the forest. They seem fascinated by the trees."

The dream from the night before flashed through her mind again. She studied the trees as they walked, their blackened trunks stark and grim in the grayness surrounding them. She broke away from Andras and headed for the closest one.

"Where are you going?" he called.

"Hang on, I want to check something." She stopped at a tree and looked at it, really looked at it. She wasn't sure what she expected to see — it was just a tree. A strange, bare, leafless one to be sure, but still just a tree. Yet she felt the strangest sense of recognition. For some reason, the sleepers in the tents in the village came to mind.

She reached out to stroke the strange bark, as smooth and dark as obsidian. There was a jolt of energy as her fingertips connected and her ears filled with the sound of singing. Not the choir from the village, no; this was a solitary voice, thin and high — a child's voice — singing a soaring, wordless aria. Irene jerked back her hand, rubbing her fingers as if she had been stung.

She turned. Andras was watching her.

"What is wrong?" he asked.

"You didn't hear that?"

He shrugged and shook his head, indicating he had no idea what she was talking about.

Irene looked at the tree, all the trees, with a mixture of fear and astonishment. Sand that wasn't sand. Trees that weren't tree. "I don't think these are trees."

"Nothing here is real," Andras said softly.

"That's not true," she replied. "In fact, just the opposite. Everything here is absolutely real. Just…differently real than expected. It's real in an absolute, literal sense." Her brow furrowed as she tried to remember an elusive piece of ghost lore. "There's this ghost story or urban legend or whatever you call it…it's Japanese, I think…about dead children that hang out under a tree or something, and they lure people there…" She concentrated hard, but the memory wouldn't come into focus. She shook her head. "I don't know; I don't remember. Something about dead children and trees.

The apple, the peel, the core — they are all one.

If the Guide was to be believed, she was still on Earth, just seeing it differently. What had he said — like seeing a leg on an x-ray? So what if, when she crossed the river, she still didn't leave Earth? What if, instead, she just became able to see things in yet another new way, like slipping on a new pair of glasses? That would mean that everything was still here, all around her, just layered—layer upon layer—and just out of sight.

Everything...that ever was and ever would be.

She backed away from the tree, suddenly afraid. *Oh God.* Samyel had said it, so had the Guide, and now she thought she was beginning to understand. A series of transformations, but the same from beginning to end.

She was going to make it back to Earth alright, and she was going to be the same—and completely and absolutely different. She was going to be stripped, layer by layer—each facet of her being laid bare. She would go under the microscope, under the x-ray, each part of her teased out and separated from the whole. She would become seeds and peel and fruit—and at each stage something would be left behind. There would be a price to pay, and it would be steep—the universe would demand a part of her.

The Greeks had said a coin symbolized the "shade's willingness to move on." What they meant was that it was the shedding of something, the shedding of the longing for home, the cutting of the ties to the past. That would be the price for leaving this place. The price would only get higher the further into the afterlife she went.

She had already started to change—the aching loneliness, the sudden caring what other people thought of her, the need to prove herself, her repulsion for being touched by strangers. A bolt of fear sizzled through her. *I can't do this*, she thought. She didn't want to be different. She wanted her old life back, exactly the way it had been—she wanted her ignorance back; she wanted her bliss.

Do you? Do you really?

Andras was suddenly close, his eyes dark and intense. "What do you see?" he asked.

"The end," she whispered.

A sudden shout from Ian simultaneous with a hiss of alarm from Andras interrupted her thoughts, squelching the sudden panic that had her dizzy and breathless with fear.

She turned to see Elvira and Bob One standing a few feet away, having slipped into view from the periphery of the forest.

Irene hurried over. Elvira was clutching something to her chest, which she now held out to Irene. It was a piece of paper, ancient and crumpled, but it was paper — blank paper — nonetheless. Elvira watched Irene's face carefully, her dark eyes searching every inch of it for God only knew what.

Elation at having finally succeeded in something drove all other concerns from her mind. She reached out and took the paper from Elvira, the rasping of the dry page as it slid from hand to hand unaccountably loud in the silence. Then Elvira backed away.

"Wait!" Irene cried, reaching for her bag. "Do you want something?" However, Elvira and Bob were already gone.

Irene stood there for a moment, stupefied. Emotions warred within her — bafflement as to how Elvira had known she wanted paper and confusion as to why Elvira hadn't wanted anything in trade, as well as joy and excitement at having succeeded at something and in being that much closer to talking to Jonah. If she was careful, she could probably get at least six notes to Jonah out of this single sheet. She ruthlessly crushed the panic and fear, driving them deep into the recesses of her mind. *One bridge at a time.*

She folded the piece of paper and carefully tucked it into the bag, checking for a note from Jonah or rocks while she did so — there were neither. Motioning to the two men to follow her, she set off once more, the flame within her burning stronger than ever before.

Nineteen

They walked for a long time now, without stopping. The flame burned steadily, unfalteringly guiding her back to the city, and she double-timed them through the forest, driven as much by fear as by hope.

They had been walking without speaking for some time when Andras put out an arm to block her and said, "Stop." He nodded, indicating something up ahead. "Nephilim," he hissed.

Irene squinted into the grayness but saw nothing. She was just about to dismiss his concerns as paranoia when she saw it, up ahead, where the landscape started to fade away into nothing.

"Come, we will go another way," Andras whispered.

Irene wasn't sure why she was whispering, too, but some instinct made her lower her voice. "Is your fear of angels based on actual experience or just superstition?"

Andras shot her a dark look. "Not everything must be experienced to be believed."

Irene made an impatient sound. "I met one of those things; I talked to it, I traveled with it, I struck a deal with it. They're not as bad as you think..." Her words died in her throat because the thing had raised its head and was looking at them. Had it heard them? Irene's breath caught in her chest and stuck.

She had never actually seen what Samyel looked like — he had worn sunglasses and a baseball cap pulled low, which, together, obscured his face. His back had been to her in the dead city—the only time she'd seen him without his accessories. Now she could see what he had been hiding.

The creature was a little like the Tolkien description of an elf: pointed ears peeked through a cascade of white-gold hair that fell to its waist, and its androgynous face had a cold and severe, almost savage, beauty. It was dressed in a kind of toga of white cloth, and a pair of wings, covered in white-gold feathers that matched its hair, was visible behind.

Its lips were pulled back, its teeth—small and sharp—exposed, and Irene's first thought was that it wasn't a very nice smile. Then she realized it wasn't smiling—it was snarling. It was then that she noticed it was rising to its feet, and, like Samyel, it was tall, so very tall. Her eyes followed the seemingly endless movement upward.

"Irene!" she heard Ian shout from somewhere behind her, his voice distant against the pounding of her heart in her ears.

There was a blur of movement as the creature moved. In one instant it was striding toward them, and in the next, it loomed over them. Up close, Irene could see that its eyes, beautiful and strange, were pink—not bloodshot, but a pretty, pale, rose color that glinted and flashed like rhinestones reflecting light.

She backed away, fumbling for words, knowing unutterably and absolutely that she was in the presence of a predator, and that she was the prey. "Uh, sorry…"

It unfurled its impossibly large wings in one smooth movement like a sail snapping open, and a blast of foul-smelling wind assaulted her. The angel snarled, a long, high, wailing note that went on and on without stopping, baring its teeth, and there was no mistaking its intent now.

Irene scrambled backwards and then turned to run. Something snagged in her hair and she was yanked back, her neck nearly snapping with the force. A searing pain sizzled through her spine. She screamed. Her head was wrenched sideways, her neck exposed, and then there was a stabbing pain in the tender flesh there. There was the stench of body odor, dirty feathers, and unwashed hair, a suffocating feeling of enveloping closeness as the angel pulled her against its chest. It bent over her, its teeth digging into her neck and its hair falling across her face as it greedily suckled.

"Irene!" Ian bellowed from somewhere far away.

She thrashed, trying to break free of the iron grip holding her, but she was pinned as effectively as a bug to flypaper. A wave of dizziness washed over her and the last of her strength ebbed away as the angel drank, leaving her boneless and limp in its suffocating embrace. She grew faint and nauseous and hot all at once, and she knew she was going to pass out.

Then Andras was there, barreling into the angel, knocking it backwards. Irene was thrown clear as Andras and the angel tumbled over and over and then they were on their feet, circling each other, both snarling in rage.

Irene was on the ground, unable to do more than hold a hand to the wound at her neck. *You can't bleed*, she vaguely told herself. *You're dead.* Laughter bubbled up, wild and crazy. *Dead. Dead. Dead.*

The world around her bobbed in and out of focus, nausea and dizziness rolling over her in waves. Around her, the horror unfolded dimly, as if from a great distance. She was vaguely aware of the need to move, to get to her feet and run. She struggled to sit up, catching sight of Andras and the angel just as one of the angel's massive wings swept forward and slammed into Andras, sending him sprawling.

"Kill it!" The words were ripped from her, as if by an invisible hand. She didn't know where they had come from. She didn't recognize her own voice, shrill and hoarse with terror. She screamed over and over. "Kill it!" she screamed. "Kill it! Kill it!"

There was an enraged animal shriek and a black blur. The ground thundered and trembled as the horse charged past, rearing and plunging, its hooves striking out at the angel. Andras sprang out of the way as the massive feet slammed into the ground inches from where he had been.

The horse plunged, rose, and then wheeled again, lashing out with its hind legs. Andras shouted a half second before Irene realized the angel was in motion again. It leapt, seemingly weightless, and then it was on the horse, hanging onto its neck, the massive wings curling round it as if in a tender embrace. Irene knew what was going to happen a half second before it did. She and the horse screamed as one as the angel sank its fangs into the animal's neck. Irene started forward, half crouched, half on all fours, too weak to stand, only to be snagged round the waist and dragged backward.

"Kill it!" she screamed, struggling to break free. "Kill it!"

"Irene," Ian shouted in her ear, "it's me!"

Then Andras was there and the two men were dragging her backwards as she swore and sobbed, kicked and scratched.

"Nonononono…" she shrieked, tears streaming uncontrollably down her face, pounding impotently at the arms holding her. "Let me go! Let me go!"

She was watching a nightmare now, outside herself, the horror close and yet so desperately far away. All she could do was watch, powerless to stop it. The horse sagged to the ground. It struggled feebly for a moment as the angel raised one hand and, with a strong deadly strike, laid the horse's stomach open, blood and guts spilling free. The horse shrieked.

Irene screamed — one long, mindless sound that blended with the horse's death cry. She was barely conscious of Andras as he bent down, grabbed her round the waist, and threw her over his shoulder.

They were running now, the pain of Andras's shoulder slamming into her stomach with every step filtering ever so slightly through her haze of terror and grief.

Finally, after an eternity, when she had grown too tired to scream and kick and struggle anymore and lay limp and nearly catatonic, they stopped to rest. Andras released her, setting her gently on her feet.

She staggered away from him, the horse's death squeals ringing in her ears. She turned and doubled over, vomiting what little there was in her stomach. She sagged to the ground, face buried in her hands, and sobbed great wracking, heaving spasms that were more convulsions than tears, wrenched from so deep inside her she felt as if she were turning inside out.

Someone crouched down beside her. She struck out viciously with her elbow to drive them away, so blinded by tears she didn't even know which man it was. Gentle hands came back a second time, and again she mindlessly struck out. "Leave me alone," she rasped, barely coherent, and only vaguely aware of what she doing. There was only one thought now — to be left alone. To forget the world, to forget everything in it. To curl in on herself and shut out everything else.

"Hey, hey…" Ian said gently, drawing her into the circle of his arms. "It's okay. Shhh…" He wordlessly soothed her as she sobbed into his chest, desperately clutching his shirt.

Finally, empty at last, the tears slowed. She lifted her head and the first thing she saw through blurry and swollen eyes was Andras, watching them with a disapproving scowl. Anger flashed through her, searing away everything but the hate and rage. She swiped at her tears, drying her face with the back of her hand.

She glared at him. "Why didn't you kill it?"

"With what?" Andras replied, his expression carefully blank. "My bare hands?"

She was drained now, exhausted and hollow, and she stared at him stupidly, trying to understand his words. Mutely she shook her head, not sure why she was doing so. Andras reached down, his hand digging into the soft flesh of her upper arm, and pulled her out of Ian's embrace and to her feet. "Come, we must go. It is not safe."

Irene tried to jerk away from him but her legs, shaking like custard, buckled beneath her. She clutched at his shirt for support as she started to fall. He grabbed her by both arms, steadied her, and then set her away from him deliberately, as if she were a naughty child. "It is only a little farther," he said, as if reprimanding her.

Ian jumped to his feet. He put a protective arm around Irene, supporting her. "Can't you see she's spent? Give her a minute to rest."

"We must go," Andras insisted.

"Well, go if you want! We ain't stoppin' ya."

Andras locked eyes with Irene, and then he leaned in close, his mouth to her ear, and softly, firmly but gently said, "There is no fatigue, no hunger, no pain."

She pulled back, her eyes flying to his, uncertain if he was encouraging or mocking her.

Conflicting emotions tussled inside—grief, anger, frustration, and the wild, crazy thought that Andras was actually trying to help. She studied his face for a moment, but it gave nothing away. Finally, she nodded. "You're right. Let's go."

Beside her, Ian let out an impatient growl. "Are you sure?"

She gave him a weak smile and a nod.

"All right then," he said doubtfully. He gave her his arm to lean on and they set off once more. They walked, double time, through the forest. Irene found herself listening hard for the horse's heavy and graceless footfalls and even turning at times to look for it when she didn't hear them. The image of the horse's entrails spilling forth from the gaping wound was permanently burned in her mind's eye, and she couldn't dislodge it no matter how hard she tried. At random intervals the tears would come again.

Eventually, she grew so tired she could no longer put one foot in front of the other and begged for a rest break. Andras agreed without argument. Ian gently tugged the bag from her shoulder and helped her sit down, as if he knew her legs were in jeopardy of giving out.

She wrapped her arms around herself. She couldn't stop her teeth from chattering and tremors wracked her body. She rubbed her arms, trying to get warm.

"I wish we had a fire," she said faintly to no one in particular.

Ian scooted closer and wrapped an arm around her. "Hey, now, it ain't so bad."

However, she wasn't reassured. Her mind kept replaying every interaction she'd ever had with both Samyel and this new angel. She didn't understand—not any of it, really. What were the angels? Where did they come from? What did they want? Samyel had appeared to be searching for something back on Earth. For what? Samyel had needed her to cross over from the land of the living to here. Why?

Samyel had said he'd come if she called him. She had thought it was a promise, but now it sounded like a threat. She shivered again.

"God!" she burst out. "I traveled with one of those things. I slept in the same room with it!"

"Hey, hey, hey," Ian said. "We don't need to know all that."

Irene tensed and pulled away from him, barely controlling the rage bubbling up. "In the same room, not the same bed."

"Oh, well now, that's alright I guess."

"I didn't know I needed your permission," she shot back, her temper boiling over. She elbowed him, hard, shrugging out of his embrace.

Unperturbed, Ian simply replaced his arm and pulled her back close again. "Why don't you put your head on my shoulder; you can close your eyes and take a little nap," he said. "You'll feel a heap better after a little sleep."

Irene was silent as the anger at being patronized and the desire for comfort and warmth warred with each other. Finally, she realized she was being an idiot—Ian was just trying to help. She took a deep breath, releasing her anger and forcing herself to relax. The tension flowed out of her, and she went loose-limbed, melting against him. However, without the anger to hold it at bay, the despair returned. She impatiently wiped at the tears welling up. *It was just a dumb horse,* she chastised herself. It didn't work; it wasn't just a dumb horse. The tears burst free, hard and fast. Ian shifted slightly and brought her in closer, tucking her head under his chin.

She soon cried herself out and lay there, empty and exhausted. She let her mind drift for a moment, but a nagging worry kept resurfacing. "Where do you think all the animals go?" she asked softly. "When they die, I mean. Do you think they go to Heaven, too?"

Andras scoffed. "Do not be foolish. Animals do not have souls; it is a sin to think so."

"I think she's in shock," Ian said.

She shifted within Ian's embrace so she could look at Andras. "Oh, really? Well, then, explain the cat I've been following around."

"The more fool you to think it *is* a cat."

"If it's not a cat, then what is it?"

"It's probably one of them Indian spirit guides," Ian said.

"Puka," Andras said, his lip curling. "A trickster."

His tone rankled. He was probably right, it hadn't seemed very cat-like, but did he have to be so argumentative about it?

She was too tired to argue, too tired to even be angry. None of it seemed to matter much anymore, anyway. She nestled deeper into Ian's arms, letting the wordless comfort soothe her.

She was on the verge of dozing when Andras jumped to his feet.

"Up," he said, curt and harsh.

Even as he spoke, she heard it—an unearthly, screeching yowl that made the hair on the back of her neck stand up. The cat.

She was on her feet in an instant, Ian springing up beside her. Andras grabbed her arm and pulled her along, breaking into a dead run away from the noise.

"Wait, the cat!" she cried, but Andras paid her no heed. Irene turned, intending to break away, and in that moment, three angels came into view, materializing out of the mist and moving fast.

She spun around and put on a burst of speed.

They ran blind, zigzagging through the trees with no thought but escape. Behind them, the angels bellowed with rage.

This time, there was no slowing, no stopping. They ran for their lives. Somehow, Irene managed to convince her lungs that they didn't need oxygen, her legs that they didn't need rest, and was able to keep running despite the burning in her side, the throbbing ache in her legs, the sharp slicing pain in her chest.

Irene didn't look back. She blindly ran, dully aware of tree branches slapping her in the face, snagging in her hair, and catching on her dress. Andras and Ian dimly filtered in and out of her line of sight, the angels crashing through the forest at their heels.

Irene had no thought but forward—no time to plan, to plead, to bargain. It took everything she had to put one foot in front of the other.

"Stop!" Andras called. "Irene, stop."

It took a moment for his shouts to register. She slid to a stop and doubled over. Falling to her hands and knees, she tried to catch her breath and soften the collection of burning, throbbing, slicing pain her body had become.

"Angels?" Ian asked, gasping for breath himself.

Andras shook his head. "We are safe here."

"How do you know we're safe?" Irene managed to wheeze out between breaths.

Andras gestured to the city. "Because we are here."

Consumed by pain and terror, she didn't notice that the forest had slowly turned to city.

Ian gave out a low whistle of admiration and turned in a circle, clearly just seeing the buildings for the first time. "You've brought us to the future!" He stared at the buildings as if he had never seen anything like them before. Andras was watching her, his dark eyes unreadable. "It is not the future," he said curtly to Ian.

"Well, then, what is it?"

Andras's eyes bored into her. "I do not know. I have never been here before. It is her place; she created it."

There was hostility in Andras's voice, something cold and accusatory. He was also talking about her as if she wasn't even there. That was the last straw. Anger surged through her, hot and suffocating. She jumped to her feet, ready to blast him with an angry retort. However, before she could say anything, a crushing wave of darkness washing over her. The buildings and sidewalks swam before her eyes, and her knees buckled.

Andras grabbed her arm and steadied her. "You need to rest."

"I thought rest was a sin," she muttered, blinking to clear the wavy lines zigzagging before her eyes.

"God forgives."

Her knees buckled again, this time giving out completely, and she went down. Andras caught her in his arms and then hefted her aloft, cradling her to him.

"The angels..." she whispered.

"We will be safe here," Andras said gently. "They cannot find this place. It is yours alone."

"Here, I'll take her," Ian said. "Give her here."

"Get the blanket," Andras said, shifting her more securely in his arms. "Prepare a bed in one of the buildings."

"Can't," Irene whispered as the darkness circled closer. "They're filled with things that bite." She chuckled faintly even though she wasn't really sure what she was laughing at. Her voice and her consciousness were fading fast. She felt Andras stiffen. Then she was roughly thrust into Ian's arms and Andras stalked off.

"Hush, now," Ian crooned softly in her ear, holding her tightly against his chest. "Shh, it'll be alright. You'll see."

She lay there, letting him hold her. His shirt was coarse and scratchy beneath her cheek, and she rubbed her face against it, liking the gently abrasive feel.

"I can stand," she said softly, hoping he wouldn't put her down.

Ian cradled her closer. "Shh."

Her eyelids were heavy and she closed them, exhaling slowly and then inhaling deeply, enjoying the smell of cotton and pipe tobacco that surrounded Ian. Her mind felt empty and fuzzy, as if she was dreaming or maybe falling asleep, which seemed ridiculous given the terror she had just experienced.

She felt herself being pulled from Ian's arms, and she whimpered in protest. It was Andras. His mouth was set in a grim line that brooked no argument. He carried her to a nearby house, a rough-hewn log cabin. The door stood open and he carried her in. "You will be safe here. I have checked — it is empty."

Irene met his eyes, confused yet grateful for the sudden consideration. Ian darted past. Andras laid her down, and she realized Ian had gone ahead of them to spread the blanket on the floor. Ian rummaged in her bag and pulled out the cup. He set it aside and then arranged the bag under her head like a pillow.

"Uh..." Ian turned the cup over in hands with a puzzled expression. "How about some whiskey?"

It must have worked because in another moment Andras was raising her head despite her weak protests and Ian was holding the cup to her lips. She sputtered as Ian nearly drowned her, pouring the burning liquid down her throat.

"Jesus, couldn't you have at least made it vodka?" she muttered darkly, turning her head away after swallowing another mouthful.

Ian grinned. "Well shoot, you must be feelin' better if you're complainin'."

"I'm not complaining."

Andras rose to his feet. "Come," he said to Ian. "Let her rest."

Ian shook his head. "We can't leave her alone!" He stretched out beside Irene, put an arm around her, and pulled her close.

"I'm alright," she said, snuggling deeper into his warmth.

"Hush now," Ian said, stroking her hair gently. "I told ya, I ain't goin' nowhere." He shifted so her head was on his shoulder, tucked under his chin. She smiled despite herself, and one arm crept across his chest to hold him tightly.

Andras stood there for a moment, and then she heard him cross the room. The sound of the door closing was the last thing she remembered before sleep overtook her.

Twenty

The next morning, Irene was reluctant to wake, to face the aftermath, and fought hard to return to sleep each time she surfaced. Finally, however, she couldn't fight it any longer. Slowly, aching as if she had been beaten black and blue, she rose from her "bed." She stumbled out of the house, bleary-eyed and fuzzy-headed, her stomach roiling as if filled with battery acid.

Andras and Ian were sitting outside and both sprang to their feet when she appeared. She waved them away, afraid she'd break down crying if they showed her the least sympathy or kindness.

They seemed to understand. Wordlessly, Ian went into the house and retrieved her blanket, which he spread on the ground, and the cup, which he filled with coffee and then handed to her.

They sat there in silence for some time. What was there to say? The only thing she wondered was if the cat had made it to safety or if it, too, had been killed by the angels. She just prayed Andras was right that the angels couldn't get into the city.

Gradually, she started to feel a little bit more like herself or, at the very least, as if she wasn't going to shatter into a million pieces if she didn't hold onto herself with every fiber of her being.

She looked around, taking in the city. It felt strange to be back here after so much had happened; in a way, she felt as if she were back at square one.

Gingerly, she felt her neck, trying to assess how much damage the angel had done, but she couldn't feel anything. She pulled the coat aside and showed her neck to Ian.

"How bad is it?"

"There is only a mark if you believe there is one," Andras said. Irene glared at him, but let the coat fall back into place. Perhaps the angel's bite hadn't left a physical mark, but she still felt it nonetheless. She shivered and wrapped her arms around herself. She wasn't sure she'd ever be warm again.

"Tell me what I need to know and I will look for the rocks," Andras said, suddenly standing. Irene felt a flare first of surprise and then reluctance. At the moment, she couldn't deal with thinking about Jonah or copying the letter or cairns or what they'd do if they actually got their hands on some coins.

She stood up. "I...please..." She shook her head, not able to articulate her feelings. "I...I'm gonna go take a nap." She grabbed the blanket and ducked back into the house. To her relief, neither man followed her. She curled up on the floor, wrapped in the blanket like a cocoon and drank deeply from the cup, which she filled with vodka. Even Jonah couldn't fault her at this moment, she told herself. Then she silently cried herself to sleep.

At some point, she thought someone came to check on her, and sometime after that, Ian joined her, wrapping his arms around her and holding her tightly. She had no idea how long she slept; when she awoke, she was alone again.

She fought her way out of the blanket and got to her feet. She still felt shaky, empty, and sick. However, the urge to burst into tears seemed to have subsided, and she found that she wanted some company. She left the house to find Ian and Andras waiting outside, as before.

They looked at her with cautious, expectant faces. She stood there for a moment, not sure what to say or do, not sure what she felt or thought.

"Okay," she said finally, exhaling slowly. "Let's see if we can find cairns."

She wrote out multiple copies of the letter and gave a few to each man. Then they split up. Ian protested — he wanted to go with her, but she convinced him that it would be more efficient if they each covered a different part of the city; there would be time for sight-seeing later. The truth was she also wanted to be by herself for a while. She was drained and tired, and she missed the horse, the cat, and Elvira. She felt empty and alone, bereft, and she wanted to mourn in private. She didn't care what Andras said — she fervently wished with all her heart that animals went to Heaven, too.

She wandered away from the campsite, letting her thoughts wander as she walked. It wasn't long before she found a cairn, despite the fact that she wasn't really looking. She pulled out a handful of cereal and set it as carefully as she could on the little shrine. Somehow, that small gesture made her feel better. She was too numb to cry again, so after leaving one of the notes there as well, she moved on.

She ambled blindly down the streets, not really paying attention to where she was going. Before too long, however, the buildings started to look familiar and she found herself in front of the hotel. She tried the door, without much expectation. It was still locked. She circled the building, looking for other entrances, but there were none — just a wide expanse of stone and soaped windows.

She returned to the front of the building and looked around, wishing for street signs or some other distinguishing landmark. *Oh well*, she thought. *If I found it once, I can find it again.* The city wasn't that big.

"What are you doing here?"

Irene spun around and was confronted with the tiny, wizened, old woman from the stone cottage. Irene eyed her for a moment, not really sure how to respond. Finally, she said, "Waiting for the mail."

"Mail?" The old woman snorted, then stopped and gave Irene an assessing look. "Well, I suppose you'll want a cup of tea then." The old lady tottered off, leaving Irene to follow.

"What is it with mystics and tea?" Irene muttered. The psychic who had given Irene the self-help book had insisted on plying her with tea—despite Irene's protests—every time they had met.

Irene watched the woman's retreating back, debating whether or not to follow. This sudden "friendliness" when she'd refused to speak to Irene at all the last time they'd met seemed suspicious. On the other hand, this might be an opportunity to get some questions answered. Maybe the old woman was a Guide, too.

What the hell, Irene thought, her curiosity piqued despite herself. *What do I have to lose?* It wasn't like she had any other pressing engagements, and she could use a distraction from thinking about the horse and the cat.

The cottage was small inside. It had one main room that served as living room, dining room, and kitchen, thanks to a large stone fireplace along one wall. A second room—a bedroom, Irene assumed—was visible through an open door in the back. Every inch of the main room—from the mantel above the fireplace to the exposed wood beams of the ceiling—was crammed with furniture and bric-a-brac so there was hardly room to move.

"We got company," the old woman barked to the chirping chorus of critters that met them at the door. Immediately, a handful of the monkey-like things scampered off, returning a few moments later with one precariously balancing a tea tray and the others carrying a motley assortment of items—a tablecloth, a crystal vase filled with dried flowers, and a dish of decorative marbles.

Irene stood back warily, afraid to get too close to them. The old woman shed her shawl, dropping it to the floor as she headed for a round, wooden tea table in the center of the room, flanked by two wing-backed chairs. Two of the "helpers" sprang forward to grab the shawl and a tug of war ensued. Meanwhile, the procession with the tea tray scampered up onto the table where they swarmed over it, arranging the items as neatly as they could, chittering all the while. With a rending sound, the tug of war over the shawl was decided. The winner jeered at the loser.

"Well, now you can go fix it," the old woman said sharply, stiffly lowering herself into one of the wing-back chairs. With a high-pitched shriek that sounded like a cry of alarm, the two critters with the shawl scampered off, disappearing behind a mountain of clutter into the back of the room.

With a scraping sound and great difficulty, one of the helpers pulled out the other chair for Irene who eyed the creature warily and remained standing. It hissed at her, baring its teeth.

"Mind your manners," the old woman said, rapping it on the head with a spoon.

Irene felt a pressure on her foot and looked down. One of the hairy little things was attempting to polish her shoes.

"What are these things?" she asked, trying to back up and shake her foot free at the same time.

The old woman chuckled. "Oh, now, you know them. They're known by many names. Urisk. Hobs. Domovoi. Tomte. You call them brownies. Always wanted some, didn't you? Always imagined they were a little cuter, huh?" The woman's chuckle turned into a deep, raspy belly laugh. Irene felt a prickle of fear flutter across her skin, raising goose bumps. When she'd been a kid, Irene had fervently believed in brownies — little sprite-like creatures that helped around the house if properly bribed — and had left saucers of milk out every night to lure one, to the chagrin of her parents; however, she had succeeded only in making the dog sick.

"How could you possibly know that?" Irene asked.

The woman just laughed. The critter holding the chair hissed at Irene again.

"You best sit," the old woman said with a malicious smile. "They hate to have their offerings ignored, and they're fierce when riled."

Irene grimaced. "Yeah, I know. A few of them attacked me last time I was here." Warily, keeping as much distance as she could from the creature, she slid into the proffered chair.

"Yes, it's a shame." The old woman tapped an empty tea cup against a saucer. "Here now," she chastised the critters standing idly on the table, "what kind of service do you call this? Pour the damn tea!"

There was a chorus of chittering and the creatures sprang into action, two of them together lifting the tea pot while a third steadied a cup beneath it.

"They aren't meant to be alone," the woman said, her sharp eyes—as bright and button-like as the creatures'—on Irene. "They need to serve. They get a little off," and here she tapped a finger to her temple, "if left alone for too long. Of course, the plain truth is that there's more than I can care for out there." She peered at Irene. "You've had some sorrow since I seen you last, haven't you?"

Tears instantly sprang to Irene's eyes and she turned her head to hide them until she was sure she could hold them in.

"Mmm," the old woman said, sitting back in her chair, a thoughtful look on her face. "Well, I'm sorry for it. My sons, they say." The old woman fairly spat the words. "Not of me, they aren't, no matter what they may say. Damn nuisance, they are!"

Irene was taken aback by the woman's sudden ferocity and was reminded of her first impression that the old woman was crazy. She thought of running for the door, but the woman suddenly chuckled and her eyes twinkled craftily. "Why don't you take some?" she said to Irene. "They'd be good company, and a young woman like you, I bet you have lots of uses for them."

It took Irene a moment to realize the old woman was talking about the "brownies," rather than the angels. She blinked in surprise. "Uh, no, thanks..." A critter pushed a cup of tea across the table to Irene.

"Here now, you're slopping it all over!" the woman scolded. Angry cries that sounded a lot like an argument over blame erupted from two of the creatures as they struggled over ownership of a tea towel.

"Two dozen should fix you up nice!"

"Two dozen...what?" Irene realized the woman was still talking about her taking some of the creatures. "Oh no! What the hell would I do with two dozen—" Irene threw up her hands. "You know what, I don't even know why I'm arguing the point. They can't even leave the houses, and I'm certainly not staying here!"

The woman waved away Irene's comment. "Don't be stupid. Of course they can leave. They'll follow their master anywhere."

Despite herself, Irene's curiosity was piqued. "What, so I just walk in and say 'hey, I'm your new master?'"

The old woman huffed with exasperation. "Didn't your mother teach you anything?"

"My mother!" The tea servers had left the table and wandered off to do other work, but the creature at Irene's feet was still there, valiantly trying to shine her shoes. Irene's eyes swept the room and took in a clump of the hairy brown things, which appeared to be fighting over a feather duster, the odd furnishings assembled from a thousand years of history, and finally the old woman herself with her piercing black eyes. "No," Irene said with absolute truth. "My mother didn't prepare me for any of this."

The old woman shook her head and muttered something about slatterns and lax ways. Then her eyes lit up with a crafty gleam as they fell on Irene's bag.

"What's in the bag?"

Instantly wary, Irene put a protective hand over it. "Why?"

"Got any tobacco?"

"Tobacco? What for?"

The woman chortled. "Come on, dear, don't you know the afterlife runs on trade?"

"That's not what I've heard," Irene said. "From what I can tell, it runs on coins."

The old woman grinned in genuine mirth. "Oh, well, a coin is no use to the likes of me. However, if you have tobacco, I have information."

Irene raised an eyebrow. She considered the old woman for a moment and then leaned back in her chair. "Who are you? What's your name?"

The woman gave her a hard look. "Be careful of names, my girl, they're dangerous—dangerous to share, dangerous to hold."

Irene knew exactly what the old woman meant. Names had never meant all that much when Irene was alive. You said your name a hundred times a day, gave it to complete strangers without a second thought, and instantly forgot the ones that were given to you. Now she was terrified of a name—terrified that she'd slip and say Samyel's name out loud and that he'd appear to rip them all to shreds, like the white-haired angel had with the horse.

What had Andras said—if one Nephilim knows your name, then they all do? Buried even deeper than her secret fear of accidentally summoning Samyel was the fear that Samyel—or any angel—could somehow summon her. What if knowing her name meant that they could whisk her away from the safety of Ian and Andras, away from the city even? She tried, unsuccessfully, to suppress a shudder.

The old woman's eyes bored into her. "Oh, so you know already, don't you?" she said softly. "You've learned the power of names the hard way, haven't you my girl?"

Irene hastily pushed her thoughts back down, burying her fear under a hefty layer of other worries and doubts. She stared at the old woman, trying to assess her intent. Irene felt like they were playing some kind of game. Clearly the woman had something she wanted to say, and though she may look like an old woman, Irene doubted very much that was what she actually was. She didn't think the woman was a Guide, though, either. She had felt—even when he was chastising her—a comforting, almost overwhelming sense of unconditional love and acceptance from the Guide. She had no such feeling from this woman. In fact, she felt almost the opposite, as if the woman was scheming and sneaking, trying to cheat her in some way.

The old woman just waited as Irene stared at her, weighing her options, trying to figure out what her instincts were telling her. Finally, Irene warily reached for her bag, her eyes locked on the bright, black spheres of the other woman's gaze. She riffled through the bag with one hand until she brushed a pack of cigarettes. She opened the pack without looking and pulled out two of the slim, white sticks.

She set them on the table but didn't remove her hand from them. The old woman smiled. "Ah, you're learning my girl, you're learning." Then the old woman leaned back and, without taking her eyes off Irene, called out, "Pipe!"

The two women sat there, watching each other, until one of the creatures appeared, like a tiny butler, carrying an ancient gray pipe made of rough, scaly clay on a small silver tray. The old woman slowly reached out a hand and put it on the table next to Irene's. Irene hesitated and then raised her fingers enough to allow the old woman to take one of the cigarettes.

The woman unrolled it and packed the tobacco into the bowl of the pipe. Irene frowned. "I'm not sure you can just…" she started to say, but the woman ignored her.

Irene watched her light the pipe with a furrowed brow. Not a smoker herself, Irene couldn't say for sure that the tobacco in a cigarette couldn't simply be packed into a pipe, but she was nonetheless skeptical.

However, the woman seemed satisfied. She took a couple of puffs on the pipe then set it aside. "You got two choices," the old woman said. "You can try to buy their allegiance or you can claim ownership of the house in which each one dwells."

It took Irene a moment to realize what the woman was talking about. "Oh. Uh…how do I do that?"

The old woman grunted. "Sweep the hearth."

"Do what?"

"Sweep the hearth," the old woman repeated, emphasizing each word as if Irene was hard of hearing.

When Irene continued to look confused, the woman added, "Not hard to understand, my girl. It's very simple magic."

Irene pursed her lips and stared at the woman. Finally, she asked, "Okay, but what's a hearth?"

The old woman gave Irene a disgusted look. "You ain't much of a housekeeper are you?"

Irene folded her arms over her chest and glared. The old woman eyed Irene up and down, leaving no doubt as to what she thought of Irene's housewifery skills. "Yes, well...I guess you better try to buy them, then."

"How do I do that?"

The woman eyed Irene's bag again. "You can't get something for nothing."

Somehow, Irene wasn't surprised. She shook her head in exasperation as she pulled out two more cigarettes. She wasn't even sure why she was pursuing the conversation. She didn't need — or want — any of the creatures; they were, at best, a nuisance. She certainly wasn't going to take them with her to the next "plane of existence," whatever that might be, and yet, she was curious. The little things were actually kind of funny — when they weren't attacking you — and if what the old woman said about the critters being driven mad by loneliness and the unfulfillable urge to serve was true, then she kind of pitied them, too.

Irene put the cigarettes on the table next to the one that was already there. The old woman cackled with glee. "Saucer of milk."

"Saucer of..." Irene cursed. She'd stepped pretty neatly into that. If she'd really thought about it for two seconds, she would have realized she already knew the answer.

Irene remembered the letter Jonah had sent with the cereal. The likelihood that she'd find any milk in the afterlife was slim, so that meant she'd have to sweep —

This was ridiculous. Why was she even thinking about this? What was she doing? She needed to be out there, looking for cairns. The most important thing right now was to contact Jonah, get a coin, and get on the boat — enough with the self-indulgent pity, enough with the avoidance and procrastination. It was time to get a move on.

Irene abruptly stood, nearly knocking the creature still at work on her shoes on its behind. It shook a tiny fist and chittered at her. "Look, thanks for the information...and the tea. I really should be going."

The old woman smiled knowingly, put the pipe to her lips, and took a couple of long drags. She grinned a Cheshire Cat kind of grin. Irene's skin prickled with unease.

"Yeah...well...goodbye." Irene turned and headed for the door. She half expected the woman to stop her, to order the creatures to attack. Instead, two of them held the door open for her. As she passed over the threshold, they jeered at her. Irene whirled around, and the door slammed in her face. She wasn't sure why, but it felt like she'd just lost at poker.

Deciding that she'd probably been lucky to get out of there in one piece, Irene left as quickly as she could. She set off, resuming her initial quest to search for cairns. She wandered around for a while, but suddenly she felt restless and anxious, her heart no longer in it. She wanted Ian. She wanted him to put his arm around her while she sipped a cup of coffee, distracting her with idle speculations about the afterlife and stupid, random conversations about nothing.

Of course, it struck her that she was now lost — she had no idea how to find her way back to where the three of them had set up camp. Actually, now that she thought about it, they hadn't agreed to reconvene there — she was just assuming that's where they'd meet up.

She ambled aimlessly for some time, going up and down various streets until, by pure chance, she managed to run into Andras. He grunted in greeting and wordlessly they trudged back to the meeting place. Ian was sitting on the sidewalk, his back against the house she'd slept in, long legs stretched out almost into the street.

"Whoo-eee!" he said as soon as they came into sight. "The future sure is amazin'!"

"It is not the future," Andras said, practically growling the words.

Irene shushed Andras with an impatient wave of her hand and went to sit beside Ian. Ian immediately opened his arms, and she was more than happy to snuggle up against him, allowing him to cradle her within the protective circle. She sighed contentedly as she put her head on his chest. Andras made an impatient noise and stalked off.

"Did you find any cairns?" she called to him.

"No," he said without stopping.

"Well, I found three," Ian said, his chest puffing up with pride. Irene rewarded him with a light kiss. Ian grinned in response.

Irene spent the rest of the evening painting word pictures for Ian of what the skyscrapers around them would have looked like on Earth—carpeting, artwork, cubicles, elevators, cafeterias, televisions, conference rooms, computers, penthouses, doormen, everything she could think of. Ian drank it all in.

"I sure hope they have all that stuff in Heaven," he said, brushing the top of her head with his lips. "It sure sounds amazin'."

"If they don't, we'll just have to find our way back to Earth," Irene said drowsily, on the verge of sleep. "Together."

"It's a deal," he said softly, resting his cheek against her hair.

Twenty-One

"Ready, cowboy?"

They had been in the city for a week, and Irene was starting to lose hope. After that first day, when they had all split up, she and Ian had, by some unspoken agreement, formed a unit. Each morning, they would set off in one direction and Andras in another. She and Ian would stroll through the city together, and she told him, as best she could, about the future as they hunted for cairns. At some point, his hand had crept into hers, and from then on it had been natural for them to walk hand-in-hand. At "night" the three of them would regroup on the blanket spread on the ground in front of "Irene's house". She and Ian, leaning together, would share a cup of coffee and a handful of cereal while Andras, sitting apart from them, was mostly silent and grim.

"We would cover more ground if you split up," Andras said behind her, a sullen note in his voice.

She glared at him, though she knew he was right. She glanced at Ian, expecting him to protest the suggestion, but instead, he looked torn. Seeing Irene's look, he grew sheepish and shrugged.

"Might as well, I guess," he said.

Irene froze, taken aback by Ian's response, not sure where his newfound desire to spend time apart was coming from. "Okay, fine. Whatever." She turned around and marched away, keeping her back straight and not looking back.

She tried to keep her mind blank as she walked, tried to stay focused on the task at hand, as she traveled farther and farther from camp. She was soon lost in the labyrinth of streets, but the anxiety kept building inside her, like a snowball rolling down a hill. Since when did Ian care more about finding coins than he did about spending time with her? And since when did he agree with Andras about anything?

She was about to pull out the cup when she tripped, pulled sideways by a sudden weight in her bag.

"What the hell...?"

The bag slipped from her shoulder and hit the pavement with a thud, spilling rocks everywhere. She stared at them, not understanding what she was seeing, until she spied a letter in their midst. With a cry, she snatched it up.

Irene,

Here are the rocks. I have a lot of questions. Please write back soon.

~Jonah

He'd gotten her letter!

Relief washed over her and her eyes flooded with tears. Her legs gave out and she sat down with a thump. Her plan had worked. It was almost too much to comprehend. *Her* plan had worked.

She stared at the page, words blurring from her tears. She trembled, but was careful not to crush the precious letter. She blinked, trying to clear her eyes so she could re-read his words and fully absorb them.

Despite how desperately she had wanted coins, somehow, the coins didn't seem important at the moment. There were so many things she wanted to ask him: How are you? Did they sell my house? What happened to my things?

Who got my office? Is someone making sure my mother remembers to pay the bills and eat?

There were things she wanted to say, too: I'm not brave. I really am trying. I don't like any of this. I want to come home.

However, she didn't ask or say any of those things. She suspected the answers to her questions wouldn't satisfy her and, like her funeral, would only upset her; the other things would only upset Jonah. Instead, she said:

Jonah,

How is school? Tell me you're going. How are things at home? Are you still in trouble for skipping school? I really need to know that you're okay.

To answer your question about Charon — I don't know if he's just a guy or what; the stories about him requiring payment to take the dead across the river are true. Unfortunately, I — and about a billion other people — didn't bring any coins (Fine, you were right. I should have hung onto my coins). We're all stuck here. Please send me pennies or dimes, as many as you can get your hands on (DO NOT ROB A BANK OR ANYTHING LIKE THAT! Just send whatever you can find).

~Irene

With trembling hands she collected the rocks and hastily assembled them into a pile. Her hands were shaking so badly she knocked the rocks over several times and had to keep restacking them. She took a couple of deep, slow breaths, willing herself to calm down. Part of her brain urged her to wait, to return to Andras and Ian, but she was too impatient.

She slipped her note under the top rock, and then sat back on her heels, clasping her hands to her lips, willing with all her might for her letter to find him. She rocked back and forth, silently praying. She stayed in that position until her legs cramped, her knees burning from the extended contact with the pavement. Slowly and painfully she shifted

217

positions to dispel the pins-and-needles prickling, sitting on the ground and stretching out her legs. She slid the bag closer, wanting a drink, willing to settle for coffee. However, a fresh letter, sitting right on top, drove all other thoughts from her head.

It couldn't be. *Already?* It had only been a few hours. How had he gotten her letter, gone home, got the coins, and come back again so quickly? But it was.

School is fine. Home is fine. What is going on? Where are you? Where's Samyel? I really need to know that you're okay.

That did it. She broke down, laughing and crying at the same time — relief, tenderness at his concern for her, and amusement at his impatient demands for information mixed together until she didn't know if she was happy or sad.

There were no coins with the letter. She frowned, shaking her head with both admiration and exasperation — he really was too smart and too stubborn. Apparently, he was holding the coins hostage for information. She began scribbling a note and then realized — due to how fast she was writing — that it was completely illegible. Luckily, Jonah had also sent the requested blank paper. Irene crumpled up the letter and started again, forcing herself to write slowly and neatly.

It's a good thing it's not an emergency or anything.

I think I'm in that 'Hel' place you talked about — there's not a lot here. I'm fine. Bored, but fine. There are other people here and I've made new friends — imagine, if you will, me traveling with a cowboy from the eighteen hundreds and a knight from the late eleven hundreds. Yeah. Exactly.

Don't get excited — it sounds cooler than it is. There are issues of "cultural relevancy" (look it up). Bill and Ted it's not.

She chuckled as she pictured Jonah's expression as he read the last two lines. She could image the red-faced belligerence with which he'd meet her assumption (which would be accurate, of course, though he wouldn't admit it) that he didn't know what "cultural relevancy" meant—and the even more belligerent look when he found out it was a fancy way of saying "we're having trouble relating to each other"—and the confused and somewhat dubious look that would greet the movie reference; he was too young to know who Bill and Ted were. She realized she'd missed having someone to tease—Ian always felt hurt and Andras just got annoyed. Maybe teasing was a twentieth century thing? Either way, it was nice to again have someone she could joke with.

She placed the letter under the rock and then settled back to wait for a response. It was here that Andras found her a couple of hours later.

"What is wrong?" he asked, as he hurried toward her.

She looked at him in surprise. "Wrong?"

"What are you doing?" He sounded both angry and bewildered.

She looked at the cairn. "Waiting for a letter." She knew she should be jumping up and down, shouting the news that her plan had worked at the top of her voice, but suddenly she felt exhausted, as if to tell him would take too much energy and effort.

A flash of concern crossed Andras's face. He surveyed the area warily. "Where is the other one?"

Irene's brow crinkled with confusion. "Other one?"

Andras gestured impatiently. "The farmhand."

She gave him a disapproving look. "You mean *Ian*? I don't know. I haven't seen him all day."

"Then why do you wait here, alone? Why did you not return to…to…"

She laughed as he fumbled for a word. "Home? Base camp? The meeting place? Yeah, I don't know what to call it, either."

He fisted his hands on his hips and glared. She realized he expected an answer.

"Jonah got my letter." There was a note of surprise and bewilderment that she didn't recognize in her voice. She gestured to the cairn. "He sent the rocks." Then she burst into tears.

The onslaught was so sudden, so unexpected, she didn't realize she was crying at first. She sat there, her arms akimbo in the air, gasping for breath as fat globs of moisture streamed from her eyes and nose.

Andras stared at her in horror. Then he came close, making as if to drop to one knee beside her. She furiously waved him away, turning her head to hide the tears. She grabbed the hem of her dress and used it to wipe her face.

"I don't know why I did that," she said, bewildered. "Cry, I mean." She mopped her eyes again, tossed back her hair and took a deep breath. When she felt calm again, she lifted her chin and turned to look at Andras, daring him to do anything other than pretend he hadn't noticed.

Andras, for his part, regarded her warily for a long, silent moment. Finally, he said, "The boy will send the coins?"

She nodded. "He'll send them. We just have to wait."

He looked at her for another long moment, then stepped back, half turning, and gestured back toward "camp." "Come. Let us return."

Irene shook her head, suddenly vehement. "No!" She grabbed the edge of her dress again, feeling new tears threaten. The thought of leaving the cairn, of leaving Jonah, of being alone and cut off again, sent a sudden panic through her, suffocating and overwhelming. She shook her head more vigorously. "No. I want to wait here."

The concern on his face grew deeper, but he gave a short, sharp nod of assent. "As you wish." He looked around, with the clear intent to sit and wait with her.

She stopped him with a shake of her head. "No. I...I'd rather be alone." Unconsciously, she reached out and protectively touched the cairn with her fingertips, as if assuring herself it was still there.

She couldn't explain it, but this felt personal and private. She needed Jonah to herself for a while—needed to be able to express her hopes and her fears, her worries and doubts, even if it was only in imaginary letters to him in her head, letters she'd never send, without Andras's sneering judgment and Ian's "don't worry your pretty little head" platitudes. She needed to be able to be scared, to be uncertain, to be full of doubt without worrying about what anyone else would think of her.

The thunderous scowl she was coming to know so well swept across Andras's face. His jaw tightened and a muscle there twitched. "As you wish." He stalked off without another word. Ian was either good and lost or Andras had told him to stay away because he didn't make an appearance.

Irene checked her bag every few minutes. Time dragged on. She didn't sleep.

Finally, there was a faint jangling sound, so quiet she almost missed it. She ripped open the bag, and there, on top, was a bulging envelope.

Her hand shook as she removed it. He had sealed the flap; she inserted a thumb and ripped it open. The copper and silver mixed and blurred together as the coins poured into her hand, their sweet jangling like music to her ears. Her palm filled and still there were more in the envelope.

She stared at the coins, shifting them back and forth in her hands, enjoying the smooth feel of them, hardly believing she had the means to leave at last.

Letters flew back and forth all night. She would hastily scrawl a reply, stick it under the top rock, then clasp her hands and breathlessly await his reply, which would appear within an hour or two.

Yes, I'm going to school (calculus is annoying).
~J

No, I don't have a girlfriend.
~J

YES, I AM PHYSICALLY, ACTUALLY GOING TO SCHOOL. STOP ASKING!
~J

In response to her inquiry regarding her mother, he assured her that her mother was still continuing on much the same as she always had — vague and a little off, but more or less healthy. Mr. Mackenzie still mowed the lawn. Aunt Betty or one of her children visited often.

If Jonah thought she was persistent in checking that he was going to school, he was worse. He kept pestering her with questions about Samyel until she had no choice but to send basically the same letter she had composed in her head all that time ago in the dead forest, explaining that Samyel had up and flown away. She left out the part about the other angels and the death of the horse.

Then Jonah asked her the question she'd been dreading:

So, what's it like there?
~J

She had to be careful with what she said. She wanted to tell Jonah about everything that she'd seen and experienced — especially the parts she didn't understand — but she couldn't figure out how to do so and still make it sound unappealing, but not so unappealing he thought she needed rescuing. The end result was that she mostly avoided answering his question, and then felt guilty that she was keeping the truth from him. In the past, he'd accused her of treating him like a child, of thinking he couldn't handle the truth. She supposed he wasn't wrong to be upset — protecting him for his own good *was* condescending. She wanted to punch Andras and Ian when they did it to her. However, she figured it was the lesser of two evils — condescendingly protect him for his own good at the risk of angering him or risk having him try to cross over and die in the process.

"City of the dead" seems to be a mistranslation — it's more of a dead city, just abandoned buildings. Not very exciting. There's a "forest," too. What do your books say about a creepy forest full of dead trees?

~I

This resulted in a long letter full of dissertation-worthy anecdotes about the afterlife, as if he was helping her cram for an exam. She laughed and skimmed this letter, the ending of which left her puzzled:

It's really important that the dead don't forget their names. It's so important that Jewish people memorize a passage from the Torah that begins with the same letter as their name, and there's several cultures where people write or sew the dead person's name into the hem of his/her clothes. You should write your name down and keep it with you at all times.

Forget her name? Not likely. She was Irene Dunphy, for God's sake. Not only was she not about to forget that, she wasn't going to let anyone else forget it either.

The next morning, she had managed to regain some of her equilibrium by the time Andras came striding into view, though the nagging thought that everything was about to change simmered at the back of her mind.

Andras must have read something in her face, because he came to an abrupt stop. "You have them?" There was a note in his voice she had never heard before — a harsh, eager quality that made her tense and wary. "You have the coins?"

She was just writing a response to Jonah. She finished her thought, signed the letter, and then stuck the scrap of paper in the cairn, trying to delay the moment a little longer. Then she drew the plain white envelope from her bag. She held out a hand and slowly poured out the coins with the other, careful not to drop any as they slithered and clinked into her palm.

She smiled, pride flooding her. She had done it. She had said she would find a way out of here and she had. She scooped up a third of the coins with her free hand and held them out to Andras. "Here," she said. "Buy yourself something pretty."

He stared at them with a hungry, covetous look that was painful to see. He raised his eyes to her, and they were full of conflict. He looked agonized, as if he was being offered something terrible but irresistible. For a moment, Irene felt a flicker of panic, like she had done something awful. In a way, she supposed she had—she had done to Andras what Jonah had done to her: she had taken his ignorance. Andras had been perfectly content to wait by the river for all eternity, content in his faith that God would provide for him, and then she had come along and given him an alternative. Now he had to make a choice: stick with the old way of being or follow the new, despite not knowing where it would lead. It was like asking someone to step blindly off a cliff. She should know—she was in the same boat.

Irene had a sudden, almost overwhelming urge to pull back her hand, to hide the coins, to tell Andras to go back to the river, to waiting, to God, to forget trying to change and be something new and different—and certainly not because of her, never because of her. What right did she have to change people? None. More than that, she didn't want that right, that responsibility; she was the last person in the world who should have it. Only an idiot would entrust it to her. She couldn't even live her own life without help; she certainly had no right to tell others how to live theirs.

Slowly, Andras held out his hand, his eyes locked on hers. Irene hesitated, torn between handing them over and refusing, suddenly feeling the decision was of monumental importance.

"Are you sure?" she whispered, almost hoping he'd change his mind.

Andras nodded. "I am sure."

The sound of the coins falling into his hand was harsh in the pin-dropping silence of the city. He stared at the coins for a moment, and then slowly, almost fearfully, he closed his hand over them.

He met her eyes once more. "Come," he said. "Let us go."

"Go? What…now?"

"We have the coins. Why needs must we wait?"

She looked at the cairn. "I…no, not yet. I need more time."

"For what purpose?"

For some reason, her heart had sped up and her palms began to sweat. "I'm just...I'm not ready. I need to prepare...to get some other stuff."

He tilted his head. "Such as?"

"Well...food and such."

Andras scowled.

"Yeah, yeah, I know. I don't have to eat. However, I still prefer to. Look, it won't take long. You can go if you want. You don't have to wait for me. You said we're safe here, so I don't need you to protect me. And I have Ian."

His scowl deepened to outrage. She held up a placating hand.

"Yeah, yeah, okay. Fine. Whatever. Then you'll have to wait until I'm ready. Why don't you go find Ian, tell him I got the coins."

"At least bring the altar back to camp. It is not good for you to spend so much time alone."

She raised an eyebrow. "I'm not alone. I've got Jonah. Besides," she quickly added as Andras opened his mouth to argue, "I don't know that I can." She thought of the cairns they'd encountered—if an altar could simply be picked up and moved, or even taken along with you, then why had those altars been left behind? Surely no one who knew their worth, who knew how they worked, would have left them if it was possible to take them. "I think, once it's built, taking it apart destroys the connection."

Andras opened his mouth a second time, but Irene turned away, ending the conversation. "I said no."

Twenty-Two

Over the next week, goods as well as letters appeared—more candles, a steak knife, granola bars. When she'd been on Earth, Jonah had tried desperately to get her to buy a sword at the ghost market, and she had resisted. Now she asked him to send one, thinking she could give it to Andras as a peace offering. Jonah's reply was succinct:

Where am I going to get a sword?

True—she hadn't thought of that. There had been swords aplenty in the ghost markets of the city, but for a fourteen-year-old in the suburbs, there probably weren't a lot of places he could get a sword without including his parents in the endeavor—which would be incredibly awkward.

She had been just about to ask him to send her some other clothes when she realized his ability to procure women's clothes in her size was also pretty limited. His sister and mother weren't a match, and she couldn't really see him walking into a woman's clothing store to ask for a shirt and pants in her size. She compromised and asked for more socks and another blanket.

Andras came by twice, urging her to leave and then growing angry when she insisted she still wasn't ready. Part of her knew that Andras was right—she had the coins, it was time to go—but still she couldn't bring herself to leave. She was so close to the land of the living right now; if she left, if she paid the fare and boarded the boat, she would be going farther away from her old life, farther from where she wanted to be. Here actually wasn't so bad – no angels, no insane ghosts, and an endless supply of her favorite foods and items from Earth. Those first few weeks immediately after she'd crossed over had been the worst of her life – when she'd realized that she'd only ever have the stuff in her bag, it had been a dose of incredibly painful cold water. The thought of *never* eating another hamburger, of *never* hearing another cheesy pop song, of *never* being able to curl up in a pair of fuzzy slippers and flannel pajamas – *forever* – had terrified her in a way nothing else had.

Maybe "the other side" would have "stuff," like Ian hoped; maybe it would be even better than the stuff on Earth. She didn't know. What she did know was that it was a gamble – the security of what she had here for the uncertainty of the other side – and she wasn't a gambler.

Speaking of Ian…she was just dashing off a reply to Jonah when he strode into view. "There's my girl," he said, snaking an arm around her waist and bringing her in for a kiss. She shrugged away from him, annoyed. Ian tensed.

"What's wrong?"

"Nothing," she said, trying to give him a reassuring smile. "I just don't want to lose my train of thought." After the first day, when he hadn't come by at all, Ian seemed to always be underfoot, popping up at the most inopportune moments – times when she was either composing a letter to Jonah or had just received one – and hanging around asking questions about the future, Jonah, and the items he sent and pestering her to "get a move on" so they could leave. He also grew bolder, more physical, as the days went by, which also exasperated her – couldn't he see she was busy? He always seemed to pick the most inconvenient moment – like when she'd just gotten a new letter – to try something.

Ian frowned, but she turned her back to him so she wouldn't have to see it. However, the damage was done – her concentration was broken. She felt edgy now, annoyed and impatient, as if his presence was stifling, and she wanted him to leave so she could finish her note. She sighed, aggravated by Ian's intrusion, and tucked the note to Jonah under the top most rock of the cairn, unfinished.

"So," she said turning back to him, forcing a bright smile to her lips. "What can I do for you?"

Ian's grin returned. "I was just checkin' on you," he said, stroking her hair and running his thumb down the side of her face. "Seein' if you was ready to go yet."

She wanted to push him away, her skin shuddering at his touch. Ian didn't seem to notice because his grin widened and he stepped closer with the clear intention to kiss her. She felt guilty in some way, as if she was doing something wrong, and the wild, crazy thought, "Not here. Not in front of Jonah," went skittering through her brain. A flash of panic went through her, and she turned away, squatting down beside the cairn quickly to snag a bag of fast food Jonah had sent her.

"Here," she said, thrusting the bag at Ian while avoiding his eyes. "I thought you might like this." Ian's brow furrowed with confusion, but he accepted the bag. "They're called french fries."

However, the distraction didn't work. Ian, never taking his eyes off her, set the bag aside and then caught hold of her again. Irene tried to move away, but Ian didn't let go. Instead, he pulled her to him, crushing her against his chest, and brought his mouth to hers.

"No," she said, turning her head. He hesitated, looking hurt. Then he leaned in a second time, twisting her in his arms to turn her face to his as he bent to find her lips. She leaned away, and turned her head even farther, pushing against his arms.

"No," she said more firmly, growing annoyed. Then she quickly softened her tone to try to ease the bite of her words. "Not here." She looked at the cairn and felt a protective rush of emotion. She looked back at Ian. "Please...don't ruin it."

She could tell he was angry; he'd gone rigid and was shaking slightly, and for a moment she thought he wasn't going to let her go. She'd fought off unwanted advances before, but the thought of doing so with Ian made her stomach twist. Ian was so laid back, so sweet, she couldn't seriously believe he'd try to go too far, would actually try to force himself on her. However, there was a look in his eyes she'd never seen before, and for a moment, she began to think he might. She tasted bile in the back of her throat, and her breath caught.

"Ian…" she said, a note of warning in her voice. She hit his arms with her fists, trying to knock them aside. Instead, they tightened around her. Her eyes widened, her heart jackhammering in her chest. She swallowed hard, not believing this was going to happen. "Please, Ian…" Her voice was soft, barely more than a whisper, and she was truly begging. "Don't…"

A muscle jumped in his jaw. Time seemed to stop. Then, stiffly, Ian eased himself back and released her. "All right," he said, and there was no kindness in his voice. Irene felt sick. She exhaled in a rush and realized she was shaking. Before she could say anything, Ian put his back to her and walked away. She wrapped her arms around herself, hugging tight to ward off the sudden chill. Irene could feel tears, hovering just on the edge of being shed, but they seemed to be frozen inside her. In fact, all of her seemed to be frozen. She was numb.

Ian disappeared, and she didn't see him for the rest of the day or night. In the morning, he returned, his usual chipper self as if nothing had happened. Unfortunately, Andras came with him, which meant not only did she and Ian have no privacy to discuss what had happened, she also had to deal with two impatient men rather than just one.

"How much longer?" Andras asked.

"Good morning to you, too," she said.

Andras glared at her, and she looked away.

Ian dropped into a sitting position beside her. "Well, can't you just take those rocks with you? Then we could get a move on."

Irene shrugged. "I don't know, and I'm not ready to risk it until I'm sure I have everything I need for the journey."

There was a portentous silence, thick and full of meaning. She glanced up to see a look pass between Ian and

Andras. A thunderous scowl descended on Andras's face. Ian held up a hand. "We waited this long, we can wait one more day."

Irene beamed at him, feeling a sudden rush of affection, and passed him a piece of chocolate, newly arrived from Jonah. She shot Andras a smug look. Andras looked murderous.

"How about we go for a walk," Ian said to Irene. She started to protest. "I know, I know," Ian said, holding up his hands, "but a little walk ain't gonna kill you, and any letters will be here waiting for you when you get back. It would do me—and you—good to stretch our legs, and I want to hear some more about the future. I want you to explain how they built all these tall buildings and such. What do you say?"

He was wearing the hopeful puppy-dog face that she couldn't say no to, and she was eager to make up for the previous evening, so she reluctantly nodded her agreement. Ian beamed.

She stood up, dusted herself off, and held out a hand to help Ian up. He grinned at her. "Hey, there's my girl!"

Andras made a sound, like a deep-throated growl, of disgust. Ian laughed, put an arm around her waist, and gave Andras a smug look. Then the two of them set off, choosing a direction at random.

Ian peppered her with questions as they walked until she had no choice but to give up thinking about Jonah and home and focus on him. She laughed. "Okay, okay. I'm all yours. What do you want to know?"

He smiled at her. "Awww, see, there's the girl I love!" He snagged her around the waist and pulled her in close. She laughed but didn't move away. They were far enough away from the cairn now that she didn't mind. For the first time since she'd built the cairn, it felt as if they were alone. The secret, furtive feelings of guilt and annoyance had dissipated. Plus, after the previous evening, she felt that she owed him at least a kiss

Ian lowered his mouth to hers, and she felt a tingle from the top of her head to the tips of her toes. This time Ian didn't stop with a quick, sweet peck. This kiss was deep and achingly thorough. She was surprised. She'd had no idea that nineteenth century men knew how to kiss that well. Her arms snaked around his neck, and she kissed him back, pouring all her fear and longing into it.

He lifted his head and beamed at her. "There now. See? That's all I wanted, just a little kiss."

Irene felt a little unsteady on her feet and her stomach fluttered with anticipation. Her lips twisted in wry amusement. "That's not all you want."

Heat radiated from his body and his arms tightened around her. He was still smiling, but now his eyes darkened with desire. "No," he said slowly, "it's not."

She lifted her mouth to his and that was all the encouragement he needed. In another moment, she felt something cold and hard against her back and realized he had backed her against the nearest building. He lifted her slightly, setting her up and back onto a granite windowsill, deep and low like a small ledge.

She expected him to be in a rush, to cut directly to the chase, or, at the very least, to lack finesse—did nineteenth century men even know anything about foreplay or g-spots?

She was wrong on both accounts.

He teased her with his mouth and hands, stoking the fire within, maddeningly thorough and taking far too long to find the fastener on his trousers. Soon she was mindless with need, the tension building unbearably inside her. She tried to wrap her legs around him, to pull him to her, but he wasn't having any of that. He pinned her legs and pushed her back until she had to use her arms to brace herself, preventing her from using them urge him on.

She groaned, the ache inside her nearly intolerable. "Ian...hurry up. Please..."

"Oh no, ma'am," he said, his voice low and deep, his mouth close to her ear. "I'm gonna take my sweet time."

His words sent a thrill of electricity sizzling through her, and she couldn't stop a whimper of anticipation from escaping.

Ian was as good as his word. He made love to her with long, slow, deep strokes that brought her to the brink and held her there, making her beg for release.

"Ian...please..."

"Not yet," he whispered.

When he finally pushed her over the edge, wave after unending wave washed over her, turning her inside out until she thought she'd pass out. They collapsed against each other, panting and soaked with sweat, as they came back down to earth.

Gradually, her heart slowed, leaving her drowsy and half dozing as she enjoyed the feeling of security and safety in his arms. His fingers stroked down her spine from between her shoulder blades to the small of her back with whisper-soft movements, leaving little eddies of electric warmth within her. For once, her mind was blissfully empty—no thoughts, no worries, no regrets. In fact, she felt relief—relief that it had all turned out alright. She had Ian, and they had coins. Everything was going to be okay. No, it was going to be great. They'd find a way back to Earth, together, and then maybe, just maybe... She suppressed a giggle as she pictured Ian in the twentieth century, navigating escalators and cube farms.

Finally, it was time to come back to reality. Ian planted a gentle kiss on the top of her head and helped her down. She slid from the window sill, her back stiff, shoulders cramped, and deliciously sore all over. He watched her dress, and she found herself blushing, which both exasperated and exhilarated her. She couldn't remember the last time a man looking at her naked had caused her to blush.

Jonah had asked her once if she thought people could fall in love after they died. She hadn't had an answer for him. Partly because she had no concept of love—she'd never been in love and had no idea how you could tell if you were. The longer she was dead, the less likely it had seemed that ghosts could love—as far as she had been able to tell, ghosts only took into the afterlife whatever they had with them in terms of thoughts and feelings and experiences at the time they died.

However she'd never had this in life—never had someone who tried so hard to make her smile, to make her laugh, who actually enjoyed her company and her companionship, who found her interesting and funny and sexy—so now she didn't know.

She supposed it didn't matter—they were together and they had all the time in the world to figure things out. All of the things that usually drove couples apart—money, arguments over the housekeeping, whether or not to have children—didn't apply here. Time was an infinite resource—they didn't have to make "or" choices. If Ian wanted to go and visit Romanian goat herders in nine hundred B.C. then they might as well as not—it wasn't like there was anything better to do.

She felt a sudden rush of guilt over her recent cold-shoulder behavior, unsure what had gotten into her. Maybe it had been cold-feet or fear of success. She kicked herself. She had almost ruined this, almost driven him away, and she didn't even know why.

Ian put a finger under her chin and raised her face to his. "Don't be embarrassed. What we just done was natural and beautiful. Ain't no shame in it."

Irene laughed. "Ian, that was hardly my first time..." Then she blushed again, realizing how that probably sounded to a man from a time in which a woman was expected to be a virgin on her wedding night. It was probably pretty shocking. "Uh...I mean...things have changed a little since your time."

Ian grinned at her. "Well, shoot, I been around here long enough to know that." Then he shot her a quizzical look. "Is that what you were worried about?"

She felt the tension flow out of her and realized she had been worried, in some small part, about the compatibility of their views and experiences in this area.

"So, when you come from, is it like with them Greeks?" he asked, and she thought she detected a note of hopefulness in his voice.

She laughed and playfully smacked him on the arm. "Uh, no...no bacchanals and orgies..." She hesitated. Well, that wasn't exactly true — just, not quite to the level of the Greeks. She struggled for a moment, trying to find a tactful way to explain the sexual revolution that wouldn't give Ian the idea she was used to just walking around naked, having sex twenty-four seven with anyone who came along. "It's more that everyone — men and women — gets to choose when and with whom they have sex, and we don't have to wait until we're married anymore."

His grin widened. "Now *that* sounds like Heaven."

She laughed. He took her hand, laced his fingers through hers, and then raised her hand to his lips. He planted a soft, sweet kiss on her knuckles.

"I suppose we have to get back," she said ruefully. They were lucky Andras hadn't come wandering along looking for them. God, how mortifying if he'd caught them. She could only imagine the scowls and sermons that would have netted them.

Ian grinned at her, as if reading her thoughts. He handed her the jacket, which she elected to carry, enjoying the thought of teasing Ian with a show of bare skin the entire way back. Then they set off, hand in hand. They took their time, ambling along, dreamy and lost in thought, basking in the afterglow, with Ian dropping occasional sweet, soft kisses onto her shoulder or neck.

All too soon, however, they were back at the site of the altar. As soon as they came within sight of the area, Irene knew something was wrong. Andras was sitting there, waiting for them, a grim and determined look on his face. The cairn was gone.

Irene dropped Ian's hand and raced forward. "What happened?" she cried, disbelief washing over her. This couldn't be happening. The cairn couldn't be gone. It just couldn't.

Without waiting for an answer she began a frantic search, tossing items without fully thinking, moving the blanket to check that the cairn hadn't somehow magically moved underneath it.

"Irene…" Ian said gently, reaching for her arm, but she shrugged him away.

Andras hadn't moved. "It is time we left."

"What?" She wasn't even fully registering what either of them was saying as she turned in a circle, frantically searching the area. "This can't be happening!"

"Irene," said Ian gently but firmly, taking hold of her arm to stop her. She paused and looked at him, confused, and then froze, suddenly understanding what they had done.

She yanked her arm from his grasp. "What did you do?" she cried, looking back and forth between the two men. "Where are they? Where are the rocks? What did you do with them?" She was shaking now, with both terror and anger, the blood pounding in her ears so hard she almost couldn't hear their responses.

Andras stood and she launched herself at him, blinded by a red haze of rage. "This was your idea, wasn't it?" she cried, striking out with both fists. He easily caught her wrists, deflecting her blows, but in the same instant, she brought up her knee, nailing him solidly in the groin. He grunted and released her, his face registering more anger than pain.

Ian grabbed her from behind, pinning her arms to her sides. She writhed and bucked, trying to break free, trying to smash his face with her head, trying to kick any part of him she could reach, intent on one thing—breaking free so she could murder Andras. She screamed incoherently at Andras, obscenities mixed with mindless cries of fury. She lashed out, alternately trying to kick Andras and then Ian.

"Irene!" Ian shouted. "Stop! Just stop!"

She flailed so fiercely he couldn't hold onto her. He dropped her and stepped away, and she spun to face him, panting with rage. "And you! What the hell was that?" She gestured wildly in the direction they had just come from. "Just a fuck to distract me so he could dismantle the altar?"

"It weren't like that—"

"To hell it wasn't!"

"Look, just settle down for a moment—"

"Settle down? *Settle down?* Did you just tell me to *settle down*?"

He put up placating hands and took a step back. She wheeled and turned on Andras again. "Where are they, you son of a bitch? Where are the rocks?"

He met her eyes for a moment and then had the grace to look away. He gestured to a nearby building.

She spun on heel and raced away, stumbling in her haste, nearly tripping over her own feet. She shoved open the door so hard it banged into the wall. The rocks were tumbled in a haphazard heap in one corner of what appeared to be a living room. Four of the small, brown creatures were huddled in one corner, as if in conference, and a fifth sat on the pile of rocks, as if guarding it.

Irene didn't pause as she marched across the room. "So help me God, I'll smash your little head in if you don't get away from those rocks!"

The critter didn't even hesitate—it scampered off the rocks with a shriek of terror and raced for the far side of the room and the sheltering protection of its brethren.

Irene dropped to her knees by the rocks and put her hand on the pile, reassuring herself it was real. She took deep, panting breaths as she tried to calm down, to slow the pounding of her heart, the thundering in her ears.

The hot rage was slowly replaced by a freezing, numbing anger, deeper and fiercer than anything she had ever felt. She honestly thought she might kill someone, given the chance.

She rose to her feet and marched back outside, grim determination driving her forward. She stopped before the two men, who now had the grace to look sheepish.

"Get out of my sight. Both of you," she said, her voice so cold, so hard, even she didn't recognize it. "I can't stand the sight of either of you, and if I ever see you again, I swear to God I'll smash your fucking heads in."

"Irene—" Ian said, but Andras put a hand on his arm and stopped him. Without a word, Andras turned away, guiding Ian away as well. Irene stood there, unmoving, as she watched their retreating backs.

When they were out of sight, a bleak and desolate numbness settled over her. She felt empty and bereft. In a fog, she picked up her jacket and headed back to the building to retrieve the rocks. She carried them back outside, into the light, and then dropped to the ground and began rebuilding the cairn, rock by rock. She set each stone in place with reverence, stroking it tenderly and saying a silent prayer over it — *Pleaseohpleaseohpleaseohpleasework…*

She found a piece of paper and a pen among her scattered belongings and scribbled Jonah a hasty note, her hand shaking so badly the words were barely legible.

> *This is just a test. I want to see if the altar still works. Long story — it got taken apart. Please let me know if you get this ASAP.*

She picked up the top rock, placed the note underneath it, and then replaced the stone but didn't let go. Somehow, she couldn't bring herself to release it as if she could will the altar to work through her connection to it. After a time, her hand began to cramp, but still, she couldn't let go. She had no idea how long she kneeled there, clutching the rock, silently begging the universe for this one thing, this one favor, this one miracle. Her legs grew stiff and her fingers became numb, and still she held on, waiting for a reply, afraid of what would happen if she didn't get one.

Twenty-Three

The long minutes ticked by, measured in heartbeats.

I got your note. Is everything okay?

She stared at the simple message, blinking back tears. The relief was too huge, her recent anger too draining, and she felt numb, unable to process the immensity of the emotions his letter evoked. In a daze, she scribbled back a reply, and immediately, the flow of messages resumed.

However, something had changed. She didn't feel the same joy, the same expectation, the same elation as she had before the fight with Andras and Ian. She paced between messages and didn't always respond right away. She had a nagging feeling of guilt and self-doubt. She had proven that the cairn could be moved, that it could be taken apart and reassembled, so why was she still here?

She tried to force herself to leave, even went so far as to ask Jonah to send her a backpack so she could carry the rocks. As she wrote the note, she imagined his smug expression at receiving her request. He had tried to give her his backpack early on in their adventures, and she had refused, telling him it didn't go with her dress.

Two days later he sent her a heavy canvas backpack. The reply that accompanied it was short and to the point:

However, still she remained at the site, unable to bring herself to dismantle the cairn...or to check and see if Andras and Ian were still waiting for her. She should just leave without them, just slip off and leave them behind. She didn't owe them anything, not any more, not after the way they had acted. Ian especially. Whenever she thought about how he had tricked her, had used her, had screwed her—both literally and figuratively—just to get what he wanted, she vacillated between heartbreak and an almost overwhelming urge to beat him to death with the tire iron. Even greater than her anger at him was her anger at herself. How had she not seen it coming? She'd been around long enough, had enough one-night stands, dated enough jerks, that she should have been able to see it coming a mile away. Even worse, what an idiot she was, thinking that he'd liked her, that he'd actually felt something for her, that they had a future together. God, what was she, fifteen? She was such a moron.

"Hello, Acorn."

She tensed for a second, startled, and then turned, correcting him automatically, like a reflex. "Don't call me that."

Somehow, she wasn't surprised to see him. In a way, she was relieved. She could use some advice; at the same time, though, she had an uncomfortable feeling, like a child caught doing something wrong.

"Well, I see you've come full circle," he said, gesturing to the city around them.

A momentary surge of pride triumphed over all her other feelings. "You have to go back to go forward."

"And forward to go back," he agreed.

She smiled, feeling like she'd just gotten an "A" on an algebra test. She'd been right! "Because all things are one—the seed, the peel, et cetera, et cetera. Backward, forward, they're irrelevant concepts now. Just like time. There's no day or night here, just...existence."

He smiled approvingly. "Clever girl."

"Yes, I am," she said, unable to keep the smugness out of her voice. "Sometimes it takes me a while, but eventually,

I always manage to catch on." She also couldn't keep a note of bitterness out of her voice. If only she'd caught on to Ian sooner.

He didn't appear to be listening. His eyes roved over the landscape, taking in the buildings, the street, the sidewalk. He seemed to be looking for something or trying to make up his mind about something. "Interesting place you've got here," he said conversationally.

"Andras says..." her voice cracked and heaviness returned as the mention of his name brought back the raw, burnt-edged memory of his betrayal, "that none of this is real — that it's some sort of mass hallucination or something."

"How very Buddhist of him."

She didn't know what he meant by that. She shot him a quizzical look and waited. When he didn't say anything further, she prodded him impatiently. "Is any of it real?"

"Real enough," he said absently, still studying the scenery.

"What is it with mystics and ghosts? You can never just give a straight answer." She stooped to tuck the letter she'd been writing when he appeared under the cairn's top-most stone and then straightened up. "So, to what do I owe the pleasure of this visit?"

"You were a little rough on the fellas, weren't you?"

She stiffened, first in surprise and then with anger. "Me? What about them?" Her voice rose. "Do you have any idea what they did?" She stopped. Of course he did.

She felt the blood rush to her face — how dare he put this all on her! How dare he act like she'd been to blame...they were the ones who had lied and tricked and betrayed. She opened her mouth and he raised an eyebrow a fraction of an inch. That was all it took. Her ire deflated as quickly as it had gathered, and the flush of anger changed to one of embarrassment. She looked away.

"Whenever you ask a question, the universe is happy to give an answer. Just be sure you're really ready to receive it."

Had she asked a question? She supposed she had in a way — the unsettled feeling that had descended over her, the reason she had lingered here, despite having no reason to. She'd wanted to know "why" — why Andras and Ian had done what they had; why she was unable to move on, to leave without them.

Now, here it was: they had been wrong — but so had she. She'd been afraid to leave, and in clinging to this place, she had selfishly held them all back. She'd defended her decision by telling herself that if they had really wanted to leave, they could have left without her, that in choosing to stay they were choosing to wait for her to be ready — however long that might take. However, they really couldn't have left. In a choice between tricking her for what they perceived as her own good and dishonorably abandoning her, they had chosen what they saw as the lesser of two evils.

Hadn't she rationalized the same kind of thing in her decision to not tell Jonah the truth about Samyel or the details of the world in which she now found herself? So how could she hold Ian and Andras to a different standard than she'd set for herself? How much of a hypocrite was she?

"Why does it all have to be on me?" she asked, trying to hide the sulky note in her voice. "Why do I have to be the one to fix this?"

He was looking up, as if admiring the clouds — that is, if there had been any clouds. Absently, he said, "I was just making an observation."

She frowned. "Uh huh. Because there's no judgment, right?"

"Exactly."

Of course there was judgment, and she was clearly getting some of it right now — in abundance. She could feel it radiating from him. "Why do I have to be the one to forgive them? Huh? They started it."

He gave her the kind of look a parent might give a particularly exasperating child. "What are you, two?"

"Now you sound like Jonah!"

"Maybe he has a point."

"Okay, well, you know what? I didn't ask your opinion." She crossed her arms, a flood of the old determination washing away all other feelings. "However, since you're here, you can answer a few questions for me. I think I'm starting to understand what all this is about, about the transformation that you were talking about. But I still don't really understand how I'm going to get back to Earth, as myself, when I'm being asked to move farther and farther from my life on Earth, to forget about everything that has to do with that life."

"That's because you're not actually ready to move on yet."

She fisted her hands on her hips. "I am ready to move on! I've been ready to move on since the moment I sent foot in this place. Believe me. Andras. Ian. All those people at the river. We're all ready to move on. Have been for quite some time."

His eyes caught and held hers. "Are you? Are you really, Acorn? Have you truly embraced all that moving on entails? Are you truly willing to go through all the transformations, to give up all that you are? All that you were? All that you might yet be?" His eyes bored into her, as if he could see inside her—her thoughts, her hopes, her fears. "What's holding you here, Irene? What is it that you're holding on to? And are you truly willing to let it go?"

Of course she was holding on to something—she was holding on to everything. She was clinging to every facet of her sense of self, her "Irene-ness"—her body, her memories, her emotions, her thoughts. More than that, she was holding on to hope—hope that she'd somehow end up back on Earth as herself with her life, her identity, and her body intact. Isn't that what he'd told her to do?

However, at the same time, she knew that those were the same things trapping her here. To move on, she would have to surrender *everything*, including hope. She'd already come to understand the transformations to come would be a stripping away, layer by layer, of everything that made her her.

Without hope, though—and without memories, without a concept of herself as a physical entity, without even a name—what, exactly, would she be? What was left?

"You said the acorn retains the core acorny-ness. Was that a lie? What's 'acorny' about me? What, exactly, do I get to retain?"

He gave her a gentle smile. "You're a clever girl. I'm sure you'll figure it out."

She felt as if she'd been punched. He was making fun of her. She hadn't expected that. Not from him. Was this whole thing a game to him? Well, it wasn't a game, it was her life, her future. If she made the wrong choice she'd be stuck here forever, or worse, she'd lose herself, dissipating into nothingness.

An anger so huge she wasn't sure it could be contained filled her, filled her until she thought she would burst. She jerked away from him without a word, grabbed the backpack from the ground, squatted down beside the cairn, and began shoving rocks into the bag.

"What are you doing?" he asked.

"Leaving," she snarled.

"Where are you going to go?"

She thought she detected a trace of smugness in his voice.

She zipped the backpack, stood up, and slung it over one shoulder while grabbing the beach bag with her free hand. "Your universe sucks. I'm gonna go get my own." She brushed past him and stalked off without looking back.

A trickle of laughter followed her down the street.

She found Andras and Ian sitting in front of "her" house at their camp. They rose to their feet when they saw her. She was too angry at the Guide to be angry or uncomfortable with them.

"Fine," she said, glaring at them both. "Let's go."

Ian looked sheepish and shuffled his feet. "Irene..."

Andras was as stoic and impassive as usual.

She shook her head and held up a hand to stop Ian. "Just to be clear, you guys still suck, and I don't know that I'm ready to forgive you just yet, but I get why you did what you did. So let's just leave it at that for now, okay?"

Ian relaxed, looking relieved. He gave her a shy half-grin and nodded. Andras's brow creased, as if he was confused or preparing to argue with her.

"Let's just go," she said, hefting the backpack higher in an attempt to settle it more securely. Ian reached out and stopped her, taking the heavy bag from her in a wordless offer to carry it. She let him slide the straps from her shoulder, relieved to have the back-breaking weight gone. She turned and set off toward the hotel.

"Where are you going?" Andras asked.

She shot him a smug look over her shoulder. "It's this way." Andras's look of confusion increased, but he didn't argue.

They walked in uncomfortable silence. Irene was afraid that either or both men would try to talk, to explain, or worse, demand an explanation, and she had no answers and no forgiveness.

They were soon at the hotel. Irene grabbed the door, feeling the cool smoothness of the brass in her hand. Her heart lurched unevenly. This was it; this was really it. She was about to put her old life, her life as Irene Dunphy – on Earth – completely behind her. Opening this door meant embracing change and the need to move on; it meant taking a leap of faith that leaving everything behind would result in her getting it all back again.

"What are you doing?" Andras asked.

"Going to the boat, of course."

His brow furrowed. "Do we not return to the river?"

Irene shot him another smug smile and shook her head. "No. That's the beauty of this plan – the boat's right here."

"Inside a building?" Ian asked with a frown of his own.

"Trust me. This is where I crossed over and there's a boat in the lobby. It's hard to explain. You'll just have to see it."

She reached for the door again, but Andras's frown deepened.

She sighed in exasperation. "Is there a problem?"

"What of all the others?"

"Others? What others?"

"Those that wait at the river. How can we go with a free heart, knowing of their suffering?"

"Whoa! Whoa!" Ian said, raising a hand. "Nobody ever said nothin' about helping all of them out. I thought this was every man for himself."

Irene released the door and gaped at Andras, momentarily speechless. "You can't be serious!"

She could tell by his face that he was.

"What happened to having faith? Isn't God supposed to take care of them?"

Andras's voice gentled. "He has. He sent you."

"Ha. Ha." Then she looked at him, really looked at him, and realized he wasn't joking. Her eyes widened in alarm and she took a step back. "Whoa! Whoa, whoa, whoa…are you nuts? I mean, like, certifiably fucking insane? Where the hell did you get that idea?"

Ian hooted with laughter. "Irene here ain't no heavenly messenger! She's about as ungodly as they come."

"Hey!" she cried, shooting Ian a dirty look. "Watch it."

She shot him another dark look and then turned back to Andras. "He's right. I'm not part of any great cosmic plan — trust me. The only person I'm capable of saving is myself — and it's a toss-up as to whether I can even manage that." She wasn't all that smart, and she certainly wasn't special. If she could get coins, then anyone could. Maybe that was the real test, a test of each individual's worthiness, and people who couldn't figure it out for themselves didn't deserve to cross over.

She reached for the door again. Andras was staring at her, as if reading her thoughts, his gaze sure and steady, full of absolute conviction. She shook her head again, more vigorously, but his look didn't change.

She had a sudden flashback to her recent conversation with the Guide — she'd asked why she had to be the one to fix this. The Guide hadn't answered her question; he hadn't had to — the answer was self-evident: someone had to fix it; why not her?

A thread of anger twined with the rising panic; the Guide had known. Or he'd guessed. Or he'd set her up. Either way, he'd known that she would reach this point, that she'd be faced with this decision.

She shook her head, silently arguing with...herself? The Guide? The universe? Maybe all three; she wasn't really sure. *I do not have to be the one to fix this. Someone else can do it.*

Terror swept over her, and she backed away. "Oh no. Oh no, no, no... It's not my job to save the universe. If you want to do it, fine, you go right ahead, but leave me out of it." The words, however, didn't seem to be penetrating either one of them. Instead, a slinking feeling of inevitability was creeping over her. She kept shaking her head, trying to shove the feeling away, to dismiss the crowd of faces waiting at the river, who had, in her mind's eye, all turned to stare at her with hopeful, pleading looks.

"Perhaps in their salvation lies our own," Andras said softly.

Speaking of salvation was a low blow. Her death had been stupid and senseless, and she would have to answer for that if the stories about there being a final judgment were true. In a silent, unspoken, not even fully realized way, she had promised herself she would make amends, that she'd find a way to erase her mistakes before she reached that point. If ever there was such a way, this was it.

"Listen, I feel for them, I do," Ian said, "but it's a dog-eat-dog world. Every man for himself. Now, we got coins, they don't. I'm sorry, but that's the way it is." He put a hand on the door and frowned at Irene. "Come on."

"What you're asking is impossible," she said to Andras. "We could never get enough coins for everybody—Jonah would have to rob a bank and then it still wouldn't be enough."

"Besides," Ian added, "those angel things are still out there. We might not even make it back to the river. No sir, I say we get while the getting is good."

Andras didn't respond; he just kept looking at Irene, and, damn him, he had that same look Jonah had worn when he'd handed her that bottle of gin, begging her with his eyes not to take it, to be good, to be noble, to be strong.

She was still shaking her head. "How would we even get everyone—there are always new people arriving. I'd have to stay there forever, doling out coins to the newcomers."

"You could leave the rocks there. Build a shrine so the dead can ask for coins."

"Is that why you...?" She looked back and forth between the two men. "It doesn't even work like that!" she cried, the mounting terror turning into a crushing black wave that threatened to sweep over her. "Stuff left at my grave comes to me..." She trailed off as a realization struck. If Jonah took the rocks from her grave and built a separate shrine with them, then the coins would, in all probability, go to the cairn instead of her—a direct phone call, shrine to shrine, the essence of the rocks here connected to the physical rocks there.

She clutched the bag to her chest. "No! Absolutely not! You have no idea what these rocks mean...what they represent..." There were tears now, caught in her throat, cutting off her air. She could barely choke out words around the mounting panic and hysteria. "These rocks are my link— my *lifeline*—to Jonah, to the land of the living, to everything, to everything that means anything. After everything we went through to get them...the horse and the angel and then...how could you even think of asking me to give them up? How could you?" She looked wildly back and forth between the two men, looking for an answer.

Ian put a protective hand on her arm. "You don't have to do anything you don't want to," he said soothingly. "I'm sorry about before. You were right...it weren't our place to interfere. You don't got to listen to him. Come on, you and me. We'll go get on that boat. If he wants to stay, then let him."

Andras, his eyes still locked on Irene, held out his hand. His gaze didn't waiver. "Then please, give me as many coins as you can spare, and I will return to the river myself."

"Then what? You'll be able to take like five people. There'll be a riot when people find out you have coins; you'll be lucky if you aren't killed."

"If that is God's will, then so be it." Neither Andras's look nor his open-palmed stance changed.

"Please," Irene whispered, her heart sinking. Her hands convulsed on the bag. "Don't ask me to do this..."

"Now hold on—" Ian said, his voice rising dangerously.

"It is her choice," Andras snarled.

Instantly, the "conversation" between the two men dissolved into a shouting match, the exact words lost in a hail of spittle and red faces. Irene looked back and forth between them. Angels. Demons. Here were her two personal ones—they were like the cartoon figures who sat on a person's shoulders, urging him toward temptation or salvation. The only problem was that she wasn't sure which was which in this case. Maybe Andras was trying to trap her here. Maybe Ian was urging her to throw away an actual chance for redemption. She couldn't be sure. The only certain thing was that she was going to have to choose.

Clearly, it had been Andras's idea to take the rocks. Ian wasn't that impatient or that clever. Ian was a "go with the flow" kind of guy.

However, he'd had no problem having sex with her just to keep her occupied while Andras destroyed the shrine. Maybe that could be chalked up to cultural differences—did nineteenth century men even know that women had feelings when it came to sex, that they weren't just things you had sex *to*? Maybe he hadn't meant to be a jerk.

On the other hand, the emergence of this sudden "every man for himself" attitude would suggest that his actions had been carefully calculated. Andras might be insufferably arrogant, but he'd never do something that might jeopardize his chances of getting into Heaven.

Faces danced before her eyes—Elvira, Gao, her father, her grandmother, Ian's wife, and all the rest trapped by the river, waiting to be ground down to nothing. *It's part of the circle of life*, she thought wildly, trying to convince herself, to allay the guilt. It didn't seem to work. The nagging voice of her conscience was yapping away in her head, and she still felt that sick, sinking feeling in the pit of her stomach.

She dashed away the tears streaming down her cheeks with an angry hand. Fuck. How could Andras ask this of her? After everything they'd gone through to get this far — and after what he'd done! — to ask her to risk her life, for strangers to boot, was too much; and, certainly, to ask her to give up her connection to Jonah was beyond anything. Worse yet, why was she considering it? She owed Andras nothing, could barely stand the man, and he could barely stand her. Better to choose Ian, who actually seemed to like her — possibly, maybe. And yet…

She ran a hand through her hair, tempted to pull handfuls of it out, and attacked the door of the hotel, kicking it — once, twice, three times — before turning away with an incoherent shriek of rage.

She had known, once, who she was. She had been Irene Dunphy — unwilling daughter, uncompromising girlfriend, unreliable friend — and she'd been happy. Or had she? Maybe it was more true to say she'd been unconscious of being unhappy. Ignorance really had been bliss.

Either way, that Irene would have gone through the hotel door, no questions, no hesitation. Now it felt as if she was standing at a crossroads, that the decision she made was of monumental, life-changing importance. Only now the stakes were higher. She wouldn't just be disappointing one person. Oh no, there was the entire human race to think about.

"Shut up!" she screamed at the two men, who appeared to be about to come to blows. Andras had Ian by the collar and Ian's fists were raised, as if ready to punch Andras in the jaw. Instantly, both men quieted and looked at her. Andras let Ian go and stepped back.

"I hate you, you know that?" she said to Andras. "You and your self-righteous, goody-goody bullshit…" She turned and aimed another vicious kick at the hotel door.

"I have not constrained you in any way or forced your assistance. You are free to do as you wish."

249

"Oh right! Sure you haven't. You and Jonah are two peas in a pod, you know that? The two of you would get on like a house afire. You both ruin everything and make everything harder than it has to be!"

Andras's brow furrowed.

"Fine," she snarled, turning away from the hotel. "Let's just get this over with."

"Now hold on..." Ian said, putting out a restraining hand.

"It won't take that long —" she started to say, but Ian cut her off.

"I'm sorry, I really am." His eyes were sad.

"Wait...what do you mean? What are you saying?"

Ian shook his head. "Darlin', I've been stuck here a good, long time. I've waited long enough. If you say the boat to the next life is just on the other side of these doors, then I'm going to have to take it."

The words didn't seem to be penetrating the sudden fog cottoning her thoughts. She blinked at him, trying to understand what he was saying. He gave her a rueful grimace, then leaned down and kissed her cheek.

"But what about...us? I thought you..." She bit back the word 'love,' unable to bear hearing him say flat out that he didn't love her. She made a helpless gesture with her hand, impotent and useless. "So...what? Everything you said...that was just to get into my pants?" She felt her face flame as she remembered Andras's presence. She edged around so her back was to Andras, cutting him out of the conversation.

Ian reached out and cupped her shoulders in his hands. "'Course not, sweetheart," he said. "I meant every word. I truly would have married you in a heartbeat. Shoot, I still mean it."

"But you won't stay?"

"Darlin' I think you're lookin' at this all wrong. I ain't the one that's doin' anything. It's you doin' it. You're the one refusing to go."

She goggled at him. "Ian, I'm asking you to stay."

"And I'm askin' you to go."

They stared at each other for a moment, and Irene realized this was it. He was going. There was nothing she could say to make him stay. If she wanted him, wanted to be with him, she would have to give in. She would have to go…and leave everyone else behind.

She looked at Andras. "I'm not the only person who can do this. There has to be someone else."

His gaze didn't waiver. Her heart sank. Of course she had to be the one to do it. Andras didn't understand how the shrine worked. Plus, the link was to Jonah — if he suddenly got a note from Andras, a complete stranger, telling him Irene was gone and asking him to move the rocks off her grave, he would flip, and there would be no way to stop him from coming to find her.

She looked at Ian again, who gave a half-hearted shrug and held the backpack out to her. "I'll be waitin' for you, on the other side."

When she didn't take the bag, he set it down on the ground between them.

"Ian…" she said. "Can't you just give me a minute to figure something out?"

His hand was already on the door. He didn't look at her as he yanked it open.

"Just wait!" she cried. She had never begged a man to stay with her — not once — but she was dangerously close now. "Ian, please, just give me a little time —" But he was already through the door. It closed behind him with a decisive click.

She started forward, ready to yank open the door and go after him, but a touch on her shoulder stopped her. She turned. Andras regarded her with soft, sympathetic eyes. A mixture of disbelief, anger, hurt, and sorrow swept over her, knocking her legs out from under her. She sagged against the building and slid to the ground.

Her head dropped to her knees as she tried to stop the world from spinning. Was he really gone? Was she really letting him go? Her brain screamed at her to get up, to go after him, but her legs didn't seem to want to comply. She was too stunned to cry, too overwhelmed to breathe. She held onto herself with every fiber of her being, knowing that she would split apart if she let go, even for an instant.

She felt a movement nearby and knew that it was Andras, crouching down beside her.

Softly, his voice gentle, he said, "He was not worthy of you."

She kept still for a moment, until she was sure she wouldn't cry or break, and then lifted her head. She met his eyes, feeling bleak and brittle. "I know," she said, "but it hurts anyway."

The worst part was that she did know—had known since the incident at the cairn. In fact, she might have known it all along. Whenever Ian had tried to kiss her, she'd had the same feeling as she'd had in the village and with Ernest, the ghost she'd hooked up with back on Earth—a sense of horror and wrongness, as if she was committing some kind of betrayal.

She'd thought it had to do with Jonah, had tried to blame him in fact, even though he was a million miles away. The truth was, it had been herself that she was betraying— she'd known that Ian wasn't right for her. She'd spent half their time together being exasperated by how shallow and vacuous he was. They had nothing in common, nothing holding them together except his fawning adoration, which had turned out to be nothing more than an act so he could get laid. Even worse, part of her had known that he was a phony. She'd seen the truth when she thought he wasn't going to stop his advances when she'd asked. She'd wanted so badly to believe there was one person in all the world who genuinely liked her and thought well of her that she had been willing to make excuses for him—hell, to take the blame onto herself, something she would never have done in the past.

Andras's eyes softened and, to her surprise, he leaned forward and planted a gentle kiss on her forehead. He rose to his feet and held out a hand to her. She stared at it blankly and then raised her eyes to his. She was about to refuse to get up, wanting to wallow in her grief for a moment, but somehow the look in Andras's eye put steel into her spine.

She'd cry later—when she was alone—but she'd be damned if she'd cry in front of him.

She put her hand into his and allowed him to pull her to her feet.

"The best cure for a sad heart is to help others," he said.

She gave him a dry look as she smoothed and straightened her dress, trying to assess if her knees were going to hold. "And here I thought it was to get drunk."

He returned her dry look with one of his own. "You have been doing it wrong."

She gaped at him for a moment and then snorted. "Yeah, apparently." She smoothed her dress again and frowned at him. "You and Jonah really would get on great, you know that? I hope you get to meet him some day."

Andras raised an eyebrow.

"You both make me want to kick you in the shins."

He smiled, though in his eyes was a lingering concern.

"All right, come on," she said, taking a deep breath and shouldering the beach bag. She held the backpack out to Andras, who took it, eyeing it with suspicion for a moment.

Irene took it from him, gestured for him to turn around, and then helped him pull the straps over his arms. He craned his neck, staring suspiciously at the bag now perched on his back. She smiled and shook her head, then set off without a word.

"Where are you going?" he called. "The forest is this way."

"Uh uh," she said. "I'm not going out there without some protection."

Twenty-Four

Irene pounded on the door. After a moment, the door creaked open and three sets of button eyes stared at her.

"Well, don't keep them standing at the door," Irene heard the old woman call. "Let them in for pity's sake, let them in."

With a chorus of chattering and hissing that sounded suspiciously like grousing, the creatures swung open the door and moved aside. Unsurprisingly, Andras refused to enter the cottage.

"Are you mad?" he hissed. "Do not enter the demoness's dwelling!"

Irene looked from Andras to the old woman and back again, completely bewildered. "Demon? I hardly think so. Even if she is, she can help us."

"Do you not know her?" Andras replied. "Surely, even in your time they still speak of her."

Irene had no idea what he was talking about. "I know she's someone who can help us. That's all I need to know," Irene said, cutting the argument short by stepping around him and entering the cottage. "Do you have a broom that I can borrow?" However, the old woman had already anticipated her—she was holding one in her hand, which she thrust at Irene.

"I want that back," the old woman said.

Andras gave Irene a dark look as she strolled out of the cottage. "Surely, you jest. This is your idea of protection?"

Irene jerked her head at the pair of creatures in the doorway. "You know what these things are?" The creatures jeered at her and closed the door.

Andras sneered. "Duende. Yes, I know of them." When Irene raised an eyebrow, he clarified. "Every child knows his folklore."

"Then you know they're fierce when riled." She motioned for him to follow and then headed down the street. She returned to the house where she had encountered the first creature—the one that had torn her blanket. She entered cautiously, peering around the door to make sure it wasn't lurking there, ready to attack.

"Sweep the hearth," she muttered, shaking her head.

She crossed to the fireplace. Awkwardly, never having used a broom before, she began sweeping. She kept her eyes peeled and sure enough, in a few minutes, the Duende crept toward her, suspicion shining in its eyes. Irene stopped sweeping and the thing chattered at her. Alarmed, she stroked the broom over the bricks again, resuming her sweeping, her eyes never leaving the creature.

It watched the broom, as if mesmerized. Then it looked at her, seemed to look her up and down, and then gave a low, awkward bow, remaining hunched over, its head nearly to the floor.

Irene stopped sweeping and regarded it for a moment. Then she cleared her throat.

"Uh...so, I was wondering...would you like to come work for me?"

"'Erk!" the thing croaked.

"Yeah...that's right. Work." She wasn't sure what to do next. It was still bowing. She held out the broom as a kind of test. "Uh...here, hold this."

The creature straightened up and took the broom, using both hands to hold it. Irene backed toward the door. She opened the door with one hand, still watching the Duende, which was watching her.

She stepped outside and said. "Okay, come on if you're coming. Bring the broom."

The thing looked at her for a moment, looked at the open door, and then, springing to life with a cacophony of sounds that could only be described as joyful, it toddled across the room and through the door.

"This will prove to be a bad idea," Andras said darkly.

"Better idea?" she asked as she headed for the next house.

However, there was a small snafu at the next house. As she entered, the two Duende living there launched themselves at the one carrying the broom. A massive fight ensued—the Duende hissing and screeching like tom cats. Tufts of course brown hair floated through the air.

"Stop it! Stop! Stop!" Irene cried, trying to break up the fight at arm's length so she wouldn't get bitten or scratched.

Andras snatched up the broom and thrust it at her. "Here!"

"Oh, good idea!" She grabbed it and began beating at the Duende, trying to break them apart.

"What are you doing?" Andras cried. "Sweep!"

"What? Why?" she asked, but he just gestured emphatically. She raced to the hearth and began sweeping frantically. In a moment, the fighting stopped. The three Duende crossed the room and stood in front of her. She kept sweeping.

Finally, the two new ones bowed to her. She held out the broom. "Here, carry this." The two new ones snatched it from her. The original broom-carrier screeched in outrage.

"Oh, hush!" Irene said. "You had a turn already."

She headed for the door. The three Duende followed— the two new ones triumphantly carrying the broom between them, the original one mewling plaintively.

"Oh, for God's sake," Irene said to it, "stop bellyaching or I'll leave you here."

It stared at her reproachfully, but its cries subsided to the occasional unhappy murmur.

Irene visited a dozen more houses, where she collected an ever growing number of Duende. Several of the creatures refused to bow, no matter how long she swept, so she gave up and left those behind.

Now she had almost two dozen—all chittering and tumbling over themselves as they followed her, pied-piper like down the street.

Dear Jonah,

You know how I told you once that when I was a kid I wanted a brownie (the mythical creature, not the chocolate dessert)? I finally got some.

~Irene

She returned to the stone cottage, where the old woman opened the door herself. Irene handed her the broom. "Thanks."

The woman eyed Irene's hoard and chuckled. "Do you good, they will. If they don't drive you mad, first."

Irene grimaced. "Yeah, that's what I'm afraid of." She surveyed the woman for a moment, feeling a strange rush of emotions—affection, concern, curiosity, and, inexplicably, sadness. She reached in her bag and pulled out the envelope of coins. "Here," she said, holding a handful out to the woman.

The woman's face turned hard. "Don't be a fool."

Irene blinked in surprise and then offered the coins again. "Don't worry. I've got more."

The woman glared at Irene. "Well, of all the arrogance!"

"I—" Irene wasn't sure what she wanted to say. There was no point asking the woman to go with them; Irene already knew she would refuse. Still, she felt like she should offer to take her or do *something* for the woman.

The old woman's face softened, and she patted Irene's cheek with a leathery hand. "No need to be sentimental, my girl. What lies beyond isn't for me."

Irene's brow puckered. "Yeah, but—"

"Oh, don't you worry; we'll meet again," the woman said, impatiently waving Irene away. "Now go on, get."

Behind Irene, the Duende chattered impatiently, and Irene knew they were getting restless. "Okay, fine," she said to the old woman. "But here, just take one coin, in case you change your mind."

"Bah!" The old woman waved away the coin.

"Okay, fine," Irene said, giving up. "Well...thanks for the help."

"Help?" The woman cackled and turned away. Before Irene could ask her what she meant by laughing, the door shut in her face. Again feeling like she'd somehow been made a fool of, Irene turned away with a sigh. Andras was wearing a smug look, one eyebrow cocked as if to say, "I told you so."

"Oh, be quiet!"

They set off, and all too quickly, they stood at the edge of the city, the barren streetscape giving way to forest. They stopped and surveyed the landscape. Irene's stomach was a knot of dread. Andras didn't say anything as his eyes scanned the area, as if hunting for hidden dangers, but his expression was grim. He looked at her and gave her a small smile of reassurance. "You asked me before if I had experience with the angels. Before now, I had only heard that Nephilim are dangerous, to be feared and avoided, but in truth, they are rare here. In eight hundred years I have never been attacked, nor known of anyone to be attacked. I believe that what happened to us was mere happenstance."

She was about to point out that those were strange words for a man who thought everything happened for a reason, when she was struck by a sudden thought: in eight hundred years he had never seen an angel, but in the course of a couple of months she'd had run-ins with two different ones. What were the odds of that?

If one Nephilim knows your name, then all.

Irene clutched the pendant at her throat, dread shuddering through her.

"Ready?" Andras asked, cutting into her train of thought.

She gave him as much of a smile as she could muster. "As I'll ever be."

He gestured for her to proceed. "Then lead on."

Twenty-Five

"Rest break," Irene called.

Andras gave her an exasperated look.

They had left the city far behind and had been double-time marching through the forest without stopping, following the flame in Irene's chest. Irene was exhausted, but the thought of encountering the angels kept her moving. However, she couldn't ignore the fact that the Duende looked like they were about to keel over.

"It's not for me; it's for the munchkins." She gestured to the creatures who had started out as a tumbling, chittering mass but were now looking rather droopy and bedraggled.

Andras frowned but gave a reluctant nod. Irene spread out the blanket, and to her surprise, Andras sat down, too. She really wanted a drink, would have settled for coffee, but decided to refrain from either as a concession to him.

She wrapped her arms around herself and surveyed the forest, keeping a wary eye out for any danger. "I wish we had a fire."

She turned to find Andras watching her intently. She raised an eyebrow in inquiry. The silence stretched out – he seemed to be searching for something in her face. She met his searching look with one of her own.

Finally, he said, "I died in Al Andalus, on the field at Alarcos."

Irene was confused for a moment and then she understood: he was telling her about his death. Her heart skipped a beat. She didn't know what any of his words meant, but she knew he was telling her something important, something deeply personal, something that went completely against his faith to share.

His eyes were hooded, and he looked grim and sad. "It was a terrible day. The Moors swept across the field in unstoppable waves. They gained the walls and then the keep. After, they stripped the bodies of the dead and tumbled them from the walk, leaving them to putrefy in the moat. The Master of my order was there and he was afforded no more courtesy or honor than the rest."

One hand closed convulsively, and he stared into the air, as if reliving the battle. "After, we awoke in this land, on a desolate, rocky plain, thousands upon thousands of us. There was a carriage there, beautiful, bedecked with ornaments and jewels, pulled by a team of eight magnificent stallions of pure white." He bit his lip and seemed overcome by emotion. Then he mastered himself and continued. "The driver struck at us with his whip and drove us away, saying that the carriage was not for the likes of us, that we would have to proceed by foot. We journeyed together for a while, but eventually we began to split apart. Some stopped to help those we met along the way; some were lost whenever we were chased by the Fantasmos; some despaired and attempted to return to the plain where we had started. In the end, there were only ten of us left when we made it to the river."

A chattering, seething mass of Duende interrupted whatever Andras was about to say next. They were carrying fire wood, and they tumbled onto the blanket, stacking the wood in a pile.

Irene jumped to her feet. "What the — "

Andras looked both exasperated and amused. "You asked for a fire."

"Well, yeah, but I didn't think they'd actually...I mean, it was just a thought, not a request — no, not on the blanket! Not on the — "

The Duende chattered and gamboled over the blanket, clearly proud of themselves. Irene pointed. "Get that off the blanket. We build fires on the ground." Chattering merrily, the Duende complied, dragging the wood a short ways away. Irene looked at Andras in bewilderment. "Where did they even find wood?"

He shrugged. "Your job is to require. Theirs is to fulfill."

She huffed in exasperation. "Gee, thanks, Confucius. That was a bundle of help."

A corner of his mouth lifted in the rare, wolfish grin. She turned back to the Duende. "Okay, well, that's great. Good work guys, but I didn't mean it."

They didn't seem to be listening. She raised her voice, trying to talk over them. "No, really...we can't have a fire...no. Bad! Dangerous!"

Her words had no effect. The Duende were swarming over the pile of wood, engaged in what appeared to be a strenuous debate, completely ignoring her. She felt like Mickey Mouse in the *Sorcerer's Apprentice*, shouting vainly at the unstoppable broomsticks flooding the room with bucket after bucket of water.

Irene gave Andras a helpless look. He shrugged.

"Do they have an off switch?"

He shrugged again. "I know nothing of these pagan things."

Irene started to glare at him in outrage before she saw the twinkle in his eyes. "Oh, suddenly *now* you have a sense of humor?"

Andras grunted in response, but Irene saw his lips twitch. She shook her head at him and then surveyed the Duende once more. She threw up her hands in exasperation and plopped down on the blanket. "Whatever. Just keep it down, guys, will ya?"

Andras's expression changed to disbelief.

Irene shrugged. "What? It's not like they're actually going to be able to start a fire."

There was a sudden whoosh of air, followed by the tangy smell of wood smoke.

"You were saying?"

Irene rolled her eyes and silently counted to five. Then she turned back to Andras. "So...*you* were saying?"

When he gave her a blank look, she said, "What happened when you arrived at the river?"

Instantly he looked grim again, and she was sorry she had brought it up. She kicked herself for being an idiot. She should have just let it be, rather than risk angering him, as she invariably did.

She didn't think he was going to answer and was desperately searching for some other topic of conversation to cover the blunder when he said, "We could not be counted among the Sabaoth. The Moors had taken not only our dignity but our honor as well."

"What do you mean?"

"A warrior without a weapon is no warrior at all, and a knight who allows his sword to be taken is not worthy to wield one."

She was silent for a moment, almost afraid to ask the obvious question. "Okay, but what's a Sabaoth?"

His lips thinned, as if he couldn't believe she had to ask. "The heavenly host. The army of God."

Irene digested this for a moment. "So the guys guarding the camp—it's like an afterlife fraternity, but open only to those who were buried with weapons?"

"To those who received the sacred burial of a warrior, yes."

Jonah had spent countless hours detailing—at great length—the different cultures that buried weapons with their warriors. He had assumed it was so they could defend themselves in the afterlife. While it did have that element, as well, she realized now that the real purpose was as a sort of badge of honor. It was a way for warriors to recognize each other in the afterlife and to determine who was eligible to join their special club.

"Well, okay, but what about martial artists? They fight with their hands."

"A warrior's honor is measured against the staff of his choosing, not against the staff of others."

Irene narrowed her eyes. "Yeah, well, your tongue is much more cutting than any sword, trust me."

Andras grunted.

"So...what then? What happened to what was left of your order?"

"Each went his own way, to redeem himself and recover his honor as best he could, in the hopes of earning a place among the holy host."

A light bulb went off in Irene's head. "That's why you were wandering in the forest when we met? You've spent the last eight hundred years looking for lost travelers to help?" It was also why he'd been so insistent on helping her, even though she'd refused his help, and he clearly hadn't liked her very much. He thought he needed to earn his way into Heaven through good deeds, and she'd presented the opportunity for a very big good deed.

The Duende suddenly swarmed over her bag, interrupting anything else she might say. Apparently rested and feeling bored, they had decided to be "helpful" by "organizing" her bag. They already had half of the items pulled out before she realized what they were doing.

"No!" she cried, grabbing the bag from them. A tug of war ensued, her against ten Duende. The little bastards were strong, and she couldn't budge them. Finally, fearing the bag would rip, she let it go. Two Duende jeered at her while a third hissed.

"Bad!" she said. "No! Put that stuff back. Put it back!" The Duende ignored her and went about their business. "Damn it!" she muttered, climbing to her feet. "Okay, fine, you want to play rough? We'll play rough. You three," she pointed to the closest Duende, "polish the rocks in my bag. You two, put all this stuff back—neatly! The rest of you, go stand guard and keep a look out for danger." None of the Duende moved. "Now!" she barked. "Or I'll fire your asses. I know plenty of other critters back in the city who would love this gig." With a cry of alarm, the Duende sprang into action.

Beside her, she heard Andras choke back a chuckle. "You would have made a good commander," he said.

"Watch it," she said. "I can still fire your ass, too."

They remained for a few more minutes, but since the Duende seemed rested there was no point in lingering. By unspoken agreement, both Andras and Irene wanted to get through the forest as quickly as possible.

It took only a moment to pack and be off. Irene followed the flame in her heart, which she had locked onto with thoughts of the camp, mixed with Jonah — or, more precisely, thoughts of Jonah being proud of her. Feeling the flame and knowing which way to go were quickly becoming second nature, and she felt a small surge of pride when she realized she had conquered this new skill. *See with no eyes — check.* Maybe she'd be able to do okay here after all.

For some reason, this made her think of Ian and her spirits plummeted again. There was a nagging question in the back of her mind, and it grew more and more insistent as they walked. Finally, she looked at Andras out of the corner of her eye.

"It was you, wasn't it? With the rocks. It was your idea to take them."

Andras looked at her, solemn and grave. He hesitated a moment and then slowly shook his head.

It was as if a knife had been plunged into her heart. She'd thought Ian's duplicity and betrayal couldn't hurt her any more than it already had, but apparently she was wrong about that because the pain burst forth anew. She felt her face crumple and tears sprang to her eyes. "Really?" She turned her head away so he couldn't see her face. "Why did you go along with it, then?"

"He convinced me that it was for the good — that your worship at the shrine had become a sickness. However, it was not part of the scheme that he should seduce you."

Irene grimaced and shook her head. "It's okay — I only sleep with guys I don't actually like." She risked looking at Andras long enough to flash him a rueful smile. His brow furrowed. Irene shrugged. "A shrink would say that I have trust or daddy or some kind of issues." She shrugged again. "The good thing is that when they leave, it never really matters." *And they always leave.*

This time was a little different, though; it did hurt, though she couldn't really say why. Maybe it was humiliation because she'd let him play her like a love-struck teenager. Maybe it was the mortification of realizing how easily she could lie to herself, how willing she was to put on blinders to the truth—she'd talked herself into thinking she was in love with Ian when, deep down, she'd known that was the farthest thing from the truth. Maybe it was embarrassment because she'd opened herself up to the possibility of love and had failed so spectacularly at it. Maybe it was the secret terror and shame of having finally confirmed that there was nothing about her that anybody wanted.

"I am sorry," Andras said. "I should not have interfered. I should have known better than to come between you and your god."

"My god?" She nearly choked in surprise. "What? No...Jonah's not...he's just a boy."

"You believe in him, have faith in him."

Irene's brow creased with confusion. "Well, yeah, but...that's because he...well, he believes in me."

"You rely on him when you are weak or afraid; you draw strength from him."

"It's not like that...it's just...it's complicated."

Andras smiled. "Faith always is."

Confused, she shot him a dark look and surged ahead. When they next stopped to rest, she opened the back pack and started pulling out rocks.

"What are you doing?" Andras asked.

"Well, it occurs to me I should test my theory that a direct altar-to-altar phone call works before we get to the river. I don't want to get anyone's hopes up. Plus, I should check in with Jonah, let him know what's going on. If he suddenly stops hearing from me, he'll get worried."

She hastily assembled the rocks into a pile and then dashed a note to Jonah, explaining that she was testing a theory, and that she needed him to take the rocks off of her grave, build an altar with them, send her a note via the new altar to let her know when he was done, and then wait to hear from her.

When she was done, she sat down across from Andras, her legs curled under her. The silence stretched out around them. "Sooo…" she said. "We can't talk about the past, we can't talk about the future, and the present isn't all that interesting. What do you want to do to pass the time?"

He studied her for a moment, his eyes crinkled in amusement. "You would have made a good commander but a very poor nun."

She narrowed her eyes, giving him a playful look of disgust. "Come on, tell me something else about your life. Something happy this time."

"Like what?"

"I don't know…like, did you always want to be a knight?"

He looked solemn for a moment. "When I was very small, I wanted to be a fish."

"A fish!" She gaped at him and then saw that his eyes twinkled. She glared in exasperation and looked around for something to throw at him.

The Duende chattered and rustled with sudden alarm. Irene looked to see what was the matter and found that there was a piece of paper and something else sitting beside the altar. With a cry of elation she sprang up to retrieve the items.

The note said simply, "Okay, done." Then, below that, as if it was an afterthought, was a hard to read paragraph, hastily scrawled. Irene squinted, trying to make out the words, and recognized one of Jonah's treatises on the afterlife.

> *The Egyptians thought people were made up of six parts: the body (Ha), heart (Ib), life force (Ka), personality (Ba), name (Ren), and shadow (Sheut). The parts all end up in different places/play a different role in the afterlife but remain connected.*

Andras was watching her. Irene opened her mouth to share what Jonah had written, then realized that getting Andras up to speed on the whole "every story of the afterlife is true" thing would take way more time than they had at the moment. She wasn't even sure he'd accept it, anyway;

such a revelation went entirely against everything he believed in.

"What does he say?" Andras asked.

"Uh...he says we're all set." She stuffed the note in her bag.

The other item Jonah had sent turned out to be a bag of black licorice. Irene turned it over in her hands, feeling a strange mixture of joy and melancholy.

Andras frowned. "What is that?"

"My favorite candy," she said around the lump in her throat. She couldn't believe Jonah had remembered.

Andras shot her a probing look, but said nothing. She hugged the candy to her chest for a moment, and then secreted it away in her bag. "Let me just send this note and then we can be off again."

She dashed another note to Jonah, explaining about the altars and the need for the dead to be able to get coins and warning him it might be some time before he heard from her again.

If you need to reach me, send the letter via my grave. I'll get that even if I don't have the altar set up.

As she tucked the note into the altar, the sight of Andras's stockinged feet caught her attention once more. "You know, I could ask him to send you some shoes."

Andras gave her an exasperated look. "Vanity of the flesh."

"Okay, okay, I'm sorry. God, please don't start with that." She shook her head but couldn't hide a smile, though she sighed in resignation. "At least you're consistent."

267

Twenty-Six

The angel came out of nowhere.

One moment they were walking through the forest; the next, Andras was barreling into her, shoving her out of the way as something swooped by. The Duende screeched, and as Irene turned, they swarmed over the Nephilim, its white-blond hair and wings barely visible under the layer of screeching brown fur.

Andras bellowed, but Irene didn't have to be told twice. Adrenaline pumped through her, and she was operating on instinct. She stumbled to her feet and ran. Andras was beside her in a flash. They bolted blindly through the forest, zigzagging between trees. Behind them, they heard enraged screams and knew that the Duende hadn't managed to buy them much time. The angel was coming.

The flame that had signaled Jonah and home flared within her, and she felt a momentary tug, as if her clothing had snagged on a branch. She veered toward the pull before she even realized what it was.

Home. Safety. Escape.

It was just a feeling, an instinct, but it overrode everything else. She latched onto it, holding on for dear life. She reached out blindly for Andras, grabbing a fistful of his shirt near the shoulder just as the feeling of being pulled down a chute kicked in.

In a moment, they were stumbling forward, tripping and struggling to stay upright, as they shot out the other end of the invisible tunnel.

Irene doubled over, hands on knees; Andras whirled in a circle, terror etched on his face. "Where have you brought me?" he cried.

Irene straightened up, trying to assess their surroundings. She stifled a groan. No wonder it had felt familiar—she was back amidst the teepees and tents of the village where she'd first met the Guide. Andras was staring at her now, as if he thought an alien was about to burst out of her stomach.

"What?" she said. "Why are you looking at me like that? I just saved your life!"

"Where have you brought us?"

"Somewhere safe," she said, her face heating at his suspicious tone.

Andras stared at her, his eyes hard.

Irene gritted her teeth. "Just be thankful we're here." When he continued to stare, she said, "You mean you've never been here before?"

"No."

"Really?" She blinked in surprise. "In eight hundred years, you never came across this place?

"No."

Irene huffed, not sure what to say. "Great, so I've developed magic powers. I invent whole villages and cities out of thin air." She looked around, trying to take stock. Everything looked the same as it had before. Memories of the horse came flooding back to her, so real she expected to feel its velvet nose against her hand any second. She clenched her fists and tried to push the memories away.

She frowned as she turned in a circle. "Wait...where are the Duende?" It was obvious, however, that the Duende had not managed to follow. "Shit! We need to go back."

Andras grabbed her arm. "You brought them to protect us; they have done so."

She shook him off. "I don't bring them to be cannon fodder! I thought maybe they'd scare the angels off, is all! Jesus!" She glared at him. "I'm not heartless, you know."

Andras gave her a look she couldn't interpret. "The Duende can take care of themselves. I am certain they will be fine."

She frowned; she wasn't sure she agreed with him but did realize that rushing right back into the forest would just put them back into the path of the angel, which would be suicide. "So what now?"

Andras shrugged.

"Why do I have to come up with all the ideas?" She looked around, not sure what to do next. Her frown deepened as a vague feeling she couldn't quite put her finger on crept over her.

Andras must have seen the change in her face because he asked, "What is wrong?"

"I don't know...I'm getting a weird vibe. This place feels...familiar, somehow. I mean, it is familiar—I've been here before..." She scanned the line of tents, trying to figure out what she was feeling. Inexplicably, she felt drawn to a nearby tent and she crossed to it, followed closely by Andras. She flipped back the flap and peered inside. In the dim light, she saw a middle-aged woman in a fur coat lying on the floor, images flashing in the air above her head.

"I know her!" Irene cried, looking at Andras in wonder. "She was at the hotel when I first arrived. She got on the boat there." She dropped the flap and turned to Andras, suddenly understanding the feeling of familiarity. "Ian's here!"

"How do you know that?" Andras asked, his voice dark with suspicion.

"I don't know—but I can feel it."

"Is that why you brought us here?"

Irene shot him an exasperated look. "Puh-lease! No, it was just blind instinct at the time." She turned in a circle again, trying to make sense of where they were. "Okay, these people got on the boat at the hotel. The bell boy there said...that boat was the express.... Oh...oh, hey, I get it!" She looked at Andras in astonishment, not quite believing that she really understood. "Oh my God, I get it! It's a short cut." She let out a whoop of joy and jumped up and down. Andras looked at her as if she had lost her mind.

"Look, these people are on the boat—they're in transit, on their way to the next stage."

"If they are on the boat, then why are they here?"

"They're not here. Not really. Or, more correctly, they're in both places—at the same time. It's hard to explain but it has something to do with the fact that everything—and I mean everything—in the universe is all sandwiched together, layer upon layer. Have you ever looked at…" She cast around, trying to think of a metaphor Andras would understand. "Okay, have you ever seen light reflecting off water? Or a rainbow? The light is always there, right? But usually you can't see it. However, sometimes, if you look at just the right angle, you can see it."

Andras nodded slowly, his face still wreathed in doubt.

"Well, it's like that. Something about this place lets us see these people, even though they're on another plane of existence from us. They just look like they're sleeping because that's the best interpretation our brain can make of what we're seeing."

She grinned, extremely proud of herself for remembering Jonah's lecture on the Buddhist afterlife belief that the deceased battle hallucinations created by their subconscious as part of the process of reaching Nirvana. This must have been what the Guide was referring to when he'd referred to Andras's belief that nothing here was real as Buddhist. She groaned; another clue the Guide had been trying to give her that she'd been too stupid to see.

Dear Jonah,

Today I actually needed to know about the Buddhist state of Bardo AND I was able to explain it to a guy from the eleven hundreds. See? I was paying attention.

Andras still looked doubtful but didn't say anything.

Irene frowned as a thought struck her. "You know, I think you're right."

"About what?"

"About forgetting that we used to have bodies."

Andras raised an eyebrow.

Irene gave him a quelling look. "Don't get excited. I just meant that I think this place, all of it, this entire plane of existence—the forest, the city, the river, this village—are designed to help accustom us to not having bodies. I think, wherever we go next, we're not going to need them."

Like everything else about being dead, it made sense in retrospect. This place was like a sensory deprivation tank—there was no day or night, it wasn't hot or cold, it was nothing. The only stuff here was what you were capable of seeing with your new, non-physical, ghost senses—basically your mind's interpretation of what you were "seeing" or "hearing" or "feeling." The trees that weren't trees, the cat that wasn't a cat, hell, even the city that wasn't a city. Since there weren't any other cities here, Irene suspected that the city was more like the village—it existed on a different plane or "layer" from where they currently were. Somehow, her ghost senses had connected with it, and she'd been temporarily and entirely unconsciously able to navigate to it, to jump to another plane of existence. She couldn't really see the people she sensed here because she wasn't fully here, not having learned yet how to exist in whatever state this plane existed in.

Irene shook her head. "Damn it; he kept telling me to go back to sleep and I wouldn't listen."

Andras raised his other eyebrow.

"The Guide. He was trying to help, trying to encourage me to take the short cut, and I wouldn't listen." She mentally kicked herself. "Why do I never listen?"

Andras raised both eyebrows higher and opened his mouth.

"*Don't* say it," Irene warned, raising a finger to stop him.

The wolfish grin appeared. "Do not ask a question, if you do not want the answer."

Irene gave him a mock glare. She was interrupted from saying anything further by the sudden appearance of the chattering, tangled horde of Duende who tumbled into view out of thin air. They appeared to be in high spirits and clustered around her feet, chirping and croaking happily. "Hey, you made it," she cried, surprised to find she was actually happy to see them. "All here?" She tried to count them, but they wouldn't stand still long enough. She frowned. "I need to get you guys name tags or something." She looked at Andras. "Do you think this means the coast is clear?"

Andras shrugged. Irene bit her lip and frowned. "Maybe we should wait a while longer; better safe than sorry."

Andras nodded his assent.

"Well, I guess we might as well take a load off," she said as she set off, heading for her favorite rock, feeling a pang as horse-related memories surfaced. She still had one more paper horse; she could bring it to life.

She quickly dismissed the thought; it would be in danger from the angels. Plus, she might need it for something later. Better to save it for an emergency.

She hunkered down on the rock, rested one elbow on her hip, and leaned on her hand. She stared at Andras thoughtfully for a moment, as a doubt nibbled at her.

"You said that you've never had a run-in with an angel before," she said slowly.

Andras cocked his head and gave her a puzzled look. "Few ever see them—they are considered more myth than truth."

"So, it's weird that we've been attacked twice, then?"

Andras's eyes narrowed but he didn't say anything, just waited for her to share the theory that was slowly forming.

"Do you think it's following us?" she asked.

"To what end?"

Irene reached up with her free hand and clasped the pendant at her throat. "I think it's my fault. I can see them. I mean...I think they're on another plane of existence from us. Like this village and the city and everything else. So normally we wouldn't even be able to see them. But I can, and I think it's because of this." When she'd bought the necklace, the trader had intimated that it was something special — hence the outrageous asking price of six dimes. She hadn't even met Samyel until after she had the pendant. In fact, the first time they'd met he'd stared at her chest. She'd thought he was staring at her breasts. She realized now that he was probably staring at the necklace. The second time they'd met, when he'd attacked her, he had tapped the pendant and said a word that she didn't understand.

She fingered the stone and considered ripping the necklace off, throwing it on the ground, and leaving it behind. However, she wasn't entirely convinced that would solve the problem. She sighed and dropped the stone. Whether or not the necklace was the reason she could see the angels, it still might be valuable. Samyel had seemed interested in it, and she'd had the impression that it had protected her, somehow — either as a badge of some sort or as a talisman. It wouldn't be smart to get rid of it until she knew exactly what it was.

Andras seemed to be waiting for her to say something else. She shrugged. "I don't know. I don't have any answers. Just...I'm sorry. If it is my fault, I'm sorry."

"It is not your fault. They exist. Nothing we do changes that."

Irene grunted. Somehow Andras managed to be both depressing and comforting at the same time. She looked around. The Duende were clearly bored — half of them were wrestling and the rest lolled around theatrically, as if sitting, doing nothing, was killing them. Irene glanced at her watch and then remembered that was stupid. She sighed and stood up. "I'll be right back. I'm going to go check on something."

Andras grabbed her arm. "Seeing him will not change anything."

She hesitated; her gut reaction was to lie, to deny that she'd been going to seek out Ian. However, it seemed Andras could see right through her so it would be useless to lie. Was she really so transparent?

Though she hated to admit it, Andras was right; seeing Ian wouldn't change anything. He was already on another plane of existence—to her eyes he'd appear to be unconscious, deep in the strange dreaming shared by the sleepers in the tents. Even if he'd been awake, she wasn't sure what she could or would say to him. She couldn't make him love her, and honestly, she didn't want to. Mostly, she just wanted to knee him in the groin, though part of her did want to hear him say that it hadn't all been pretend, that he had cared for her, if even just a little bit.

With a heavy sigh, she stepped back, and Andras instantly released her arm. She sat back down on the rock, and they both settled down to the business of waiting. It didn't take long for her to be reminded that they were both terrible at it.

Andras got up to pace.

Irene glared at him. "You're killing me."

With a dark look, Andras stalked off. Irene let him go. After a moment's hesitation, she sent several of the Duende after him, to keep an eye on him just in case. There wasn't any trouble Andras could get into here, as far as she knew, but better safe than sorry.

Irene absently watched the Duendes' antics. Time passed very slowly. Another letter arrived from Jonah. She was just finishing reading it when Andras appeared.

"For someone who came on this trip to protect me, you sure do disappear a lot," she said as she folded up the letter.

"I am never far."

Irene sighed and stood up. "Do you think it's been long enough?"

"Send the Duende to see if it is safe."

"Hey, good idea!" Irene snapped her fingers at the closest Duende, which was lying on its back, legs straight up in the air, theatrically conveying it's boredom. "Hey, you, I've got a job for you." The Duende immediately sat up with a chirp and gave her an attentive, hopeful look. "Yeah, you. Take a friend and go see if the coast is clear."

With a happy cry, it jumped to its feet and set off. A nearby Duende chirped excitedly and set off after it as fast as its stubby little legs would carry it. A mournful, dissatisfied cry went up from the rest of them.

"Yeah, wah, wah, wah," Irene said. "You're all so bored."

More than a dozen pairs of button eyes all turned to stare reproachfully at her.

"I would not bait them if I were you," Andras warned.

Before Irene could respond, the Duende who had gone to scout returned. They chirped in chorus, jumping up and down at Irene's feet. Irene looked to Andras for guidance. "I think that's the all clear," she said, doubtfully.

Andras shrugged.

Irene slid off the rock and shouldered her bag. "Okay, then, let's go."

The rest of the Duende jumped to their feet, chittering excitedly. "Yeah, yeah," Irene said. "Back to work."

This time, there was no trouble leaving the village. She knew exactly where she was going. She took Andras's hand, settled the bag more firmly on her shoulder, and walked straight out of the village and into the forest.

"So," Irene said, glancing at Andras out of the corner of her eye. "I asked Jonah about…the place where you died." She hesitated, expecting Andras to tense up, but he said nothing. Taking his silence for permission to continue, she went on. "It turns out it's actually sort of a big deal. The fortress is still there — ruined, of course. It's an historic site. They've preserved it, and people can go there and tour it. The battle of eleven hundred and ninety-five is remembered still, to this day. More than eight hundred years later, they still talk about it. Seventeen years after that battle, in twelve-twelve there was another big battle — only you guys won."

Several long minutes of silence went by. Irene felt her face heat. "I just thought you'd like to know," she said, feeling foolish.

"Thank you," Andras said quietly, not looking at her. His voice shook, and Irene realized he wasn't angry, he was touched. She smiled to herself and looked away.

They walked through the forest, comfortably silent but always on the alert for danger, until the Duende began to droop and they were forced to stop. Irene didn't even spread out the blanket. She and Andras each found a large rock to share, ready to bound up and run at a second's notice. The Duende milled aimlessly, never really stopping, though some lay down on their backs, feet straight up in the air as if they were dead, for a few minutes. Often, another Duende would pounce on one of those lying down, tackling it, and they would fall to wrestling, like kittens. Irene watched them with detached amusement, her thoughts drifting and not really on the Duende.

She looked over at Andras, studying him thoughtfully. He noticed and gave her a quizzical look. "Can I ask you a question?" she asked.

He nodded.

"When you were talking about how you died, you sounded pretty angry—or like you were at the time—about the way your enemies treated the dead, stripping the bodies and not giving anyone a proper burial. To then find yourself sharing the same afterlife with them...that must have been hard to swallow."

Andras looked down at his hands, which had clenched into fists. "Yes."

"So how come you aren't out here?" She nodded to the forest. "How come you didn't become one of the angry, resentful ghosts wandering around?"

He looked up, meeting her eyes with a clear, unwavering gaze. "I was. For a time."

"What changed?"

"I realized my anger changed nothing."

She nodded and looked down. She supposed that's what the Guide had meant when he'd goaded her into making up with Andras and Ian—staying angry wouldn't have changed what had happened. Anger didn't change the past, just the future.

"Do you ever think about your life—on Earth, I mean. Your beliefs, the reason you went to war, how angry you were with the Moors? After eight hundred years, do you still feel the same or do you wish you could change things?"

Andras was silent for a moment. The burble of the Duende chattering amongst themselves filled the space, a kind of soothing white noise. "I do not think we were wrong. On Earth, we focus on earthly matters. If we are invaded, we have the right to defend ourselves. If we are stolen from, we have the right to reclaim what is ours."

Irene picked at the rock, digesting this. Then she looked at him and gave him a self-conscious, half-grin. "I'm sorry I threatened to beat your head in with a tire iron."

A slow grin spread across his face. "I believe we have already agreed that you would make a very bad nun."

Irene laughed but was cut short by something streaking out of the woods toward them. Instantly, the Duende were on their feet, chittering and hissing. The streaking object skidded to a halt.

It was the cat. Irene's heart leapt at the sight of it. She was halfway to her feet before she realized something was wrong. The cat was emitting the most unearthly screech Irene had ever heard, and its fur was standing on end.

"Nephilim!" Andras shouted a second before the angel burst from the gray nothing twenty feet away. The Duende shrieked with rage, rushing toward the angel as one. Irene just had time to see the angel cut through the mass, as if they weren't even there, before Andras shoved her aside.

"Run!" he shouted as he stepped into the path of the angel.

Irene screamed.

Everything happened in an instant. The angel grabbed Andras by the shoulders at the same moment the Duende, who had turned a hundred and eighty degrees as crisply as a flock of birds, swarmed up its back, tearing and biting as they went.

The angel gave a guttural cry of rage and pain. In one swift movement it threw back its head to shake off the Duende and lifted Andras, throwing him as if he were a toy. Andras hit a nearby tree, and Irene heard the crack of his skull connecting with the obsidian-hard bark in the same moment that she wrenched the heart-shaped pendant from her throat, breaking the flimsy cord that held it there.

She raised the pendant high just as the Duende reached the angel's shoulders, scratching and tearing, marring its beautiful face with a thousand angry, bloody lines.

"I am everything that lives and everything that dies!" Irene shouted. "Do you hear me? I am everything that was and will be!" She shook the pendant and bellowed the words, struggling to be heard above the screams of the Duende, the shrieks of the angel, the roar of her heart in her ears.

The angel froze and looked at her, its lip curled in a scornful snarl. Its strange, glittering eyes made her own eyes water and she wanted to look away, but held her ground. The Duende were still swarming over the angel, biting and scratching, ripping and tearing, and she called them off. "Stop! Get back. Leave it alone!"

The Duende froze and collectively looked at her, as if assessing whether or not she was serious. For a moment, she thought they weren't going to comply. Then, reluctantly, with angry hisses and squeals, the Duende backed off, clambering down off the angel.

Irene held her ground, her eyes never leaving the angel's though she desperately wanted to see if Andras was moving, trying her best not to show how badly she was shaking.

"You can understand me?" she asked the angel, shaking the pendant again to make sure she had its attention.

The angel lifted one lip in a disdainful sneer.

Irene's fingers tightened on the cord of the pendant until her fingernails cut into her palm. "I know you understand — answer me!"

The angel's sneer deepened. "You are not Utukuu." It spoke as Samyel had, with long, sibilant syllables that slithered over her nerve endings, like dry leavings rasping together. "You have no right to those words."

"They were given to me, by one of you, one of your kind." She shifted her weight, digging into her stance, hoping her legs didn't give out. She took a deep breath, not sure what to do with the angel now that she had it. "Why are you following us? Why did you attack us?"

The angel's beautiful face twisted with scorn and it turned its head, disdaining to even look at her.

Behind her, the Duende hissed and chittered with anger, and a collective rustling went through them, as if they moved as one.

"Answer my question," she shouted, a sudden flare of anger cutting through her fear, "or I'll feed you to them."

The angel's lip curled again, but she saw its eyes flick to the horde of tiny monsters, and then it looked at her. "Attack?" It seemed genuinely surprised. Irene had a flashback to her first and second encounters with Samyel—he had attacked her. At least, she had thought he had, but he'd been offended and surprised by the suggestion—the same as this angel. Clearly angels and humans had very different codes of conduct.

"What is it you want?" she asked. "Why are you here and why are you following us?"

The angel's lip curled with contempt, but it was silent.

"I met one of your kind on Earth, with the living—"

"*Your* living."

She hesitated and then continued, not wanting to be distracted from her original question. "Fine, *my* living. What was he looking for?"

The sneer deepened.

Irene stiffened as another flash of anger sizzled through her. "I see."

The angel bared its teeth but was silent.

Irene narrowed her eyes. "The one that was on Earth—he owes me a favor. What will happen if I call his name, if I try to collect?"

The angel drew back its lips in a horrible parody of a smile, its sharp teeth flashing into sight. "Regret."

That was the last straw. A red haze of rage descended over Irene—it had killed her horse, attacked her, hurt Andras, and now it stood there laughing at her, daring her to call in her favor from Samyel. Her knees were in danger of buckling, and she had no out. She had a tiger by the tail, and if she let go, it would kill her. Even worse, the angel knew it. It was laughing at her, biding its time. She risked taking her eyes off of it long enough to check on Andras. He was lying at the base of the tree, not moving. Her heart skipped a beat. Was he dead?

She was in a stalemate. She couldn't run away, abandoning Andras, and she couldn't let the angel go, since it would attack as soon as her back was turned. The inevitably of her death, here and now, at the hands of this angel, washed over her. Her hand tightened on the pendant, clutching the talisman as if her life depended on it.

She looked at the chittering hoard of Duende and a strange, disjointed sense of icy calm washed over her. She looked at the angel and let her arm go slack, lowering the pendant. The angel's eyes widened with surprise even as its look of disdain deepened.

The Duende were all staring at her now, two dozen pairs of eyes watching her with expectation. She nodded toward the angel. "Get to work," she said.

They didn't need to be told twice — they swarmed.

Irene watched impassively as they mobbed the angel, drowning out its screams with their enraged cries. She stumbled away from the carnage, her legs barely carrying her as she ran to Andras.

He was unconscious, or possibly dead — she had no way of telling which. "Andras! Andras!" She shook him but he didn't stir. She had enough presence of mind to pull the cup out of her bag, ask for cold water, and then throw the water in his face. He came to instantly, spluttering and coughing.

"Oh my God," she said, covering her face with her hands as she tried to get hold of herself. She was still shaking from adrenaline and fear, and she thought she might throw up. She took a deep breath and ran her hands through her hair. "Are you alright?"

He touched his face, peered at the moisture on his fingers, tasted it, and then looked at her. "Why have you doused me?"

She laughed and sat back on her heels. "You son of a bitch. You're lucky to be alive." She gestured for him to turn his head so she could check the goose egg that had surely formed there, but he waved her away.

"Where is the angel?"

Irene didn't bother looking. "It's dead. The Duende killed it."

She helped Andras climb to his feet. He appeared unsteady, and Irene reached for him, intending to hold him up, but he waved her away. "Vanity of the flesh," he said.

She sighed in irritation and glared at him. "Okay, fine, Hercules. Let's go. We have people to save, and there are still more angels out there." She studiously avoided looking at the corpse—the once beautiful wings, torn and mangled covering the angel's remains—as she collected her bag, retied the necklace around her neck, and took stock. The cat had disappeared. The Duende were fine—triumphant and smug, but fine. Andras insisted he was well enough to continue carrying the backpack full of rocks.

Irene surreptitiously filled the cup with vodka, and as they set off, she drank deeply from it, trying to still the palsied shaking of her hands.

Twenty-Seven

They didn't stop again and soon the edge of the forest came into sight. The ground changed to sand, they crested the rise, and then the encampment spread out before them. As before, the outer ring had expanded as thousands more joined the camp in the time since they had passed this way. Irene noticed that despite the fact the outer ring kept expanding, the distance between the forest and the edge of the camp seemed to remain the same, and there was still a vast, empty expanse of sand to cross before they reached the camp.

Something about her and Andras must have seemed different — perhaps it was the pack of Duende — because, as they moved through the crowd, people stopped talking, moved aside to let them pass, and then turned to follow them with their eyes. Irene stared straight ahead, setting a determined course for the river.

Home. Home. Home.

It took two non-stop days to reach the river. In that time, she hardly saw what was around her. She was only vaguely aware of people, of changing time periods, of a crowd that gathered to follow them at a discrete distance. Irene tried to blot out the burble of whispered conversation from the growing crowd and the memories of Ian, of the horse's death screams, of the angel's outraged last cries, focusing instead on the bright flame in her chest and the river ahead.

When they finally reached the river, she surveyed its vastness and wondered how she was supposed to know where the best place was to build the altar so the dead could find it. Then she supposed it didn't matter. Eventually, they would find it — they had nothing but time to look for it.

She held the backpack while Andras shrugged out of it, and then she handed it to the nearest Duende. "Build an altar," she said. "A big one, like Manea had, and then attach the rocks, in a ring, to the top of it."

The Duende tumbled off in a chittering mass to comply.

As she turned away, wondering what to do next, her attention was drawn by the assembled crowd. Everyone was silent, having that "wait and see" kind of vibe, but it occurred to her that things were very likely going to get ugly once it became clear there were coins. Very possibly there would be a riot.

She turned to Andras. "Suggestions on crowd control?"

He seemed to be thinking the same thing because he was eyeing everyone warily. "I will fetch the Sabaoth." He started to move away, stopped, and turned back to her. "I will not be gone long."

She raised a questioning eyebrow, not sure why he thought she would be concerned. "Okay." Then she thought maybe he was the one who was worried. "I won't leave without you. Scout's honor."

His brow furrowed for a moment, and she thought he was about to say something. However, he turned away and set off without another word.

She wandered closer to watch the Duende work. They seemed to be fighting, flopping around at the water's edge and splashing a great deal.

"Are you working or playing?" she asked. There was shriek of alarm, as if they had been caught doing something wrong, and a sudden redoubling of effort. She shook her head and watched them for a bit until she was certain they were working, and then she wandered farther down the river, not sure what to do with herself while she waited. There was no Ian to distract her, to make her laugh, to help keep all the anxious thoughts at the back of her mind.

She slowed to a halt and looked across the vast expanse of water. What lay on the other side? She couldn't even begin to guess. She and Jonah had made a list of all the things the stories said awaited—a palace, a city, a desert, a lake of fire, mountains made of razor sharp glass. Well, she supposed it didn't much matter. She had beat this, hadn't she? She'd found a way across when everyone told her it was impossible. Whatever lay on the other side, she'd beat that, too.

Suddenly, she was tired—tired and sad. She ached, body and soul. She wanted to lie down, right here beside the river, and sleep for a thousand years and maybe a thousand more after that, but then she remembered the hippos and decided she should probably move inland.

She turned away and walked on, lost in thought. She hadn't really had a chance to digest what had happened with Ian; she tried to now, but it felt too big, too raw, too awful, so she nibbled at the edges, examining discrete conversations, individual looks, finite moments, in the hopes of achieving some understanding. Why hadn't he loved her? How could she have thought he did?

The old anxiety returned. She wasn't sure what she was afraid of, but it had something to do with love and what waited on the other side. The dream from the village, oh-so-long ago, came back to her—the haunting music that had taken form and the empty, aching feeling she'd had when it had left her. Some elusive truth flitted on the edge of her understanding, but before she could reach out and grab it, something appeared on the sand ahead.

It was the cat, sitting smugly on its haunches. It jumped to its feet, purring loudly, vibrating with excitement.

Irene smiled. "Yeah, I'm happy to see you, too."

The cat flung itself against her legs, rubbing furiously.

She watched it for a moment. "I don't suppose you're going to tell me what you really are?"

The cat sat down, looked up at her, and yawned. Irene laughed.

"Yeah, that's what I thought." She grew sad again, the heavy melancholy settling over her once more. "You're not coming with me, are you?"

The cat gave her a long, slow blink.

She swallowed back tears, feeling the fear of what awaited on the other side creeping back in. She reached into her bag and pulled out her last paper crane. She held it out to the cat. "Thanks for saving us from the angel. Twice."

The cat studied her for a moment, its vivid green eyes meeting hers. Slowly, it winked. Then it very delicately stepped forward and took the crane from her hand. It paused, and, through the crane, they were connected for a second. Irene wasn't sure but thought, just for an instant, she felt a small jolt of electricity. Then she released the bird, and the cat stepped back. It turned, and walked away with quiet dignity, disappearing into the distance.

Irene dashed a hand across her cheek, wiping away the single tear that had managed to escape. She realized this was just the first of many goodbyes to come. With a heavy heart and no particular destination in mind, she continued on her way.

"Hello, Acorn."

She sighed as she turned around. "*Please* stop calling me that."

"How's it going?"

She crossed her arms and tossed back her hair. "Actually, really well. I'm about to get out of here and take every single dead person in the place with me."

"I guess I'm going to need a bigger boat."

"Ha. Ha."

"Don't ruin it for me. I've been waiting forever to use that joke."

"Did you want something?" she asked.

"Oh, I just thought I'd check on you, see how you're doing. I thought you might be discouraged, thinking about throwing yourself in." He nodded toward the river.

"I don't give up that easily."

He smiled. "No, you don't." She thought he sounded proud. He contemplated her for a moment. "So, have you finally figured out what's acorn-y about you?"

His words were a splash of cold water, puncturing her self-satisfaction. Her shoulders drooped. She looked down at the ground, the overwhelming sadness returning. "Yeah," she said softly, "I'm stubborn. That's the essential truth about me. That's what I'll take to the next life."

His look gentled even further, to one of almost pity. "Everything serves a purpose, Irene — even stubbornness. Sometimes what's needed is that one person who won't give up or give in."

"Okay, fine — I'm stubborn. Let's not act like it's a good and noble thing, though. Even I'm not that deluded."

He frowned, as if exasperated with her lack of enthusiasm. "Oh, well, I guess it's lucky for all these people stuck here that you and your stubbornness came along, isn't it? What an amazing coincidence."

She hesitated, uncertainty creeping in. He couldn't be serious...could he? "You've been talking to Andras," she said, trying to make a joke, but a tremor of fear had crept into her voice as that feeling of overwhelming expectation — all focused on her — returned.

The Guide smiled and shook his head.

Panic washed over her. She had thought she was being clever, that she'd found an end-run around the problem of getting across the river, that she had been "sticking it" to the powers that be. Instead, the Guide was telling her that she'd only done what was expected of her, what she'd been purposely designed for, what she'd been sent to do — that everything about her, including and especially her stubbornness, had been created on purpose.

Irene took a step back, raising a hand as if to ward off his words. "No! Stop! Don't do that! Don't act like this was all part of some grand cosmic plan, like this was all pre-ordained from the beginning. There's no scenario in which there can be both a being powerful enough to control everything in the universe and yet stupid enough to make a plan that depended on me."

"Irene, you're looking at this all wrong. The Universe asks no more and no less than that you be exactly what you are. You don't have to accept or deny, choose or decide. You simply have to be."

She shook her head, a defiant twist to her mouth. "Andras at least has the grace to dress it up a little nicer, to make it sound all noble and messianic. In your version, there's no free will. I'm just a cog in a machine."

"So you're terrified of being given responsibility and miffed if you aren't? Interesting."

She glared at him. "That's not the point. The point is — "

"Does it really make a difference? Divine providence or a cog in a machine — you are as you are meant to be. Stop wishing to be different than you are. Learn to accept what you are, Irene, whatever that may be."

"But I don't want to be stubborn!" She practically wailed the words, and she bit her lip, suddenly embarrassed. She looked down, unable to meet his eyes, as the words bubbled to the surface against her will. She didn't want to speak them — in fact, hated herself for saying them — but somehow she could keep nothing from him. "I don't want to be remembered as the chick who was too stubborn to give up. I want to be remembered for something good, for helping people…for — "

"You want to be loved."

She looked up quickly to see if he was laughing at her. Instead, his eyes were filled with pity.

"Irene, you *are* loved."

Her track record with people — the disapproving parents, the shallow friends, the superficial romantic relationships — would seem to indicate otherwise. She gave a half-hearted shrug. "Yeah, well, I'd settle for liked."

Gently, the Guide put a hand on her shoulder and turned her. As they turned, the river faded away, replaced with the wide, verdant strips of lawn and stark white headstones of a cemetery. Irene blinked in surprise.

"What the…how did you do that?"

"I sense you're still not quite getting the 'time and space are one' thing."

She glared at him. Then she looked around, trying to get a sense of where they were. It took only a second. They were near a grave, and she knew without looking that it was hers.

"There," said the Guide, nodding toward the headstone, "is your immortality."

In front of her headstone was a modest-sized pile of rocks, on top of which was a small granite statue of an angel, wings spread, holding a shallow bowl in both hands, as if in supplication. A small, hand-written sign tacked to the base of the statue said, "Leave a penny and a prayer for the dead." The angel's bowl was already overflowing with coins.

It was beautiful. Perhaps the most beautiful thing she had ever seen. Tears threatened to overtake her, and she had to turn away.

"Every person who passes by here will be reminded that the dead are still with them," the Guide said, "that they have a responsibility to them, even though they can no longer see them. You did that, Irene." His voice was gentle, almost apologetic. "And there," he said, nodding to a small figure huddled beside the grave, burrowed deep into a coat, "is your love."

She knew at first glance that it was Jonah. Her heart leapt at the sight of him. She wanted to throw her arms around him, wanted to cry with relief. Somehow, though, she knew that they were invisible, that Jonah couldn't see them. The Guide had not actually transported her to Earth; he had just peeled back the curtain that obscured this plane of existence from the one she was on.

The Guide cleared his throat meaningfully. In response to Irene's quizzical look, the Guide nodded at the sky, motioning with his eyes toward the sun high overhead.

Irene looked around, assessing their surroundings. When she had left Earth, it had been fall, but now the sun shone brightly, the grass was green, and the trees were covered with new leaves. The sun-warmed chill of early spring — April or May — was in the air.

Just as quickly, her initial elation at seeing Jonah drained away as other details began to stand out — his wan, pale face.

The stockpile of food. The sleeping bag and blanket. Irene had no idea what month or even what day of the week it was, but she suspected she knew what all these things indicated. Her heart sank.

"Is he skipping school again?" That would explain why his responses came back so fast—he was sitting here night and day, waiting for her letters.

The Guide spoke gently. "Don't you think it's time you let the boy go?"

She started to protest, to say that she hadn't done this, but she looked at Jonah, so sad and small, sitting there, his life on hold, waiting for a word from her, and the arguments died in her throat. Hot, burning shame washed over her. She had known she shouldn't contact him—hadn't she said repeatedly that she couldn't tell him this or that about the afterlife because he might try to cross over? Yet she'd submerged those fears, those instincts, and reached out to him anyway, once more pulling him into both the world of the dead and her problems—problems she should have been solving on her own, rather than relying on a fourteen-year-old.

Irene turned away, hiding her burning face. One last small piece of her heart rebelled. She had already sacrificed so much, lost so much—Ian, the horse, the cat, Elvira and the rest of the Hungry Ghosts. How much more was she supposed to give up?

The Guide seemed to read her thoughts. "This isn't sacrifice, Irene. It's the right thing to do."

She knew he was right, though the thought of breaking ties with Jonah was like a knife to her heart. Jonah was truly the best thing that had ever happened to her. He was the best person she'd ever known, the best friend she had ever had, and she was a better person because of him. And it was because of him, of what he'd taught her, that she now understood why she had to let him go.

Jonah, for all that he was fourteen, was so much braver and wiser than her. He understood about love, about friendship. He was one of those people who put their entire heart and soul into their being. He cared, really cared, about everything, including her. His friendship with her had been unrestrained, without conditions. Even when it was hard, even when it hurt, even when he knew it would hurt, he hadn't held back. He'd looked out for her — was still looking out for her — consoled her, worried about her, had risked his life for her, and what had she ever done for him? The exact opposite. She claimed she wanted to be loved, wondered why Ian hadn't loved her, but the truth was, she wasn't worthy of it, wasn't ready for it. To get love, you had to give love. You had to be generous and kind with the other person's heart as much as you were with your own. You had to care for the other person more than you cared for yourself, and you also had to be willing to surrender yourself to something greater. You had to be willing to let go, to trust, to have faith — which she had never done. She had never been able to surrender herself, to stop being so very *Irene* even for a second. She was afraid to — what would be left of her if she did?

Instead, she had reached for Jonah, like a life raft, before she'd even tried to swim on her own, and in doing so, she threatened to drown them both. He had become a crutch, a way to avoid doing what she knew needed to be done, the same as she was a way for him to avoid what he didn't want to deal with. That wasn't love and it wasn't friendship; it was cruelty.

But now, at last, here was her chance to prove herself worthy of the selfless care and regard Jonah had shown her. To do so, however, she would have to stop clinging so very hard to things, stop trying to force them to be immutable and unchanging; instead, she'd have to find the courage to be selfless and brave. In that moment when she finally realized the worth of what he'd offered her, she would have to find the courage to let him go.

She turned to the Guide, swallowing the lump in her throat. He was watching her carefully. She avoided his eyes as she nodded. "Take me back." She turned away and they were at the river once more.

They stood silently for a moment as Irene tried to collect herself. When she was finally able to speak, she said, "What of the Hungry Ghosts — Elvira and the rest? They're not here at the river — they won't know there's a way to cross now."

The Guide shook his head, his eyes sad. "They can't cross, Irene. Surely you must know that."

Yes, she supposed she did. Crossing meant entering a higher plane of existence, it meant continuing on one's journey to enlightenment or reincarnation or Heaven or whatever it was they were all trying to achieve. The Hungry Ghosts didn't have enough memories or reason to make the trip. There was no further plane for them — this was their reality from now on.

"Well, then, I'd like to say goodbye, at least."

"They wouldn't understand goodbye," the Guide said gently. "They remember you, and that's more than most people can say. The one you call Elvira, especially — she remembers kindness. She'll never forget."

That was it. There was nothing more to be said, no more excuses to be made, no more ways to delay the inevitable.

The Guide walked with her, all the way back to where the Duende were building the altar. Irene felt like she was being escorted to her execution. She and the Guide didn't speak, and Irene kept her face turned away so he wouldn't see her silent tears.

A handful of the Duende bounded up to her, chittering proudly as she approached, and she knew that they were done. She hastily wiped her face, drying her tears before allowing the Duende to lead her forward.

Andras had returned, and he had brought friends — a man clothed in furs holding a stout club, a loin-cloth clad man with a bow and arrow, a tall strong-looking woman with a spear, and a man in a military uniform holding a rifle. Andras and the others took up position in a perimeter about fifty feet from the altar, though they didn't appear to be needed at the moment. The small crowd that had followed Irene and Andras was standing nearby, silently waiting, dull and somber, as if unsure what was about to happen. Otherwise, all was still and silent — the next nearest dead, too far away to be seen, were lifeless statues, turning to dust, inch by inch. They, also, were too far gone to board the boat.

Her pain and sorrow must have been etched on her face because, as she approached, the crowd moved aside, opening up a path to the altar. Andras silently watched her pass, his eyes dark and hooded as he followed her progress.

She stood in front of the altar and studied it for a moment. It was magnificent—everything she could have hoped for. The Duende had mixed together sand and water to make a soft clay and then shaped it into a pedestal like Manea's, standing waist-high. They had affixed the stones around the perimeter of the smooth, flat, table-like surface, in effect using them to form the sides of a bowl. Already, she could see a few coins glinting dully in the center of it.

She looked at the Duende, who all stared back with a sort of hopeful, expectant expression. "You did good," she said softly. "It's just what I wanted."

A ripple of soft chittering ran through them, as if they were grateful for her words.

She swiped away the new tears that had managed to escape and then reached into her bag for paper and pen. She swallowed hard, trying to keep her mind empty; if she thought about what she was about to say, what she needed to say, she wouldn't be able to say it. Unlike last time, this goodbye had to be final, the door firmly shut. It had to be clear that there was no hope that they would ever see each other again, that it was time to go their separate ways.

The pen touched the paper and her mind shut off, letting the words write themselves. She didn't think, didn't breath, just let them spill forth, each one a stab to her heart.

Dear Jonah,

This will be my last letter. I'm leaving the rocks by the river so that future arrivals will always have a way to get a coin so they can cross. Someday, very far in the future, when you finally make it here, I hope you'll see the altar and think of the woman you once helped.

We both know I couldn't have gotten this far without you, but now it's time for us to go our separate ways. Don't send me any more letters – I won't read them. Stop visiting my grave. I need to move on and you need to forget about ghosts and the afterlife. It's not good for you to spend so much time with the dead. You need to live your life – your real life. Go out and see and do and experience everything that the world has to offer before it's too late. Life is short, Jonah; the afterlife is forever.

Her hand shook as she folded the letter, addressed it, and set it on the altar. Just as quickly she turned away so she didn't have to see the hateful thing, didn't have to fight the temptation to snatch it back and rip it to shreds. An iron fist squeezed her heart, the stabbing pain of it so great she thought she might die, and for a moment, she almost wished she would. Anything, even death, would be preferable to the agony.

Then Andras was there, his hand on the small of her back, guiding her away from the altar, wordlessly lending her the strength and the courage to walk away. She leaned on him, taking comfort from his stoicism and his belief that something better waited for them across the river.

"Are you ready now?" the Guide asked. At the water's edge, a long, multi-oared and dragon-headed boat – like something the Vikings might have used – bobbed gently.

Irene nodded.

Andras left her side and approached the milling crowd. Irene was too far away to hear what was said, but she could see that there was a lengthy discussion with Andras repeatedly holding out the coins and then gesturing to the boat. Finally, one brave soul warily took a coin and broke away from the crowd. It was as if everyone collectively held their breaths. Then the woman stepped onto the boat and all hell broke loose. There was a pandemonium of cries, shouts, and cheers.

The rest of the Sabaoth stepped forward, ready to come to Andras's aid, but there was no need. The crowd quickly quieted, as if their jubilation had been an involuntary and shameful thing, and once more stood somber and silent. As Andras handed out the rest of the coins, they formed a line and slowly and somberly made their way to the boat, where they helped hand each other in. Apparently, a few thousand millennia of waiting had indeed made them patient, or perhaps they were all in shock to finally find themselves free.

Some of the pain in Irene's heart lifted as she watched them. *I did that*, she thought. *I freed them.* Somehow, that dulled the ache.

Irene looked at the Guide. "I guess that's it, then?"

The Guide nodded.

"Okay, so where to?"

"That depends — where do you want to go?"

"What are my choices?"

"Hey, this is your afterlife, not mine."

"Is anyone I encounter on this adventure ever going to be the least bit helpful?"

"Define helpful."

Irene groaned, but only half-heartedly. She recognized that he was teasing her, trying to lift her spirits, and she appreciated the effort. "Yeah, that's what I thought."

"Cheer up," the Guide said gently, but with a touch of irony in his voice, nudging her in the direction of the boat with a hand on her back. "You've managed to completely change the natural order of things, to overturn a system that's been in place since the dawn of time." He jerked his head toward the line of the dead slowly making their way past the altar and toward the boat. "Good job."

Irene grimaced and shook her head, but was forced to smile despite herself. He wasn't really chastising her; it was a compliment.

She sighed. "Okay, fine then, onward and upward. Take me to where I need to go to get back home."

She stepped forward to join the line inching toward the boat. Andras returned to her side, and she said, "How are we going to get the word out that there's a boat and coins to the rest of the people?"

Andras nodded to the warriors. "The Sabaoth will see to it."

They were interrupted by the chattering hoard of Duende. They clustered around her feet, chirping like birds.

"What? What's the problem?" she asked.

Their cries increased.

"What, you don't wait in lines? Too bad. We need to get on the boat."

Andras touched her arm. "Duende cannot cross water."

Irene blinked in surprise. "What?"

Andras's face remained impassive.

"I thought you didn't know anything about these pagan things?"

Andras gave a sheepish, half-hearted shrug. "Every child knows his folk tales."

"And you're just mentioning this little problem now?" When he didn't say anything, she looked at the Guide for confirmation. The Guide gave her a gentle smile and shook his head.

"Oh come on," she cried. She had an urge to add, "that's not fair," but knew that would only be mocked by both Andras and the Guide as childish.

She looked at the Duende, who had grown silent, watching her with their button eyes. She was responsible for them. They had been stuck here, abandoned, losing their minds, and she'd managed to rescue them. With that, however, had come the responsibility to protect them, to take care of them. How could she just turn around and abandon them?

Yet…there was a fitting rightness in leaving them. They needed to serve, to have a master and a purpose. She had no idea what awaited across the river, but she suspected the farther she went from the physical realm, the less need she'd have for the Duende. By rights, they shouldn't even be here. This wasn't their world. They belonged to the physical plane—to the place where there were hearths and the need for manual labor. These Duende were only here because they had been dragged along when their master—and the house he or she was in—crossed over. If not for that, they would have crossed directly to wherever it was that animals went.

She reached down and patted the nearest one on the head. It began to wail and the rest picked up the cry, as if they knew what she was about to do. Her heart was heavy as she crouched down to their level, looking each one in the eyes as she spoke. "Stop that," she admonished gently. The wailing went on. "Stop or I'll be very angry with you." Gradually, with much coaxing, their cries lessened to a soft keening. "You've done a very good job, all of you. Now, I have one last task for you." She couldn't keep the quaver out of her voice. "See this altar that you built? I want you to care for it. I want you to clean it and keep it in good repair. I want you to distribute the coins that appear, and I want you to go into the forest and guide lost travelers here. Is that clear?"

The Duende were silent, watching her carefully, as if hoping she'd change her mind. There was a soft, sad croak from somewhere amongst them.

"Go on," she said softly, standing up. "I gave you a job. Now go do it."

The Duende shuffled off, heads bowed, shoulders slumped. All except one. It stood by her feet, gazing mournfully up at her.

"'Erk," it croaked unhappily. From somewhere it produced the missing corner of her blanket, which it held out to her. Then it wrapped its stumpy arms around her leg and clung to her, whimpering pitifully.

She gently shook it off. "Go on," she said. "Stop loafing about."

With a mournful sigh, it released her leg and waddled off to join its fellows.

She looked around, but the Guide had disappeared. She frowned, but knew that she had not seen the last of him.

She rejoined the line, coming to stand beside Andras. She gave him a rueful look. "Well, I guess this is goodbye." She held out her hand, offering to shake.

Andras's brow furrowed.

"Well, we're going to different places, right?" she asked. "Following different paths from here on out. You're looking for Heaven and I'm heading back to Earth."

"Your path is my path."

She shook her head. "Yeah, I know you have this crazy idea that I'm your ticket into Heaven and all, but really, that's not where I'm going. I'm trying to go back to Earth."

"Yes."

She stared at him, not sure he understood. "I'm talking about the totally heathen concept of reincarnation here, okay? Couldn't be further from your God if I tried."

"Then so be it."

Her heart gave an odd lurch, but she shook her head, not daring to believe. "Andras—"

He reached down and took her proffered hand in his own. "I have faith," he said softly.

Her mouth gaped open. She knew it did and couldn't stop it. She stared at him, unable to find any words.

He smiled at her, warm and rich. "It is good to know you can be quiet, when the occasion calls for it."

Before she could retort, he raised her hand to his mouth and brushed her knuckles with his lips, his eyes never leaving hers. An odd warmth spread through her, buoyant and comforting. She smiled.

They had reached the head of the line, and now Andras led her forward to the boat. "Come," he said. "Let us make our own Heaven."

She groaned and shook her head, but couldn't hide a smile. "That is the *worst* come-on line I've ever heard."

EXTRAS

THEREAFTER Discussion Guide

1. *Hereafter* was set in the real world. *Thereafter* is set in a fantasy world. Does the fantasy setting make the story any more or less believable? Does this change the story or your perceptions of the story in any way? If so, how?

2. In some ways, *Thereafter* is much easier to classify than *Hereafter* — *Thereafter* is much more clearly fantasy. Do you agree? In what ways does it adhere to genre conventions and in which way does it deviate from them? Does *Thereafter* cover any new ground or add anything unique to the genre? What are some other books that *Thereafter* reminds you of? In what way is it similar to those books? In what way is it different?

3. How does Irene in *Thereafter* compare with Irene in *Hereafter* — is she more or less sympathetic than in *Hereafter*? Has she grown/evolved since the first book, and if so, how?

4. How would you describe Irene's character at the beginning of the book? At the end of the book? Does she grow or change during the story?

5. How would you describe Irene and Jonah's relationship in this book compared to in *Hereafter*? Do you think this relationship, as presented in *Thereafter*, is good for each of them or bad? Why? Do you agree with Irene's decision at the end of the book to cut off all contact with Jonah?

6. Irene continues to struggle with her alcoholism in *Thereafter* — did this seem realistic? Why or why not? Were you frustrated by her inability to overcome her addiction or did you sympathize? Why?

7. Andras and Ian have very different outlooks on life and the afterlife. How much of their views do you think is influenced by their personalities and how much by the time period in which they grew up?

8. Did you like Ian and Irene as a couple? Why or why not? Do you think Irene should have gone with Ian? If she had, do you think they would have stayed together as a couple?

9. How would you describe Andras's and Irene's relationship throughout the story? Would you describe it as a romantic relationship or as something else?

10. Why is Irene so afraid of Andras and the Guide believing in destiny and pre-ordination? Do you believe in pre-ordination? Why or why not?

11. The mystery of who or what Samyel is was finally revealed — were you surprised? Why or why not? Samyel's purpose in the land of the living and in traveling to the land of the dead with Irene, however, was not revealed. Why do you think he was on Earth? What do you think he is doing in the land of the dead? Do you have any theories about what lies ahead for this character?

12. In *Thereafter*, Irene believes she is in the Buddhist state of Bardo, an indeterminate/intermediate state in which the spirit wrestles with temptations and demons that are a manifestation of the person's subconscious. Do you believe this is where Irene is? What are some other explanations for where she might be or the things she sees and experiences during *Thereafter*?

13. Who or what did you think the Guide was — was he God? A buddhu? Something else?

14. Which afterlife myths did you recognize in *Thereafter*? How were the myths similar or different from the way you knew the story(ies)? Which myths were new or unexpected? What was your favorite part of the afterlife, as depicted in *Thereafter*?

15. Some readers felt that the version of the afterlife presented in *Hereafter* was depressing or bleak. How did you feel about the version presented in *Thereafter* — was it hopeful or bleak? Was it more or less hopeful than the afterlife of *Hereafter*? Which parts of the afterlife as depicted in *Thereafter* do you hope are true? Which parts do you hope are not? What would your ideal version of the afterlife look like?

16. What are some of themes in *Thereafter*, and how did these compare to the themes of *Hereafter*? Did any of these themes resonate more strongly with you than the others? Why or why not?

17. Overall, did you feel that *Thereafter* was a hopeful or a bleak story? Did it have a "happy" ending? Why or why not?

18. Did you have any favorite quotes or scenes from the story? What made that quote or passage stand out to you?

19. Was the author fairly descriptive? Was she better at describing the concrete or the abstract? Was she clear about what she was trying to say, or were you confused by some of what you read? How did this affect your reading of the book?

20. Which was more important to the story, the characters or the plot? Was the plot moved forward by decisions of the characters, or were the characters at the mercy of the plot? Was the action believable?

21. What events in the story stand out for you as memorable? Was there any foreshadowing and suspense or did the author give things away at the beginning of the book? Was this effective? How did it affect your enjoyment of the book? Has the author foreshadowed things to come in the remaining books of the series?

22. Have you read anything else written by this author? How does *Thereafter* compare in terms of voice, tone, and style to the author's other works?

23. The *Afterlife Series* is planned to be six books total. What do you think will happen to the characters next? What do you wish would happen to the characters? How would you like to see the series progress? What, for you, would be a "happy" ending, given that Irene is dead?

Interview with the Author

When did you start writing and has it always been your passion?

I've always written; in grade school, they had us write a story every year, which we then made into a book – we printed it neatly on nice paper, drew pictures to accompany the story, and then sewed it all together with a cardboard wrapped in wall paper for covers. I think that was my favorite thing we did all year and I still have those stories (thanks Mom for keeping them!). It wasn't until 2001, however, that I really set out to write a novel "for real," and that's when I started working steadily toward becoming a professional author.

What is the genre of *Hereafter*? Are you going to follow the same genre with later books?

Good question! My stories tend to be cross-genre and a bit hard to categorize, which is one of the reasons it took so long to get *Hereafter* published. Technically, *Hereafter* is categorized as contemporary fantasy, but it has elements of romance, women's fiction, literary fiction, and fantasy. My first novel was future noir/science fiction. I'm working on two other novels that fall within the speculative fiction umbrella (one sci fi, one fantasy), but I also have an idea for an historical fiction based on the Bread and Roses Strike that is demanding to be written and a very serious literary fiction story that has been banging around in my head for years.

Through all of my writing I explore a few key themes – the fantastical and miraculous all around us, man's relationship with the universe (and a supreme deity if one exists), and the struggle with issues of identity and self – and I hope that regardless of the genre framework I use for any given story, those themes will come out and satisfy fans.

What do you like to do in your spare time (other than writing)?

Spare time? What is this thing of which you speak? I must learn more – it sounds fascinating! ☺

I work full time, as a grant writer for a non-profit, and fiction writing is a second full time job on top of that, so there isn't a lot of free time right now. When there is, I love horseback riding, hiking, quilting, and gardening. Now ask me the last time I did any of those things! However, if "Hereafter" does well, my husband has agreed to let me buy a horse, so hopefully there will be more horseback riding in my future.

Is Irene modeled on you? Are you and she similar in any way?

I'm actually more Jonah than Irene, and I definitely shared his experience of being an outcast as a teen. I remember very strongly what it felt like to not really fit in and to desperately want to be taken seriously by adults. However, Irene and I do share a love of snappy come-backs and an inability to deal well with frustration.

Which character from a book do you most relate to, if any? And why?

Setting aside the betrayal of his best friend, Lancelot from T.H. White's "Once and Future King." I spend a lot of time setting impossible standards for myself and then feeling like I'm not good enough. I also want to do something great, just once in my life—something miraculous and wonderful. I'm hoping that someday I write a book good enough to touch people and endure long after I'm gone.

About the Author

Terri Bruce has been making up adventure stories for as long as she can remember. Like Anne Shirley, she prefers to make people cry rather than laugh, but is happy if she can do either. She produces fantasy and adventure stories from a haunted house in New England where she lives with her husband and three cats. Visit her on the web at www.terribruce.net.

Keep up to date with all the latest news and sign up to be notified of new releases in the Afterlife Series at:

Website/Blog:
http://www.terribruce.net

Twitter:
http://www.twitter.com/@_TerriBruce_

Made in the USA
Columbia, SC
22 November 2017

WHEREAFTER (Afterlife #3)

How Far Would You Go To Get Your Life Back?

Stuck on an island encircled by fire and hunted by shadows bent on trapping them there forever, Irene and Andras struggle to hold onto the last vestiges of their physical selves, without which they can never return to the land of the living. But it's not just external forces they'll have to fight as the pair grow to realize they have different goals. Irene still clings to the hope that she can somehow return to her old life—the one she had before she died—while Andras would be only too glad to embrace oblivion.

Meanwhile, Jonah desperately searches for a way to cross over to the other side, even if doing so means his death. His crossing over, however, is the one thing that could destroy Irene's chances of returning home.

Too many obstacles, too many people to save, and the thing Irene most desperately wants—to return to her old life—seems farther away than ever. Only one thing is clear: moving on will require making a terrible sacrifice.

Coming Soon!